Dreaming Sophia

...because dreaming is an art

By

Melissa Muldoon

Matta Press • San Francisco

DreamingSophiaBook.com

Cover Illustration, Cover Design,
Interior Design & Layout
by
Melissa Muldoon

MATTA

PRESS

Matta Press
46509 Mission Blvd, #162
Fremont, California 94539

Cover Design by Melissa Muldoon
Interior Book Design by Melissa Muldoon
Character Illustrations by Melissa Muldoon

Manufactured in the United States of America

1st Edition
Muldoon, Melissa.
Dreaming Sophia

ISBN: 978-0-9976348-0-8

ISBN: 978-0-9976348-1-5 (E-Book)

Dedicated with love to...

My mother who first inspired my creativity.
My father who gave me wings to fly.
My husband who encourages my big, beautiful Italian dream.

"I believe in dreams. Dreams become reality."
Sophia Loren, 2016

non smettere mai
di sognare!. Never
stop dreaming.
Melissa Muldoon

...because dreaming is an art

Dreaming Sophia

Giuletta Capuleti

Michaelangelo

Leonardo da Vinci

Marcello Mastroianni

Simonetta Vespucci

Dante Alighieri

Eleonora de' Medici

Casanova

Sophia Loren

Garibaldi

Filippo Brunelleschi

Lorenzo de Medici

Lucrezia Borgia

www.DreamingSophiaBook.com

www.pinterest.com/DreamingSophia

Visit the Dreaming Sophia Website and Pinterest site for posts, images and video clips about the art, artists, and music featured in the book

Cari lettori / Dear readers,

Thank you for joining Sophia on her journey to Italy! I hope like Sophia, you, too, will be inspired to walk the fine line between fantasy and reality.

It is my pleasure to bring you Sophia's story, but I also want to take you on a trip to Italy to discover more about her music, history, culture, art, and cinema. I want you to experience the Italy I know and love. I want to tickle your senses with sights, sounds, tastes, and cultural anecdotes.

After reading Sophia's story, I hope a few readers will be inspired to learn Italian! It happened to me several years ago. As an art student in Italy, I was more interested in painting than language learning. I used to skip class and sit on the steps of the Duomo and sketch. Years later, a book filled with a smattering of Italian phrases inspired me to start a journey, much like Sophia's, to learn the language.

With this book I also want to make learning about artists and paintings as fun, entertaining, and enriching for you as it is for me! I want art to "speak" to you as well!

As I wrote the book, I began to wish I could have Italian music play when I mention a song or have a picture pop up when I talk about a piece of art. So to experience the book visually and aurally, I have created the Dreaming Sophia website and Pinterest page. On both sites you will find links to music, film clips, and lots of delicious images of food and the many places Sophia goes—Florence, Lucca, Viareggio, Rome, Venice, Verona, and Val d'Orcia. In the e-book there are clickable links that will take you to an image, a song, or a video to enhance your reading experience!

Keep dreaming your dreams—they do become reality! Happy reading! Buona lettura!

Melissa Muldoon

...because dreaming is an art

Dreaming Sophia

Antiquity

Antiquity refers to ancient classical civilizations of the Mediterranean, especially Ancient Greece and Rome. The humanist aesthetic and high technical standards of Greek art has influenced generations of artists and, during the fifteenth and sixteenth centuries, inspired the flowering of the Renaissance in Florence.

Chapter 1

A Train Bound for Italy

*T*he doors slammed shut, and the train lurched forward. Momentarily losing my balance, I was pitched headfirst into the aisle. To keep from falling completely, I grabbed the back of a seat to steady myself. Slowly I moved through the rocking cars and connecting passageways, stopping every so often to set my suitcases down and rest my arms. When I found my reserved couchette, I shoved my things inside and settled myself next to the big window.

From a paper bag, I took out a sandwich and nibbled it slowly, savoring the taste of peppery olive oil and salty prosciutto. After a few minutes, the door to the compartment slid open, and a girl in a purple dress tumbled in. She looked at me and apologized for her clumsy entrance. Swaying with the uneven movements of the train, she placed a small, round case onto the overhead rack. Smiling briefly at me, she made herself comfortable the best she could on the hard, narrow seat opposite of mine. At first, she busied herself with her cell phone, but realizing there was no service, she shook her head in exasperation and gave up. Unzipping her purse, she tossed the phone inside and pulled out a paperback novel covered in Florentine marbled paper. I thought the improvised book jacket pretty but wondered if its real purpose was to hide the title of a trashy romance novel.

The girl and I sat in companionable silence, she reading her book and I looking out the window. As the engine snaked its way through the train yard, past abandoned wagons and walls sprayed with colorful graffiti I sighed in relief to be on the last leg of my journey. As we picked up speed, things began to blur together like a saturated watercolor painting.

Soon I lost interest in the scenery. My eyes drooped to a close, and my head lolled against the headrest. Warm pulses of sunlight flickered across my eyelids, and I began to relax. As I drifted into a state of semi-consciousness, random images began to take shape. I saw a woman wearing a crown of laurels holding two chalkboard erasers. She clapped them together, sending a cloud of dust high into the air. As she backed away into the swirling mist, her image was replaced by that of my mother, who leaned forward to kiss me good night. Dark clouds floated behind my lids, illuminated by flashes of lightning. Soon a marble statue of a boy came into focus. Over it flew a hawk. It circled the statue several times as if it were lost, searching, searching for something. Gracefully it alighted on the shoulder of a woman with a perfectly oval face and alabaster complexion. She was seated in a radiant meadow, and her full brocade skirts billowed gently around her. The silver and gold threads of her dress glistened in the sunlight. Raising her hand, she reached out and beckoned me closer. Insistently she called out, "Sophia...Sophi...*Svegliati!* Can you hear me, Bella? It's time to wake up."

Hearing the sound of someone biting into an apple my eyes fluttered open. Across from me, the girl in the purple dress was observing me intently. Seeing that I was awake, she smiled. Without saying a word she reached into her bag, drew out another apple, and offered it to me.

Cozily ensconced in the small train compartment, we were soon munching our apples, sharing an unspoken intimacy often forged when people are randomly thrown together in transit. We traveled on without speaking, listening contentedly to the *tchjk tchjk tchjk tchjk* sound the train's wheels made as they hit the joints between the rails.

Finishing the last bite of her apple the girl, looked at me, cocked her head to one side and uttered the most surprising words, "You did the right thing, you know. It was good you trusted your instincts and boarded this train to Italy."

I paused mid-bite. "Excuse me?" I wondered how she knew my ultimate destination. She rolled her eyes as if it was evident. Leaning over, the girl undid the latch and lifted the window letting fresh air into the compartment. Raising her arm over her head, she tossed the apple core into the flashing fields beyond.

The young woman turned back to me and said again, "You did well to choose this train bound for Florence."

Narrowing my eyes, I raised one eyebrow and waited for her to continue. "Listen, I know it was difficult, but you were wise to follow your heart to Italy and not let yourself be pulled off in another direction." She shrugged her shoulders. "Take it from me. Love is wonderful, amazing even, but you don't have to fall for the first good-looking guy who comes along—even if he is a Romeo. Sometimes there are even better things waiting for you—things you haven't even begun to dream about yet."

Picking up the book resting on her lap, she turned a couple of pages. When she found the correct one, with a slim finger, she pointed to a passage and said, "Here, take a look at this, and you will understand."

Squinting I tried to read the barely legible text, a task made more difficult by the rocking train. She took pity on me. Bookmarking the spot, she snapped the book closed and tossed it onto my lap and said, "Keep it, I'm done with it. I was never a fan of tragedies I prefer happy endings instead."

I thumbed the corners of the pages gently. They made a soothing sound as they rippled together. I was so tired. Had I made the best decision? As though reading my mind the girl replied, "You have lost so much, but a new life awaits you in Florence, and it's about to begin. You will find your joy."

Her words echoed in my mind as I turned my head to look out the window. Night had fallen. Instead of quaint villages and tidy fields, what I saw instead was my reflection in the glass. The woman staring back at me resembled a photo of my mother I had tucked away in my suitcase. Shifting my weight upon the hard cushion, I let my head fall back again.

As the train wheels ground on, taking us to higher altitudes, my thoughts drifted again. I recalled the dark place I had been dragged down into and how I had come to be sitting aboard this train bound for Italy. I smiled conspiratorially at the reflection as if I shared a secret with the girl in the glass. I began to think about the voices that had called out to me from that elusive place where sensibility leaves us and fantasy carries us further.

I closed my eyes and continued to dream.

Chapter 2

The Phone Call

*O*pening my eyes wide, I took a deep breath, and as I let it out, I said in a rush of words: "Triple-venti-half-sweet-non-fat-caramel-macchiato-latte-hold-the-cream." Stopping in front of my door, I collapsed in a fit of laughter knocking into the side of one of my girlfriends. All the way back from the coffee shop, we had been competing with one another to see who could say the words the fastest, a tongue twister facilitated by the generous amounts of caffeine, syrup, and sugar we had just consumed. It was silly how complicated American coffee drinks had become. Let's face it. I was a coffee snob. My mother had made sure of that. Give me a simple shot of rich dark Italian espresso, with a spoonful of sugar, and I was perfectly happy.

My friends sang out their good-byes over their shoulders as they drifted down the corridor. Digging around in my bag for my keys, I could still hear them shouting and laughing as they continued stumbling over the words "...non-fat-caramel-macchiato-latte-hold-the-cream." Using the best Sophia Loren accent I could muster, one that dripped with movie diva charm, I called out after them, "*Ciaaoooo* daaarlings!"

Jangling my key ring, I selected one and inserted it into the lock and gave it a firm twist. As I pushed the door open, I heard one of my friends, who was almost out of earshot, cry out, "Don't forget, Sophi. We're meeting up tonight at that new pizza joint over on University Avenue. See you later."

I raised my voice so she could hear me over the commotion in the hallway and said, "Save a glass of wine and a slice of the pie for me. I'll try my best to be on time."

I kicked the door shut with my foot, and I dumped my books onto the desk. Before slinging my purse onto the back of the chair, I pulled out my phone to check my messages. There were four. I had a tendency to keep my device on mute so hadn't realized it had even rung. My friends were always complaining I was a terrible correspondent and never returned their calls. Most of the time I was too busy or distracted to bother with my phone. Before I forgot, I decided to listen to my messages just to prove to them, and myself, that sometimes I could respond promptly like a responsible adult.

When I dialed into my mailbox, I heard Luciana's familiar and well-loved voice. In a cryptic message, she said: "Ciao, Sophia—please call me back as soon as you can." I listened to the second recording and the third. They were all from the same caller, each one more insistent, conveying the same message: "Chiamami! We need to talk." Holding the phone to my ear, waiting for the fourth one to begin, I heard yet again Luciana's voice. This time, her urgent tone made me smile. I thought to myself: *Well, somebody sure misses me.*

Standing by the window, I looked down at the campus below me. Checking my watch I calculated the three-hour time difference between Philadelphia and California. I decided now was as good a time as any to phone her. I punched the callback key. The phone rang once, and in a heartbeat, Luciana was on the line.

"Sophia. *Finalmente...*" She stopped abruptly, and there was a long, drawn-out pause. For all the urgent messages she had left, it seemed now she had nothing to say to me. Then in a somber tone, she said, "*Non so come dirtelo,* Sophia..." Her voice trailed off again as if she were searching for the right words to say in English. "How do I even begin to tell you this..." Then giving up, she pressed on in Italian. "*Carissima, mi dispiace così tanto.*"

I realized she was trying to comfort me and was telling me how sorry she was. I had no idea where this was leading. I waited for her to continue. The unstable line cut in and out making it hard for me to hear her words clearly. Several seconds passed, as she tried to speak, and then finally I heard her murmur, "*Un incidente...non ce l'hanno fatta...*"

What had she just said? Something about an accident...they didn't make it? That made no sense at all. My Italian must be slipping. I held the phone to my ear and waited. When I didn't respond, Luciana coughed slightly, as if the words had become lodged in her throat, and she switched back to English so I would fully comprehend her meaning. In a wavering voice, she said, "Sophia...your mom and dad...they are gone." She paused again before saying, "There was a plane crash."

The static I had heard previously on the line turned into a vicious buzz. As Luciana continued to talk, from the rasping sound of her voice and her convulsive breathing, I realized she had been crying. In broken words, she told me that earlier that morning she had received a call from Italian authorities. Because of my busy school schedule, my parents had listed her as an emergency contact in case of difficulties while traveling abroad. During a brief exchange, they told her there had been a mechanical malfunction caus-ing Flight 1599 to veer off the tarmac in Rome during takeoff. The plane had crashed into a fuel tank. Only a few seated in the back rows had managed to escape before the aircraft had exploded, killing the rest of the passengers.

Wait! What? Slow down. It simply wasn't possible. People don't die on take-off. There were precautions for those kinds of things. Even in English, the words didn't make sense. Obviously, this was a translation error.

I had no words. Holding the phone to my ear, I forced myself to focus on Luciana's voice as she spoke in a mix of Italian and English. Finally, I stopped trying. I gazed instead out the window. Catching sight of a small bird perched on a slender tree branch, I watched it preen its feathers in the late afternoon sun. Now and then it cocked its head to look at me. In a flash of yellow it took off, disappearing into the cobalt sky. A mundane sight. An ordinary day. The world had been minding its own business, spinning along on its orbit and then this...this...this "thing"—what had Luciana called it? *"Un incidente"*—had happened on the other side of the ocean, causing it to tilt lopsidedly and grind to a shuddering stop. I couldn't acknowledge it, or say the word out loud in English, or even begin to fathom the terrible scene and what they must have endured during those last awful moments before the plane spun out of control.

Suddenly the enormity of Luciana's message was too much to process. My brain shut down completely. It was all I could do to mumble a few inane responses before I told her I'd call her back later.

But my hand shook as I hung up the phone. Stepping closer to the win-dow, I pressed my hot forehead against the smooth glass. As my brain began to reboot, two random things crossed my mind. First, I thought what a co-incidence it was that my father, who envied the flight of birds, had tragically been struck down while attempting to learn their secret. Then I envisioned my mother's colorful tubes of paint and the canvases left in stacks in her art studio. Who now, I wondered, would finish her paintings?

Turning, I gazed dully around my dorm room taking in the all-too-familiar objects: the standard-issue oak desk, the metal blinds, a disorderly stack of books, and a pile of CDs. On the other side of the door, I could hear graduate students talking as they passed each other in the hall. Looking up at the mirror over the dresser, I made eye contact with a woman with long, dark curly hair. I didn't recognize her. The stranger staring back at me was a pale shadow of her former self, who just an hour before had been clowning around with friends in an off-campus coffee shop. The laughter was gone.

Slowly I replayed the phone call again in my head. With a bang and a crack, the reality of Luciana's horrific words exploded in my brain, and my temples began to throb. The firm ground upon which I stood was deteriorating into loosely shifting sand, and it felt as if I was being pulled down, down, down into a dark quagmire. I took a deep breath and tried to claw my way back to the surface, but the harder I struggled, the faster it pulled me back under.

Light-headed, my legs gave out from under me. I sank slowly onto my narrow bed. Slumping over, I pulled my knees up to my chin. Why had I even bothered to call Luciana back? Trembling uncontrollably, I willed the phone call to be an unfortunate dream. Make it stop! Wake me up! I waited, but I felt no gentle tap on my shoulder. No one wrapped loving arms around me.

I closed my dry, stinging eyes and began rocking to and fro. The rhythmic movement caused the stalled gears in my brain to pick up momentum. Suddenly my mind was fraught with images. At first, I couldn't make sense of them, but then out of the swirling confusion, the faces of my mother and father rose up before me. I reached up to touch them, but my hand met nothing but air. My arm fell limply back to my side.

A sob escaped my lips. Doubling over, I turned my head into the mattress and thought: *This can't be happening. This isn't the way things are supposed to turn out.*

A wave of nausea hit me. Then another. Sorrow completely engulfed me; the tears finally began to well up. They coursed down my cheeks, flooding my pillow. Struck by another wave of pain, I was pushed over the edge and into total darkness. The last thought I had before going completely under: *My brilliant father and my magnificent avant-garde mother—they are gone.*

They were my inspiration—my guiding stars. Gone.

Chapter 3

A Golden Valley

My mother, always petite but never small, had been a free-spirited student at Berkeley who studied art in Italy during the 1960s, at a time when the Mud Angels saved Florence. She was a gifted painter, inspired more by Piero della Francesca's architectural structure and Giorgio Morandi's compositions than by the loosely applied brush strokes of Fragonard and Monet. Always headstrong and independent, she looked for beauty in unusual things. She loved life, appreciated a robust red wine, and chatted easily with strangers. But, more than anything, she was an impassioned dreamer. What she imagined more often than not came true.

At Berkeley, she majored in art and Italian and embraced a bohemian lifestyle. During her junior year, she studied in Italy for a semester. When she set off for Europe, she expected to have a lark, travel like a gypsy, visit art museums, and paint Italian landscapes. She hadn't expected to become so enamored with the country and its people.

She used to sigh and tell me, "Sophi, that is where I fell in love for the first time." Throwing back her head she hugged herself tightly as if she were embracing an ardent admirer. Spinning around the room, she said, "Can you believe that? I didn't fall in love with just one man. *Oddio*, my God, no. Leave it to me to fall in love with an entire country!"

It was true. In just a few short months in Florence, the puzzle pieces of her life fell together, and she felt she had finally found her place in the world. She returned to Berkeley to finish her degree, but far too restless to settle down and remain in California; she decided to go back to Italy.

Looking down at me, she often laughed and said, "It's what all proper aspiring artists do. They go to Italy to wander the ruins and learn from the Masters and put the finishing touch on their art educations."

She thrived in an environment that had been fueled by countless generations of artists, tapping into the wellspring of creativity that emanated from the very stones upon which Italy was built. But art was only one side of the coin. She also adored the culture. She embraced it all—the language, the traditions, and the food. Oh, the food!

In Italy, she also discovered something exquisitely delicious. Something that would come to define her outlook on life, right up until the day she died. She learned *il dolce far niente*, the sweet joy of doing nothing. Her mentors were her hardworking friends who embraced the sweet bliss of letting it all go—*lasciare andare*. She was a quick study, patterning herself after her Italian movie idols Marcello Mastroianni and Sophia Loren, and she learned how to appreciate the million tiny, inconsequential things that made life so abundant and rich and well worth the living. And just like Fellini's Cabiria, she believed that even on the worst of days, if she kept going, just around the corner she would find something beautiful to cheer herself up.

My mother spent six joyful years in Italy but, when the money ran out, she packed little pieces of Italy into her suitcase and reluctantly boarded a plane back to the States. It broke her heart to leave Florence, but it was time to go back. Always at this point in the story, which I must have heard a hundred times, she looked over at me and said, "Yes, I had to return to San Francisco, Sophia. I could feel something pulling me back." Then she hugged me tightly and kissed me on the head and added, "I returned to find you, my darling girl. You were out there waiting for me to be your mother."

Still holding me close, she whispered into my ear, "But you know what, Soph? Italy is my destiny; it calls to me to return home."

When she eventually arrived back in the city by the Bay, my mother, who always danced to a different tune than others, didn't come alone. No, indeed. She returned convinced she was carrying Italian muses inside her.

"Really?" I asked the first time she had told me, excited by the idea that spirits possessed my mother.

Seeing my face, she smiled and said, "*Oh, mia cara.* They aren't really ghosts, my dear." Tweaking my nose, she said, "I have always welcomed the 'fantasy' of Italia to dwell within me." Waving her arms dramatically like an Italian movie diva she exclaimed, "I'm inspired by the art, the music, the history, the cinema, and all the magical things that make Italy, well, *Italy.* " Then she hugged me again and said, "Even if I was coming back to California, I couldn't bear to leave any of it behind."

I believed her. But if uninspired, less imaginative people interpreted that to mean she was slightly touched in the head, so be it. Her creativity was boundless, and when she was feeling blue, she conjured up the most fascinating personalities, past and present. She was a born actress and cast herself in her own whimsical dramas. One day she might dine with a Renaissance artist, another a crazy Neapolitan king, or perhaps a Medici duchess. She invited each and every one of them, all the Italian personalities past and present, to fill up the empty spaces inside her.

In the morning as she brewed thick, dark espresso in a silver Bialetti coffee pot she reeled off Italian expressions. At night she whirled around her apartment mimicking Italian pop music stars like Mina and Patty Pravo, pretending to croon like the divas into the back of a spoon.

She often told me she had hoped someday to return to Italy, but while restocking her bank account, she was content to live in San Francisco, in the big beautiful Italian life she had created, fueled by her imagination and moonstruck dreams.

But my mother's plans to return to Italy were seriously derailed when she met my father. She ran into him—quite literally—as she dashed across a busy intersection to avoid an advancing trolley car. She had been at a gallery opening at the MOMA on Third Street, and he was returning home from his office on the tenth floor of the Flood Building.

According to my mother's version of the story, when they collided, he was startled by the exclamations she cried out in Italian: *"Accidenti! Aiutami!* Damn it. Help me up."

My father said he thought he had bumped into a flustered Italian tourist who had wandered astray from Fisherman's Wharf.

"Excuse me, ah, um...*signorina?*" hesitantly he said, as he held her arm to keep her from falling out of her three-inch Prada heels. When she removed her dark glasses, and he looked into her eyes for the first time, he knew he was a lost man. Taking in the psychedelic Pucci print skirt and the art portfolio she carried under her arm, he was intrigued and bemused by the quirky, if not exasperated, woman standing before him. How curious he thought—at first glance, they were opposites in every way.

Regaining her equilibrium, she slipped her oversized Armani shades back into place. From behind the dark glasses, she sized him up, admiring the length of his legs in neatly pressed trousers. She observed how his well-tailored jacket fit smoothly across the breadth of his shoulders and swooned just a bit when he put on a pair of black-rimmed glasses. She thought they gave him a bookish demeanor in the manner of a handsome film star—à la Gregory Peck. Judging by the set of his jaw and the directness of his deep blue eyes, just like Atticus Finch, she instinctively felt he was a trustworthy man.

My mother told me later she had dreamed him into existence. "You see," she said, "I so adore romantic Italian films, you know, like in *Houseboat* when

Sophia Loren dances with Cary Grant...*così affascinante*. So charming. Or no, wait. Make that Marcello Mastroianni in...let's see...oh, I can't decide. In any one of the dozens of films, she made with him. Yes. I always fantasized about meeting a wildly good-looking man like Marcello who would sweep me off my feet."

As I said, my mother was a dreamer, and what she imagined often came true. In fact, she was indeed knocked off her feet that day by the man in the black-rimmed glasses. Soon they found themselves in a quaint Italian café in Little Italy ordering Bellinis. As my mother sipped on prosecco flavored with peaches, she contemplated the handsome stranger sitting across from her. With a flirty smile and an enticing tilt of her head, she leaned in and said, "So tell me about yourself, *caro*."

According to the story, my father had gazed at her thoughtfully, opting to stay silent a few seconds more. But relaxed by the foreign, fizzy cocktail, something he'd never tried before, and charmed by my mother's unconventionality he began to open up and talk about himself. It was something he rarely did with friends, let alone strangers—especially outraged crazy women he ran into on the street.

She learned he was a local San Francisco boy who had graduated with honors from Stanford Law School. While she prided herself on being independent and not easily tied down, she couldn't resist the sense of security that enveloped her at just the touch of his hand. The young lawyer, in turn, despite being taciturn and fact driven, was drawn to the chatty brunette, enchanted by her spontaneity and amused by the fact that she preferred a dish of *spaghetti alla carbonara* to a good, old-fashioned hot dog.

So, like the cable cars on the turnstile at Market and Powell, the young couple's course swiveled and rotated. It took only a few weeks for them to fall in love and they married on a late summer afternoon in a simple chapel in the Haight District. Of course, my mother couldn't possibly orchestrate her wedding without a touch of something Italian, so as they exited the chapel she had asked one of her friends to sing *Nel blu dipinto di blu*.

As she finished her story she used to sing the song for me too: "*E incominciavo a volare nel cielo infinito Volare, oh oh oh oooh...*" Pausing she smiled at me and inevitably added, "The sky *was* the limit, as was the uncharacteristically blue sky that graced San Francisco that day. Just like the words of the song, we wanted to be abducted by the wind and fly away, hand in hand, into the infinite blue sky."

On the very day, they discovered I was on the way my father also learned of a legal practice for sale in Sonoma, a small, dusty farming community north of the city. Set in a valley between two rugged mountains where cool ocean breezes blew in from the Pacific, it was a fertile spot for growing grapes and home to a fledgling wine industry.

My mother said she would miss the metropolitan galleries and multi-cultural neighborhoods of San Francisco, but, on the other hand, Sonoma was home to a large community of Italian immigrants. The woman who fantasized about living in Italy, teased her husband saying, "*Tesoro,* darling, don't worry. I can survive without the tiramisu and the espressos in North Beach because living in Sonoma will be the next best thing to living in Tuscany, *and* it will be a good place to raise a family."

In the end, my father bought the practice in Sonoma, and my parents found a place to live a few miles out of town. My mother, bursting with energy, set about decorating their new home. Every so often she reined in her nesting fervor and set down her dripping paintbrush to pick up *Dr. Spock's Baby and Child Care.* The book was a present from a new friend, Luciana Marano she had met at the market in town. She was a young mother, who had moved to Sonoma from Italy with her husband, Giovanni. They were intent on becoming California winemakers.

My mother accepted Luciana's hand-me-down book gratefully, realizing she had much to learn about raising a baby. She was amused that the good doctor suggested giving up alcohol *and* coffee. Reluctantly she followed his advice about the wine but couldn't quite bring herself to forego a shot of espresso, claiming that both she and her baby could benefit from a caffeine kick now and then.

According to my mother, it seemed an eternity from Bellinis to birth, when I finally kicked myself, forcefully, into the world. But actually, I arrived early. Whether it was from the espresso shots my mother wouldn't give up or her refusal to sit still and stop painting, I came into the world two weeks prematurely. It was probably the only time in my life I ever arrived anywhere ahead of schedule.

My mother suggested my name and given her love of Italy and La Loren, my father readily agreed. She told me the first time he held me he let the soft syllables roll around in his mouth: "Sooo-phiii-aaa." But later he simply called me Bella. In Italian, *bella* means beautiful. He used to tell me, "From the first moment you opened your eyes I could see your beauty inside and out."

As I grew up, when I looked into the mirror I tended to disagree, thinking myself a bit scrawny with eyes too big for my narrow face. Despite my protests, Bella remained his special pet name for me. In his opinion, I took after my mom. Not only had I inherited her dark hair and almond-shaped eyes but also her gift for dreaming.

"Just like her," my father once said, "you keep company with a league of imaginary friends." With a grin, he confided, "I so enjoy eavesdropping on your conversations. You have even fooled me a couple of times. Sometimes when I pass by your door, I think you are talking to a real person...that is until I peek around the corner and see you all alone in the room."

For many years, fantasy and reality existed side by side in a golden valley. While my father penned documents seated behind a large mahogany desk, my mother painted canvases in a studio she had converted from a garage at the back of the house. She was a new mother, but that didn't stop her from painting. She set my bassinet next to her easel, and when I cried, my father told me later, she leaned over and whispered soothing words in Italian, *"Dormi, tesoro, dormi."* Sleep, darling, sleep. Then she rocked my cradle with a hand that still held a paintbrush.

As I grew older, my mother taught me how to mix cadmium yellow, crimson red, and cerulean blue paints. At night, she filled my head with delightful stories starring the Italian muses who resided within her. As the moon rose over the Sonoma Valley, my mother told me fanciful tales of Roman soldiers, plotting Machiavellian princes, and radiant Renaissance duchesses. She spoke to me of movie divas and opera singers, cavaliers and generals. Like an Italianized Scheherazade, my mother held me captive. Concluding her story she turned out the light and whispered, "Dream, Sophia, dream!"

My world had been safe and secure, full of love and laughter. But due to a senseless mechanical malfunction, it had been blown apart on an ordinary spring afternoon. When the news sank in that my parents would never leave the land of terracotta pots and sunflowers to cross the chilly, blue Atlantic and return to our golden valley, my world drained of color. Somewhere out there, my parents had vanished. They were flying...flying...into the infinite darkness, moving farther and farther away from me.

Chapter 4

Pandora's Box

*L*uciana's phone call transformed me into an exhausted, soggy wreck. I wept for days. Weeks, even. I must have called my mother's friend back at some point, but I can't remember when or the specifics of the conversation. The days ran together in a dismal, moist blur. I moved through life in slow motion. Nothing made sense. Nothing mattered anymore. In retrospect, I don't even know how I managed to buy toothpaste—let alone brush my teeth—or purchase a plane ticket to return to California for the funerals

I thought I was all cried out and not another drop could be squeezed from my red, swollen eyes. But I was wrong. When I returned to the Sonoma Valley, the dam broke again. Tears welled up and spilled down my face at the least provocation. It couldn't be helped. There were just too many memories, and they descended upon me at every turn, suffocating me.

For my own preservation, I couldn't remain in the town where I had grown up. Directly following my parent's simple memorial service, I fled the Valley. I told myself the farther away, the better. I needed a place to grieve on my terms and timetable. I didn't have much of a family. There were no grandparents, brothers, or sisters to take me in. So I grabbed the car keys and took off on my own, headed south in the direction of San Diego. But after a couple of weeks of aimless driving, depressing hotel rooms and deserted beaches, I decided it was time to return home.

The Oakland hills were brown and dusty from late summer heat when I passed by the city on my way back up to Sonoma. Continuing to follow the expressway north, I crossed the bay at Vallejo until it turned into the Valley of the Moon. When I pulled up to Luciana's ranch house, she was waiting for me on the porch. She clucked over me like a mother hen, helping me settle into a spare room that had belonged to her eldest daughter. At first, I didn't mind the cramped quarters, as I spent most of my time in bed. After a few days, however, I grew edgy again. Perhaps it was the familiar smell of aromatic coffee brewing on the stove or the scent of Luciana's fragrant basil pestos that made me restless, but it felt like I was drifting backward, wasting time, taking up space in the houses of others.

I've turned into such a pathetic blob of a person, I thought, as I lay in bed, staring at the sun-dappled ceiling. Listening to the sounds of a vacuum cleaner on the other side of the door, I dully remembered the previous year, when my parents had told me they were treating themselves to a second honeymoon. Over the years they had traveled many places, even to Italy three or four times. It had always been my mother's fondest wish to take me with her but the timing was never right, and things kept getting in the way.

Once, I had thought about going on my own to Florence. During college, I had been enticed by a study abroad program offered through Berkeley. But like a silly co-ed, I had opted out to travel to Mexico instead. I told everyone, including my art history professors, during the months I lived south of the border I would spend my time studying Frida Kahlo's surrealist paintings at her home, La Casa Azul, in Mexico City. But in reality, my priorities were slightly skewed. I had fallen for a cute guy and wanted a mini-sabbatical. So I kissed goodbye the chance to study abroad in Italy, deciding instead to embrace the beaches of Cozumel and drink margaritas out of glasses dusted with salt, hoping for a little romance.

I admit, too, I was showing a bit of defiance, wanting to strike out on my own path and not follow directly in my mother's footsteps. When she found out, she shook her head in dismay. We argued considerably over that and in the end, even though I hated to admit it, I realized my mother had probably been right.

So on the occasion of their twenty-fifth anniversary, when my parents began planning a three-week trip to Italy to mark the event, I was happy for them and yes, a tad bit jealous. When I came home for Christmas break, I watched in amusement as they bantered back and forth, arguing about where they should go. My father innocently suggested Hawaii, but my mother simply snorted and replied without hesitation, "Why, we're going to Florence, Rome, and Venice of course."

Before flying off on their romantic adventure, they made a layover in New York so we could all meet up in the city. I took the train up from Philly to say good-bye and wish them *Buon viaggio!*

After landing in Florence, they climbed to the top of the Duomo and walked across the Ponte Vecchio. From the mail I received, I knew in Rome they sipped an excellent Chianti and ate big bowls of *spaghetti alla car-*

bonara in a small trattoria near Piazza Navona. They had the trip of their dreams, but now all that remained of their adventure was a stack of souvenir postcards.

Suddenly I was angry. Angry at the world. Angry with my parents' carelessness to go off and get themselves killed. But mostly I was angry with myself. I was wasting away. Disgusted by my lack of energy, I threw down my pillow forcefully, and it landed with a less than impressive *plop* onto the hardwood floor. Gritting my teeth, I swung my legs over the edge and planted my feet firmly on the ground. I sat there a few more minutes, trying to muster the energy to confront the past. Surely by now I was ready to be useful and could handle the mundane chore of preparing the house for sale.

Defiantly I thought: *What's the problem, you stupid girl? It's just a house. It's just a bunch of silly knickknacks. A good spring cleaning is just what you need.*

I padded into the kitchen, where Luciana was busily washing out Mason jars, preparing to start canning her last batch of summer tomatoes. When I leaned against the counter and casually mentioned I was going to visit the house and start clearing it out; her eyes grew wide. A shadow of grief passed across her face as she grabbed a dish towel to wipe her hands. Looking at me intently, she offered to set aside her plans for the day to help. But I shook my head, refusing her assistance, assuring her I would be okay.

Eyeing me skeptically, she said, "*Sei sicura, Sophia?* It will be a difficult thing to handle all on your own."

Seeing the concern etched on her brow, I said, "Yes, I'm sure. It's no big deal. Really. I'll take some garbage bags and a couple of boxes and decide what I want to keep and what to toss. I'll be fine. Don't worry, Luci. It's time. I can't stand living like this anymore. I have to do something."

She hugged me and insisted on joining me in a couple of hours with a thermos of homemade lemonade. Then she looked me in the eye and said, "*Sophia, non sei sola. Chiamami se hai bisogno di me.* You're not alone. Call me if you need me."

Shrugging I pulled my hand out of her grasp. Driving up Highway 12 in Giovanni's truck, which had been borrowed to have room for the load I intended to drop off at the Goodwill and the local dump, I thought: *But I am alone. I am the only one left now.*

When I came to my turnoff, I slowed the truck and waited for oncoming traffic to pass before entering the rutted, rocky lane that led to a large yellow house. Climbing out from behind the wheel, I stood for a moment, seeking signs of life. But as I strained my ears, all I could hear was the wind whispering through the grape leaves in the adjacent side yard, eerily accentuating its vacancy. To break the silence, I slammed the door of the truck cab with a decisive *thunk*.

Gazing at the house that had been my home forever, it seemed tired, as if it, too, had suffered a loss. The lavender beds were choked with weeds and debris and to the right of the porch was an out-of-control rosemary bush. My dad was forever pruning that tangled old thing. We used to laugh and say it wasn't content to be an ordinary shrub but rather aspired to be a tree. At the moment it seemed to be obtaining its goal.

As I navigated the overgrown path, I breathed in the heady scent of green grass, moist dirt, and tangy lemon verbena. I paused for a moment with one foot on the bottom step and looked up to see three familiar green rocking chairs idly swaying to the left of the front door. I recalled how we used to sit together, sipping sun tea—or when I grew older, gin and tonics—watching the hawks in the distance as the sun sank into the evening shadows.

I listened again for signs that my parents might still be inside, but all I heard was the whir of more insects and the far off crow of a rooster from the neighbor's hen house, despite it being a quarter past one in the afternoon. I smiled, thinking Sonoma roosters were crazy birds that apparently couldn't tell time.

Leaning over the railing, I saw my old bike chained to a sturdy gutter. As a young girl, I used that bike to explore abandoned dirt paths and join friends on wild adventures. On bright days we created forts in tall grasses or swam in creeks, and when night fell, we played Kick the Can, hiding in mysterious, dark places. But on rainy days, when confined to the house, my mother stepped in and released me from my doldrums. She often told me the world was a more interesting place when you loosened your mind and dreamt with your eyes open. In her lovely Italian, she said, "Sophia sweetheart, did you know the Italians call it *sognare ad occhi aperti'?*"

Then swiping a cloth off the dining room table, she said, "Bella, let's pretend." As she wrapped the lace around my shoulders, she proclaimed me Donna Bianca, the white lady from the Vincigliata Castle in Fiesole, the hill town overlooking Florence. Adjusting the tablecloth to form my bridal dress, she said, "On the lady's wedding day, the groom tragically died in a duel instigated by her conniving brothers. So instead of feasting on Tuscan boar and drinking sparkling wine, she died of a broken heart and was buried alongside her fiancé."

When the story came to an end, my mother plucked a silver candlestick off the table and began dueling with a phantom swordsman. Then suddenly her eyes flashed open. Clasping a hand to her chest, as if she had been pierced in the heart, run through by a saber, she collapsed to the floor. In an exaggerated death dance, she wiggled on the carpet until finally lying stock still.

I rushed to her side, my hand upon my forehead. In mock despair, I cried out, "Take me with you. I cannot go on without you." Smothering a giggle, I twirled around before dropping down on top of her.

Chuckling, my mother opened one eye and whispered, "But Sophi, you don't really die. Donna Bianca became a spirit forever trapped within the walls of the castle. There she remains to haunt the palace, protecting all kinds of loves, especially the more challenging ones."

Taking my cue, I rose and began traipsing around the room, moaning like a haunted spirit. "Oooooohhhh. Aaaaahhhhh."

With the tablecloth slipping over my eyes, I didn't see my mother sneak up behind me. When she grabbed and tickled me, I screamed in surprise. I tried my best to squirm out of her clutches but eventually fell to the floor, laughing uncontrollably.

Smiling at the memory, I walked across the porch to the front door. As clever and silly as my mother could be, she was also fearlessly unique and unconventional. She often said to me, "Who decides what is normal? Normal is the invention of those who are without fantasy."

During my teen years when I was feeling awkward and insecure, she placed her hand under my chin and tilted my face up to observe it from several angles. Then she quoted Sophia Loren, "Remember Sophi: Nothing makes a woman more beautiful than the belief that she is beautiful."

When I rolled my eyes, she added, "Did you know, my darling Bella, that when Sophia Loren was a little girl, she was nicknamed 'Sofia Stuzzicadenti,' Sofia the toothpick? Everyone thought she was too scrawny and thin. But eventually, she blossomed from an ugly duckling to become a beautiful swan."

"Oh stop!" I said, "Now, you're just making things up."

Laughing at my disbelief, she said, "No, I'm not. When Sophia stepped in front of a movie camera for the very first time, the cameraman complained she was impossible to photograph. They said her face was too short, her mouth too big, and her nose too long."

I thought about this, but before I could respond, my mother brushed the hair back from my face and said, "La Loren grew up in a time of war and poverty, without a father. Life was harsh and demanding, so she learned how to cope by nurturing a rich fantasy life. She learned to dream with her eyes open." Pausing a moment she added, "But Sophia Loren was also very practical. She knew that a fairy tale loses its magic without real life and that the opposite is also true. The most beautiful thing in life is to learn how to walk between the two."

Remembering my mother's poignant words now, with an ache the size of the Atlantic inside of me, I wondered if I could once again walk the line between fantasy and reality. Would I find beauty in the world again?

The call of the confused rooster brought me back to reality. I wiped a tear away as another of my mother's favorite "Sophia-isms" sprang to mind: "If you haven't cried, your eyes can't be beautiful." I choked back a little hiccup, a cross between a laugh and a sob.

Taking a deep breath, I exhaled slowly. It was time to go inside. I turned the key in the brass lock and gave the door a little push. It resisted slightly before swiveling open with a mournful groan. I was immediately confronted by a large oil painting of our golden valley done by my mom. She said it was the perfect way to greet people and draw them into our home. Looking at it now, I didn't feel very welcome.

Under the painting was a long, narrow table filled with an odd assortment of books and bric-a-brac. Amongst the clutter was a jar filled with foreign coins and forgotten keys and a basket holding seashells, river pebbles and a rough piece of Carrara marble. I picked up the stone and caressed it. I held it up to the light and admired it before slipping it into my pocket.

At the far end of the table, resting on top of some legal notepads, I saw my father's leather binocular case. I opened it, pulled out the glasses, and began fiddling with the viewfinder. I recalled how he had enjoyed stomping about the fields of Sonoma in galoshes in search of a new species to add to his "Life List." As a child, I often joined him in his quest.

Seeing a pair of wings soaring in the distance, he would call out, "Bella, did you see that? Look at the Osprey over there." Another time, hearing the trill of a blue-winged teal, he cocked his head to one side and said, "Listen Bella. Listen carefully to their voices. They are calling to you. Can't you hear them telling you to open your wings and fly free?"

During those long afternoons in pursuit of a wild bird call, my dad told me there was something magical about watching a bird fly. Just like da Vinci, he had studied the mechanics of flight. I often imagined while La Loren was whispering into my mother's ears, Leonardo and the birds were singing sweet messages into my father's.

Turning, I crossed the hall and glanced at the shelves that lined the walls of the living room. So many books! Only about a few hundred biographies, novels, and art history tomes. They covered every age from the dawn of the Egyptian pyramids to the trendy New York ateliers of Andy Warhol and Roy Lichtenstein. My mother often pulled a book from the shelf and then, in a way only my mom could do, she took me by the hand and introduced me to Giotto, Michelangelo, and Leonardo. She had the creative power to turn stuffy old art historians into entertaining geniuses in the same league with Walt Disney. As she recounted amusing anecdotes about the lives of artists, it seemed she, too, had painted in their studios and afterward attended their salons and soirees.

Wistfully I pulled a banged-up book off the shelf. The oversized volume opened of its own accord to a well-worn page, and I found myself looking at a picture as recognizable as any in our family photo album. It was that of the Renaissance duchess Eleonora de' Medici and her son Giovanni, painted by the sixteenth-century artist Bronzino. Now, as always, the woman's gown held my attention, as did her lovely oval face. Lingering over the page, I traced the design of her magnificent brocade dress with my finger.

As I continued to gaze at the familiar image, a film of moisture blurred my vision, and a tear fell onto the page. Swiping the drop from the Medici duchess' face it seemed she was crying too as if she shared my grief. I shook my head to regain my composure and closed the book with a snap. Setting the book down, I swiftly exited the room, moving toward the kitchen. I paused in the doorway, caught once again by an unexpected memory. As I looked over at the kitchen table, I heard girlish giggling and a misty image of my mother emerged. She was seated comfortably in a chair, pouring out coffee for her friend Luciana.

"Luci," my mother said leaning over to stir a spoonful sugar into her cup, "*devo raccontarti una storia favolosa ma è solo per noi.* I have a story for you...but it is for your ears only. *Non dire nulla a Giovanni, ti prego.* Don't tell your husband pleeeaaaassse...or for that matter, mine."

Hearing the first part of the story, my mother's friend threw up her hands, giggled, and said *"No, dai! Incredibile. Dimmi di più.* Incredible.

Don't stop. Tell me more."

As far back as I could remember, the Italian language had been a part of my upbringing. My wanna-be-Italian mother never passed up an opportunity to converse in the language. Intrigued with the melodic words, I started to learn Italian in high school and continued well into college. Over time my mother and I used it as our own private language.

Repressing the nostalgic memory, I turned to mount the back stairs. When I peeked inside my bedroom, things were just as I'd left them. But now, instead of laughter, I heard teenage wails and a door slamming. When my mother and I argued and voices were raised, my father hid in the den, battening down the hatches to ride out the storm. As a teenager, I was stubborn and impulsive. I'll admit I have always preferred to move at my own speed, operating according to my own clock. I wasn't one to be on time. Ever. My father called it "Bella Time", and if anything, it seemed to amuse more than annoy him.

Gently I closed the door to my room. Perhaps I wasn't up to cleaning it out just yet. Turning around, I hesitated a moment before slowly walking down the hall towards my parents' bedroom. I listened carefully half-expecting to find them still inside, laughing together at a private joke. To dispel the shadows, I raised the wood blinds. Turning around, I caught sight of my reflection in the mirror and jumped slightly. For a split second, I thought my mother was in the room with me. I glanced down at the bureau. Judging by the scarves, brushes, and tubes of lipstick scattered about, it looked as if she had hastily fixed her hair and dabbed her lips with color before rushing out the door. I held a brilliantly colored scarf to my face and breathed in the scent of my mother. I draped the silk around my neck, feeling the lightness of her touch.

When I looked in the mirror again, another one of my mother's "La Loren-isms" popped into my head, "Remember what Sophia used to say: There really is a fountain of youth. It is your mind, your talents, and the creativity you bring to your life and the lives of people you love. When you learn to tap this source, you will truly have defeated age."

What a waste, I thought. She died too early. In the end, she hadn't been defeated by old age, but by a stupid plane crash. Life was so cruel. But perhaps, in the end, it was rather poetic. If my mom had to die somewhere, it might as well have been Italy. Now like the Donna Bianca, she would remain there forever, holding the hand of her beloved husband—dragging him along on another one of her crazy adventures.

I looked over at my mother's closet. As a child I used to hide inside, pretending it was a secret room in a magic castle. Pulling out the shoe boxes stamped with fancy Italian logos, I admired the spiky high heels and the Audrey Hepburn Ferragamo flats. To me, the soft, supple Italian leather was as exotic as any fairy tale shoes made of fragile glass.

Pushing the closet door open, I was greeted again by the scent of her perfume. It lingered everywhere. As I let my hand caress the colorful silks and satins, denim, and suedes, I was hit by another wave of nostalgia. But this time, I wasn't able to curb it. Slowly I sank to the floor. From deep inside of me, the vengeful Furies clawed their way out. As they were released, I cried out in rage. Ripping off the lids of boxes, I pulled out leather sandals and high-heel shoes and flung them roughly against the wall. I wanted to punish something or someone for her insensible death.

I carried on with my crazed destructive attack for several minutes, but when I touched a familiar wooden chest hidden at the back of the closet, my outburst came to an abrupt halt. Silence descended. Momentarily distracted, I looked at the antique wooden chest, no bigger than a shoe box. I gently brushed my hand over the lid, removing a layer of dust, revealing an image of a fleur-de-lis and a name engraved beneath it.

Was this Pandora's box? Inside I knew, I'd find a random jumble of souvenirs my mother had collected in Italy years before. I held the chest up to my ear and shook it gently. The objects inside shifted and gently rattled. I held my breath, contemplating my next move. I reached for the lid, but when I heard the voice call out from deep within, "Bella, my love, Italy is the answer." I gasped in shock. By agitating the box, it seemed I had aroused whatever lay hidden inside.

As if burned by a hot coal I flung it away. I sharply exhaled any thoughts of hope and healing. Heartache and desperation rushed in to fill the void. I gave up in defeat and fell to the floor, reduced once again to a helpless hot mess of tears. A half hour later, Luciana found me still sitting amongst the mangled chaos in my mother's closet. She gently drew me out of the closet and back to reality, crooning, "*Mi dispiace, Sophia. Mi dispiace così tanto.* I'm sorry. So very sorry."

I surrendered myself to Luciana's warm embrace. She had been right. This wasn't the time to deal with my parents' things. Looking at my mother's friend, I pleaded with her to do the work instead. She was the executor of their estate, and I trusted her completely. It was cowardly on my part, relinquishing my daughterly responsibilities, but I knew it wasn't something I could handle in my current state of mind. And perhaps not for a long, long time.

"*Sì, Luci, mi fido di te.* I trust you completely to take care of things." Choking on a sob, I wrapped my arms around her shoulders and said, "I have to leave. This house...these things...everything is just too painful."

I glanced over at the chest with the fleur-de-lis. Resting on top of the pile of shoes, it sat there taunting me, daring me to run away to Italy as my mother had done years before. I quickly dismissed it as utterly ridiculous. What a stupid, stupid idea. Absurd. Wouldn't it be just as bad to flee to Italy? The memories of my mother were intricately intertwined with Florence. Wouldn't it be a constant reminder of my loss?

Stumbling to my feet, I leaned heavily on Luciana for support. Looking around my parents' bedroom one last time, I remembered the love they felt for one another and the life they had created. It had been a beautiful life—a marvelous life, the one in which they had nurtured me. But now that chapter had concluded. A new one was about to begin. The pages were blank, waiting to be written.

What remained of the story was now up to me.

Medieval

With the onset of the Black Death, which destroyed at least a third of the overall population in Europe, the Middle Ages saw a decrease in prosperity and stability. Medieval art in Europe grew out of iconographic traditions of the early Christian church, mixed with barbarian artistic cultures of Northern Europe. Classical proportion and perspective were forgotten. Instead, medieval art was one-dimensional, often surrealistically elongated and distorted.

Chapter 5

Waking Up to Italy

Not knowing what else to do I packed my things and returned to Philadelphia to finish my MFA in painting. Perhaps it wasn't the greatest escape plan. I wasn't throwing caution to the wind, hiking the Pacific Crest Trail, or joining a yoga commune in Tibet. I definitely wasn't running off to Italy to eat pasta. A year earlier, however, the decision to pursue a master's degree in painting had helped me get back on track and jump-start my artistic motor.

Graduating from college with a double major in art history and fine arts, I immediately began pelting the San Francisco Bay Area with my resume. I wasn't entirely sure what kind of job I wanted—teaching, gallery work, painting—anything to get my foot in the door. But instead of being welcomed into the city's creative community, I received not a single response. I soon came to the sinking realization that the diploma with my name engraved in gold was a worthless scrap of paper. I promptly fell into a million pieces, not knowing what to do or how to earn a living.

With no promising career options, I reluctantly moved home to Sonoma. Instead of a posh San Francisco apartment, I took up residence in my old room at the top of the stairs. Eventually, I found work at local wineries, pouring out splashes of reds and whites in tasting rooms for tourists. Even Luciana and Giovanni took pity and hired me to help out around their farm in the spring and assist with the grape crush in the fall. During the winter months, when there was no other work to be had, I waited tables at the Play it Again Sam Bar in Glen Ellen.

I was so busy eking out an income there wasn't time to paint, or for that matter, anytime to date. Driven by boredom and fed up with a lack of direction, I took out my frustration on my poor dad. In a voice dripping with annoyance and desperation, I moaned, "Why did you let me become a painter? What the hell am I supposed to do now? Why didn't you make me study something useful, like law or science? Then I'd have a marketable skill and could move out of this backwater farming town."

When I was in my most pitiful state, my father calmed my nerves and helped to replace the pieces of self-esteem that had started to crumble away. Sitting on the porch steps, he said, "Sophia, relax. I have always known you weren't meant to be a lawyer like me or even a doctor. Ever since you were a little girl, I have been delighted by your fanciful nature. You are an artist, Sophia. Plain and simple."

When I sighed heavily, he chuckled and said, "Look, Bella girl, the world has plenty of judges, dentists, and tax men, but what it desperately needs is more beauty. You need to follow your own path and astonish us with the things you create."

Without ever telling me what to do, he helped me remember what was important. Ripping a page out of Frost's book, he had told me to forge a new path and strike off in a new direction. But a year later, now headed back to a school outside of Philadelphia, it seemed my path had dead-ended. I had wandered astray, and no longer had the energy to keep forging ahead, but mostly, I lacked the desire. Frost hadn't warned me about this.

Sitting on the floor of my mother's closet, I thought I had hit rock bottom and hoped things would be different when I got back to the university. But I was wrong. Things progressed normally for others, but I remained in a state of apathetic depression, barely caring about my own life, let alone anyone else's. My grad school friends, whom I had previously found entertaining, now seemed overly gregarious. Some offered words of compassion, but it sounded to me like artificial sympathy; others didn't know what to say and avoided me altogether. At any rate, I was in no mood to go drinking with my friends or banter lightheartedly about trivial matters with classmates, so instead of hanging out in pubs or pizza joints, I pushed everyone away.

Now the only parts of the campus I found remotely desirable were the less inhabited areas where few ever set foot. On the east side of campus stretched a field of dry grasses. On the opposite side lay a dark, tangled forest where militiamen had fallen. That autumn, I found those retreats infinitely more appealing. I took refuge in the bleak abandoned spaces, burying "Bella" deep inside me.

As the weather turned cold and biting, I bundled myself in a heavy coat and dragged booted feet through piles of crackly leaves, which later turned into mounds of dense, wet snow. I attended classes but stared listlessly out frosted windows, barely hearing what my professors were saying. Christmas arrived, but I didn't return to California. I couldn't face spending time with Luciana's happy family. On New Year's Day, I wandered deeper into the woods and sat on a cold stone bench. I was alone in the eerie woods, which echoed with the lonely caws of blue-black ravens. Looking up, I noticed the lacy patterns the tree branches made against the ashen sky. Drawing my coat tightly around my shivering frame, I blew out my breath and watched it freeze in the cold winter air.

Like a sleepwalker, observing herself from afar, I struggled to wake up. I tried desperately to move forward, but it was useless. I remained immobile; my feet encased in frozen blocks of ice. It seemed I was a prisoner of Hades, the gatekeeper of the underworld. Like Persephone, the wife, he released only in the Spring, I too remained cut off from life in an isolated tomb waiting for someone to awaken me.

In the end, I wasn't saved by a handsome prince on a white charger or brought back to life by a kiss from a dashing duke with a sword. *I* was saved by a short, stout Italian man with a dour face and beak-like nose. It was Dante, the famous poet and father of the Italian language, who came to *my* rescue. Once he started snapping his fingers in my face, crying, *"Ehi, svegliati bella addormentata!* It's time to wake up, sleeping beauty," I began to come back to life, and my path became much clearer.

To graduate, I had to demonstrate a writing and speaking proficiency in a foreign language. Thinking it would be an easy "A" to brush up on my college Italian I had left the requirement until my second year. But when I returned to the university, I struggled with the idea of hearing the language, let alone studying it. In a bold move, I decided to start afresh and elected to learn German, the language of Bavarian kings. But after two tedious days listening to Herr Herriman's guttural pronunciations of *"Guten Tag"* and *"Ich habe einen roten Rucksack,"* I was plenty full of sauerkraut and threw my books into my backpack, dropped the class, and transferred into Mademoiselle Babineaux's beginning French.

Unfortunately, I had no more patience for the flighty Mademoiselle than I had for the exuberant "oompah-pahing" Herr Herriman. The French teacher resembled a sack of flour and reeked of expensive Parisian perfume and stinky Camembert cheese. Just as I had quickly grown bored of German, so, too, I tired of phrases like *"Je veux un petit chien."* It took me less than two weeks to say *"au revoir"* to Mademoiselle Babineaux and her *petit chien*—her puppies.

Left with no other choice, I returned to Italian. But I wasn't a willing participant. For the remainder of the fall, I sat at the back of Signora Zeffirelli's classroom, my arms crossed over my chest, staring at the leaves dropping from the trees, trying not to be captivated by her words and phrases. But as the semester progressed, the professor's familiar tones began to penetrate my stubborn brain and instead of a nasty-tasting medicine, her thick, rich accent made me think of *pane caldo* and hot chocolate. In spite of myself, I recalled happier moments listening to my mother chat with Luciana in the kitchen. The words wrapped around me like a comforting embrace and despite my resolve to let things remain in the past, the tug and pull of Italy were too strong. I surrendered.

Toward the end of the semester, instead of staring at icicles dripping outside the window, I abandoned my seat at the back of the room and concentrated my attention on my Italian professor. Following the holiday break, I even surprised myself, by enrolling in an advanced Italian lit class. I watched with new interest, as the weather grew warmer, as Signora Zeffirelli wrote with great flourishes, the opening lines of a poem on the blackboard.

When the professor finished, she let the chalk clatter into the tray and admonished her lethargic students to pay attention and wake up, *"Ehi. Fate attenzione. Svegliatevi!"* She explained having just read short stories of the *lirica popolare* and *giullaresca*, the Italian troubadour stories of the Middle Ages we would next be tackling something a bit more challenging, Dante's La Divina Commedia.

In jest, a guy in the back of the class groaned, *"Aiutami!* Help me. I see dead people!" When others started laughing at his reference to the movie the "Sixth Sense" the professor raised an eyebrow and gave him a look. The boy grinned back and shut his mouth contritely. Shrugging his shoulders, he pointed to the poster of Dante on the wall and then lifted his hands in fright as if he had just seen a ghost.

Shaking her head, she shrugged her shoulders and conceded his point. *"Boh. Hai ragione.* Well, I guess you are right. We are about to see dead people. Lots of them. We are about to enter the realms of Hell with Dante. We follow him as he meets and speaks with sinners, artists, lovers, and poets, who, due to popular belief at the time the poem was written, were destined to spend all of eternity in the netherworld as a result of their particular sin."

Glancing around to make sure she had everyone's attention, she explained, "Dante's poem is a famous medieval allegory of the soul's journey to find God—true enlightenment and joy." Briefly, she recapped Dante's story, which started on Good Friday, culminating in Paradise on Easter Sunday in 1300. She spoke of a dark wood where the poet woke to find himself completely alone. "Just imagine how it must feel to be all alone in a terrible place, full of despair." Pausing she asked, "What would you have done if you had lost your path?"

I shifted nervously in my chair. I glanced up at the professor, but she wasn't making eye contact with anyone in particular. Clearing her throat, she continued, "Out of the dark forest, Virgil the Roman poet materialized to lead Dante on a journey into hell and out again. Along the way, he meets all manner of individuals who give him words of advice and encouragement."

As the professor said this, she looked directly at me. She held my gaze for a moment before turning back to the blackboard. In swift strokes, she wrote "Dante Alighieri," the year of his birth, 1265, and the year of his death, 1321. As she worked at the board, several students began whispering among themselves again, making a few off-topic jokes. Signora Zeffirelli looked over her shoulder and frowned. To regain control she called, "*Ragazzi. Attenzione! Basta con le chiacchiere. Smettetela di fare chiasso.* Settle down. Stop making noise."

To emphasize her point, she picked up two chalk erasers. Swiveling to face the class, she clapped them together, sending a cloud of powdery chalk dust into the air. But instead of curbing the student's amusement, her absurd action only provoked more laughter. Wiping excess chalk dust from her hands, she laughed herself and challenged the class, "You are all a bunch of *saputelli.* Ok, wise guys—open your books. Go on, *provateci voi*! Try translating the poem. Let's see who's laughing now."

Picking up my book, I flipped to the opening lines and started to read: *Nel mezzo del cammin di nostra vita mi ritrovai per una selva oscura.*

Drumming my pencil on the desk I pondered the words, but like a Shakespeare sonnet, the language was so antique I guessed at some of the meanings. When I finished, I read my translation: *Midway upon the journey of our life, I found myself within a forest dark, For my pathway had been lost.*

Looking up, I caught sight of the poet's image in a poster on the wall. He was shown in profile, which accentuated his prominent nose. Around his head was entwined a crown of laurel leaves indicating his high-ranking academic status. I imagined how pleased my mother would have been to see me reading Dante. Hadn't she told me he was the father of the modern Italian language, the great uniter of Italy through the Tuscan dialect?

Continuing to stare at the image of Dante, I imagined my room in Sonoma illuminated by moonlight as my mother told me about the poet's love for a beautiful Florentine girl. "Sadly," she said, "their love was not meant to be; Beatrice was promised to another."

Feeling sorry for Dante and Beatrice, I said, "Couldn't they just tell their parents they wanted to get married?"

Shaking her head, she said, "Well, Bella, sometimes life can be a bit unfair. Beatrice's family wanted her to marry a wealthy Florentine merchant. Perhaps they thought a poet wasn't a suitable match."

"You know," I said, "they should have just run off together."

My mother cocked her head to one side and said, "Yes, my little *saputella*. But things were different back in Dante's time. People followed the rules of society and obeyed the wishes of their parents.

Impatiently I motioned for her to continue. My mother smiled and said, "Well, Dante loved Beatrice so much he waited every day by the Ponte Vecchio for her to pass his way. He never gave up hope of talking to her. According to legend, one day during a morning walk Beatrice finally stopped and chatted with Dante...about...oh, I don't know, perhaps the weather. Maybe he complimented her dress. But whatever words she uttered back, it is said his heart burst with joy. He returned to his rooms and that night had a dream that would eventually become the world's greatest poem, *La Divina Commedia*."

Waiting for Signora Zeffirelli to begin her lecture, I thought about Dante's love for Beatrice. If you asked me, he suffered not once but twice from a love story that ended badly. Dante who also dearly loved his home in Florence had been banished from the city because he found himself on the wrong side of a political argument. He wandered Italy, a lost man until he eventually landed in Verona, where he lived out his final years. He never returned home; he never set foot on the Ponte Vecchio again.

Chewing my pencil, I was brought back from my reverie by my Italian teacher. Resting a hand gently on my shoulder, she praised my work. *"Complimenti, Sophia. Che buon lavoro."*

It meant a lot to me to be singled out by Signora Zeffirelli, or simply La Signora, as most of her students called her. She was a demanding teacher, who pushed her students to do their very best. Because she was a hard grader, she had also garnered the title "Lucrezia Borgia", the Renaissance femme fatale rumored to have killed off a lover or two with poisons hidden in her ring.

From what I could gather, however, La Signora was single—there was no evidence of a husband and no ring on her finger, engagement or otherwise. Sometimes I, too, invented stories, imagining she had suffered a tragic love affair. Other times I decided she was the daughter of an Italian prince, accustomed to masked balls and equestrian outings but faced with the dissolution of fortunes, she had been forced to wander far from her native land, much like Dante.

La Signora could be severe with her students, but I didn't see her as a merciless professor, as the others did. On the contrary, I rather liked her and that spring we developed a mutual appreciation. Perhaps she respected me because I cared about Italian verb conjugations and proper pronunciation. Approvingly she nodded, when I rolled my "r's" and created the "gli" sound, almost like a true Italian. On more than one occasion, at the end of class, after the other students had sprinted out the door, she invited me to stay and talk. During our chats, she warmly encouraged me to travel to Italy where I could put my language skills to good use.

At first, I shook my head, distressed by the suggestion. Hadn't I already rejected the thought of escaping to Italy? But now I realized I was feeling less ambivalent about the idea. In fact, La Signora made it sound rather appealing. Her classroom was a source of delight and inspiration as well. All around the room hung art posters featuring Caravaggio, Botticelli, Michelangelo, and Leonardo. I found it a particular coincidence that behind her desk was a copy of Bronzino's painting of Eleonora de' Medici in her lovely black-and-white gown embroidered with gold thread.

Travel advertisements also papered the back wall. One featured the Cathedral in Florence, another the Coliseum in Rome. In yet another, gondoliers rowed lovers down the Grand Canal in Venice. If that wasn't enough to pique your interest or make you want to learn Italian, pinned to the bulletin board was a medieval map featuring fantastic Disney-esque castles and jousting men from Arezzo on white chargers.

The room was a bubbling cauldron of Italian culture and creativity. And Dante, the great poet himself, watched protectively over it all.

When classes were done for the day, I gathered my books and headed to the cafeteria. Tonight's meal consisted of sticky, neon yellow macaroni and mushy green beans. Scooping up a forkful of food, I let small pieces of yellow pasta plop down onto my plate. This was a far cry from the *"maccheroni cacio e pepe,"* the cheesy black pepper pasta my mother made. I pushed away my half-eaten plate of spongy mush and slumped back into my chair. Just like the food in front of me, life was so pointless and dull.

This was crazy. This was no way to live. Something had to change. I thought about La Signora's classroom and Dante's journey. I remembered a kitchen in Sonoma where the Italian language took center stage. I recalled

La Donna Bianca and all the princes, duchesses, and artists my mother had introduced me to over the years and realized I already knew how to make a dreary world more interesting. If I couldn't have an interesting life, then it was time to invent one. *È ora.* Yes, it's time.

Dumping my depressing plate of food in the trash, I left the cafeteria and walked deep into the woods. The weather had turned warmer—I didn't even need a jacket. Sitting on the stone bench looking up, I noticed the tree branches, previously barren, were now misty green, and the black crows had been replaced by comical goldfinches. They flitted across the daffodil-strewn hollow, making the yellow flowers seem animated and buoyant.

As I listened, I heard the melancholy cooing of a mourning dove. I wondered if it was calling to a mate hoping to find its lost family. I remembered my mother's last words, before stepping into the cab on her way to the airport. She had pulled the scarf from around her neck and draped it lightly around my shoulders saying, "Some day Sophi, we will see Italy together."

Then she had twisted a gold ring with a fleur-de-lis, the symbol of Florence, off of her finger. It had been a gift from my dad on the day I was born. Placing it in the palm of my hand and curling my fingers tightly around it, she said it would be a constant reminder that nothing could ever keep us apart and that someday she hoped I, too, would go to Italy. As the cab pulled away, I heard her say one last time: *Sogna Sophia. Non smettere mai di sognare.* Never stop dreaming.

Looking back up at the night sky, I felt a tendril of hope awaken inside of me. A cool evening breeze sent a shiver down my spine, and I heard a small voice whisper in my ear, "Dream Sophia. Keep dreaming."

I looked around expectantly but could see no one. Glancing down at the park bench, I saw a bouquet of yellow daffodils I had absently gathered as I had walked through the woods. I picked up the flowers and imagined Persephone, released from her winter prison, had placed them there for me.

As I caressed my cheek with the fragrant flowers, something clicked in my head. I made a decision. Standing up, I took a step forward. I realized where I needed to be. Italy. It was a fantastic idea—hardly obtainable—but now I was ready to let my imagination take me away and believe the impossible. In my dreams, I was already there.

Chapter 6

The Dreams Begin

I looked about in wonderment. It seemed I was standing in the middle of a long narrow street flanked by Renaissance palaces. All around me, people were laughing and calling out to one another. I turned around in a slow circle as the crowd ebbed and flowed about me. Was this Florence? From behind, I felt tap my shoulder. Glancing back, I saw a man in a red cloak. Urgently, he said, "Ehi! Svegliati. Andiamo! Wake up girl. Of course, this is Florence. Let's go."

Not quite sure where I was going, I started to follow him. But, it was hard to keep up with his brisk pace; there was just so much to see. I paused to look into a gelato store and admire the banks of multicolored ice cream. Hearing someone call out my name—Sooo-phii-aaa—I glanced over my shoulder and realized I was now standing on a medieval bridge. I paused on top of a bridge and looked over the stone ledge at the river below. Below me, I saw a young boy paddling a boat. When he glanced up, I gasped in surprise to see the fierce and determined expression of Michelangelo's *David*.

Bemused I pressed on walking, walking, walking, past crenulated towers and classical archways. I turned a corner and came to a full stop. Before me stood a magnificent cathedral. The light from the late afternoon sun reflected off the tiled dome turning it a fiery orange hue. The image was just like one my mother had painted once. I reached up my hand to shield my eyes from the bright light. I could just make out the silhouette of a woman standing at the top of the cupola. She waved a hand and said, "Sophia its time. It's time to get going."

Abruptly I opened my eyes. Coming to my senses, I saw the librarian shining a flashlight down the aisle. I heard her call out in an exasperated raspy tone, "Sophia. The library is closing. I'm making my last round. It's time to go." Turning away she clicked off the overhead florescent light and darkness descended over the stacks.

With only a small desk lamp to illuminate my study carrel, I shook my head a couple of times, trying to get my bearings feeling more than a bit disoriented. How long had I been asleep? I had been studying for midterms, but the long hours, late nights, and a less than healthy diet, combined with shots of espresso, were making me jittery and light-headed—not to mention exhausted.

I turned my attention back book in front of me. It was still open to the passage I had been reading. I flipped the page and found myself staring at a glossy plate of Eleonora de' Medici. Despite my groggy state, I was transfixed once again by the duchess' elaborate gown and the serene expression on her face. As I often did, I imagined what it must be like to wear that gorgeous dress and feel the weight of her pearls around my neck. What would I say to this woman if I were to slip back in time and be welcomed into her home in the Pitti Palace in Florence?

Shoving my things into my bag, I exited the building as lamp posts flickered on, illuminating shadowy bats that swooped drunkenly through the evening sky. I glanced at the foreign languages building and saw light emanating from Signora Zeffirelli's classroom window. Like me, she preferred to work beyond the witching hour. Yet somehow I wasn't entirely convinced she was alone. I smiled, imagining her surrounded by her milieu of Italian friends, perhaps deep in conversation with Dante as she tidied her classroom. Other times I envisioned the Medici duchess peeking over her shoulder as she wrote on the chalkboard.

Often when I passed by my professor's window on late spring evenings, I heard her singing. Sometimes she hummed a classical melody by Vivaldi, or she would sing an Italian pop song that was sweet and bright or pulsed with lover-lorn sentimentality. Tonight I recognized a ballad Mina had crooned. As I slowed my pace, I looked up at the sky. From beyond the realm of the stars, my mother's voice joined with La Signora's. *Guarda, io sono da sola ormai*...Look, I'm all alone now...*Credi, non c'è più nessuna*...You think there's nobody...*ricordati di me*...remember me...

Looking over my shoulder, convinced I was alone in the dark, I tested the main door, half-expecting it to be locked. But, at my insistence, the door gave way with a gentle push. At the far end of the hall, light spilled into the corridor. I bit my bottom lip and took another step forward, hypnotically drawn to the brightness. As I drew nearer her room, Signora Zeffirelli's voice became clearer: *La cambio io la vita che non ce la fa a cambiare me*....It's going to be *me* changing life, life won't change me....*Portami al mare, fammi sognare*...Take me to the sea, make me dream...

I stopped in front of the classroom door and looked inside. Instead of La Signora, there stood a woman in a full-length gown. The woman had stopped singing the lyrics but proceeded to hum the melody softly under her breath. Unable to move forward or step back, I remained in the doorway, watching her write Italian phrases on the blackboard. As her hand dipped and rose in great flourishes, chalk dust shimmered and floated about the room, giving her the ethereal air of a radiant angel.

I shook my head. Clearly, my brain was overstimulated by the effects of caffeine, and I was hallucinating. I let the fantasy play out watching curiously as the woman rolled her shoulders to alleviate the weight of her long, full dress. As I scanned the room, I became aware of a flurry of activity. The posters on the walls had sprung to life, and in my befuddled state, it seemed spinning movie projectors were casting cartoon images onto the walls. I shook my head in amusement to see the medieval map filled with cavalrymen galloping from one castle to another.

Seeking signs of sanity in this improbable situation, I looked at the stoic image of Dante. But instead of the poet's usual impassive demeanor, he now leaned out of his frame and was carrying on a lively conversation with Caravaggio's heavy-lidded lute player.

I closed my eyes and opened them again. Now the travel posters at the back of the room were spirited and lively. I heard splashing water and the melodic call of a gondolier. A short distance away in a movie flyer, Fellini's Sylvia reached up to feel the spray of the Trevi fountain. As she turned her head, she smiled and wiggled her fingers at a Roman soldier. He tipped his feathered helmet and whistled in return. Next to them, a young Renaissance miss blushed at something Marcello Mastroianni had just said. The movie divo took a long draw on his cigarette and blew a puff of smoke into the air.

Wrinkling my nose, I only detected the scent of powdery chalk. It tickled my nose, causing me to sneeze violently. My unexpected outburst reverberated around the walls. All eyes turned in my direction, and a hush fell over the room. The woman at the chalkboard, aware of a disturbance behind her, stopped humming. Slowly she turned around to face me. When our eyes met, we both gasped.

I could readily understand her shock and alarm. I was sloppily dressed in a gray flannel shirt, frayed blue jeans, and dirty old sneakers. Devoid of makeup, with my hair, pulled back into a ratty ponytail, I was an unsightly mess. She, on the other hand, was stunning. Not a hair on her head was out of place. On the contrary, it was securely fastened by a gold net encrusted with jewels. Even at this distance, I could smell her perfume. Unlike me, she smelled divine.

We stood for a few moments, considering one another. The woman tilted her head and narrowed her eyes as if she was trying to identify a rare bird that had just materialized before her. Cautiously she moved toward me. When she was just a few steps away, she stopped and placed her hands on her hips. She said not a word, but by the way she stood proudly before me, I could tell she was inviting me to notice every aspect of her fabulous dress.

And indeed, it was a thing of beauty. The bodice fit snugly over her bosom, and the wide, full skirt flared out, draping heavily to the floor. But what made the dress so unique was the design of the fabric. The black-and-white arabesque pattern was further enhanced with shimmering strands of silver and gold. Peeking from under the cuffs of her puffy sleeves was a hint of lace.

The woman examined me with a puzzled frown. I said nothing, hesitant to break the spell. Who was this elegant creature? Had I just I fallen into the pages of a magical book? Hearing giggling, I glanced up at the walls. Some of the characters were now pointing at me. Others, concealing their mouths behind cupped hands, whispered urgently.

Several moments ticked by and then the woman in front of me broke into a radiant smile, the characters beamed as well. Some even clapped in delight as she exclaimed, "*Santo cielo, ma certo! Devi essere proprio Sophia.* Heavens, but of course. You must be Bella." Laughing she said, "How silly of me not recognize you immediately."

Bobbing her head, she added, "It's been a while since you last visited me and...my, my, my, how you have changed, but I still remember those eyes. They are beautiful. Just like your mother's. Sorry not to have put things together sooner, but lately my mind has been occupied with many things. You can't even begin to imagine how many decorating decisions I have yet to make regarding the palace. It makes my head spin."

I cast about recklessly as to who she was and how she knew my name. The woman had called out to me familiarly—and not just any name. She had referred to me as Bella. I looked at her in confusion. What could she possibly be talking about? Palace? Decorating? Duties? Decisions?

She lifted her dress, revealing a shapely foot in a bejeweled slipper that matched her attire. Catching my eye, she agreed, "Yes, I know. Aren't my shoes divine?" Then she took a step toward me. I hesitated ever so slightly and stepped back. I decided it best to keep a wide berth between us. Clearly, the woman was quite crazy.

Seeing my reluctance to approach her, she gently pleaded, "Bella, *tesoro*, don't be frightened. Surely you know who I am. Think. Think carefully. Why, dear child, I have felt the trace of your small finger and the warmth of your breath on my face. Loosen your mind and let the memory out. The dress. The pearls. Focus. Surely you remember the pattern. Why it took ten gold and silver weavers to create this gorgeous thing. In my experience, it has certainly been a conversation-stopper. Well worth its weight in gold." Once again, she giggled at her joke. "I've turned my fair share of heads stepping out in this beautiful creation. It's a piece of art, no?" She nodded her head delightedly as she held out the wide skirt to display the admittedly intricate work.

When I only shook my head in disbelief, the woman stamped her foot. From the pockets of her wide, full skirt, she pulled out two chalkboard erasers and clapped them together, sending a cloud of chalk dust high into the air. Then she tossed them aside and placed her hands on hips again, and said in an exasperated tone, "Sophia, my dear, dear girl. Remember those moonlit nights when you used to study my picture?"

I narrowed my eyes and began to make a connection. Seeing the dawn of recognition light my eyes, she laughed delightedly and said, "*Sì, signorina, sì!* It is I, Eleonora."

Of course. Standing in front of me was the Medici duchess. Glancing at Bronzino's print behind my professor's desk, I noticed the woman in the picture was curiously missing. The little boy, who had stood by her side, was now all alone. I watched in amusement as he climbed onto the cushion of the chair. Dangling his legs, he played with a small ball as he waited for his mother to return.

"Yes. I *do* know you," I slowly admitted. "You are Eleonora, the wife of Cosimo de' Medici, the great Duke of Florence and first Grand Duke of Tuscany."

Delighted to be recognized at last, she nodded in agreement. "Yes. It is I. The very one and only Duchess of Florence. Daughter of Don Pedro de Toledo, Marquis of Francavilla, the Viceroy of Naples." Raising her arms in a mocking gesture, she added, "Oh and lest we forget—because *he* certainly never does—the senior officer to the Emperor Charles V."

Leaning in my direction she chuckled and said, "Men. What is it with those incredibly long titles? You'd think they were overcompensating for something." She laughed uproariously at her bawdy joke.

I smiled at her quip and comical expression. She was beautiful in person as she was in her pictures *and* it appeared she had quite a wit. Cosimo, her husband, had taken quite a shine to her face based on the numerous portraits he had been sent before their nuptials. When the two had finally met, I'm sure it was a bonus to discover she had a sense of humor. She must have also been a saucy little lady in their marriage bed, for the union produced eleven children. But, in the final analysis, I imagined her noble lineage and political connections hadn't harmed her chances of snagging a marriage proposal from the powerful Medici ruler.

As if she had read my mind, Eleonora giggled and said, "I'm quite flattered, to the point of blushing. It seems you know quite a lot about me. You are *una vera saputella*."

She was right. Hadn't I just been reading about how clever she was and how she had supported the arts and commanded the respect of the Florentine people? And although it was reported she ran through money like a bandit and was a notorious gambler, the fates had smiled kindly on her. Instead of losing money, she had increased the family's fortunes through astute property acquisitions, like the Pitti Palace in Florence. She had snapped up that crumbling monstrosity for a song and through lavish renovations had overhauled the interiors, creating a sumptuous palace for the Medici family. As for the backyard, well, she had turned it into a sanctuary of earthly delights, calling it the Boboli Gardens.

Lost in thought, I barely realized she had moved another step closer. She stood so near I could clearly see the shine of the metallic threads and the luminosity of her pearls. Her dress was truly a masterpiece. I *had* always wondered what it would be like to wear it, to run my hand over the fabric and feel its weight upon my shoulders.

When I was about ten or eleven, my mother, realizing my fascination with Eleonora and her beautiful dress, had surprised me one Halloween by fashioning a miniaturized version of the duchess's gown. To complete the look, she had tied golden beads into a hair net to hold back my curly hair, and at the local dime store, she had bought a string of plastic pearls to drape around my neck. When I tried the dress on, I dipped and swayed, curtsying like a Renaissance princess. Then my mother turned me around, and together we gazed at our images and were transported back in time to a stone palace in Tuscany.

Clearing her throat loudly, Eleonora began snapping her fingers in front of my face, "*Ehi! Fai attenzione. Svegliati!* Hey Bella. Pay attention.

Startled, I looked at her exasperated expression. Lifting a bejeweled hand, she tucked a lock of hair behind my ear. Seeing my posture relax, she leaned over and gently kissed me on the forehead. Holding my gaze, she said, "There. You see? You can feel it, can't you? You are not alone." Leaning over she whispered, "It is time to move on with your life, Bella, and I am here to help you. Your path has been lost, but together we will make it through."

I sucked in my breath in astonishment. Was this magical vision quoting Dante to me? Was Eleonora de' Medici implying she would guide me through the dark and lonely woods? I glanced up at the poster of Dante on the wall. Across his face was spread a smug grin. He tilted his head and winked.

Eleonora smiled up at Dante before turning back to me. "I am not the only one who cares for you. You will be surprised to know how many others there are looking out for you. We are here to guide you along your journey."

Seeing my confusion, she said, "Yes, there are many more for you to encounter. I know a certain ancestor of my husband, Lorenzo de' Medici, is particularly interested in making your acquaintance. He is waiting for you in Florence."

I tilted my head and regarded her thoughtfully. The idea of Lorenzo de' Medici, the Florentine prince who had encouraged so many artists, having any interest in me at all was rather curious and a little exciting.

Eleonora said matter-of-factly, "Yes, my dear, you must go to Italy. It is your destiny. I know it seems impossible right now. But just remember, dreams can become reality." Resting a hand gently on my shoulder, she added, "You are lucky I am here to get you started."

"*Mamma!*" Eleonora's little boy Giovanni demanded, "When are you coming back? I'm getting lonely sitting here by myself." Hearing her child, she turned to him and said in a sweet voice, "*Amore mio. Ancora un'attimo.* Just a few more minutes, sweetheart."

Looking back at me, she continued, "Dearest Bella, like my darling Giovanni, I consider you my child, too. After all, I have watched you grow up. You and I share a special bond. Where you go, I follow—and where I go, you follow. You see, our paths are one and the same."

She held up her hand and pointed to a gold band with a fleur-de-lis.

Smiling, she began twisting it off her finger. When it refused to budge over her knuckle, she stamped her foot, bit her lower lip, and gave it another swift tug. Finally, success. Raising the ring up to the light, she carefully examined it, reading the engraving etched inside.

Gently she placed it into my palm and closed my fingers over it. Looking me in the eye, she said, "Take this. It belongs to you now. It will be a reminder that I am always near. The past is the present, and the future is the past. We are walking in a magical circle, you and I." Then she said, "This ring unites us. When you are sad or lonely, just touch it and know I am always here for you. I will return."

I shook my head in confusion. "Wait! What? What did you just say? Hold on...why exactly did you come here tonight?"

Letting out a small chortle, she said, "Well, that's a silly question, my dear girl. I'm here because it's time. You are ready now. I heard you call out to me." She paused and sympathetically added, "Listen you have a lot going on in that lovely head of yours. *Tranquilla!* It is all going to work out just fine. One step at a time. The important thing is to keep moving forward on your path."

She waited a moment as if expecting a new question, but I was still puzzling over her words. Seeing this she clapped her hands together and said, "*Allora. Sei proprio in gamba.* Well, you're a lovely and capable girl." Pausing to take in my rather unattractive "studying-for-midterms" look, she leaned in and whispered, "Perhaps I can even give you some advice about your wardrobe...and a splash of my cologne."

She straightened and gave a hard little tug to her jewel-encrusted headpiece. "But right now, my dear, I must go. I have so many things to attend to when my husband, Cosimo, is away."

Waving at her little boy, she blew him a kiss, and said, "Coming, my love. It's time for a bedtime story. The hour is growing late." As she turned, I heard her say, "What a relief it will be to get out of this heavy dress. I love it dearly, but it puts a strain on my shoulders *and* my pocketbook." She laughed at her quip. Then she resumed humming her song.

I closed my eyes and counted to ten. When I opened them, Signora Zeffirelli in her black sweater and sensible flats was gazing at me with concern. In her hands, she held a copy of Dante's poem.

She shook her head in amusement, saying, "*Ehi! Fai attenzione. Svegliati!* Wake up Sophia. You forgot your book."

When I didn't respond immediately, she asked, "Are you okay? Seems like your mind is a million miles away."

I shrugged my shoulders apologetically, as she placed the book on the desk. Turning around, she walked to the chalkboard. As she resumed writing, she began to sing softly again *La cambio io la vita che mi ha deluso... Portami al mare, fammi sognare...I will change my life that has deluded me... Take me to the sea, make me dream again...*

Reaching out to pick up my copy of Dante's cantos I realized my hand was curled tightly into a fist. Slowly I let my fingers splay open. There on my finger was a gold band with a fleur-de-lis. I touched it and rotated it around and around on my finger.

La Signora turned back to me and said, "Sophia, remember what I said. With your grasp of the language, I believe you would do well in Italy. It seems a little daunting right now, but you will make it through. Everything starts with a single decision, a single step, and we are all here to guide you.

Remember tonight, Sophia...for it is the beginning of always."

Chapter 7

Saving Lorenzo's Legacy

*A*fter my last midterm paper was turned in, I crawled into bed and slept for days. When I awoke again, it was with a clearer head. Raising a hand to cover my eyes to avoid the bright sun streaming in through the window, I realized how uncomfortably warm the room had become. Annoyed, I kicked off the tangle of cloying sheets, sending them up into the air where they floated, suspended for a few moments before sinking like a deflated ghost onto the floor in a billowing puddle. No need for alarm, I thought with a smile. No magical visitors hiding under the covers this morning.

I rolled out of bed and walked to the window, and I raised it. Taking a deep breath of air I picked up the scent of wet, fertile earth and heard the birds chirping just a tad too gleefully. Perhaps I had been too quick to dismiss the idea that messages were being telegraphed from beyond. As I inhaled the scent of new life and listened to the calls of the birds, I heard my father whisper into my ear, "Bella, return to your art! That is what gives you the greatest comfort and solace. You have real talent. Trust your instincts." Once again, his words restored and inspired me.

Remembering there were others like La Signora, looking out for me wanting to help when my friends returned from spring break, I began reconnecting with them. I eased my way back into the campus social scene and was greeted with warm smiles and open arms. It didn't take long before I was resuming old habits, meeting my classmates at coffee bars and local dives to drink wine and talk about art or simply dish up campus gossip.

Occasionally Glenninghall, our painting instructor, joined us at the bar. He liked to hang out with grad students to swap stories on "two-for-one-drinks Tuesdays." He was a welcome addition to our group, as he was always quick with a witty retort or entertaining story tell. He was the epitome of a modern Renaissance man, loved jazz, mathematics, and Plato and was a virtual walking catalog of the arts. You could ask him almost anything, and he could tell you what books the library owned on the subject and the merits of each.

At the same time, none of his students would ever complain he was too bookish. Instead of a conservative tie, he often showed up to lectures in paint-spattered khakis and black army boots. Judging by the messy state of his full mane of white hair, it seemed it was rarely tended to by a comb. The most charming and curious thing about Glenninghall, was his deep-throated laugh, which began in his toes and burst out of his mouth in a series of hearty hiccups.

The man's lectures were also lively and entertaining, frequently embellished by stories of his outrageous past. Often he meandered off topic or stopped to stare at an image on the screen lost in thought. Springing back to the podium, he inevitably pushed a wrong button on his computer, causing the slide show to either shut down or shoot too far in advance. When this happened, he softly cursed under his breath, and his lectures came to a halt. After rummaging about for the correct image, and it flashed onto the screen, often he stepped back in triumph and exclaimed, "Now, isn't that sexy?"

On one occasion he was referring to the square jaw and hooked nose of the Duke of Montefeltro. Dumbfounded the class looked at the crooked profile of the man in the portrait, confused by his comment. Laughing at our reactions, he said, "Federico, you see, bless his little mercenary heart, was no stranger to assassination attempts. After losing an eye, he had surgeons remove the bridge of his nose to improve his field of vision with the other—ouch! Well, the operation rendered the Count more agile at seeing and dodging surprise attacks, but...it turned his profile into anything but seductive."

Leaning over the podium, he said, "It isn't that Federico, that ugly, old, conniving devil, was sexy. People, people! Just look at the colors. Look at how the artist Piero della Francesca rendered the texture. Look at his forms, the shape, and the brushwork. Now *that* is sexy!"

It was quite customary to hear such bizarre things spring out of his mouth. I drank up Professor Glenninghall's stories and enjoyed the fact that he, like my mother, referred to the artists as his intimate cronies.

One particular "friend" he liked to talk about was Lorenzo de' Medici—Florence's sage and benevolent Prince. Glenninghall explained, "Because he ruled his city wisely, preserving its independence, increasing its wealth and protecting its citizens from famine, Lorenzo had been nicknamed il Magnifico." Laughing he added, "But what made the Prince, even more, *magnifico*—at least in my opinion—is the fact that he was a patron of the arts. And *what* a patron he was. He eased the way for lots of local talent—folks like Leonardo, Michelangelo, and Botticelli. They were just a few of the many gifted individuals Lorenzo invited into his home, granting them commissions and freeing them from financial burden so they could focus on their art."

Clicking a button on his computer, an image of Lorenzo swathed in a red cloak flashed onto the screen. Immediately I recognized the aristocratic Medici profile, the aquiline nose, and the dark, intelligent eyes. The professor pointed to the slide and continued, "Due to the prince's appreciation of beautiful things *and* his sponsorship of young artists, he cultivated an atmosphere in which the arts flourished in Florence, giving birth to what we now call the Renaissance."

Replacing the prince's image with that of a portrait of *Ginevra de' Benci* painted by Leonardo, Glenninghall stepped back and exclaimed, "Simply amazing. Astounding! Look carefully. It's almost as if you can see the woman's throat pulsing. Yes, Leo was certainly "one cool cat".

Of all his colorful expressions, I think I loved that one the most.

"In Lorenzo's fertile city," Glenninghall went on to say, "da Vinci began dabbling with oil paints, a radical Northern invention. Instead of traditional tempera paints made from egg yolks that dried far too quickly, he experimented with pigments suspended in oil. This new medium gave him the flexibility to manipulate and build up layers of color washes to create greater depth and subtle nuances. We call this *sfumato*. In Italian, it means "veils" or something vague. It appropriately describes da Vinci's style, because it seems he blended smoke into the colors on his palette."

To Glenninghall the refined and elegant Leonardo was "one cool cat", but Michelangelo on the other hand, he described as "diamond in the rough". Elaborating, he said, "Michè was a gifted child, who Il Magnifico singled out when he was a very young boy. The prince invited him to live in his palace to be educated with his children. Despite his undeniable talents, Michelangelo was a melancholy sort, one who kept to himself, answering only to the visions in his head and those he saw in his marble stones."

Switching slides again he showed us one of the sculptor's unfinished works, inviting us to examine the technique that he referred to as "draining the water out of a bathtub." He said, "Instead of working in the round, Michelangelo hacked away pieces from the front of a piece of marble, carving in relief. In this way, the figure emerged up toward the artist, as if it were being lifted out of a bath of water."

Glenninghall's stories about the artists were endless, but having lived and painted in Italy, he also delighted in talking about the time he had spent there. I was fascinated to learn that he, like my mother, had been in Florence during the time of the great flood in 1966. While running his fingers through his hair in an agitated way, he referred to the weeks and months following the flood as "simply far out" and told stories about everyone banding together like pre-Woodstock groupies. They cleaned by day and hung out together in the evenings in the loggias, talking politics, art, and music.

He shook his head as he told us that not even Leonardo, a scholar of civil engineering, could devise a plan to contain such an unbridled river system. But, he said, if any good came out of the flood, it was the advancements made in the fields of art restoration and book preservation. As he talked about the intense rains that had poured down on the city, I heard my mother's voice pick up the story. Waving her paintbrush high in the air, she used to tell me: "We were called the *Angeli del fango*...Mud Angels. It was our mission to save the art of Florence."

She told me the Arno River, so engorged by torrential rains, had risen dramatically, menacing the Ponte Vecchio. The ancient bridge shimmied and swayed under the strain and pressure of the *acqua alta*, the high waters threatening to explode the pilings. The storm had no mercy and was ready to topple the medieval bridge that even the Nazis had been too respectful to destroy. But the forces of nature can be crueler than the evil intents of men. With nothing to restrain it, the unbridled river water continued rising, preparing to carry out its brutal attack.

Finally at midnight on that miserable night, the Arno's soggy embankments gave way and river water gushed into the city. When the gongs and sirens blared, the Florentines panicked. In fright, they ran out of late-night discos or sat shaking in their beds as the floodwaters poured into the narrow medieval streets. Never before had they seen such a menacing tide. They were shell-shocked and helpless to protect their city from imminent, watery devastation.

The Arno first rushed into the Santa Croce neighborhood, where it filled the sanctified spaces of the church with six and a half feet of muddy water. Gurgling and churning, it lapped at the colorful frescoes painted by Giotto and drowned Cimabue's Byzantine crucifix. The people were faced with a vengeful river god, who attacked the very heart and soul of the city.

For two days the waters engulfed the city. Fortunately, the human casualties were relatively few. The real victims of the flood were the thousands of paintings and gold-leaf, hand-stamped books that floated away on a gilded slime. The rest of Prince Lorenzo's treasure trove was facing a terrifying last judgment. What would survive, or be lost forever, hung in precarious balance.

As the river retreated into its lair, my mother told me that the people of Florence were left with the task of cleaning up six hundred thousand tons of mud, rubble, and sewage that now clogged the streets as well as the basements of Renaissance palaces. Even well before the age of the Internet, it didn't take long for the world to hear the desperate pleas of the Florentine people. From all parts of Italy and every corner of the world, young people descended upon the city like salvation's angels. Picking up brooms, shovels, and buckets they began to clean up the streets where Eleonora had once strolled, and Dante had dreamed of his Beatrice.

In my mind's eye, I watched as my mother pulled on boots and waded fearlessly into icy cold, sloshing waters. Side by side with other Mud Angels, she shoveled muck and debris from churches and alleyways. I saw her nimble hands, so used to holding a paintbrush, wrinkled from river water, and her lovely face streaked with mud and oil. Watching in fascination, I observed as she and the others formed long human chains passing soggy, medieval books hand over hand, rescuing them from waterlogged basements.

Both Glenninghall and my mother, along with countless others, had toiled for weeks, helping the Florentines protect their Medici heritage. I wondered if my professor had seen my mom during those dark, traumatic days. Had he stood next to her, shoving pulpy books into her hands as they emptied the soddened basement of the National Library? Or maybe he had helped her lay damp manuscripts out to dry in big open barns outside the city. There in the golden fields of Tuscany, had they diligently flipped pages made from animal skins to keep them from permanently fusing together?

Finishing his story Glenninghall gazed off into the distance for a moment before slowly turning his attention back to the podium and his lecture notes. As I waited for him to project the next slide, I looked down at my tablet and saw a series of random drawings I had made while listening to him talk about the flood in Florence. In one I had sketched Cimabue's crucifix. Below that were hasty portraits of fashionable Renaissance ladies, each with the aquiline nose of a Botticelli goddess. The face of one of the women resembled my mother's. Or was it mine?

In the manner of fifteenth-century portraits, I had paired this woman's profile with that of a distinguished nobleman. He wore a cape and about his neck swung a chain with a fleur-de-lis. Bemused at the sight of the aristocratic profile, I sketched in more details to accent the man's face. I retraced the line of his strong jaw and darkened the hatchings of his beard. With each stroke, I defined more clearly his prominent nose and mesmerizing eyes. When I finished, I smiled. Then beneath the drawing, I slowly penned the name "Lorenzo de' Medici". The tug and pull of Italy were becoming more insistent. The voices were becoming firmer.

I could hear Prince Lorenzo calling me home.

Early Renaissance

The Early Renaissance was a period of great creative and intellectual activity, during which artists broke away from the restrictions of medieval art. Throughout the fifteenth century, artists studied the natural world in order to perfect their understanding of perspective and anatomy.

Chapter 8

The Angel in the Marble

*W*hen the lights came back up, I lingered a few moments, allowing the last stragglers to leave the lecture hall. Slinging my bag over my shoulder, I approached Glenninghall, who was taking his time packing up his notes and computer.

Seeing me, he said. "So Sophi, what do you think of the Mud Angels? I don't think I've ever seen so much gook and goo in all my life. Well, let me tell you, we certainly deserved the name. I cleaned so much mud from cracks and crevices all over town...not to mention from my own body. Man, what a disaster. What a mess!"

"It must have been an incredible time," I said. "I meant to tell you, my mom was in Florence during the flood. Who knows, maybe you two slid into each other in all that slime?"

I paused. I was now ready to verbalize something that had started percolating around in my brain. My dad had always said, "If you articulate a plan if you put it out there, the universe conspires to help you. Nothing ever comes about if you keep your hopes and dreams locked up inside of you." My mother had called these hidden desires *'sogni nel cassetto'*—golden dreams in a drawer. Well, I was now ready to open that drawer up and let my *sogni* fly out. I took a deep breath. "Hey, do you have a minute? Can I ask you something?"

Glenninghall rested his arms on the podium, raised an eyebrow and said, "Ask away!"

"Well, you know...I've been thinking..." I began slowly, "I want to travel abroad...to Italy. Florence. I'd like to paint there. I'm trying to figure out how to go about it. What do you think? Where do I even begin?"

At the first mention of Florence, Glenninghall's face lit up. "Listen," he exclaimed, "I think that is an absolutely brilliant idea. Firenze. Good choice. It cures a lot of things, including heartbreak, writer's block...and it fuels an artist's imagination."

With a raised eyebrow he added, "It ain't half bad either for having a pretty good time. Oh, and the food...it is fantastic! You haven't lived until you've tried a bowl of *ribollita* soup."

When I confessed, I didn't have a lot of money to play with he said, "Sophia, my dear girl, you've come to the right place." With an exaggerated wink, he said, "I'm very well connected. For starters, there is a very fine program at the Scuola Normale Superiore di Pisa. And, oh, hell's bells! There is another beaut' offered through the Art Institute of Chicago. I think they have locations in Rome and one in Florence, too."

Listening to him, I started to see possibilities where before I had only seen obstacles. Looking at Glenninghall I asked, "It's kind of last minute. Is it too late to apply for this coming fall?"

Glenninghall shrugged his shoulders and said, "Well, for this year it might be kind of iffy. It all depends. It wouldn't hurt to apply. Who knows? Someone might drop out at the last minute. There might be an opening. And listen, some of these programs offer grants, or there are sponsors who help exceptional students..." Stopping mid-sentence he grinned, "Hey, hold on there a sec. I just got this really interesting idea." Patting me on the back, he hurried on to say, "Gotta get on the horn first and make a couple of calls. I'll let you know what I'm thinking in just a bit."

I looked at him gratefully, but my smile quickly faded when he narrowed his eyes and vigorously wagged a finger at me. "You've gotten lazy, Sophia," he said. "You need to get back into the studio and paint. You aren't going to Florence or *anywhere* for the matter until you put in the hard work here and finish your graduate degree."

He was right, of course. Over the past few months, I hadn't been very prolific. In fact, it had been a couple of weeks since I'd even stepped foot in the studio. One day I had just given up, shoving everything, paints, and brushes and palettes, into my oversized locker and slammed it shut.

But now with new incentive and energy, I returned to the studio. Opening my storage bin, I pulled out a couple of canvases I had finished, and a couple that had yet to be completed. Standing back, I regarded my work with a critical eye. Ugh. They were truly hideous. At the time I had thought them intellectually profound, some kind of personal statement—a mantra about the miserable and tortured condition of humanity. Looking at them now, I wanted to cry. They were so dark and full of Gothic despair.

It was painfully apparent I needed to kick everything up a notch to pass the final year-end review.

To make up for wasted time, I kept an erratic schedule, painting at odd hours, even past midnight. I worked companionably alongside other students or, like today, in the studio all by myself. Pausing, I studied a still life I had composed earlier. The apples, lemons, and chipped coffee cups scattered upon a blue scarf seemed randomly arranged, but it had taken me thirty minutes to assemble everything to my liking.

Tilting my head from side to side, I considered my canvas and the progress I was making. I sighed. I hated it. Annoyed, I wiped down the canvas with an oily rag. Now all that remained was an ugly, brown stain. I let the word *"pentimento"* roll around in my head. It was the Italian word for repentance and referred to an alteration in a painting. Often with the passage of time, the ghosting of an artist's underdrawing appeared below the surface. It seemed many of my canvases these days were filled with *pentimenti*. But I took to heart. Changing one's artistic vision happened to the best of artists, even Picasso, Caravaggio, and Vermeer. There was nothing wrong with abandoning one's first idea in search of one more visually compelling.

Resignedly I also scraped down my palette, adding blobs of new colors from well-used grimy metallic tubes. I cast about my tackle box looking for my favorite color—Alizarin Crimson. It was an intense, dark magenta pigment that when mixed correctly was perfect for creating dusky evening shadows the color of midnight dreams. Still, Glenninghall often warned me, "Just a little dab'll do ya." A small amount was the right touch to make a painting vibrate with energy. Too much could turn an artist's color palette drab and lifeless.

I picked up a tube, twisted off the cap, and began squeezing. It resisted my efforts. Nothing came out. Having not used my paints for a while, some had dried up or formed thin crusts at the top. Squeezing the tube with my fingers, I could feel it flex and give way. I was confident that inside there was paint left to salvage, so I pressed a little harder. As I applied more force, the obstruction gave way. Like an uncapped geyser, a juicy glob of Alizarin Crimson splattered onto the table and on my denim shirt.

"Porca miseria!" I cursed. It was mild Italian explicative Giovanni, Luciana's husband, often bellowed out. *Cavolo."* I grumbled. It was another one of Giovanni's expressions that literally translated as "cabbage". It was a handy substitute for a far more vulgar word...kind of like saying "Darn"

instead of "Damn."

Scrutinizing the canvas in front of me, I frowned, and swore again. On more than one occasion Glenninghall had told me that to see contrasts clearly, you have to close your eyes and squint. I set to work again, switching between mixing paints and squinting. Mixing. Squinting. Mixing. Squinting. Now as I looked at my painting, although still highly critical of my work, I decided I liked what I saw.

I glanced up when I heard the cheery salute of my painting instructor, "Sophi! You are a sight for sore eyes. Good to see you in here again. Don't let me interrupt you. Just passing through." Knocking into easels, he noisily collected charcoal renderings from his life drawing class and began pinning them to a board at the back of the room. Dawdling a few moments more, he turned on his heel and whistling a Beatle's tune, disappeared in the direction of his office.

Glenninghall's impromptu entrance brought to mind his morning lecture. We were discussing Giorgio Vasari's *Lives of the Artists*. It was an important little book in the field of art, and Vasari himself was considered to be the very first art historian. It contained a listing of all the artists of his age, including Michelangelo and Leonardo, as well as Donatello, Verrocchio, and Giotto—the artists who had preceded them.

I remembered my mother telling me, "Vasari wrote a marvelous piece, filled with colorful tales and anecdotes. For the most part, the stories are true; others are based on gossip and popular legends. What made the book so valuable, is its impact on the people in the 1500s. They began to realize artists had big ideas to convey. Before that, they were regarded as working class craftsmen, very low on the totem pole of society. Vasari also made it clear that art is the progression of one artist learning from another. Each artist stands on the shoulders of another, looking back to the past, reinventing old ideas."

One of my favorite stories she used to read from Vasari's book was about Giotto. He was the artist who had painted an indigo sky filled with gold stars on the ceiling of a chapel in Padua. According to Vasari, Giotto was a skilled draftsman and had astounded everyone by dipping his brush in red paint and in one stroke, had drawn a perfect circle. It seemed a small miracle. Soon the Italians coined the term *perfetto come la 'O' di Giotto*—perfect like the "O" of Giotto—to express a job well done.

So many fabulous stories. So many talented artists. So many triumphs and tribulations. Glenninghall had ended his lecture talking about Michelangelo and Leonardo and their not so "peachy keen" relationship.

Standing at the podium, Glenninghall asked the class, "Why would two such notable men, the pillars of Renaissance art, harbor such animosity?" Not waiting for an answer, he leaned casually over the dais and said, "For starters, they were two entirely different men. They were nothing alike, physically or emotionally. Naturally, they went about creating art in opposite ways."

He added, "Then, of course, despite being opposites in every way, throw into the mix a little jealousy and artistic rivalry and voilà! The plot thickens, stirring up all kinds of conflicting emotions."

Striding center stage, he said, "Michelangelo would have been aware of the *Mona Lisa*, as well as *The Last Supper*. He would have known all about Leo's brilliant inventions. From countless men, he would have heard them drone on and on saying, 'Isn't he amazing? Wouldn't you agree? Isn't Leonardo the world's greatest living artist?'"

Tossing his hands in the air, he exclaimed, "How annoying for Michelangelo. After all, wasn't he still alive and kicking? Hadn't Vasari called him the 'Divine One'?"

Studying my painting, I absently mixed my paints thinking about the two great artists who had harbored such dislike for one another. I wondered what it would have been like to see them working side by side in the Palazzo Vecchio creating murals to decorate the wall in the Salone dei Cinquecento.

I was so deep in concentration that at first, I didn't hear the sound, but soon I detected an odd sort of noise, like that of a dripping water faucet.

Plink. Plink. Plink.

With my brush suspended midair, I glanced over my shoulder to see if Glenninghall had reentered the room. But I saw no one. Then the sounds began again.

Plink. Plink. Plink.

I tilted my head. Clearly, something or someone was there. Curious, I followed the sound to a large storeroom that contained a deep sink that was used to clean out brushes. I stopped in front of the door and breathed in the scent of turpentine and oil paint. When the noise began again, I recognized the sound: not dripping water—chisel upon stone.

I moved forward slowly but stopped when I heard a cry of pain and a deep masculine voice boom out, "*Owww! Porca miseria. Il mio povero dito.*

Damn it! My poor finger.

From the other side of the room, I heard a male voice respond, *"Poverino!* Can't you be more careful with your tools? It's no wonder you hurt yourself all the time. Those hands of yours are massive. I swear if I didn't know any better I would say Titans had conceived you."

The first voice replied indignantly, "Why you arrogant peacock. I know exactly what I am doing."

The second voice rebutted, *"Smettila. Basta! Non lamentarti più*— stop moaning. Keep your voice down. You are going to disturb Sophia. Can't you see she is trying to concentrate? I see she is having a few difficulties with her painting. Perhaps I can help her finish it up."

There was a snort of laughter, and the first voice replied rudely, "What are you talking about? You can't sit still long enough to finish your own paintings, let alone that of another. Your attention span is about as short as the hairs on your paintbrush."

Cautiously I peeked into the room to get a better view. Standing in the center was a large impressive man. His blue-black hair and beard stuck out in a wild way, giving him the savage look one might expect of a marauding Roman soldier. He wore a tattered linen shirt so well-worn, you could see through it. He had a well-defined muscular chest and his rolled back sleeves revealed a pair of bulging forearms. It appeared he was no stranger to heavy lifting. Sucking on his finger for a moment, he shook it a couple of times before picking up his hammer and began chipping away again at the large block of marble.

I scanned the room for the other man. I saw him sitting on a stool in front of a small easel. Unlike his companion, he had a slim physique and a short, trim beard. Around his shoulders was an elegant green cape. On his head was a jaunty cap decorated with an ostrich plume that bobbed when he nodded his head. Curiously I watched as the elegant dandy leaned in to examine the portrait of a woman he was working on. I instantly recognized his subject. She had pale skin and a mysterious smile. Apparently satisfied with his progress, he lifted his arm so as not to drag a sleeve across the palette, and began applying paint to the canvas in gentle, controlled strokes. He paused again, and I was amused to see him squint. Mixing. Squinting. Mixing. Squinting.

Turning my head back to the other man and the large block of marble, I realized now that an arm and a well-muscled leg were starting to emerge out of the stone. As I watched, I saw a big toe wiggle and move. How very curious. Wanting a closer look, I inched into the room. At the same moment a chip, loosened by the man's chiseling exploded, landing directly in front of me. Stepping on it, I skidded haphazardly across the floor, ending in a heap at the base of the marble block.

My clumsy entrance, combined with a banshee shriek, caused both men to look up from their work in surprise. As if it were a common occurrence to see a girl fly across the room and crash land on the floor on her face, the elegant chap leaned back in his chair, only smiled and exclaimed, "Bella my dear. There you are! How wonderful for you to drop in on us like this."

The other man quickly set down his tools. In one smooth movement, he picked me up. I imagined compared to the block of marble my weight was a trifling thing. He cradled me in arms for a moment, giving me a chance to recover from my spill. Then with concern in his eyes, he asked if I could walk. When I nodded yes he gently placed me on my feet.

Not to be outdone by his companion, the slender man stood up, pulled out a long white silk scarf and proceeded to dust me off. Seeing the stone that had caused my fall, he bent down and picked it up. He held it up to the light and admired its milky hues. Weighing it in the palm of his hand, he looked over at the other man and said, "Ah, Michè, I see you are working with a rather excellent piece of Carrara marble. This will polish up nicely."

Turning in my direction, he offered it to me. I took the marble and rolled it between my hands. Soon it felt warm and pulsed with energy as if a heart beat deep inside.

Touching me on the shoulder, the slender man said, "Well, then. Everything all right, Bella? It seems you have had a go of it lately. Rough spills can knock the wind, as well as the feet, right out from under a person. The important thing is to get back up. Don't let a fall keep you down."

As I slid the stone into my pocket, I looked from one man to the other and inquired, "If you don't mind my asking, just who are you both? I overheard you talking about my painting. How could you possibly know anything about it?"

The man with the plume didn't answer my question directly. Instead, he scrutinized me, then gesturing broadly, declared, "Who are *we*? That, my dear Bella, should be obvious." With a laugh, he looked over to see if his friend agreed. "As for your painting, well, are we not working in the same studio, my dear girl? One can't help but be a bit noisy and sneak a peek at a fellow artist's work."

The tall giant slapped him on his shoulder and scolded him, "Don't play games. She asked for your name, dear sir." Taking pity on me, he said, "It is nice to finally meet you, Sophia. But may I call you Bella? Unlike *some*," he said looking pointedly at his friend, "*I* don't take any liberties."

Looking back at me, he said, "My, how I like that name. Now then. Allow me to introduce myself. I am Michelangelo. Michelangelo di Lodovico Buonarroti Simoni. Perhaps you have heard of me? Come. See what I'm working on."

Together we looked up at the block of stone he was carving. I circled it, observing it from all angles. It was curious. Only the front of the stone had been touched. As I watched, Michelangelo picked up his chisel and began to work the stone again. As chips started to fly, he looked back at me and said, "Did you know I was born in the small town of Caprese, near Arezzo? At the age of...hmmm let's see now...I must have been about fourteen...I moved to Florence. I was an apprentice in the workshop of Ghirlandaio."

He looked off into the distance. "How I enjoyed my time in that marvelous city. Ah, those were the days." Turning back to me, he said, "If ever the opportunity presents itself, Bella, go to Florence. It is alive with the energy of countless artists. I learned much in Ghirlandaio's studio, but, after making the acquaintance of Lorenzo de' Medici, the Prince invited me to live in his palace with his family."

His eyes sparkled with remembrance. "Ah, Lorenzo il Magnifico. What a brilliant man. With his guidance and support, I was given all the materials needed to hone my skills and perfect my artistic vision. With Lorenzo's encouragement, I learned to really see. I found a way to capture the struggle and power of nature and translate it into my stones, bringing them magnificently to life."

Hearing his friend's praise of the Medici prince and his poetic words about his stones, the other man raised his arms and exclaimed, "*Sì, sì. Molto bello, amico mio.* Very well said, my dear fellow. For such a brute who lives like a hermit, you keep such beautiful images deep inside that massive skull of yours. I suppose, you *do* show a little talent for carving figures out of rock and stone." Putting a hand to his mouth, he whispered to me, "He also fancies himself to be a painter."

At that, Michelangelo rolled his eyes in disgust. Huffily he said, "Well, I've introduced myself. Tell her *your* name, my dear friend."

The man looked at me and said, "Ah, yes, well now that you've met the *great* Michelangelo, let me introduce *myself.*"

Doffing his hat, he bowed over an extended leg and said, "I am the one—the only—Leonardo da Vinci." He rose up and leaned casually against the marble statue, sending me a dazzling smile. I wondered what he would say if he knew Glenninghall called him "one cool cat." Well, I decided he probably would have enjoyed it very much.

My eyes panned from one man to the other. In an amused tone, I said, "Okay, so about my painting. Since you both seem so interested, can you offer suggestions for improvement?"

Michelangelo opened his mouth to speak, but Leonardo cut him off, "Well, for starters, don't go overboard with that Alizarin Crimson." Reaching over, he gently rubbed a bit of paint off my cheek with his scarf. "Such an intense color—too much and it is sure to turn any palette drab."

"Now...let me see, where do I start? Yes, well...naturally an artist must begin by carefully studying all the inconsequential things around them— horses, gears, muscles, cats, dogs, noses, fingers, and toes. Look closely. Let nothing escape your inquisitive eye."

Examining the items on the table next to him, he picked up a rotting lemon from a bowl. Gingerly holding it up he said, "For example, observe carefully how the light plays on the surface. See the change in color and texture. An artist can take the most mundane object and see great beauty where others see only ugliness." Placing the lemon back into the bowl and wiping his hands with his scarf, he said, "Beauty abounds in many ordinary things. Uncovering and capturing it, ah! That, my dear, is a gift only a few have." Gesturing to the sculptor, he said, "Take for instance my good friend, Michè."

Suspiciously Michelangelo stopped and looked up. "What's that you say? Are you speaking of me? Did I just hear my name?" The dust from the stone had turned the giant's hair gray, making him appear an aged man. Sweat dripped from his brow, leaving wet rivulets in the powder dusting his face.

"Calm down old man. I was just saying that you see things in those blocks of marble that you drag from your quarry in Pietrasanta. The rocks speak to you. You hear their calls and emancipate the figures buried deep inside."

Leonardo turned back to me. "This one once told me he saw an angel in the marble and carved until he set it free."

Thoughtfully I looked at the stone. "You see a figure in there?"

Michelangelo nodded his head as if the image in the marble was as clear to us as it was to him. "Yes, of course," he said. "I see the shape of its head. I see the expression on its face. I won't stop until it is liberated."

Leonardo chimed in, "I am as driven as Michelangelo. But not surprisingly, we work in different ways." Reflecting a moment, he added, "I allow my creations to build up through layers and layers of luminous paint. The oil tints are like life lessons. Each new experience, good or bad, makes us all a little more complex. Learn to appreciate the artistry in that."

The sculptor nodded in approval and slapped Leonardo on his back causing the slender man to pitch forward a step. Gesturing with his other hand to his work in progress, Michelangelo said, "Remember, Sophia. See the inner beauty. See the angel in the marble. Set the angel free."

The two men looked at one another slightly in awe, as if they couldn't believe they had agreed on something. Glancing back at me, Leonardo said, "Oh dear, I missed a spot. You've still got a bit of paint on your face. Here let me fix that." Studying my face, he exclaimed, *"Che occhi!"* You have such beautiful eyes. Wait! Where is my sketchbook? You my dear girl...are an angel."

Embarrassed by his words, I looked down at the concrete floor. I was accustomed to seeing its dirty surface caked with years of dried paint. Now, however, it was covered by a fine layer of marble powder. Touching my shoulder, Leonardo pointed toward the spot where I had previously fallen. There in Michelangelo's dust was the impression of an angel. As I watched, the broad outspread wings began to tremor and flutter.

I turned around to see if either of the artists had seen the same thing. But I was alone in the room. Instead of a stone block there stood the plaster urn that Glenninghall sometimes used as a still-life prop. I walked over to the sink, stained by years and years of turpentine and paint. From the faucet, little drops of water splashed one by one into the basin.

Plink. Plink. Plink.

I tightened the valves and smiled. When I returned to my easel, Glenninghall was standing in front of it, legs stretched wide apart, hand to his chin, studying my painting.

When he saw me, he exclaimed, "Ah, there you are, Sophia."

Nodding at my painting, he said, *"Perfetto come la 'O' di Giotto!* Nicely done! Your work has new energy. I can see the vitality in your strokes." Then, with his usual clarity, he offered a couple of suggestions where improvements could be made. Before returning to his office, he patted me heartily on the back and said, "Keep up the good work."

I rolled my neck and flexed my fingers feeling the creative energy in the studio. As I reached for my brush and palette, I became aware of a heavy weight tugging lopsidedly on my shirt. I reached into my pocket and pulled out a familiar piece of Carrara marble. I held it up and examined it, hearing ever so softly the steady sounds of a chisel on stone.

Plink. Plink. Plink.

Soon an angel would be set free.

Chapter 9

Kiss Me Again / Baciami Ancora

*L*ike the beating heart inside Michelangelo's piece of Carrara marble, mine too had started to come alive. But while I was up for meeting friends for drinks at the bar, dating anyone in particular, seemed a ridiculous notion. My track record wasn't all that great, to begin with. If a guy had no wit or imagination, I was the first to end things and move on. But, now, I wasn't even sure I would ever be ready to love again or trust a romantic relationship. Love. What was that anyway? It was just the promise of happiness that ultimately left you aching and vulnerable.

Despite my resolve to protect my fragile heart, my romantic nature couldn't be denied when it came to old films and classic love stories. Earlier when I had passed through the media section on the way to my study carrel, my eyes had caught a vintage poster of Sophia tempting Marcello in a seductive striptease. I couldn't resist grabbing the Vittorio de Sica film and popping it into my laptop. As the Italian film drew to a conclusion, I glanced at my watch realizing a bit guiltily I needed to get back to work. Clicking the pause button on my computer, a close-up image of Sophia and Marcello froze on the screen in a passionate kiss.

Pushing the laptop aside, I pulled off my headphones and dropped them into my purse. Inside my bag, I saw a recent letter I had received from Luciana. I withdrew it and held it under my nose. I detected just a hint of lavender. Since leaving California, I had received dozens of letters from her. Death in the family, I thought a little sadly, left not only a large, gaping hole in one's life, but it also generated a lot of tedious paperwork. There were so many estate details yet to be sorted through, and money was still tied up in probate. But Luciana with her usual efficiency had handled both the legal mumbo jumbo, as well as cleaning out the house. She had gone through everything, boxing up belongings and putting things in storage for me to sort through later.

To keep me in the loop, she had phoned and forwarded all the lawyers' letters and had bombarded me with questions about what I wanted to hold on to. But even from a distance, it was too much for me to deal with. Hoping to ignore the whole tired, sad situation, true also to my nature, instead of picking up her calls I started to ignore them, letting them go to voice mail. Poor Luci. She was doing the best she could to keep me involved, but early on, I couldn't stand the thought of rehashing the past and talking about my parents, and I definitely hadn't been in the mood to chat with her in Italian.

If I was completely honest with myself, I was ashamed for dumping everything—the house, the legal junk, and the nostalgic baggage—all in her lap to cope with. But, to her credit, Luciana hadn't given up on me. When the phone calls and emails failed to attract my attention, she had started writing letters.

Her notes started off in a sensible way, but inevitably at mid-point she slipped in a random personal recollection about my parents. Initially, it caught me off-guard—scanning boring legal information in one paragraph, and then reading in the next an amusing anecdote Luciana had remembered about my mother. At the point her flowery handwriting became even loopier, I stopped reading and refolded her letter and stashed it away in a box under my bed.

Throughout the fall and winter, the shoebox had filled up and just like the wooden chest I had found in my mother's closet I was afraid of what this Pandora's box might contain. As the spring progressed, however, I began to wonder about the letters. Suddenly I wanted to know what Luciana was finding hidden away in the house. I was curious to know what she and my mother had conspired about over tiny espresso cups and biscotti. I was finally ready to process the personal clutter, all the odds and ends and surprises that remained for the living to discover.

Yet, every time I started to pull the box out, something held me back. Curiously it was encouragement from an unexpected source—a new friend—that helped me overcome my fears. His name was Marc, and he was an architecture student from Chicago. The first time I met him, it had been in the library. He studied in a carrel near mine. We had struck up a random conversation about being the outsiders here at this Eastern school, me from California and he from the Midwest. I soon discovered he was a fan of classic films from the forties and from those two things, we established an immediate connection.

An hour later, we still stood in the same spot in the stacks as I listened to him tell me about his favorite architects from the Windy City: Frank Lloyd Wright, Mies van der Rohe, Holabird, and Roche. Despite his love for Chicago, however, after graduation he had big plans to set New

York on fire. In fact, he had already lined up an associate's position with a prestigious architectural firm.

Listening to Marc discuss his work, interspersed with funny quips from Cary Grant and Humphrey Bogart movies, I realized he had a wry sense of humor. His chiseled profile and wavy blond hair also made me think of dashing lords and stubborn Scottish chieftains. But despite the whisper of attraction I felt, I didn't pursue things. Checking my watch, I smiled politely and said good-bye. I thought to myself: *Some things are better left alone.*

But things changed late one night at a new bar on Cherry Street. I was out with my girlfriends, and we were doing a number on a bottle of red wine. Marc and his friends stood at the bar drinking beer. Nudging her shoulder against mine, my friend Patty leaned over and whispered into my ear, "Hey Sophi, I think that guy...what's his name again? Marc. That's it! I do believe he has a thing for you. He keeps turning around to look at you."

"Are you crazy?" I asked and took a sip of wine. "Leave it alone Patty, or I swear I will go back to the dorm on my own."

My friend set down her wine glass a little too emphatically, and some splashed out. Reaching over she patted my arm and whispered so only I could hear, "Listen, Sophi, I think it would do you good. Let yourself go. It's time to start dating again."

Glancing back at the bar, I caught Marc looking my way. When our eyes met, he lifted his mug and gave me a brilliant smile. My well-intentioned friend missed nothing. In her thick Texan drawl, she called out, "Hey, guys. Why don't y'all come over here and join the party? There's plenty of room for a few more."

It didn't take any more encouragement before the guys ambled over, offering to buy another bottle. When the wine was polished off, our group dispersed leaving me alone with Marc. We sat talking, drinking wine and listening to music thudding softly through the bar's speakers. At first, I kept to safe topics. I talked about the plans I was formulating to live abroad in Italy. But relaxed by the wine, I began to open up and talk about my parents and the plane crash. My new friend from Chicago listened sympathetically, and soon all the pent-up emotions spilled out. When I told him about Luciana's letters and my resulting guilt, he scooted his chair closer to mine and urged, "Sophi, it's time. You should read the letters."

So later that night, warmed by the wine and Marc's words, I pulled out the box of letters and gazed at it in apprehension, bracing myself for an assault on my senses. When I finally opened and read the first letter, it wasn't as painful as I had anticipated. In fact, I found the contents soothing and refreshing like the limonata Luciana used to make on hot summer days in Sonoma. I quickly downed the letters one by one, finding each one sweeter than the last.

In her own special way, she brought my mother's indomitable spirit back to life. How self-centered I'd been. I realized Luci needed to share her memories with me as much as I needed to hear them. I now considered my correspondence with Luci a lifeline and her letters my greatest treasures.

Included with her letters, she sometimes sent small packages containing watercolor sketches, or scarves, or perhaps small pieces of jewelry. Other times she simply recounted an amusing story like the day she had met Mom in the market in Sonoma. In one funny letter, she recalled a wacky New Year's Eve party when my mother had entertained us by dancing and singing *Tu vuò fà l'americano,* like Sophia Loren had done to catch the eye of Clark Gable in the movie *It Started in Naples.*

I loved the thought of two grown women, devoted wives, and mothers, going absolutely bonkers for their film idol Marcello Mastroianni. All you had to do was throw a tabloid on the table with Marcello's picture and watch how they swooned. I could hear my mother say, *"Oh, Luci, guarda! Che bello.* Look, how handsome." They rolled their eyes when they read stories about his *scappatelle*—meaningless trysts, and screamed when they learned about his more intense affairs—the *storie d'amore.*

They also followed Sophia's love stories with interest. I had once overheard my mother say incredulously to Luciana, "How any woman could turn down a proposal from Cary Grant is beyond me."

Luciana had responded, "But, *cara,* Sophia knew what she was doing. She allowed herself to be romanced by a fascinating film star, but in the end, she found true love with a man she knew she could build a life with—Carlo Ponti. If you ask me, that is the stuff of true romance."

Sighing, my mother agreed, "You're right Luci. In love, as in life, Sophia knew the line between fantasy and reality. She made a wise choice, and she's been happily married ever since."

Seeing Luciana's unread letter, I was distracted again. I decided studying could wait just a little longer. My mother's friend had sent this letter inside a small box which had also contained a red coral hair clip. It was a beautiful piece, decorated with intricate carvings and I'd often see my mother wear it on special occasions.

Unfolding the thin sheets of her letter, I quickly skimmed the first page.

As always, Luciana began in a newsy way, writing about vineyard business and how Giovanni was transforming a barn into a tasting room. When I came to the word "Capri", I stopped reading. I repeated it out loud. Just uttering the word conjured up sun-dappled waters, emerald green hills, and enchanting blue grottoes, a place made famous by movie stars and wealthy socialites.

Backtracking, I read again: *Off the coast of Naples, floating in the Tyrrhenian Sea is the island called Capri. That is where your mother spent one of the most romantic holidays of her lifetime.*

I paused again over the words "one of the most romantic holidays of her lifetime". Well, this sounded very interesting. Turning the page, I read: *I thought you might like to know the story of the hair clip I sent with this letter. Keep in mind, Sophia, this all happened long before she met your father. But I think it made her realize he was the right man for her. Sometimes you have to take chances to know what your heart wants.*

Intrigued and a little mystified, I continued reading. In confidence, my mother had told Luciana a story about a fascinating Italian man she had met during her holiday on the Amalfi coast. *There, where the air smelled like lemons and ripened pomegranates,* Luciana wrote, *your mother met a handsome man—his name was Pietro—and fell in love for the first time.*

According to Luciana, it had occurred during a boat excursion my mother had taken from Amalfi to Capri. *From the moment she had laid eyes on his slim physique and handsome dark hair she fell for him, and he was instantly taken with her. Together they spent the rest of their summer holiday together, playing in the waves and basking lazily in the sun on sandy beaches. She said in the evenings when they got hungry they ate plates of fish dripping in savory sauces, that had been caught in the very waters in which they had swum.*

Flipping the page I read: *I remember quite clearly at that point in the story your mother stopped and asked, "Luci, can you keep a secret? Please don't tell your husband...or mine!" When I replied my lips were sealed, she laughed and admitted, "Well...one hot afternoon we stole a red dinghy and rowed to a secluded grotto. Peeling off our clothes, leaving them on the boat, we jumped into the water hand in hand. I remember how our laughter echoed off the walls as if sea nymphs were secretly spying on us. It was all so terribly exciting and romantic."*

Looking up, I exclaimed, "Oh mamma mia!"

Turning back to Luci's letter, I picked up the story: *Your mother was deliriously happy. But it all happened so fast and ended almost as quickly as it began. Her young man, he was some kind of businessman I think, received a phone call from his boss telling him he had been transferred from Milan to London to work in a branch office. He would be away from Italy for at least a year.*

Luciana concluded with these words: *They tried so hard to convince each other a long distance relationship would work. But in the end, your mother decided she couldn't be tied down, and it would be too difficult. They thought it better to keep their days on Capri a lovely memory and not turn it into something difficult and bitter. When your mom finished telling the story, I remember she removed the coral clip in her hair and held it up for me to inspect and said, "Look at this, Luci. Just before we parted ways, Pietro kissed me and gave me this clip. It was so hard to let him go. I remember that awful train ride back to Rome. How I cried and cried. I guess some loves are just not meant to be. But despite how things ended, I never regretted for a moment the time I spent with Pietro on Capri."*

Laying Luciana's letter down on the desk, I gazed across the room realizing there was a side to my mother I had never known. I released the coral clip from my hair and turned it around in my hands, observing it with fresh eyes.

I jumped when I felt the touch of a hand on my shoulder. Instantly I was transported from the blue grotto back to the musty library. Looking up, I saw Marc standing over me. With a warm smile, he said, "I was hoping to find you here." Noticing the letter I held in my hands, he asked, "Do you want to go check mailboxes to see if you've gotten another?"

Returning his smile, I readily agreed and scooped up my books, laptop, and purse. When we reached the mailroom, I opened my box and was delighted to find amongst the junk mail a yellow slip indicating I had received another package. I called over my shoulder to Marc that I had something to pick up, telling him to go on without me.

Turning around quickly, I bumped into his chest; I hadn't heard him step up behind me. Laughing, he reached out to keep me from stumbling. Then spontaneously, he bent down and kissed me. When we pulled away, we were slightly out of breath, both astonished by the gravitational pull of our first kiss. I took a step backward.

Marc seemed disoriented as well, but instead of retreating, he took a step closer. Leaning down, he whispered into my ear, "That was really nice. We...well...we should try that again sometime soon. Why don't you come over for dinner tonight? I can throw together a batch of spaghetti. I've got a great bottle of wine..." Pulling out the stops, he added in a poor imitation of Cary Grant, "*You* are a particularly attractive package I'd like to unwrap and get to know better."

He raised his eyebrows a couple of times, making fun of his own double entendre, and then said, "I'll see *you* later."

Alone in the mailroom, I laughed in spite of myself at his silly Cary Grant-esque banter and was both intrigued and curious to know where our next kiss might take us. But in typical Sophia fashion, I was also ready to slam on the brakes. Once again I exclaimed, "Oh mamma!" Where was advice from La Loren when a girl needed her? I hugged myself tightly, quickly glancing around to see if there had been witnesses to our first kiss. I was relieved to find no one around. It was, in fact, curiously empty for this hour of the day.

Remembering the yellow slip I held in my hand, I walked to the post-master's window and waited. When no one arrived, I stood on my tiptoes and looked through the opening in search of the postal clerk. He was a friendly man everyone knew as Charlie. Most days you could find him behind the counter sorting mail, chain-smoking Lucky Strikes. Today, however, Charlie was nowhere to be found.

Leaning over, I called out, "Hello. Charlie, are you back there? Is anyone there?" Sitting on the little ledge outside the window was a small bell. I pushed it softly, sending a pathetic little "ding" into the quiet room. Growing impatient, I rang the bell again.

Ding. Ding. Ding!

From the back of the room came a rush of words. I strained to hear the man better. I called out loudly, "Excuse me, what did you say? I need to pick up a package. Can you help me, please?"

This time, when the man responded, I understood his words, even though they were spoken in another language "*Un attimo. Arrivo!* I'll be right there. A woman interjected with a laugh, "*Caro Marcello. Smettila! Tesoro.* Stop. Darling, you had better go see what Sophia needs. She doesn't have all day you know."

The man poked his head around the corner and stepped fully into the light. He wore a suit and tie, but his appearance was rendered informal by the sunglasses that were perched at a rakish angle on top of his head. When he saw me, he cocked an eyebrow and flashed a charismatic smile.

Then, on cue, a woman entered the scene. She draped her long arms over the man's chest and rested her chin on his left shoulder. Beaming broadly, she looked at me. She had big brown eyes accentuated by thick dark eyeliner, and her lips were covered in red gloss. When she stepped out from behind the man, I saw a form-fitting top hugged her hourglass figure. Black leggings covered her long legs, and around her neck was tied a silk scarf that matched her lipstick. She had a natural elegance and moved like a cat despite her four-inch stiletto heels.

As I stared at the woman in those fabulous shoes, I recognized her immediately. She was Sophia. La Loren! Looking at her, I understood why the tabloids called her a diva *and* why the paparazzi chased and adored her.

As I watched the film reel flicker and spin, the man glanced over at the woman and arched an eyebrow flashing a provocative grin. Reaching into his pocket, he withdrew a pack of cigarettes, offering one to his companion. After he lit hers, Sophia took a long draw and blew out a white stream of smoke. When their eyes met, they chuckled at a private joke.

Glancing back over at me, Marcello said, "So, Bella, what can I help you with?"

I was completely starstruck and barely managed to stammer out, "I believe you have a package for me somewhere back there. Can you help find it for me?"

Turning the full wattage of his brilliant smile upon me, he said, "*Certo. But of course, carissima.* My apologies. Sophia and I got a little distracted while we were waiting for you to arrive." He looked over at his leading lady and raised one eyebrow. "You know, Bella, this delicious woman never fails to charm me, and what better things does a man have to do with his time than to kiss a beautiful woman?"

Sophia shook a finger at her leading man. "Marcello, you are so foolish. Never forget it is *I* who allowed *you* to kiss *me*! Besides, we were only rehearsing for a film."

Dismissing him for the moment, she tossed her head and sauntered over to the window. Gazing affectionately at me, she said, "*Ciao Bella, come stai? How are you?*" Cupping a hand under my chin, she tilted my face up, observing it from several angles. Then she looked at me directly and smiled knowingly. She arched an eyebrow and said, "Well, Bella, my dear, by the look in your eyes and the flush upon your cheeks I can tell you are thinking about falling in love. How wonderful. Who is the lucky man?"

I stared at her, not knowing how to respond. Love? It was much too soon to tell. Before I could respond, however, Marcello interjected, "*Cara,* do you recall the first movie we filmed together? Do you remember how madly in love I was with you?"

Scoffing Sophia answered, "*Senti,* Marcello...we filmed so many movies together...and you, sweetheart, have a tendency to fall in love with all your leading ladies. Each woman you meet is another apple on the tree. You are always tempted, but after the first bite you are after another, a rounder and juicier apple."

Leaning against the counter, he crossed his ankles and blew out a long breath of smoke before retorting, "Well, *tesoro,* there is no one rounder or juicer then you." He swatted her backside before pushing off the counter and began nudging the packages strewn about the floor with his foot.

Rolling her eyes, Sophia countered, "You are such a prince, Marcello."

Turning back to me, she urged, "*Dimmi tutto.* Tell me everything. What is his name? Giovanni? Stefano? Ooh, Lorenzo?"

When I didn't reply, she waved her hand and said, "*Va bene! Non importa.* Your secret is safe with me. I won't say a word to anyone. Not even him." She flicked her cigarette at Marcello who had squatted down on his heels to better study the postage labels. Raising an eyebrow, she continued, "You don't have to tell me anything, but if it helps to talk, I am happy to be your confidant. You can trust me, you know."

I considered for a moment. I did trust her. Touching the gold ring on my finger, I twisted it a couple of times before whispering, "If you really must know, I don't even know if I'm capable of falling in love."

Sophia looked at me and sighed sympathetically. Taking my hand, she said, "*Oh, ragazzina mia.* You have lost so much in your young life. Loving someone and allowing him into your heart will be quite difficult."

And there it was. The thing that worried me the most.

Seeing my confusion, Sophia said, "My advice to you, dearest Bella: *Lasciati andare!* Let yourself go! It is the only way you will actually discover what your heart wants." Squeezing my hand, she added, "There can be many special men in your life. Look at me, I had a lovely affair with Cary, but in the end, my heart chose Carlo. You will never know what you really need or want until you start taking chances. Yes, you may get hurt in the process..."

Waiting a moment for her to collect her thoughts, I heard her gently whisper into my ear, "*Ama prima te stessa e tutto andrà bene.* Love yourself first, and everything will be okay. In this world, you have to love yourself to love others."

Letting her words sink in I realized she was right. To love and offer love in return, I had to make peace with myself. I needed to find my inner confidence. I was more than just a girl, someone's daughter, and a victim. So much more. This new emerging Sophia was stronger and wiser.

Marcello stopped sorting packages. Standing up, he pulled Sophia back into his arms. He looked over at me and said, "And if you want some really helpful advice about love, here it is: Kiss often *and* kiss like you mean it. Men love that in a woman!" In a gallant gesture, he leaned his leading lady back and kissed her on the lips.

Sophia responded enthusiastically, as she had done dozens of times before in their films. Laughing musically, she straightened up. Then she kissed him again lightly on the cheek, as she had done a thousand times before as his friend in real life. Rubbing her lipstick stain from his amused face she said, "Darling Marcello, you are such a lovable idiot."

Reaching for her scarf, she untied it. She draped it gently around my neck and said, "Well, now. That suits you beautifully. I kept it safe for you. I think the color..."

Before she could continue, Marcello sang out, "*Eccolo!* Here it is! I found your package."

Tearing off the brown paper, I discovered inside a familiar wooden box inlaid with mother of pearl. The last time I had seen this box, it had caused me so much pain. Now I lovingly ran my hand over the polished surface. I tested the lid, but it was locked. Taped to the bottom, I found a small key. I shook the box slightly and heard a soft clattering of objects. Previously I had rejected its contents, never wanting to open the box or see what was inside. But now I was ready to open my *cassetto dei sogni*—my box filled with golden dreams.

I looked up at Sophia and Marcello, but they had disappeared. The mailroom was vacant and quiet. Only a faint trace of cigarette smoke remained. I picked up the box and moved toward the door.

As I pushed it open, I heard Sophia call out from behind, "*Carissima, mi raccomando.* My dear girl, take a few chances. But remember, in the end, your heart knows what it wants. It will lead you to your true destiny.

Before the door closed, I heard Marcello chuckle and say, "*Cara. Baciami ancora!* Come here darling...kiss me again!"

Chapter 10

What Ifs...

*H*earing the story of my mother's love affair, I decided it was time to let myself go, take a few chances and start dating again. I wanted to test out this new, more confident Sophia. Maybe, just maybe, I was ready to allow a real person into my head and heart. It would be a change from the usual suspects who already crowded that space.

So I gave in to the feelings I was developing for Marc. Soon I was intoxicated, not only by the wine we drank late at night but by the warmth of his lingering kisses. Behind closed doors, we talked for hours. When we ran out of things to say, we gazed up at the ceiling and listened to Coldplay and old Police CDs. As we lay entwined on the couch, Marc kept rhythm, tapping his fingers lightly on my arm, reminding me that his heart was aching with every step I took and that he was lost without me. There was something intimate and appealing about the way he looked deep into my eyes.

I couldn't believe how fast things were moving, but it felt good to laugh again. For too long I had been tossed about in a dark sea of grief. Now in Marc's arms, I had found a safe harbor. Italy and my Italian dreams drifted out with the tide, and I allowed myself to be seduced by the possibility of a happily-ever-after with Marc. As nights waned into wee morning hours, now with every breath I took and every move I made—someone was watching over me. I began to wonder. Could this be a love worth holding on to? A love like my parents had found?

A state of total blissfulness, however, can last only so long. As with all new relationships, when the first rush of passion subsides, real life and insecurities sneak back in. Leave it to me to overanalyze things. It started with a wisp of chilly spring air that wafted into the studio. I was stretching canvases with a friend, getting ready to work on one last painting.

When the Police song came on the radio, I sang along softly. Hearing me, my friend looked over at me in disbelief and said, "Sophia. Really? I can't believe you like that song."

I looked at her blankly.

"Don't you get it? Don't you find it just a tad disturbing?" she asked, waving her paintbrush at me. "Think about it...it's about a guy who can't leave his girlfriend alone for a minute. The girl in the song is entitled to her own life without a man watching her every move."

The thought hadn't even entered my mind. That song was terribly romantic, wasn't it? Why wouldn't any girl want to be the object of someone's unrelenting and intense affection? By the time Sting's voice was replaced by Mick Jagger's, reminding me I couldn't get no satisfaction, a seed of doubt had been planted.

I quickly squelched the idea and turned my gaze back to Marc. Over pizza and cheap red wine in a little pub called Ruffini's where the tables were covered with cheap plastic tablecloths, we held hands and mapped out summer plans. Since I hadn't heard back from any of the programs I had applied to, Marc had suggested I move to New York with him. At first, I was disappointed that my Italy plans hadn't panned out—but as I got to know Marc better, I warmed to the idea of pursuing an art career in the Big Apple.

Reassuring me, he said, "Don't worry Sophia, someday we will go to Italy together. In the meantime, if you don't find your dream job right away. Just think...all famous writers, actors and artists pay their dues slinging hash or serving coffee at one time or another."

As we clinked wine glasses, I smiled a bit ruefully. Once again I was changing plans to go to Italy because of an enticing romancing. Looking into Marc's eyes and encouraged by his lopsided grin, I told myself, this time, it would work out. I convinced myself I was headed in the right direction.

But on a humid afternoon, the kind of day that promised a big, blow-out thunderstorm, everything came crashing down. I was working in the studio, trying to envision myself handing out "Triple-venti-half-sweet-non-fat-caramel-macchiato-latte-hold-the-cream" to Wall Street stockbrokers when Glenninghall sauntered into the room whistling an intriguing, off-kilter melody. Hearing it, I immediately forgot the Police tune I had been humming. By the devil-may-care gleam in his eye, I sensed he was up to something.

Running a hand through his unruly mane, he told me his hunch had paid off. Seeing my puzzled look, he reminded me of the program in Italy he had alluded to previously. "For the love of Mike, Sophia!" he exclaimed. "This morning I got word that it's definitely a thing."

He let out a wild whoop and began telling me about La Scuola Artistica di Belle Arti di Firenze. He said he was personal friends with the director,

Roberto Guerrieri.

"Roberto's school," he said with a broad smile, "is a bit unconventional and eclectic. You will dabble in various media and art styles while perfecting your unique way of painting. It will be the finishing touch on your art education. He also insists his students follow a curriculum of art history courses." He added, "It's hard to escape the shadow of the Renaissance masters in Florence. Lorenzo de' Medici made sure of that."

Gesturing excitedly, he exclaimed, "It's a two-year program. Imagine that. You will spend *two* whole years in Florence. Sophia. What do you think of that! Sweet. Right?"

I bit my lip trying to take it all in. For once in my life, I had nothing to say. The idea of moving to Florence stunned me. All I could think was: two years! My two worlds had just collided, and one of them was about to implode. If I went to Florence, the life I was starting to envision with Marc would be jeopardized. If I went to New York, I would forever regret not going to Italy.

Not noticing my apprehension Glenninghall continued, "After our conversation a few weeks back, I got in touch with Roberto. I even snapped some photos of your work and sent them to him in an email."

Nodding his head enthusiastically, he teased, "Yes, even *I* know how to send emails—even attach a few files. I was delighted to hear from Roberto so quickly. My friend owes me a favor, big time." As he said this, he elbowed my ribs. "I'll spare you the details right now, but next time over a beer, I'll tell you the whole story."

Growing serious again, he said, "But really, Roberto was impressed with your work. He wants you to apply." He waved some papers at me, which I assumed were applications. "Oh, and by the way, it comes with a small one-year stipend."

When I said nothing, Glenninghall frowned slightly. Arching an eyebrow, he exclaimed, "Well, son of a biscuit! I didn't realize this would be such a tough call to make." Then he added, "Take a moment. Collect your thoughts. Go pour yourself a glass of wine and think it over. Not to rush you or anything, but you have until the end of the week. If it's a go, bring me the filled-out application so I can attach my recommendation."

He tossed the papers onto the table, turned on his heels, and walked out of the room resuming his upbeat tune. As he departed, the blood rushed back into my head, making me dizzy. Suddenly I was being forced to choose between two dreams.

When I told Marc about the possibility of studying in Italy, he was happy for me, but quickly reminded me of the plans *we* were making together. "Sophia, I've signed a lease for an apartment. We are going to New York. Think of our life together." Then leaning over he kissed me and said, "You must know, I'm falling in love with you Soph."

At the mention of the word "love", my heart did a somersault, only adding to my confusion. Italy or New York? Love or career? But mostly I thought: *Was this the man I could build a life with?*

In a state of indecision, I allowed the application to sit on top of the chest with the fleur-de-lis. The papers reminded me of what I might give up, as well as the things I might achieve if I returned them to Glenninghall. When I woke in the morning, they taunted and beckoned me. At night in my darkened room, I could hear them calling out to me, "Think of the possibilities."

The "what ifs" began to accumulate, filling me with hope and admittedly some hope and dread. My stomach was in knots. What if I woke up in Florence instead of New York? What if I walked along the Arno instead of the Hudson? What if I climbed Giotto's bell tower instead of the Empire State Building? Should I go to New York and sketch urban graffiti, or should I paint Italian scenery?

As I weighed my choices, the easy camaraderie I had enjoyed with Marc now vibrated with an unfamiliar tension. I began to pick small fights, and we bickered over silly things. The attentiveness I had once found attractive was suddenly irritating and restrictive.

Confused by my vacillating moods, he cursed and said, "Damn it, Sophia, what is going on with you? It's like you are two different girls. One day you're the girl I met in the library. The next day you're like Lucrezia Borgia, and I fear for my life.

Me? Lucrezia Borgia? Where had that come from? That was a little extreme. Sure she was rumored to be a Renaissance "man killer", but that was probably just rumors and gossip. Just like La Signora, who had also earned that nickname, I thought Lucrezia had gotten a bad rap. She may have been just like my Italian teacher, a lovely encouraging woman with extremely high standards. The only thing La Signora threatened was a person's mediocrity.

None the less, I felt bad for snapping at Marc. To make amends I squeezed his hand and drew him back to my room where I whispered reassuring words in the dark. After he had returned to his apartment, I leaned my head against the door, plagued by nagging doubts. Had I fallen in love with Marc or with the idea of love? How could I love anyone else if I didn't understand myself first?

But the question that repeatedly pulsed in my brain: *How could I possibly not go to Italy?*

The day the application was due, I overslept. Following a night of wild, unresolved dreams I felt groggy and exhausted. I lay in my bed surveying the ceiling but was distracted by the whir of an errant mosquito.

Zzzzzz...zzzzzz...zzzzzz...

"Zanzare."

For such a pesky insect, in Italian, the word "mosquito" sounded quite pleasant. I turned to look at the clock, watching idly as the minute hand ticked rhythmically forward. My thoughts began to follow along in pulsing staccato beats:

Tic. Where do you want to be?

Tic. What if...*Tic. Tic. Tic.*

Coming to my senses, I realized if I didn't get moving I would be late for class. Leaping out of bed, I grabbed my toothbrush and hurried to the bathroom and splashed cold water onto my face. I reached for my towel, but it wasn't where I had left it. I groped about blindly as water dripped from my face. Cursing softly under my breath, I muttered, *"Cavolo!"*

Then I felt a light tap on my shoulder, and a cheerful, feminine voice said, *"Eccolo!* Here. Is this what you're looking for?"

I straightened up, water streaming down my face. As I did, I felt the weight of a towel draped lightly over my shoulder. Slowly I opened my eyes and beheld a lovely young woman. Although I hadn't heard her, it seemed she had been in the shower. I could see droplets of water shimmering in her hair as if diamonds were entwined in her braids.

I sank back against the counter and looked at the woman. I was not surprised. Raking a hand through my hair, I asked, "And you would be?"

The girl struck a suggestive pose, resembling a Grecian goddess. She seemed quite chic and shameless. A long pink towel gracefully draped her body and even though it was evident she was nude underneath, a colorful strand of Venetian beads hung around her neck.

Flashing me an exasperated look, she said, "Well, surely you recognize *me*, Sophia."

Picking up my toothbrush, I swirled it around, shaking my head indicating I didn't have a clue. She took a step forward and said. "Oh, all right. It is I, Lucrezia! Lucrezia Borgia. Remember me now?"

She did a jaunty pirouette, revealing a shapely leg. Clutching the towel to keep it from slipping, she nodded in the direction of the shower. "Those water closets are simply divine. *Una favola!* What a marvelous invention. To think hot water rushes out at the touch of a silver lever. What a treat. I could stay in there for hours."

I laughed at her appreciation for modern technology. She seemed so open and curious, not at all what I imagined a conniving murderess would be. This slender girl behaved no more like an assassin of lovers than I a NASA engineer.

"I know what you are thinking," the girl scoffed. "They are all vicious rumors, my dear all started by jealous spinsters who despise me for my beauty... perhaps even by my very own dear brothers."

Leaning over the sink, she cleared a spot on the foggy glass and checked her reflection. Satisfied her complexion remained intact and unblemished, she straightened and turned back to me. Seeing my impatient expression, she said, "Well, since you are in a hurry, I'll make this quick. Tell me please, what are you thinking?"

Perplexed, I raised an eyebrow. "What are you talking about?"

She reached for a gold brocade dressing gown hanging on a hook nearby. Cinching it firmly at the waist, she demanded again, "What *am* I talking about? I want to know what is the matter with *you!*"

Hands on her hips, she said: "*Senti, mia cara amica.* Listen my friend, it has come to my attention you are considering moving to New York."

She cocked her head to one side. "Granted you have a rather handsome reason. But *please*...this is your future we are discussing. Do you really think you are going to be happy living anywhere other than Italy? Wake up! This is your *second* chance to go to Italy.

When I didn't respond, she added, "You do remember Mexico, don't you? All you got from that brief affair was a nasty sunburn."

I shuddered at the memory. Instead of a tan I had come home an awful peeling mess and had suffered many margarita hangovers. As for the guy, that hadn't turned out so great either. He had barely noticed me and once we hit the beach had taken off with a dark-haired chiquita. Definitely not the trip of my dreams.

Lost in thought, I forgot about Lucrezia. I came back to attention a few moments later when she began slapping my face between her two hands crying out, "*Ehi! Attenzione. Guardami!* Look at me, you silly girl."

Pushing her hands away I said, "Hey. Cut that out."

She only laughed and took hold of my hands and squeezed them. "Bella, Bella, Bella, you are an artist. You have a gift for the language. You need to go to Italy. Don't deny your real destiny!"

As she talked, I began to replay all the "what ifs" that had been filling my head lately. Seeing my expression she snapped her fingers and exclaimed, "Aha I knew it. You are thinking about Florence."

Placing her hand on my cheek, she turned my head and urged, "Just look at your face in the mirror." "Go on. Look."

By now the glass was no longer cloudy, and I could see my image clearly. Yes, even I could see the desire in my eyes.

From behind me, Lucrezia's face blended beautifully into that of La Signora, and I heard my Italian teacher say, "Everything starts with a single decision. A single step. It is time to turn the things you have been dreaming about into reality."

She was right. I knew she was right.

I leaned back over the sink and splashed more cold water on my face. When I looked up, I saw a new look of determination on my face. I grabbed my things and hurried back down the hall.

Standing in the center of the room, I realized that now I wore the string of Venetian beads that had graced the throat of Lucrezia. I slipped them over my head and held them between my fingers, rolling one of the beads around and around. Then I began reverently touching the others as if the necklace were a rosary. As each bead slipped down the silk thread, I recalled an image or a story my mother had told me about Italy. Each represented a connection to the past as well as a vision of the future.

Thinking about a budding love I was potentially extinguishing, allowing a new one to bloom in its place, I blinked back sudden tears. I gently put the necklace next to the box with the fleur-de-lis. The beads made a soft clattering sound as they settled onto the wooden desk in a little pool of promises.

I picked up the application and rapidly filled in blanks. Now all I had to do was sign it and submit it to Glenninghall. I held up my pen and examined it in the light. Lost in thought, I let it bounce lightly against my lower lip. Time stood still, and the world held its breath.

Tic. Tic. Tic. Italy. *Tic. Tic. Tic.*

Who was I kidding? All along, this had been a foregone conclusion. I couldn't hold back the inevitable. Time was moving on. I had to take the chance or forever regret not trying.

Springing into action, I signed my name with a flourish. Pulling on a pair of jeans and a T-shirt, I grabbed my purse and swung out the door. Taking the stairs two at a time, I flew around the stairwell and into the dewy, hazy morning. As I sprinted across the campus, a lone bird trilled out triumphantly, heralding a new dawn.

By the time I reached the studio, I was out of breath and my shoes were completely soaked through. I ran down the corridor and burst into Glenninghall's office. Hearing my squishing sneakers, he looked up, and a broad smile spread across his face. Without saying a word, I thrust the completed application onto his desk. He gave me a thumbs up and said, "Delighted to see you. I've been expecting you."

I decided not to say anything to Marc. I didn't want to rock the boat or upset him prematurely. Although Glenninghall seemed fairly convinced my candidacy would be accepted, I was still a bit skeptical. I knew all too well nothing in life was guaranteed. But more quickly than anticipated, I had my answer. Opening an email, I read: *La Scuola Artistica di Belle Arti di Firenze is proud to accept you into its fall program.* I let out my breath in a long rush and began whirling around the room until it was a blur of color. After my giddy outburst, the next thought I had was: *Marc.*

Coming back to earth with a thud, I was suddenly out of breath. I realized I needed to find a way to tell him the news. I knew a two-year stint abroad would test our relationship. Still, I believed we could find a way to make things work. I hoped he would understand and ultimately be happy for me...for us.

But, I was wrong. When I told Marc the news, he listened patiently, up until the point I said I'd be gone for two years. At that, his eyes narrowed in disbelief, and we began to argue. Eventually in a fit of frustration, he threw one of my Italian books against the wall and walked out of my room. He called over his shoulder, "Listen, if you change your mind, you know where to find me."

Despite his words, the next day, Marc appeared at my door holding a bouquet of sunflowers he had picked in the fields near campus. Smiling a bit thinly, he said, "Hey, Sophi. Wanna go for a walk?"

Slumping against the door frame, I nodded and accepted his peace offering. Side by side we crossed the hot campus headed for the shelter of the cool, dank woods, the familiar place I retreated to in times of trouble. Sitting on a bench by the creek, with clearer heads we began to talk more rationally.

"I'm sorry," I said as I reached for his hand. "I never meant to hurt you. I wanted to go to New York. I mean I still do. But you have to remember I've been thinking about Italy for a while now...practically my whole life."

Taking a deep breath, I pressed on, "I told you from the first. Remember the night we got together—how I outlined the plans I was making to go to Italy. Then we got closer..." I gave his hand a gentle squeeze. "I thought following you was the answer. When I got accepted into the school in Florence, it...well it changed everything."

When he didn't respond, I knew I was blundering things. This is not what he wanted to hear. I looked down at the ground and picked up a small stone. I tossed it back and forth a couple of times. Then taking careful aim, I sent it skittering across the surface of the creek. When it sank into the water, I said, "Italy is no longer a dream, now it's something tangible. This is happening, Marc. I can't pass up this opportunity again."

Looking at his rigid profile, I said, "If I do, I will always have regrets. If I stay here, I think I will end up resenting you. You mean so much to me and that would break my heart."

I glanced down at the ground again. This time, instead of searching for pebbles to skip, I was trying to find the words that would make this difficult conversation easier. Marc offered no encouragement. He remained mute, clenching and unclenching his jaw.

Placing my hand on his right cheek, I gently turned his face toward mine. I stroked the stubble of his beard, realizing he hadn't shaved. Noting the dark circles under his eyes, I thought regretfully: *Am I actually doing this? Am I leaving this intelligent, sensitive guy for Italy? Am I a total idiot?*

Then sighing through the trees, I heard Sophia whisper into my ear: "*Cara,* before you can fall in love with another person, you have to know yourself first."

Caressing his face again, I said with a little more conviction, "You have been such a big part of discovering who I am. You have helped me grow stronger *and* brought laughter back into my life. But now I have to follow my own path. I have to find myself first. I believe if we love each other, we can make a long-distance relationship work."

Letting out a low groan, he turned fully toward me. As I studied him, I noticed his face muscles had relaxed. Then he smiled weakly at me. I finally saw the familiar lopsided grin I found so attractive.

Resting his chin on top of my head, he said, "I'm sorry, Soph, for not understanding or realizing what this opportunity means to you. I care so much for you. Fear makes people do crazy things, like hold on tighter, when in fact, they should relax and let go. I want you to be happy, Sophi." Clearing his voice again, he added, "So if going to Italy is the right step for you, then, of course, that is what you should do."

Encouraged by his response, I relaxed and leaned into him. We promised ourselves we could handle the separation and it wouldn't last forever.

A week after school ended, Marc purchased a one-way ticket to New York and moved into a studio apartment on the Lower East Side. He started his new job and was quickly pulled into the company's corporate fast track. Throughout the summer we spoke nearly every day. He told me about the friends he was making and the neighborhood hangouts he was frequenting. Every time I hung up the phone, and we said another long goodbye I thought about Marc's new life in the city and wondered if this was going to work.

I pondered my decision over and over. I feared I had made a colossal mistake, but then I remembered Italy. With a lot of guilt I realized when I closed my eyes, instead of Marc, I saw Eleonora in her beautiful golden gown opening her arms wide, beckoning me closer.

For now, Italy was my future.

Chapter 11

Over the Alps Into Italy

I had made the decision to go to Italy, I had even put a romantic relationship on hold, but still, things didn't seem completely real until I held a new passport and an airline ticket in my hand.

Acting as my own travel agent, I searched online for an economical airfare. At first, I was elated to find a super-saver low-cost deal that would take me from Philly to Germany. Reading about an add-on option, an overnight train ride to Florence—advertised as "the scenic way" to travel—I impulsively selected it. The idea of traveling by train had immediately captured my imagination. What a way to see the world! But after purchasing the nonrefundable package, I experienced buyer's remorse. Calculating the time spent onboard the train to cross the Alps and arrive at Santa Maria Novella train station, I immediately regretted my decision. And so much for a "scenic" ride. I would be passing over the Alps at midnight.

"Seriously?" I moaned to Glenninghall. "What was I thinking? First, I travel eight hours in a plane, and then *another* twelve to get to Florence."

Glenninghall only laughed. "Relax Sophia. Italy isn't going anywhere without you. You'll get there in the end." Then he said, "Taking the train is a marvelous experience. When I was a student, I traveled all over the place on a Eurail Pass."

Encouraged by his words, I turned my attention back to packing. As the piles of clothes began stacking up, realizing I'd need another bag, I began scouring local thrift shops in search of a cheap solution. When I came across an oversized vintage Louis Vuitton leather case with weathered travel stickers, I knew I'd found the perfect thing. Despite being a tad bit heavy and lacking wheels, it was a gorgeous piece of nostalgia, and it appealed to my romantic nature. Even better, I bought it for a song. Into the deep, silk-lined interior I fit in all my belongings. Before closing the lid, I gently placed the wooden box with the Florentine fleur-de-lis.

The weekend of my departure, Marc drove down to Philly, and we savored our last moments together. We ate dinner at a fancy restaurant and drank copious amounts of red wine. We laughed and kissed and talked, then kissed some more. It was truly a magical evening. But when Marc checked his messages in the morning, he looked at me and sighed, "Oh my God, Soph...they're telling me I have to go back. There is a problem with my client's proposal. I have to return immediately."

My heart broke a little more when I realized he wouldn't be there to see me off. He apologized profusely, saying, "I love you so much, Sophia. I'm missing you already." Then with that endearing smile I found so attractive, he said, *"Buon viaggio!"* Come back to me soon."

After Marc had left, I called Glenninghall in a panic, asking if he could give me a ride to the airport. "I know it's very last minute," I said, "but I could really use a friend right about now."

He readily agreed "You got it, kid! There's nothing I'd rather do today than help get you on that plane." To further cheer me up, he said he'd bring Signora Zeffirelli along for the ride.

It wasn't quite the romantic send-off I had been envisioning, but in the end, it turned out perfectly. Who better to see me off than my two mentors—La Signora, who had inspired me to go to Italy and Glenninghall, who had encouraged me to keep painting?

At the curb in front of the airport, La Signora embraced me. In her hands, she held a gift. Peeling back the tissue paper, I discovered her newly published book on Giuseppi Garibaldi. He was one of the red shirted generals of the Risorgimento, Italy's unification wars, who had helped liberate the country from foreign rule in the 1860s. I had often heard La Signora refer to the Italian military hero as one of the founding fathers of Italy. She had told us, despite Italy's ancient roots, it was a fledgling child still learning to crawl. "You see, modern-day Italy was forged from many regions, each with various traditions and customs—even different languages and dialects. It's a cauldron of paradoxical diversity. Just like the vegetable soup I make." Rolling her eyes, she said: *"Italia! Mamma mia che bel minestrone."*

Opening the book I flipped to the first page and read: *"Coraggio!* Courage!" Giving me a firm nod, she said, "Trust your instincts, Sophia. You will do just fine. Just like Italy...this is your moment to invent yourself."

"Oh and don't forget," she said, "promise me you will stop by my hometown of Verona. You must visit Juliet's house, just off Piazza delle Erbe—the city's main square. I used to play in her courtyard under the famous balcony where Romeo declared his love for his fair lady."

Delighted to learn something about La Signora's past, I readily agreed.

Setting my bags down, Glenninghall said, "Sophia, Think of me when you paint the skyline of Florence." Then with a flourish, he pulled out from behind his back a bouquet of brand new sable paintbrushes.

And so with Garibaldi and a new set of paintbrushes stowed away in my bags, I boarded the plane, bound for Europe. As the engines hummed and the aircraft came to life, I was not afraid. Instead, I was lighthearted and giddy. Looking down at the world through the puffy marshmallow clouds, I believed I could conquer Italy like Garibaldi. But as the plane descended into Düsseldorf, my bravado and euphoria evaporated. Inexperience, coupled with jet lag, made negotiating a strange city overwhelming.

Initially, I was relieved to see my bags again, but as I dragged them through the airport, my stride, once self-assured, was now awkward and tedious. My impulsive purchase—the vintage bag without wheels—now seemed a foolish idea.

Passing a shop window, I caught sight of myself and shuddered in embarrassment. I was nothing like the sophisticated high-heeled models in airline magazines, who seemed to travel effortlessly from country to country. Instead, I wore sneakers, and my hair was a tangled mess from sitting up all night in an uncomfortable coach seat.

I stopped and set my luggage down. My arms ached, and a rivulet of sweat dribbled down my back. Rolling my shoulders a couple of times, I gritted my teeth, picked up my bags and soldiered on. By the time I reached the rail station, I was completely exhausted. The noise, the crowds and the grim enveloped me, causing further disorientation. But it wasn't until I scrutinized train times posted in military hours that true panic set in. There wasn't one train going to Florence; there were several. Just when I thought I'd figured things out, the clicking train board flipped over in a confusing display of digits and decimals.

Hearing the station bells chiming and unintelligible announcements over the loudspeaker, my heart started beating faster As passengers whisked past, rushing to board their trains, I paused again to collect my wits. This time, my unanticipated stop made a short, stocky man with round glasses plow into my back. The impact knocked my legs out from under me, and I plopped down on the pavement along with my suitcase. The jolt caused the old locks on my "new" suitcase to spring open, spilling my belongings onto the dirty floor.

As the man babbled meaningless words at me in German, I snatched up a sweater and to my mortification a couple of bras. Despite my limited exposure to the language, the man's words seemed overly brusk. But, then again, most things said in German sounded that way to me. Before he could rush away and dismiss me altogether, I waved my ticket in the air, pleading for help. He mumbled something I couldn't understand and pointed to the opposite track.

I glanced over and saw two trains waiting to depart. Which was the right train? This one or that one? How was I going to make it to the other platform in time? Alarmed, I called out frantically to the conductor to please hold the door. As I hastened toward the closest hissing train, a hand on my shoulder stopped me.

Startled, I turned around. Behind me stood a distinguished looking man. He wore black boots, green pants, and a red shirt adorned with gold buttons. On his head was a velvet hat with gold braiding. He had an air of a military man about him. As if that wasn't enough to give away his identity, from his belt dangled a sword.

The gentleman sized me up and said in a formal, yet gentle tone, "*Mi scusi, signorina, posso aiutarLa?* Excuse me, miss. Can I help you?"

The man spoke Italian.

"Oh, thank God!" I cried out in relief. He clicked his heels together and bowed. I smiled in delight. Out of my suitcase had just popped the Italian Risorgimento general, Giuseppe Garibaldi.

"*Gentile signore*, kind sir," I said addressing him formally, "*mi sono persa*. I'm lost. I don't know which train to take to Florence."

The general nodded and said, "*Cara*, relax. You are in luck. This is an easy task. Am *I* not Garibaldi, an expert at battle stratagems and logistics? Follow me. Let *me* escort you to your carriage."

Without waiting for a reply, he reached down and picked up both my cases. Turning on the heels of his boots, he walked in the opposite direction. I noticed the train I had been about to board was now chugging down the rails, about to slip into an underground tunnel. Hastening my steps, I pointed to the locomotive. Calling out, I asked, "Hey wait a minute! Wasn't that my train?"

With a tilt of his head and a broad sweep of his arm, Garibaldi indicated a train on the opposite side. "*No signorina*. You will take that train. *L'espresso*—the fast train to Florence. *Sbrighiamoci*. Let's get a move on! It's about to leave."

As we hurried, he shouted to be heard above the commotion, "Florence is such a lovely city. You are a lucky girl. I spent some time there in my youth. I had a *zia,* my mother's sister, who lived there. She prepared the best *ribollita,* a soup made with Tuscan vegetables and day-old bread. So delicious. *Che minestrone!* What a soup."

Seeing my eyes glaze over at the mention of food, he took pity on me. "You are hungry, yes? Don't worry. You can buy sandwiches on the train. You should eat something soon. You will feel better when you do."

Stepping up to the waiting train, I smelled grease and diesel fuel. Once again the station chimes clanged, making a terrible ruckus. The general tilted his head and said, "Climb on board and settle in. Before you know it, you will wake in Italy. From the looks of it, you will be asleep as you pass over the Alps." With ease, he hoisted up my bags and deposited them into the first compartment.

"*Buon viaggio, signorina.* Have a pleasant and safe trip."

Thankful for the general's assistance, I gave him a quick hug. When I stepped back, my jean jacket snagged on one of his gold buttons. It now dangled loosely by a thread. I looked at the general in dismay, but Garibaldi only squeezed my hand and said not to worry. Unsheathing his sword, he expertly sliced the thread, severing the button completely. Polishing it on his soft jersey, he clicked his heels together again and offered it to me. "*Per Lei, signorina.* I would like you to have it."

Taking the button, I held it up for inspection. I saw two olive branches encircled by the words: *Per l'onore d'Italia—Siamo uniti.* For the honor of Italy—We are united.

"Just as I helped make Italy a country," he said, "the work to unite the Italians remained." Eyeing me thoughtfully, he added, "Your life has fallen apart, and that is understandable. But you are on your way to Italy now. It is time to put those puzzle pieces back together." Leaning down, he whispered, "*Buon lavoro!* You have your work cut out for you."

I nodded as I slid the button into my pocket. Grabbing the iron guardrail, I stepped into the train compartment. I turned around to wave at Garibaldi, but he had disappeared into the dark passageway.

Finding my seat, I settled in and let my head drop back against the headrest. I glanced up when the door slid open, and a conductor with a broadbrimmed hat poked his head inside asking to see my ticket. When I handed it to him, he studied the card for a moment and then began punching it rapidly. As he did bits of chaff floated into the air, and he said, "Enjoy the ride. We will be in Florence first thing in the morning."

After a few minutes, the door to the compartment swooshed open again, and a girl in a purple dress tumbled into the compartment. I acknowledged her with a weary smile, but too tired to make conversation, I closed my eyes and drifted to sleep.

I awoke when I heard my traveling companion opening the window. Coming fully to my senses, I looked up. Dawn had broken.

The girl in the purple dress pointed out the window. "Look!" she said, "We are getting close to Florence."

I blinked and stood up. In the early morning light, I had my first glimpse of Italy. We were now descending into the plains of Tuscany. Together the girl and I slid the glass higher, letting the fresh morning air wash over our faces and gazed with delight at the mist-drenched fields.

As the train slowed to take a curve, I leaned into my companion, and we laughed out loud in unison. The train righted again, pushing relentlessly onward. I swayed forward with the motion, knowing with every fiber of my being that I was on the right track, moving in the right direction.

I rubbed my eyes removing the last traces of sleep, elated to be waking up in Italy. Somewhere over the Alps my dreams had turned into reality.

Leaning farther out the window, I cried, "*Ciaoooooo Italiaaaa! Sei bellissima!* You're more beautiful than even *I* could have imagined."

Golden Renaissance

During the Golden or High Renaissance, the ideals of classical humanism were fully implemented in both painting and sculpture. During this glorification of man as worthy subject matter for art, artists continued to refine painterly techniques as well as master the use of linear perspective, shading, and other methods of realism.

Chapter 12

Welcome Home!

*S*tepping off the train at Santa Maria Novella Station and onto Italian soil, I was assaulted by a cacophony: bells chimed, train engines hummed, wheels screeched, and compartment doors banged open and shut. I stood on the platform smiling broadly, observing the bustling station and the throng of passengers hustling past me. The scene was similar to the one in Germany, but now I relaxed into the chaos. Rather than feeling lost as I had in northern Europe, in Italy I felt found.

A musical whistle made me turn around. Advancing rapidly toward me was a porter pushing a luggage trolley. As he drew nearer, he called out for me to move, *"Signorina. Attenzione! Scusi. Scusi signorina."* Hastily I picked up my cases and stepped out of his way to avoid being knocked off the platform. He smiled brightly and tipped his hat. As he passed by, he bellowed out over his shoulder, *"Buona giornata, signorina. Benvenuta a Firenze!*—Welcome to Florence!"

Flushed and giddy, I replied, *"Buon giorno! Grazie."*

My heart beat faster to hear Italian spoken to me for the first time in Italy. The porter's good humor was contagious. A delighted smile spread across my own face—one I didn't think I'd scrape off easily or anytime soon. I was here, I had done it, this was real! This time, I wasn't dreaming.

I picked up my bags and made my way to the end of the platform. There, a tall, bearded man in his early thirties was holding up a sign that read, "Sophia—La Scuola Artistica." He was wearing a leather jacket and over his shoulder was slung a satchel. Seeing me wave he called out, *"Salve, Sophia. Benvenuta."*

With a friendly tilt of his head, he introduced himself as Alessandro Mazza, one of the assistant directors at the art school. As he spoke, he leaned over and kissed me on the right cheek. As he turned to address my left cheek in a similar manner, I swiveled my head in the wrong direction, and we awkwardly bumped noses. I knew about the Italian two-kiss greeting from watching films and seeing my mother and Luciana affectionately greet one another, but in practice, it was quite another thing. Half the time I wasn't ever sure which side of the face to start with. Inevitably I got it wrong. Groaning inwardly I pulled back, my face flushed red with embarrassment.

Alessandro waved his hand in the air, and said, "*Non si preoccupi, Sophia.* Don't worry. You will get the hang of it soon."

Picking up my heavier case, he led me out of the station to the street, where buses and taxis waited to carry passengers deeper into the city. To help me get my bearings he pointed across the square at the back side of the church of Santa Maria Novella, designed by the Renaissance architect Alberti.

Looking back at me, he said, "*Allora*...okay are you ready to see the rest of the city? *La pensione,* where you will stay the first couple of days before settling in with an Italian family, is down the street a couple of blocks. It is just a short walk from here, practically next door to the Duomo."

When we reached the crosswalk, Alessandro held out his arm to keep me from being run down by a Vespa. With a wry smile, he warned, "*Stia attenta!* The motorbikes can sneak up on an unsuspecting pedestrian, gunning their engines and blaring their horns. They often scare newcomers to the city half to death. *Figurati.* Sometimes they startle me too."

As we pressed on down the sidewalk, I was jostled by morning commuters who gushed out of the station. Despite having traveled all night, my mind, like the Vespas, was now alive and racing. But it took just a few blocks before my pace began to drag again. It was a chore keep to up with Alessandro's long legs, and my arms ached from carrying my luggage in Germany.

Glancing back, seeing my discomfort, Alessandro gestured to an open bar and asked, "Do you want to rest a minute? *Le va un gelato o un espresso?* I'm buying."

Although it was barely mid-morning, the idea of an ice cream sounded marvelous. Leaning over Alessandro joked, "Listen, you are now in Italy. If you want, you can have gelato anytime you like. It is served practically on every corner here in Florence. I think it's just the thing to *tirarsi su.* You know, pick you up."

"Yes," I laughed in agreement. "I could use something to *tirami su.*" I suddenly realized how the famous Italian dessert called tiramisù—made with sponge cake soaked in coffee, powdered chocolate, and mascarpone cheese—got its name. With *those* ingredients, it certainly was a "pick-me-up" cake.

To Alessandro, I said, "I think I have died and gone to heaven. I've only just arrived, and we are talking about tiramisu and having ice cream for breakfast, lunch, and dinner."

Standing on the sidewalk outside the bar, I scrutinized the display case containing stainless steel bins of ice cream. Reading the handwritten cards placed above each one, I let the names of the flavors roll off my tongue as if I were reciting a poem written by Dante: *Stracciatella, Nocciola, Frutti di Bosco, Lampone*—Chocolate Chip, Hazelnut, Wild Berry, Raspberry. I pondered my choices for several minutes. Then I looked up and asked the *proprietario* behind the counter for a cone with two scoops—peach and chocolate.

It was a brief exchange of words, *"Vorrei un cono gelato. Posso avere pesca e cioccolato?"* Hearing me speak in Italian the man looked at me in surprise and praised me, *"Complimenti, signorina. Ma come mai parla così bene?"*

I flushed with pleasure. Tasting the ice cream, I raised my eyes heavenward and gave him a big smile in return. He grinned back. Looking at my suitcases, he said, "Welcome to Florence. Enjoy your visit."

Turning to Alessandro, I said, "I already like this city. Everyone is so friendly, *and* the gelato is divine. I may never leave." Without wasting any time, I devoured the ice cream. So as to savor every last bit, I licked the melting drops that slid down the side of the cone. Alessandro chuckled at my less-than-ladylike conduct. Handing me a napkin, he asked, *"Allora, è pronta?"* Are you ready to continue, or perhaps you'd like another?"

Smiling sheepishly, I assured him I was all set. As we continued down the street, I walked in a daze, feeling like a stranger in a strange land. I glanced at the elegant shop windows, the smooth gray paving stones, the small three-wheeled trucks and the signs written in another language. I tuned into the strange sounds, the curious horns, the roar of unfamiliar engines, even straining my ears to eavesdrop on Italian businessmen conversing on cell phones and teenage girls chatting with their boyfriends.

So caught up in the sights, sounds, and smells, as well as the never-ending parade of people, when we turned a corner, and the red dome of Florence's cathedral loomed large in front of me, I came to a complete standstill. I gazed in wonder, and the crowds melted away. My mother had created so many visual and verbal pictures of Florence that it seemed I had just walked into one of her paintings.

Alessandro turned and looked at me with a worried face. Clearly, I was proving to be quite a handful already. *"Che c'è, Sophia?"* When I didn't respond, he repeated in English, "What's the matter?"

I merely pointed at the confection of pink and green marble before us and shook my head from side to side.

"Ah. This is the first time you have seen our magnificent Duomo in person, no? *Non è bellissimo?* It's beautiful, right?"

"*È meraviglioso.*" Nodding, I agreed—it was indeed a marvel.

He leaned over and said, "*Caspita.* I pass the cathedral every day, and it never grows old. *Che magia. Ha un bel fascino, no?* There is something very magical and charming about it."

I stood transfixed a few seconds more. Then feeling a tug on my arm, I realized Alessandro was ready to move on. Despite his words, it seemed he was already over the fact that he lived with this astonishing cathedral on a daily basis. As he started to walk across the piazza, I picked up my case and hurried after him.

Alessandro left me at the pensione, giving me time to settle in. He returned a short time later to lead a few other students and me to La Scuola for a brief orientation. I thought the walk would be longer, but I quickly discovered how small Florence was. With Alessandro urging us on, it took just a few minutes to go from the pensione to the school, located in a building in the Lungarno, near the river.

As we walked down the street, Alessandro called over his shoulder, "This takes you directly to Piazza Signoria. There you will find the Palazzo Vecchio and a copy of Michelangelo's statue of *David*. We will veer off here, in the direction of Santa Croce church. In that piazza you will meet another very important Florentine, Dante Alighieri. He stands next to the church on a pedestal where he keeps an eye on the tourists and pigeons."

Strolling backward so we could hear him better, he said, "The Florentines may have booted Dante out of the city, but we are quite reasonable people. We were more than happy to welcome Dante back *after* he became a famous poet." He admitted ruefully, "It took only a couple of hundred years for us to say 'Let's forget about the past...welcome back home. But apparently, Dante had the last laugh. When the Florentines finally got hold of his casket, hoping to bury his body in Santa Croce, we discovered it was empty. So, who knows where Dante really is these days? Perhaps he is still traipsing about Italy, content to keep an eye on the whole country."

I smiled to myself, imagining that somewhere, maybe just across the square, Dante, my mother, and my father were sipping cappuccinos together, content in the knowledge that their Sophia had arrived in Italy where they could keep an eye on her.

When we reached the river, Alessandro stopped in front of a building with an arched doorway and said, "*Ragazzi!* Guys. This is it. Welcome to your new home. The school is on the top floor of this building."

Holding open the door he ushered us into the atrium. Pointing to a rickety, wrought-iron elevator Leonardo da Vinci himself could have designed, Alessandro indicated we could take the lift, or if we preferred the eight flights of stairs to the top. Weighing the alternatives, we stepped a bit reluctantly into the lift. Pressed together in the tiny space, we held our collective breaths, as it ground slowly and noisily up to the top floor.

When the doors opened, we were greeted by the director, Roberto Guerrieri, Glenninghall's friend. Unlike my American professor, he was dressed fashionably, in a well-fitting jacket, silk tie, and designer shoes. No army boots for this refined gentleman. When he saw me, his face lit up. As Alessandro had done, he kissed me on both of my cheeks. Once again I hesitated. I leaned to the left when I should have moved to the right. In the end, to connect with at least one of his cheeks awkwardly.

He only laughed at my blundered kisses and said, "I've been told by my American friend to keep a special eye on you. And whatever stories he may have alluded to regarding our student days..." he said with a roguish smile, "*Beh*. I can assure you they are all untrue."

Patting me on the back, he called out to the others to join him in the main studio. There he introduced us to the instructors and told us about logistics, as well as the idiosyncrasies of the school's facilities. Next, he explained the curriculum. Pausing a moment he scanned the room before telling everyone that to graduate and receive our degrees, we would be subjected to oral interrogations. Hearing a few good-natured curses, he started to laugh.

As I looked around at the unusual faces, physiques, hairdos, and tattooed arms, it appeared some had never cracked open an art history book. But then again, I thought, of course, this eclectic, creative bunch had been drawn to the city for reasons similar to my own.

To settle things down, Roberto said in a reassuring tone, "*Tranquilli!* Relax. Everyone will do just fine." Then he informed us, "All lectures will be taught in venues around the city. Why study slides and pictures in books, when the actual paintings and sculptures exist just around the corner? Just think of Florence as Medici headquarters. It certainly is not an accident that their offices are right below us. Take a look out the window. Right there on the corner is the Uffizi Gallery—a treasure trove stockpiled with all you need to know and more. It's an open book full of things just waiting to be discovered." With that, he dismissed everyone.

About an hour later I popped my head around Alessandro's open office door to tell him I'd signed up for one of his seminars. "It seems you aren't going to get rid of me anytime soon..." I stopped mid-sentence. Gazing about his office words failed me just as they had earlier in front of the Duomo. Covering his walls was an impressive array of canvases featuring scenes of a crazy, futuristic cities. Alessandro's paintings combined various mediums with computer-generated images. Upon closer inspection, I noticed the panoramic scenes hid subliminal messages and irreverent jokes that poked fun at modern society rivaling the wit of a Dutch master's iconography.

I realized there was so much more to the man than I had originally imagined. I could see he had a sly sense of humor and enjoyed a rich fantasy life that rivaled my own. My hunch was confirmed when I saw on his desk an extensive collection of superhero figures—Captain America, Wolverine, and the Hulk, as well the Star War heroes Luke, Leia, and Han. Looking back at Alessandro I noticed he was tossing a mini-replica of Darth Vader back and forth between his hands.

Thoughtfully, we regarded one another. Then, as if on cue, we both raised an eyebrow and laughed in unison at an unspoken joke. At that moment, we forged the first link in the chain of our friendship.

Picking up a miniaturized light saber that lay on his desk, he unfurled it and pointed at me. "I can see the force is strong with you, young Padawan." Grinning, he added, "You have chosen your path well. We will guide you on a path back to the Light." I bowed my head in deference to my *new* Jedi Master. I had safely arrived at starport in a galaxy far, far away and now the sword had been passed, from one painting master to another. Despite the new surroundings and foreign faces, I felt I had landed in the right place.

A week after my arrival, just as I was getting my bearings, finding my way easily from the *pensione* to the school, I discovered I was to be placed with a family in Pian dei Giullari. Alessandro told me it was an affluent area beyond Piazzale Michelangelo. Initially, I was dismayed to be placed so far out in the suburbs. I would need to take a bus to the school. On the other hand, Pian dei Giullari would be more peaceful. Finally, I could get some rest. Due to the change in time zones, I was lucky to fall asleep by four in the morning. At the very least, there would be fewer Vespas in the suburbs. Florence was quaint and picturesque, but I didn't appreciate being awakened at odd hours by the angry whine of grinding gears reverberating off acoustically challenged medieval walls.

At first, the house and the family seemed ideal. The husband was a banker and the wife an architect. They lived in a modern house filled with gilded antiques and edgy sculptures that could have been featured on the pages of *Architectural Digest Italia*. As beautiful as it was, it was usually deserted. Everyone kept busy schedules, waking up early and working late and I was left to my own devices, even when it came to making dinner.

But when Gianluca, the couple's son, realized an international student was living in the house, he began to buzz around me like a fly circling a jar of fig jam. Each night, when I started banging around the family's spacious kitchen, I could count on him to make an appearance. He provided welcome company as I opened cans of Rio Mare Tuna and filled pots of water to boil pasta.

When we sat down to eat, he poured me wine from his family's collection. Then, either because he liked the sound of his own voice, or actually believed he possessed an above-average palate, he talked endlessly about Tuscan vintages, Ruffinos, Brunellos, and Chianti Classicos. But, his expertise wasn't limited to wine it included a vast range of subjects—cars, horses, and soccer. As I sipped my wine, I listened to him talk, smiling and nodding politely.

Initially, it was nice having a member of the family pay me attention. I was a bit disoriented, missing Marc and my friends from home, and found Gianluca's interest in my well-being sweet and his attentions flattering. So when he offered to drive me to Greve in Chianti to visit a local vineyard and see the *vendemmia*, the fall harvesting of the grapes, I jumped at the chance. We spent a pleasant afternoon wandering through fields of ripening grapes and dipping inside the cool cantina.

At the end of the day, Gianluca ushered me into the main building, where we sampled the estate's wine as well as its olive oil. Waving away the proprietor, Gianluca, placing a hand upon my back, directed me to a table filled with large bottles of freshly pressed oils.

"*Ci penso io,*" he said with a gracious smile, adding in English, "let *me* teach you how to taste olive oil."

Intrigued, I watched as he poured a bit of oil from a dark green bottle into a plastic cup. Covering it with one hand, he slowly warmed it against the other. After a moment he held it up and inhaled deeply. Waving it under my nose, I detected the nutty aroma of freshly pressed olives, mixed with a fresh scent of grass and pungent sage.

Then Gianluca began to slurp up the oil in small sips, sucking in air at the same time, making bizarre noises. I raised my eyebrows in surprise. He quickly assured me it was normal and necessary to spread the flavors throughout the mouth.

When the demonstration was over, he asked if I wanted to try. Without hesitation, I agreed. Despite feeling silly, I began to slurp up the oil with little gasps of air. I discovered the taste and texture was quite lovely. I was enjoying the moment, but when Gianluca moved a little closer and draped his arm casually around my shoulders, alarm bells began to clang in my head. I realized he was telegraphing an unspoken invitation to try something much more than Tuscan olive oil.

My opinions were corroborated later that evening. We had stopped at a local trattoria for a plate of *pici all'aglione*—a type of thick spaghetti smothered in a sauce made with tomatoes and garlic. At the end of the meal, having listened to Gianluca talk for hours about this year's wine crop, I was ready to go home. I raised my arm casually to look at my watch, hoping he'd get the message. Inwardly I groaned when, instead of grabbing his car keys, he leaned back in his chair and lit up another cigarette. Taking a leisurely puff, he casually said, *"Senti, cara, tu assomigli moltissimo alla mia quarta ragazza.* You remind me very much of my fourth girlfriend."

Confused by the odd turn in the conversation, I asked, "Hmmm, how many girlfriends have you had?"

Gianluca took another puff on his cigarette and answered, "Three."

I looked at him blankly. As he gazed at me with a knowing smile, I finally understood his meaning. He was suggesting *I* was to be his fourth girlfriend. I almost spit out my wine in a burst of laughter.

"Gianluca, really that's *troppo divertente,* that's too funny."

I saw however *he* wasn't amused. Straightening in my chair and trying to keep a straight face, I quickly explained I had a *fidanzato* back in the States, and friendship was all I could offer. I thought he had gotten the message, but the next day he was knocking on my door again, suggesting that we pop down to Rome for a long weekend.

I declined and to avoid further awkward conversations and encounters in the kitchen, instead of returning to Pian dei Giullari, I remained in town and attended late-night discos or ate in restaurants with friends from the school. But soon that plan fizzled. At the end of the evening, I was often left stranded in front of the Duomo, with no other alternative than to hail a cab. It didn't help matters to learn that sometimes fares were doubled at that time of night to pay for the taxi driver's return trip back to town.

It took two weeks before I threw in the towel. I could put up with Gianluca; his flirtations were harmless, and I reasoned he would eventually get the message and give up. But what finally drove me over the edge was the forty-five-minute bus commute and the taxi fares when I missed a bus, or when they stopped running altogether.

I decided to approach Alessandro about finding a new living arrangement. I worried he'd think I was a nitpicky, fault-finding American, but, to my relief, he listened sympathetically to my complaints about the long bus commute and the even longer walk to reach the city center. Chucking around a Spiderman figurine, he looked amused when I told him about Gianluca's pickup lines. I got the impression he was already familiar with Gianluca's "Don Giovanni" routines.

I was happy to hear him say, "*Mi dispiace, Sophia.* Sorry about that. Don't go judging all Italian men by Gianluca. Let's just say he is a tad over eager." Continuing he added, "You were one of the last applicants, and that family in Pian dei Giullari was the only one available. Of course, if it isn't working out, we'll find another family for you."

Tossing Spiderman high into the air for me to catch he opened a draw and pulled out a thick file. "So you want to be closer to the heart of the city, right?" When I nodded yes, he said, "There is a family in Campo di Marte that just became available. Their apartment isn't far from the center. If you stay out too late, you can always walk home." Looking at me, he said with a grin, "Even better, if you like soccer—and who doesn't?—they are just a couple of blocks away from the stadium."

Alessandro began sorting through folders until he came to one and stopped. "*Eccolo!* Here it is." Flipping open the file he pulled out a photo of three people and held it up for me to see, "Sophia, meet the Pogliani family. I think they will be a perfect match for you. *Sono buoni come il pane.*"

I looked at him curiously, wondering why he had just said the family was as good as bread.

Seeing my expression, Alessandro quickly explained, "Yeah, kind of an untranslatable expression. It means they are nice." Reviewing the file again, he said, "Yes, I think this family will work out fine."

I was delighted to be moving back into town. Around every corner, I recognized familiar places I'd seen in books and remembered special stories my mother had told me about the city. If I needed to get my bearings, I only had to look to the Duomo—my one true north—to orient myself.

As I passed the church of Santa Croce, I admired the blue-and-white mosaic marble façade. It was one of the buildings closest to the Arno and had suffered the greatest damage during the flood of '66. When I entered the basilica, I closed my eyes and envisioned water pouring into this serene and sacred space, lapping at the frescoes. Soon I began to hear sloshing water and heard my mother's voice calling out to the other Mud Angels to bring more buckets and brooms.

Opening my eyes again, the only thing I saw pouring into the church today was sunlight from the overhead windows. The voices of the Mud Angels faded away, and all was calm again. I walked down the side aisle of the church and looked at the tombs that lined the wall, reading the names of famous artists, including that of Michelangelo. Here I finally stood surrounded by the Renaissance superstars.

I exited the church and walked along the Arno River, following the steps of Medici princes. As I approached the Ponte Vecchio bridge, I saw Dante the young poet talking to Beatrice for the very first time. As I drew nearer, he turned his head in my direction, and we made eye contact. Placing a hand over his heart, he swept his other arm out, inviting me to cross over.

Circling back to the *Mercato Nuovo*, the loggia where leather merchants now hawked purses, I smiled to see the "lucky" bronze boar, *il Porcellino*. Before moving on I rubbed his snout and patted it affectionately. I imagined, perhaps with Eleonora as my confidant, I had put a coin into the boar's jowls, ensuring someday I would return.

Rounding the corner, I found myself in front of Orsanmichele in Via Calzaiuoli admiring the fourteen statutes representing Florence's medieval trade guilds. Closing my eyes, I clearly saw the commotion when men in britches unloaded bags of wheat and barley from wagons that had just trundled into the city. Milling about, waiting for the market to open, was an eclectic crowd of noblemen, apprentices, and domestic servants.

Slipping inside the church, I was reminded of Glenninghall's darkened lecture hall. I could vividly hear him proclaim, "What an amazing experience it must have been for all of Florence, from the lowliest servant to the noble Medici princes, to see the new naturalism and three-dimensionality in the statues of Orsanmichele. They knew they were on the cusp of change, entering a new age."

I felt a rush of gratitude and silently thanked my professor for helping me make the leap from the shores of America to Italy. Now instead of fingering glossy plates in books, I was touching stone and marble, making a personal connection.

Retracing my steps, headed back to the school, I was passed by a man on a bicycle. He stopped halfway down the street, turned his head and watched me approach. Calling out, he asked, "*Signorina*, are you lost? I've seen you wandering all over town. In fact, you have passed my leather shop window several times today. I couldn't help but notice you."

Flattered I had caught the eye of this handsome stranger, I was also a bit embarrassed. I thought I'd been wandering the streets of the city incognito. Florence, apparently, though had been paying attention and was watching over me. It had dispatched an emissary to ensure I hadn't lost my way.

Pausing a moment I looked at the man as beautiful as a Donatello angel and said, "*No, no. No signore, non mi sono persa.*" I thought: *No indeed, I'm not lost...I'm doing well here.*

Hearing me respond in Italian, he was momentarily taken aback. "You speak Italian. *Brava!* Tell me...have you lived here before?"

I smiled. It did feel like I'd lived here before thanks to my mother. I'd certainly been here before in my dreams. But I wasn't going to say that to him. He would think I was totally *"matta"*—crazy. So I only nodded politely.

As I walked away, he called out in a teasing manner, "So you've returned. *Bene.* We've all been waiting for you. Welcome home."

Chapter 13

Learning Curve

*T*he first morning I woke up in Campo di Marte, I flung open the shutters and looked up into the hills of Fiesole. Leaning over the sill, I saw a canal. Alongside it, a path meandered into a grove of olive trees. Lost in thought, I wondered where the path might lead. Noises on the other side of the door brought me back. *Great.* I thought: *Late as usual for first breakfast.* Snapping to attention, I promptly I organized my things and made the bed, knowing Adriana, my new Italian mamma, would not be pleased if things were left in disarray.

Ushering me into my new room the first time, beaming brightly, she had said, *"Eccoci! La tua camera. Fai come se fossi a casa tua."* In my head, I had replayed her words. Here we are. This will be your room. Make yourself at home.

I smiled thinly, a little dismayed to find my new quarters a bit miserly on latitude and longitude. If I stood in the middle and stretched out my arms, I could almost touch both walls. There was no room for a desk and just barely enough space for the oversized wardrobe. When I opened its doors, they narrowly cleared the bed frame. The nicest thing about the room, aside from the view, was the fluffy down comforter—a *piumone*—that covered my hard, narrow bed. I could handle the tiny room as long as I had could wrap myself in that. I blessed the Italian ducks that had sacrificed their feathers to keep me warm at night.

The rest of the Poglianis' apartment, like my bedroom, was modest. Despite being less than luxurious, however, the floors were covered entirely in slippery, white marble. Adriana told me solemnly that carpets were filthy things, filled with germs and dirt. In her opinion, if it couldn't be picked up, hung on a line, and beaten, it was an impractical and unnecessary evil. So although the floor was cold to the touch *and* the feet, it was the pride of my Italian mother. To keep it polished, each morning she skated around on a soft cloth, like an ice dancer gliding on a sheet of ice.

I discovered her fastidiousness also extended to matters of health. As she suffered from more mysterious complaints of the liver, sore throats and high fevers, she took great delighted in doling out advice to others. Often her remedies were rather unusual, and I'm pretty sure they didn't come from a physician, but rather from a medieval book of ailments and antidotes that she kept stashed away in a drawer.

The first day after showing me the room, Adriana advised me in a solemn tone not to keep the window *and* the door open at the same time when I slept. When I asked her why, she shrugged her shoulders and said, "*Ma dai!* Come on, Sophia. *C'è corrente. Prenderai un colpo d'aria.* There is a current. You will be struck by a stream of cold air." She was fully convinced a draft of night air, flowing from the window through the door, would be the death of me or at the very least leave me bedridden, plagued by a severe case of pneumonia.

At our first meal when I asked for a glass of ice water she emphatically advised me, "*Non si beve mai acqua gelata.* Don't ever drink ice water." She feared a glass of cold would give me stomach cramps. I made a mental note to myself: no fresh air, no ice water, no wall-to-wall carpets. I thought: *How had I ever managed to survive before without knowing all of this?*

Things became even more colorful when I met the rest of the family: Adriana's husband Settimo and their daughter, Paola. While Adriana relished her role as a sensible sort, Settimo her husband was her polar antithesis. It seemed opposites did attract. He was a large, rotund man who had a silly sense of humor, always ready with an amusing story or *barzelletta* to share. When I asked Adriana why he was called Settimo, she said his mother, after having given birth to six other children—perhaps due to a lack of creativity or just because she was plain tired—named him *Settimo*, the seventh.

The Pogliani family was indeed quite large and gregarious. It extended well beyond a small nucleus of three to include a universe of aunts, uncles, grandparents, and a thousand adoring cousins. It wasn't long before I too was pulled into this orbit and embraced as part of the clan. I was delighted to be surrounded by so much company but soon learned that everyone's lives were entwined and one's slightest movement was up for comment or debate.

On a typical day, Adriana was on the phone with her mother at least five times, as well as in constant communication with her sister via text messaging. She was also kept busy running errands for her grandmother.

Cousin Gabriele, who was between jobs, habitually dropped in unannounced to *scroccare un pranzo*—in other words, share a free meal—and Settimo's sister Zia Ilaria who lived next door was never too far behind him. As if normal, daily interaction wasn't enough, each week there was a constant rotation of birthday parties, anniversaries, and baptisms, all of which required a special sauce and hand-rolled pasta and the presence of each and every family member.

It took a few weeks, but I was starting to get the hang of Italian family life. Mealtimes were my best classroom. Adriana worked a full day as a secretary and then prepared a homemade dinner that consisted of soup or pasta dish, followed by a small portion of meat. As platters were passed around the table, when I wasn't paying attention, Settimo thought it tremendously funny to refill my wine glass. Before I caught on to his little prank, I tottered off to bed, never quite sure how much wine I had drunk. It soon became instinctual, for the sake of my sobriety, to cover my glass with my hand whenever I turned my head.

Adriana rolled her eyes at her husband's antics and then catching a glimpse of my plate, she exclaimed, "Sophia. You haven't eaten enough! *Mangia! Mangia!*" she implored. Eat! Eat!

While I welcomed almost all the plates she placed before me—roasted chickens, creamy polentas, homemade pastas—the idea of *la trippa* repelled me. In a city full of street vendors who sold tripe sandwiches —*lampredotto*—and served it up in every form imaginable, I wasn't convinced eating the third inner lining of a cow's stomach was something humans were meant to do. I had my limits and firmly told the family it was something I wouldn't enjoy.

One evening, however, having heartily consuming a plate of steaming stew, looking up to see the pleased faces of my Italian family, I realized I had been duped. I felt a little sick when I realized I had even sopped up the remaining sauce with a small piece of bread.

Watching me clean my plate, Adriana had said, "Sophia, did you know we call that *fare scarpetta*? It means to 'make the little shoe' out of a piece of bread to enjoy last remaining bite. It's fine to do this at home with us, but in a restaurant, it would be considered very impolite. Very bad manners. You don't want to make a *brutta figura*—make a bad impression."

Over the years I had done countless verb drills in school, but now over plates of tripe and pasta in the Pogliani's kitchen I was learning new idioms and expressions. Even eavesdropping on exchanges between Settimo and his friends was increasing my vocabulary. I became privy to all manner of phrases and colorful curse words. To my American ear, swear words didn't sound so bad when said in Italian. But there I'd be wrong, considering my audience. Case in point, I made a complete idiot of myself when I let slip this little gem, *"Che cazzo vuoi?"* As soon as the words left my lips, spoons were suspended, and all eyes turned on me in astonishment.

While Settimo chuckled into his sleeve, Adriana gently admonished, *"Sophia, non si dice! È molto volgare!* Oh my goodness. *Never* say that in polite company. It's very rude!"

Embarrassed, I apologized. Adriana reminded me that in the Italian language, it is important to distinguish between formal and informal situations. As usual, Adriana—or as I was starting to call her, "Signora Grammatica"—had plenty to say on the subject. "Sophia, to properly communicate in Italian, you must be aware of your audience and choose the form of speech that best fits the social context. In a formal situation, when you are first introduced to someone, even if social rank and age are similar, the *"Lei"* form is used."

Leaning into the conversation, Settimo interjected, "In informal situations the *"tu"* form can be used, around us or when you are speaking friends... or...well, the cat."

Now that I was speaking Italian much more extemporaneously, I was acutely aware that a mere slip of the tongue or forgetting to insert the right vowel at the end of a word could turn a good intention into something sour. And how many times had I embarrassed myself by not properly enunciating my double consonants. Sometimes it seemed I didn't understand anything. After my blunder at dinner, I sighed in frustration. The learning curve was proving to be quite steep.

But, after good night's sleep, I was ready to start anew. If I was running on Bella Time, Adriana the guardian of the clock made sure I was up. I could count on her to call out briskly, *"Sophia, sbrigati! Sei in ritardo. Muoviti!"* Get moving."

Each morning as I walked down the lane I stepped out of the way to let Cousin Leo pass by on his motorbike. At the corner, I waited at the bus stop for an orange Metro bus to take me to the school in the Lungarno. To avoid being fined by the Metro police, Adriana advised me to obtain a city bus pass. *"Non vuoi essere beccata.* You don't want to be caught red-handed."

I agreed, thinking it would be an easy thing to obtain. But the procurement of this innocuous document introduced me to the perplexing world of Italian bureaucracy. Italy did many things well, but the management of the civil system was about as transparent as a sea full of black ink squid.

Optimistically I approached the man behind a window at the post office, but before I got out a whole sentence, he pointed to another window and turned back to his crossword puzzle. The woman at the second window placed a hand over the phone and impatiently said, "Can't you see I'm busy?"

Really? I could hear her speaking with her mother. Seeing I wasn't going away, she flicked her cigarette in the direction of the stairs and mouthed the word *"ventiquattro".* She held up first two fingers and then four indicating the number twenty-four.

When I arrived at the office on the second floor, again I was met with a vapid stare and told to return to the main floor. As I descended the steps, my enthusiasm and optimism slid down my face, being replaced by annoyance and frustration. As I rounded the corner, finally headed in the right direction, I noticed the line was twenty people deep.

"Che palle," I swore, like a sailor, grateful Adriana couldn't hear me. The elderly woman in front of me turned around and frowned. I smiled apologetically.

After standing around for forty-five minutes, my turn finally came. Paging through my documents, however, the man sadly shook his head and quickly dismissed me, saying, "Signorina, where is your identity photo? You must first acquire a photo from one of the automated booths at the train station." Then looking past me he called out, *"Avanti!* Next."

"Uffa!" I exclaimed, and gave him a chilly look. Fortunately, for him and for me, nothing more regrettable slipped out of my mouth. This time, Adriana would have been proud of my restraint.

Eventually, when I was "bus official" I didn't fear the bus police quite so much, what I now worried about was the erratic Metro bus schedule. Sometimes I waited for over an hour for just one bus to appear, other times, three arrived in unison. Who knew why? But I was happy the buses showed up at all. It could be a million times worse if I was a casualty of a random *sciopero*—a bus strike.

Embracing the Italian art of scraping by—*l'arte di arrangiarsi*—I quickly discovered how to turn lemons into limonata. Now if the bus didn't arrive, or was too crowded to board, I flagged down cousin Leo on his Vespa and hitched a ride. Sometimes I even managed to coax him to take me all the way to the school.

Aside from these small hiccups, life was smoothing out, or as I was learning to say, everything was *liscio come l'olio*—smooth like oil. I missed Marc of course, and we kept in contact throughout the fall. He even talked about visiting during the holidays, but his work and my school commitments inevitably got in the way. We tried, but it just wasn't working. Our timing was wrong. With deep regret and many sad tears, we mutually agreed to let each other go. Our love affair ended, eventually suffocated by slow-speed Internet and an antiquated postal system, not to mention the four thousand miles and six time zones that separated us.

I probably should have been more upset than I was, but there were just so many fascinating things to take in and the new experiences helped keep my mind off of Marc. On weekends with friends, I ventured out of Florence to sample cheese in Pienza, drink wine in Montalcino or climb a tower in San Gimignano. Walking down the streets in the medieval hill towns, I pinched myself, realizing the buildings around me had been built hundreds of years before America had founding fathers. Often it felt as though I had fallen back in time. In Italy, the past really did step up to meet the present, and the present blended back into the past. Here I was walking in Eleonora's magic circle.

It also seemed ancient rivalries and medieval civic pride, dressed up in modern-day trappings, were also very much alive and kicking. Take for example the Italians' fervor for soccer. If the Florentines couldn't attack other city-states, marauding the walls of Lucca or beating down the gates of Siena, they could be conquering heroes on a modern-day soccer field. Attacker beware, and woe to anyone who came between ACF Fiorentina and a soccer goal.

I became an initiate of the sport soon after my arrival in Campo di Marte. One Saturday afternoon, Paola and I joined other frenzied Florentines in the stadium near our apartment. For the match, we dressed in purple, and during the game we clapped and stamped our feet, making a crazy ruckus with the other fans. When the final goal was scored in Florence's favor, pulses were pitched even higher when cannons exploded, just like artillery fire, sending billowing clouds of violet-and-white smoke over the crowd.

As we made our way home, we sang and waved purple flags. Nearing our apartment, I saw a young neighbor boy dribbling a well-used soccer ball. Recognizing me, he raised his arm and saluted me. Then with a nod of his head, he signaled I should get ready. Moving forward, he kicked the ball forcefully in my direction.

As the ball came towards me, I looked for the boy to kick it back to him, but he was already too far ahead of me. So instead, I deftly lobbed the ball to Paola. When it collided with her foot, she looked over at me and laughed in surprise. Rising to the challenge, she kicked it back to me. We continued volleying the ball back and forth until we reached our gate.

Taking control of the ball, I yelled over at Paola, "Get ready, here comes the winning goal." Jumping up and down trying to block the shot, she chanted, "*Dai, dai, dai!* Go. Go. Go. Come on, I'm ready. Bring it on, American girl! Let's see what you've got."

Hearing her taunts, I hauled back my foot and with a mighty punt I kicked the ball high over the fence. Paola's eyes grew wide. Together we watched as it arched high into the sky and finished with a satisfying *plop* in the canal behind the apartment.

I smiled a bit smugly. Guess I didn't know my own strength. My little Fiorentina fan was clearly impressed by my newly acquired soccer skills. She blew crazily on her kazoo in a victory salute. Hearing our gleeful cries, a couple of neighbors leaned over their balconies and called out, "*Brava* Sophia! You are learning to kick like an Italian."

Indeed I was picking up the rules and the moves of the game quickly, but then again, I had some excellent coaches.

Chapter 14

Divas

*A*s the fall progressed, after spending my days in the studio, I took to the streets, seeking out the statues in the loggias, capturing their likenesses in my sketchbook. Just as Leonardo had implored me to do—pay attention to all the small details and let nothing escape my artistic eye—I drank in everything I saw.

In the Uffizi Gallery, as Roberto had encouraged his students to do, I set up headquarters in the "Medici offices". There I learned all kinds of interesting tidbits about the paintings and the accomplished masters who had created them. I especially enjoyed a lovely chat, *una bella chiacchierata*, I had with Botticelli's *Venus*, who floated out to me on an open half-shell.

"*Ciao, tesoro.* Come here, don't be shy. It's been ages since I talked to someone. I'm getting so lonely standing here on this seashell all by myself. These nymphs surrounding me...well, I've heard their jokes and stories a thousand times. *Che noia!* I'm so bored."

Positioning myself closer to better admire Botticelli's brushwork, I obliged her. Smiling at me, Venus said, "You can't even begin to imagine how tricky it is to stand here all day and balance on this thing without tipping over." As if to prove her point, she shifted her weight, and her seashell boat dipped to the left.

Flipping open my sketchbook, I began delineating her elongated curves and serene expression. Curious, to see what I was doing she leaned over to take a peek. Satisfied with my progress, she whispered, "You think me to be Venus, but really I'm just a simple Florentine maiden—I'm Simonetta Vespucci." She blushed profusely. "Here I am, a respectable girl, standing in this public space—completely nude! Imagine that."

I was intent on sketching, but when she stopped talking, I glanced up and urged her to continue. She giggled again and said, "Well, I just wanted you to know...it's really quite liberating standing here without a stitch on."

Growing serious she said, "But with freedoms and notoriety there are consequences. It comes with the territory—you have to learn to take the good with the bad. Yes, I'm quite popular. People flock from all over the world to catch a glimpse of me on this over-grown half-shell. At times I feel adored, and it truly is lovely to be unhampered by tight corsets and long heavy gowns. But on the flip side, you wouldn't believe how drafty this room gets. Sometimes a wish I had more than my long tresses to keep me warm." I smiled when she wrapped her arms around her body and shivered dramatically.

"Nonetheless," she said, "I trusted Botticelli completely. He was a wonderful artist. He saw both my external and internal beauty and used my likeness in many of his paintings. Truth be told, the man was quite besotted with me. I confess I had feelings for him too, but unfortunately, I was already married. So, instead of giving him my heart, behind closed doors we carried on an affair of art."

She sighed, "Botticelli did love me so. When he died, he asked to be placed next to me in the Church of the Ognissanti."

Finishing my sketch, I held it up for her to see. She clapped her hands in approval. Shifting her weight, making her shell sway, she said, "You should go to the beach yourself and relax. Go to Viareggio some afternoon. Gather up all the seashells you can find. *Lasciati andare*. Let yourself go."

I nodded in agreement and resumed my walk through the galleries. When I came to the portraits of the Duke and Duchess of Urbino, Glenninghall's mercenary friend with the crooked nose and poked-out eye, painted by Piero della Francesca, I stopped. I listened in amusement as the two portraits facing one another carried on a heated domestic quarrel.

"Federico, my goodness, can't you ever be home on time for dinner?" whined Battista Sforza, the Duke's wife. "And why must you always track mud into the house? It looks like a pigsty in here."

"Good heavens, woman! Have you no respect?" bellowed Federico. "I have places to be, cities to conquer and money to collect. And the next time I catch you watering down the wine to save a florin to buy a new dress, I'm going to swat your behind."

Finally, I gave up hope of interrupting the crusty old married couple and left them to their bickering. Turning the page in my sketchbook, I walked around the room stopping to chat now and then with many of the gilded and pastel-hued Madonnas painted by Cimabue, Simone Martini, Giotto, and Michelangelo.

Because of my frequent visits, and my obsessive fascination with the paintings, I soon attracted the attention of a short stout museum guard who followed me around with a concerned frown. If I leaned in a trifle too close to a canvas, he quickly admonished, *"Non tocchi, signorina!* Don't touch."* Soon I became accustomed to his firm intonations. Each time I heard him call out, I automatically stepped back a few paces then turned and gave him an apologetic smile.

At the end of my visit, on my way out the door, I passed through the Bronzino room to pay a social call to Eleonora de' Medici. I thought it fitting she shared space with another of Bronzino's works—a portrait of Dante. I imagined the lively conversations the two of them had after everyone else had gone home. Often so lost in thought, I wouldn't see my friend, the ever-vigilant museum guard step into the room. But, when I heard him call out briskly, *"Signorina, stiamo per chiudere.* The museum is about to close",* I inevitably jumped.

Glancing from Dante to Eleonora I said to them both, "Don't worry. I will be back soon for another chat." As I watched, it seemed the duchess smiled at me as she reached up and tugged gently on her beaded headdress. I gave her a little wave and said, *"Ci vediamo presto.* See you soon."*

Turning to go, I saw the guard watching me with a raised eyebrow. I'm sure he thought I was quite touched in the head. Nodding and waving at him as well, I said, *"A dopo.* See you next time, too."*

Taking Simonetta's advice I took the bus to Viareggio. There in the warm waves, I drifted idly, letting the late autumn breezes caress my face. Going with the flow, I reached up and untied the strap of my swimsuit and pulled it off. Holding it by the string, I let it trail in the water behind me. There I floated happy and free in the current, born again like a Botticelli goddess.

As I returned home, I congratulated myself on how well things were going. Despite Adrian's strict advice not to enter the water at least four hours after eating, I hadn't drowned due to a spasm of intestinal cramping. I smiled at yet another one of her cautionary rules. But in all seriousness, I considered myself lucky. I was thriving in my new environment, benefitting daily from the living museum in which I now inhabited. Like Venus on her half-shell, I was learning to keep my balance and stay afloat.

But as Simonetta had warned, with independence came consequences. Soon a cold wave of reality washed over me causing my oyster shell to dip and sway. Overnight the weather in Florence turned chilly. Now when I opened my window, I saw the path to Fiesole was obscured by a thick bank of fog. To keep warm, I wore a wool sweater and a scarf. When I entered the kitchen, seeing me well bundled, Adriana smiled approvingly. She motioned for me to take a seat next to Zia Ilaria who had stopped in for her early-morning chat. Reaching for the coffee pot to fill my cup she asked, "So Sophi are you ready to face the day *and* the girl from Marseille? Make sure you keep your head out of the clouds and watch where you are going."

Taking a sip of coffee, I grimaced. Last night I had told her about my disastrous run-in with the French girl. Adriana had listened sympathetically and like all good Italian mamas, had immediately taken sides and was ready to dig in and give advice. This morning, however, I still felt unsettled. I reached for a pastry from a plate on the table and tilted it back and forth contemplating the calories. Throwing caution to the wind, I took a big bite.

I looked back at Adriana and said, "Oh, I'll be okay. It was just so embarrassing. Aside from being a total clutz around this girl, I seem to be suffering a small artistic crisis. You should see her work! It's amazing. Breathtaking."

Taking another sip of coffee, I added, "She creates such amazing paintings that rival the work of Vermeer. Her work is hyper-realistic, like photographs—you can't even detect her strokes."

I let out a sigh, rippling my bangs. "Our styles are, well, so different..." Taking another bite of the pastry, chewing slowly, I began again, "The other day she made some critical comments about my work...unflattering, really... and it's making me think."

I raised an eyebrow and shook my head in disbelief, "I can't believe I'm letting her get under my skin like this."

Looking over at Zia Ilaria and seeing her blank expression, I said, "You see, my style is...well I guess you'd say it's more modern. I use big, broad, painterly strokes and dabs of color to suggest form and movement, light, and shadow." Searching for examples, I explained, "Like Cézanne, or the Tuscan painters, the Macchiaioli—the artists of the nineteenth century who broke away from the traditional classical ways of painting to start the impressionist movement—many of them even painting outdoors to capture natural light, shade, and color."

"So what is the problem?" asked Adriana. "No two artists paint alike. There are classical painters, who are more traditional, as well as more modern artists, like yourself, who are a little more avant-garde. Some are realistic; some are not. There is no wrong or right way to paint."

"Yes, of course," I said quickly. "I realize that. It's just that I'm in a bit of a creative slump. I'm wondering if I should take my work in a different direction, that's all. Try something new."

Adriana looked at me and raised her eyebrow.

"Oh, okay," I said. "It isn't just my work. On a personal level, this girl is making me feel like a complete fool. She may dislike me almost as much as my paintings. You should have heard what she said the other day."

Giving me a sympathetic smile, Adriana said, "Ah well, that's just friction and sparks from two talented divas colliding."

Seeing my empty cup, she reached for the pot again and poured out the last drop of coffee before saying, "Listen, Sophia. You wanted this opportunity. Trust your instincts. You were selected to attend this art school because of your talent. It is inevitable you will encounter some who will appreciate your work, as well as those who will criticize it. *Chissà perché.* Who knows why? Maybe they are mean spirited or full of their own insecurities."

Zia Ilaria reached over the table and squeezed my arm. "*Su! Su! Forza!* Keep your spirits up. Take heart."

Nodding in agreement, Adriana looked at her watch. Raising an eyebrow, she clucked her tongue and said, "*O mio Dio! Andiamo!* It's time to go."

Before pushing me out the door, she exclaimed, *"Hai voluto la bicicletta? Adesso pedala."* As I looked at her curiously, she hastened to explain, "You know, Sophi. You wanted this opportunity. Now pedal. You have to keep going. You have to take the good with the bad."

All the way to school I thought about Adriana's words. As I pressed the buttons of the elevator, I knew she was right. I had to find a way to figure things out. So what if I was having a little artistic meltdown? The only way to get through it was to keep pedaling so as to stay on my bike.

At the top, I opened the lift door. I glanced around, cautiously looking for signs of the French girl. Relieved to see she hadn't yet arrived, I walked down the hall to the studio thinking about the moment we had first run into each other—literally. I had been crossing the studio with a jar of turpentine, headed to the sink to clean out my brushes. I didn't see her standing in my path and had inadvertently slammed into her, splattering her face and blouse with solvent. The girl was momentarily speechless. Then she let out a scream followed by a torrent of angry French words.

Embarrassed, I quickly grabbed a towel to clean up the mess. Instead of helping the situation, it only served to make her more angry. Cursing in

Italian, she said, "*Idiota!* Do you *know* how much I just paid for this blouse? It's Dolce Gabbana. *Merde! Elle est ruinée.* Now it's ruined."

Glancing over at my easel, she added, "You are as clumsy when you walk as when you paint. Look at you. You have more paint on your clothes than you do on your palette." Sizing me up, she said, "And from the look of things, you wear the paint better than your canvas does."

I bit my tongue and said nothing. The accident had completely been my fault. I hadn't been paying attention and could certainly understand her anger, but her words were unkind and uncalled for. But really, who wears Dolce & Gabbana in a painting studio? Once again I apologized and backed away, giving her space to cool down.

A few minutes later, Alessandro entered the room. He casually approached me. Looking at my painting from over my shoulder, he studied it for a moment. Then putting his hand on my shoulder, he said, "So...Sophi, I heard you met Bébé." Laughing, he joked, "I guess you two finally bumped into one another."

"Bébé?" I asked in disbelief. "*Santo cielo!* Is that her name?"

Alessandro shrugged and rolled his eyes, agreeing silently with me that she was a real pill. "Try to get along with her."

I raised an eyebrow and looked at him in disbelief. He shrugged and said, and said, "*Lo so*, I know she can be a bit of a prima donna."

I tilted my head to one side and said, "Yeah, just a bit."

"However," he said, "she is quite a talented painter, with a real gift. She is one of Roberto's protégées. It was a real coup that she decided to study with us." He coughed and added, "Best if we all keep her happy. So anything you can do to maintain the peace, I'd appreciate it."

So in spite of the girl's unkind words, I was ready to oblige Alessandro. I thought my efforts were paying off when a few days later, I found her standing in front of my easel studying one of my paintings. It appeared she was showing a glimmer of interest, and I wondered if maybe she might be about to say something nice, apologize even.

When she saw me, she narrowed her eyes and said, "Don't tell me you are finished with this one? It's a nice start, but it looks like you have a lot more work to do." With a dismissive toss of her head, she walked out of the room. When she was gone, a new rush of animosity bubbled up inside of me. Irritated, I looked at the painting on my easel and tried to see it through her eyes. She had just sparked my internal critic, touching off a whole new series of negative thoughts.

Suddenly I, too, had to get out of the studio. Grabbing my bag of paints and portable easel I left. When I reached the street, I wasn't sure where I was headed, but my feet seemed to know where they were going. Soon I found myself standing in front of the Duomo.

Turning around, I looked at the Baptistery just as a shaft of early morning sun illuminated the bronze doors. In a heartbeat, I felt inspired again. Finding a relatively secluded spot where I wouldn't be bothered by tourists, I set up my easel. As I began painting, I remembered that once Michelangelo, completely in awe of the Baptistery panels, had called them the "Gates of Paradise," deeming them so beautiful they could easily grace the portals of heaven. Judging by the size of the crowds that flocked to the Baptistery each day, Ghiberti's doors—that had taken twenty-one years to complete—continued to beckon saints and sinners alike.

Recalling my morning encounter with Bébé, who I was beginning to think of as my nemesis, I was reminded of yet another famous artistic rivalry that had existed between two famous Florentine artists: Lorenzo Ghiberti and Filippo Brunelleschi. In 1401 when a competition was announced to determine who would design the Baptistry doors, both men had set their caps on winning. Each was committed to prove to the other *and* the entire city which was the better artist.

To enter the competition, they along with many others had prepared a single bronze panel depicting the biblical story of Abraham's *Sacrifice of Isaac*. When the results were unveiled, there really was no competition. While Brunelleschi's panels had been competent and pleasingly well rendered, they paled in comparison to that of his rival. Ghiberti was the clear winner. His clever use of depth and realistic perspective outshone all the other entries.

Infuriated to have been defeated by a younger and cockier artist, Brunelleschi decamped to Rome to lick his wounds. There he studied classical architecture. When he returned to Florence a few years later, he was better equipped to compete and win another prestigious competition—that of building the massive dome over the cathedral.

Shielding my eyes from the sun with my hand, I looked back up at the Duomo. In the end, I thought, how impressive to go down in history for masterminding the majestic red brick cupola. Perhaps a bit of animosity had been useful to fuel the creative fires of Ghiberti and Brunelleschi. Would it be helpful in my case as well?

It had been a disastrous beginning to the week, but after my painting session in front of the Gates of Paradise, I approached the weekend in a much better frame of mind. As was his routine, every Friday Alessandro gathered his students for a peer review. After a rough few days, I was ready to hear feedback from other painters. So when he called us into one of the smaller studios, I eagerly put down my brush and grabbed a small plastic cup of espresso from the machine.

When nearly all of our paintings had been reviewed, and we were starting to think about dinner, Alessandro looked over at me and nodded for me to go next. As I positioned my painting on the easel in front of the group, Alessandro's cell phone rang. Indicating I should start without him, he stepped into the hall to take the call.

Looking around the room, I told the group I was having a rough week and would appreciate their honest opinions and feedback. I sat back and waited. A couple of artists responded with complimentary words, pointing out passages they particularly liked. I was feeling confident again until I heard Bébé cough and clear her throat.

Slowly she rose from her chair and slithered to the front of the room. Studying my painting for a moment, she wrinkled her nose in distaste. Then turning around, she said in an incredulous tone, "Do you call this art? This is *trés* uninspired. Smear some gray and throw in some black and yellow lines, dot it with red and blue blobs at random, and voilà! You consider that a painting? Where are the classic lines? Everything here is distorted and random. Ghiberti would not be happy his were doors were dishonored like this. *Che disgrazia!*"

I sat in shock, unnerved by her words. I felt the blood rush to my face. I glanced around when I heard Alessandro's voice from the doorway firmly telling Bébé to take a seat. I felt a second wave of embarrassment when I realized he had heard her words, too. So focused on my hyper-critical thoughts, I barely registered what he said after that. All I heard was my own voice: *Who did I think I was? I wasn't a painter. I was an impostor. My paintings couldn't hold a candle to Bébé's, which mimicked the Flemish masters.*

When Alessandro's cell rang again, he let everyone go, saying he had to take the call and would see everyone after the weekend. As I retrieved my canvas, several friends rallied around me telling me not to take Bébé seriously. Clearly, she was just in a bad mood. I shrugged and put on a brave face and agreed, but later that night behind closed doors, I recalled the French girl's comments. She was so egotistical; I tried to dismiss the unkind things she had said. Still, a niggling thought troubled my mind. What if she was right?

The following Monday when I returned to the studio, Bébé was already at work in front of her easel. She glanced over at me and raised a disinterested eyebrow. I noted again how she held her brush, painting with extreme precision. She didn't need to worry about marring *her* designer silk blouse. I glanced down at my spattered jeans and the remnants of dried paint under my fingernails. Raking the hair out of my eyes, I stepped up to my easel, ready to make a new start.

When Alessandro passed through the studios a short time later, he stopped by my side and with one eyebrow raised whispered, "*Che disastro!* What a mess! What the hell are you doing here?"

I narrowed my eyes and looked at my painting. I was trying something new. But the attempt was far from pleasing. It wasn't working at all. This was not the way I saw the world or how I wanted to capture it. Alessandro patted my arm and said, "*Senti.* Listen, Sophi, it's great to experiment and try new things, but you must trust your instincts. You must paint what you feel and see. You must paint from the heart. Don't fall into the trap of imitating someone else. You will never be successful unless you do."

Shaking my head, I reminded him of Bébé's words. He looked at me sympathetically and said, "Didn't you hear anything I said last Friday? Your work shows an organic naturalism that is fresh and remarkable." Looking over in Bébé's direction, he added, "Perhaps your painting touched a nerve with our French girl over there. It just might be that she sees something in your painting she could never achieve in her own."

I looked at Alessandro in surprise. Bébé? Jealous of my work? I considered the stack of paintings next to my easel and pursed my lips. This was a new thought that I needed to digest.

Throughout the rest of the fall and early winter, Bébé and I coolly kept our distance. But one spring afternoon, after reading a yellow flyer tacked to the bulletin board outside of the main office, I knew sparks were about to fly again. It was an announcement for an artistic competition sponsored by the La Società delle Belle Arti in Florence, and the prize was a substantial sum of money. Also, the winner would receive a *borsa di studio*, a coveted scholarship to study at the Louvre's Master Painter Program in France. It would be an amazing experience to study at the Paris, but even more, I could use the money.

As I began thinking about what painting I might submit, I heard a slight snicker behind me. At first, I hadn't felt her presence, but when I turned around, I saw Bébé leaning casually against the far wall. She gazed at me coolly for a moment as she sipped a small plastic cup of espresso. Pushing off the wall and standing up straight, she looked at me pointedly and said, "So, Sophia. What do you think? Are you going to participate? Just think. If you do, we will be competing against one another."

Refusing to be intimidated I said, "Sure, why not? May the best artist win. Good luck." Narrowing my eyes, I thought: *Game on!*

That afternoon I headed up to Piazzale Michelangelo. Pulling out the red sable brushes Glenninghall had given me, I began to paint a view of the city as I had never painted it before. As I worked, I felt the presence of Giovanni Fattori, one of the leaders of the Italian Impressionist movement, standing behind me. His warm words of encouragement guided my brush and gave me the confidence. But in reality, the voice that rang in my head and pushed me even further was Bébé's.

As the deadline of the competition drew near, the tension was palpable, but I was happy with my painting and knew I had done my best work. The night the results were announced we gathered at the Palazzo Strozzi. For the occasion, a string quartet had been hired to play. I stood next to Alessandro and toyed with my flute of champagne. Glancing up, I noticed Bébé standing in a corner on the opposite side of the room with her arms crossed tightly in front of her chest. When she caught me observing her, she regarded me with a frigid look before nonchalantly shrugging her shoulders and turning away.

When a man in a navy blue suit and tortoise-rim glasses, followed by two elegantly dressed women, entered the room the crowd clapped politely. They introduced themselves as the judging committee, and proceeding in a clockwise fashion began studying the entries whispering amongst themselves.

Midway through the gallery, the three of them stopped in front of my painting. From my position, it was hard to read their faces or guess what their thoughts might be. I looked over at Bébé and saw her biting her lip. Taking more time with my painting than with some of the others, the judges conferred a few more minutes before continuing.

As the music of Paganini filled the room, they began circulating the gallery again, admiring all of the paintings. But when they reached the spot where Bébé's entry hung on the opposite wall, they all paused as if transfixed before stepping closer for a better look. Several heightened minutes passed before one of the judges nodded his head to the others and in unison they turned around to face the crowd.

Stepping up to a podium, the man in the blue suit tapped the microphone. The crowd ceased its murmuring, and the music stopped playing. Clearing his throat, he thanked all the artists for participating. He noted that while all the paintings showed great merit, only one artist could claim the prize. Then gesturing broadly, he announced the winner's name: Mademoiselle Bissette.

Everyone applauded including me...well perhaps not quite as enthusiastically as the others. I glanced over at Bébé and saw her looking at me. Although I was disappointed I had lost, I rallied, graciously saluting her *and* her painting with my wineglass.

What she did next surprised me. Continuing to hold my gaze, she raised her glass and nodded in the direction of my canvas. This time, her smile was several degrees above freezing, and well, it seemed quite genuine.

It appeared two divas had just called a truce, each recognizing the strengths and talents of the other.

Chapter 15

On Top of the Duomo

*I*t was just as well that Bébé had been granted the scholarship to study in Paris. As with Ghiberti and Brunelleschi, the most laudable artist had won this artistic competition. I had to believe something better was in store for me. I just didn't know what it was at the moment.

If I was completely honest with myself, I couldn't see myself painting at the French Academy at the Louvre. I much preferred to paint outdoors in Florence. The one thing I did regret was not receiving the prize money. In preparation for lean times to come I was learning to *stringere la cinghia* and *incrociare le dita*—tighten my belt and cross my fingers—in hopes that the new grant I had applied for would be approved. If not, I would have to take out a temporary loan.

Following the competition, as a consolation prize, I decided it was high time for me to climb to the top of the Duomo. It seemed an appropriate moment to seek out the company of Brunelleschi. After all, he knew a thing or two about artistic differences, competition, and rivalry. He would know how to soothe my injured pride.

The Duomo, officially known as Santa Maria del Fiore, had been started in 1296 by Arnolfo di Cambio. However, it remained incomplete for more than two hundred years. With the demise of poor Arnolfo and the onset of the Black Death, work ground to a halt. The Florentines scratched their heads and furrowed their brows. No one, not even architectural luminaries like Giotto or Andrea Pisano, had a viable solution to top it off.

To medieval men, it seemed an impossible feat to create a dome that would span the space above the church without the use of flying buttresses. The Florentines turned up their noses at such ugly reinforcements, deeming them secondhand solutions. Instead, they wanted a free-standing dome, with pleasing lines and classical proportions. So instead of a "quick fix," Florence held out for a better plan. Time slowly ticked by, the cathedral remained in a state of undress, and rainwater poured in from the skies.

Filippo, the hot-tempered Florentine goldsmith, was the one who came up with the solution. Standing before the Pantheon in Rome, he had an "Aha!" moment. While gazing at the coffered ceiling built by the Romans, he found the structural formula he needed. Dusting off an ancient concept, he improved upon the idea. Instead of a single, circular shell of concrete, he created double-nesting, egg-shaped domes. To finish it off, he used light-weight Florentine bricks. It was the perfect solution to reduce stress and ensure the dome would stand the test of time.

Since my arrival, I had been inside the church and looked up into the dome decorated with scenes of the Last Judgement by Vasari. I had also descended into the crypt to see Brunelleschi's tomb. There stretched out for all eternity he gazed forever upward into his majestic dome. This was a high honor indeed, as before Brunelleschi's time very few saints, let alone common people were interred in the basement of the Duomo.

As yet I hadn't been to the top of the cupola. But on the day I decided to rise to the top, fortune favored me. As I approached the cathedral, I noticed the queue was looking kind of slim. The ticket agent was just shutting down, about to turn off his cash register. But after some lighthearted bantering, I convinced the man to sell me a ticket. He only looked at me as if I were crazy and said, "*Signorina*, there isn't much time left, and there won't be much of a view today. Look at the weather. It's been raining all day."

With a wry face, I said, "I'll take my chances. A little moisture never hurt anyone."

There was no modern elevator to reach the top. Instead, one had to climb the four-hundred-and-sixty-three stairs that spiraled upward between the two shells of the cupola. Optimistically, I approached the stairs, and up and around I went. When I put my foot on the last narrow step, I emerged into the watery light of day. I blinked my eyes a few times, adjusting to the beams of sun that had managed to pierce through the low-lying clouds to the west. It was a welcoming sign, promising a glorious sunset. Below me, the Arno gently curved along the western edge of the city, and gleaming in the distance, I could see the monastery of San Francesco in Fiesole.

I leaned over the rail and gazed down at the tiny people scurrying about the Baptistery. Up here I felt invincible and free from worries. I thought of my father and wondered if he had felt the same when he stood here with my mother. Looking up a noticed a hawk gliding on a draft of air. Gracefully it landed on the railing. As I pondered the bird's silver plumes, I believed my father was closer than I realized.

As the sun sank a little lower in the sky, the air grew brisker. Zipping up my jacket, I buried my chin deeper into my cotton scarf. A guard poked his head out of the entryway and said, "*Signorina, sbrigati!* We are closing in ten minutes."

I watched as one of the last remaining couples exited into the stairwell. It seemed I had the place all to myself. Settling against the rail, I enjoyed the feel of the cool air on my face. Wrinkling my nose, I caught the scent of cigar smoke as it wafted along with the breeze and wrapped around me like a gentle caress. Following the source, I saw an old man a few steps away. He must have sensed my presence because he turned and looked at me.

Silhouetted against the shimmering band of light emanating from the horizon, he was a formidable figure. Upon his head was a turban-like sash and he wore a long, flowing, purple cloak. As the wind began to blow again, the folds of the cloth rippled across his large frame. It appeared he had just stepped out from the narrow strip of space that separates day from night. I thought: *He has come to lead me to that elusive place where promises take us and dreams carry us further.*

The man nodded at me as if he could read my mind. Then he threw down his cigar and ground it out with the toe of his boot. Immediately, I knew I was in the presence of Signor Brunelleschi, the architect who had built this spectacular dome.

"Well," he said, "what do you think of my *capolavoro*?"

"Your masterpiece is *magnifico, signore!*" I said, gazing around me. "What you have created is astounding."

Hearing my words, he beamed with pleasure. "Yes, it is quite remarkable, no? But it wasn't easy. We started work on the dome in 1420 and didn't finish it until 1436."

"Can you imagine? They built this beautiful church a century before my birth but had no idea how to complete it." Raising his hands and gesturing broadly, he continued, "They had no idea. No idea at all. Trust the foolery of men or perhaps the confidence they have in a supreme God, they thought would eventually provide them with a solution."

"But Signor Brunelleschi..." I said, "they were waiting for you. Only you had the remarkable insight and creativity to build this dome."

He tapped a finger to his temple. "Yes, I did. I did indeed! It seems all my life I was in training to build this dome. As a boy, I apprenticed in a goldsmith's shop where I mastered drawing, painting and working in gold. But I never tired of tinkering with wheels and gears."

Leaning against the railing, he looked down at the piazza and said, "But let me tell you. It was no easy thing to design this monstrosity. It took a lot of men to raise this tricky dome of mine." Turning his head to look at me he said with a chuckle, "It was a climb to reach this height, no?"
I quickly agreed. My legs were still recovering from all those stairs, and my breath had just returned to normal.

Taking a step closer, he said, "I'll let you in on a little secret. Once my workers arrived at the top, I didn't let them leave until the end of the day. Instead, I arranged for food and diluted wine to be brought to them. Can you imagine the loss of productivity if they had to climb the stairs twice in one day? Why it would have taken another hundred years."

In my mind's eye, I could see a tattered collection of hungry men heartily consuming their noon meal as they told jokes, all the while complaining that their wine was a bit weak. But talk about a meal with a view. No one could grumble about that.

Brunelleschi cleared his throat to attract my attention. When I turned my eyes back to him, he said in a conspiratorial whisper, "Let me tell you another little secret...sometimes I wasn't even sure my ideas would work. Sometimes it seemed an impossible feat. You see, such a large dome had never been attempted before. And then I had a flash of inspiration. It came to me just like that. Oh, I did my research and I did the math. I can't tell you how many hours of calculations I did each night, burning through countless candles. Do you know where I got my biggest inspiration? Do you know how I knew my solution would work?"

Not waiting for an answer, he asked, "You've seen the Pantheon?"

"Not yet," I replied quickly adding, "but don't worry I plan on taking the train to Rome in just a few weeks."

He glanced at me in disbelief and said, "*Caspita!* Good heavens, girl." Shaking me by the shoulders, he exclaimed, "There is no time like the present. As soon as you can, you must go there...see the entire city, the Forum, Trajan's column, the Colosseum...but pay particular attention to the Pantheon. I used it as my model. Those Romans were brilliant."

Together we began to circle the narrow passage. As we walked, Brunelleschi confided, "Once I figured out a plan of action, I knew I was on the right track. But just the same I used to lie awake at night, tossing and turning, worried I had miscalculated something or added numbers incorrectly and the whole thing would come crashing down upon my head." He grimaced at the recollection. "But then I would hear a voice that encouraged me and gave me the confidence to continue."

He chuckled at my startled expression. "Ah yes, sweet Sophia I, like you, have had visitors who guide my creative process." Gazing out at the evening sky, he softly said, "We are but the work of dreams and visions, all held together by sensibility and hard work. True joy lies between the two."

I looked at him with wide eyes. "So your visitors...they are voices that speak to you from your dreams?"

He held up his arms widely and exclaimed, "*Mia cara*. But of course! Where do you think we artists derive our inspiration? From whence do you think all creative energy flows?"

When I didn't reply, Brunelleschi answered for me. "From the past, my dear girl. Ideas for the future always come from the past."

The old architect dropped his arms, took out another cigar, and lit it. Leaning back against the railing again, he added, "Why Botticelli was telling me just the other day, he is often visited by the Greek poet Homer and that Michelangelo often has conversations with the sculptors Myron, Phidias, and Polyclitus."

I slowed my steps and stopped. Placing my hands on the rail, I looked down upon the piazza.

"But remember, Sophia...only those who listen hear the voices. It is a gift." He looked back at me and said with a wise smile. "This is what moves us all forward. One discovery leads to another and another and another. But it all starts with a spark that blows from the past, propelling us upward to greater heights."

I reflected on this. The old architect had studied to learn the science of how to build, but in the end, it had been the muses he channeled that helped him realize his vision. Perhaps I wasn't crazy after all. In fact, I was in quite good company.

Brunelleschi smiled and said, "Yes, Bella my dear, you are in very good company. Creative types like ourselves are all just a little *pazzi*. But we are crazy in the most unusual kinds of ways, no?"

With a grimace, he lamented, "But some are crazier than others! Let me tell you about my nemesis—Ghiberti! He was a real thorn in my side, full of plots, always scheming to undermine my projects. It made me so mad when the Florentine council appointed him as my co-superintendent. Why that scoundrel even tried to get me thrown in jail."

Pounding his fist on the railing, he declared, "Just the thought of that man makes my blood boil. When we were competing to win the Baptistery door commission, I thought I might murder him. Such an arrogant, pompous fool!"

Brunelleschi glanced around as if to make sure no one else could hear. Leaning close to my ear he whispered, "But, for whatever it's worth..." he hesitated a moment, "Ghiberti deserved to win the Baptistery door commission. I admit it. Yes, his designs were a bit more creative and innovative than mine."

Smiling a bit ruefully, he admitted, "Sometimes, my dear, we are fueled not only by our creative muses but also by plain old human rivalry. Just ask my good friends Michelangelo and Leonardo..." Before he could go on, Giotto's campanile began to chime, causing the pigeons to flap their wings and flutter up into the air. Dusk was descending. Regretfully I realized it was time to return to the piazza below.

I said goodbye to my new friend, kissing him on both of his cheeks without any awkwardness or colliding of noses. Brunelleschi stepped back and said, "My, you did that very nicely, indeed! You are quickly catching on to our customs. Lorenzo's city has been good for you. He tells me he is more than pleased you are here. He hopes you will stay a bit longer. We are all enjoying your company."

Thinking about the Medici prince I smiled. Before I could turn to go, the wise old architect withdrew a small box from his pocket and urged me to take it. Opening the lid, I discovered a snow globe. I lifted it out and shook it. When I did tiny flakes of powdery snow swirled around a miniature version of the Duomo.

Looking up to thank Brunelleschi, I discovered once again I was alone. I leaned against the railing and shook the globe again. It felt like I was standing on top of the world. Regardless of all the Bébés out there who might drag me down from time to time, right here, right now, I was standing on the cupola of the Duomo.

Momentarily losing my balance, my confidence had been restored.

Sophia was back on top.

Baroque

The Baroque period of art, in general, was a stylistic expression of complex emotional states communicated in dramatic manifestations and in painting, sculpture, architecture, and music. Some of the qualities most frequently associated with the Baroque are grandeur, sensuous richness, drama, vitality, movement, tension, and emotional exuberance. The style began around 1600 in Rome and spread rapidly throughout Europe.

Chapter 16

Morning Symphony

*A*t the beginning of August, before the Florentines cleared out of the city and headed to the beach to celebrate *Ferragosto* and their local patron saints, I learned my scholarship grant had been renewed. I was more than ready to say hello to a new fall semester.

When I entered the studios again, the first thing I saw was Alessandro deep in conversation with a pretty young woman with a curtain of straight dark hair. Alessandro seemed unusually attentive, and I wondered who she was. I stood waiting for them to notice me but they continued chatting, oblivious to my presence. Finally, I cleared my throat loudly, and Alessandro swung around to face me. When he saw me, he grinned, and said, "*Ciao* Sophi! Good to see you. There is someone here I'd like you to meet. I think you two will get along just fine. Meet Raffaella Mezzanotte. We've hired her to work as the school's secretary. She is a genius with computers and is working on her graphic design degree."

The girl standing next to Ale turned a beaming smile on me and said in a gush of words, "*Che bei capelli!* What great hair! I wish I had curls like yours." Hearing that, I too knew we were going to get along great.

My first impression proved correct. Raffaella was the sort of person who reached out to others and made them feel good about themselves. Soon she and I became *"amiche del cuore,"* the best of friends. Together we shopped and shared confidences. She was witty and bright, as well as a bit quirky. I was amused when she solemnly told me she thought of herself as a modern-day matchmaker. "You see, Sophia," she said with a sly smile, "I've helped bring about more marriages than Venus' famous son, Cupid." Raising her eyes heavenward, placing the back of her hand to her forehead, she sighed dramatically, "What can I do? It's a gift."

I had to concur she was indeed a special goddess of love. It didn't take long before she cast her eyes upon the ever-elusive Alessandro. During the time I'd been at La Scuola, I had seen many women make a play for him. Until Raffaella, though, I hadn't seen him reciprocate so completely. In just a few weeks of their first meeting, their playful bantering escalated from a casual flirting to a serious romance.

Watching my new friend interact with Alessandro, observing the whispers and kisses they exchanged, I sometimes became wistful. A girl can get lonely from time to time, living on her own in a foreign country. Despite our mutual break up, I still thought about Marc and wondered if we should try to get back together. When I confessed this to Raffa it didn't take long before she was setting me up with every eligible bachelor she knew in Florence—every Tizio, Caio, and Sempronio—Italy's Tom, Dick, and Harry.

Knowing I was single and on my own, Raffaella and Alessandro often invited me to accompany them on weekend outings. Together we explored the hill towns sprinkled around Tuscany sampling local fare and drinking delicious wines. Often I'd show up for an excursion only to discover one of Raffaella's single male friends waiting to meet me. Once unleashed she relentlessly set me up on blind dates, or as she referred to them *appuntamenti al buio*. I smiled to myself—the phrase translated to "appointments in the dark". As yet, none of the eligible bachelors she drummed up had sparked my interest. Although many of them were quite pleasant, some even rather lovely to look at, I inevitably lost interest.

I feared Raffaella was losing her touch and I was going to ruin her reputation as an accomplished matchmaker. So as not to completely disappoint her, I played along good-naturedly and put up with her attempts to find me a *Principe Azzurro*—an Italian Prince Charming.

"*Non si sa mai.* Ya' never know," Raffaella said encouragingly every time she called the following day to hear an instant replay of my date. "You have to kiss a lot of frogs—*devi baciare un sacco di rospi*—to find a prince of a guy. Perhaps the next one you meet will be your Lorenzo de' Medici."

I breathed out heavily in exasperation and said, "*Cara,* really. I know you mean well, but you don't have to worry about me." I tried my best to explain I wasn't in a hurry to exchange my newfound freedom for whatever "thing" her eligible suitors might be offering. I liked being independent and having control over my life and could deal with a little loneliness.

Lying on my back, I gazed up at the ceiling. Into the phone I said, "I know you like to think I am *la bella addormentata* waiting for a man with a blue cloak to ride up on a white horse who will wake me like Sleeping Beauty and save me from my terrible past. But Raffa, sometimes I don't want to be disturbed. I love to sleep! Have you seen me in the morning?"

On the other end of the line, I could hear Raffaella chuckling. Wrapping my soft fluffy quilt more tightly around me, I looked around my tiny room in Campo di Marte and said, "Granted, like *la bella addormentata*, half the time I walk around with my head in the clouds. Sometimes I am more asleep than awake. But you know what, my dearest Raffaella, matchmaker extraordinaire? I'm not going to please a man by knocking myself out trying to be beautiful, punctual, sweet, and accommodating."

She laughed at my next quip. "When *my* handsome, courageous, fascinating, funny, intellectually equal arrives, *he* will know exactly how to appreciate me for who I am."

Not only did Raffaella find this funny, but it was also highly amusing to my Italian family. Since I had begun dating again, I had become the popular target of good-natured jokes and teasing from all the aunts and uncles. It also opened the floodgates to silly questions, like when I was going to settle down and get married and when did I expect to have babies. I soon tired of hearing Zia Ilaria say with a mournful tone, "*Senti,* Sophia. Listen, honey, you aren't getting any younger, you know."

I knew they all meant well, but I began to wish for more privacy. Wouldn't it be great, I thought, to have a place to call my own where I could make a mess, stack my paintings, and abandon myself to my zany pursuits? There was just one small problem with that plan. Money. I was still living on just a few flimsy Euro with barely enough *spiccioli*—pocket change—for a cone of gelato.

Still, I knew I was lucky. Even though I didn't have a real flesh-and-blood family to call my own anymore, I had managed to invent one. Of course, the Poglianis weren't picture perfect, like the nauseatingly sweet families in the ads for the Mulino Bianco brand of cookies that flooded the Italian TV airwaves. They were the real deal, warts and all. Loud and nosy, they wore their hearts on their sleeves. I had achieved a level of intimacy with the family and felt comfortable letting down my hair, dishing the dirt, and hanging my underwear on the clothesline with theirs without the least bit of embarrassment.

But later that fall unexpectedly my fortunes changed when I received an official-looking letter with a California postmark. I expected it to contain some niggling estate detail, but when I opened the large packet I was surprised to learn that money from several accounts tied up in probate had been released. With this windfall, I realized, I could afford my own place.

It was a bittersweet moment when I broke the news to the Poglianis, but they understood. And really I wasn't moving too far away. I would be just across town on the other side of the river in a third-floor studio apartment in the Oltrarno. As a departing gift, Adriana handed me a brand-new coffee pot to make my morning coffee. I hugged her gratefully, promising I would put it to good use.

I chose the Oltrarno as my new home for a couple of reasons. It was close to the school, just a short walk from the Ponte Vecchio. But in comparison to some of the older, more stoic Florentine neighborhoods, it pulsed to a hipper beat. As such, it was home to many young artists. But more important I was drawn to the area because it was where the Pitti Palace was located—the home to Eleonora and Cosimo de' Medici. It felt comforting and rather fitting to live so close to the ducal family home.

As I walked down the narrow streets that Eleonora had also traversed, zigzagging back and forth from Santa Trinità to the Boboli Gardens, I passed by the storefronts of wood carvers, gilders, and goldsmiths. Peeking in, I saw men carrying forward ancient Florentine crafts, applying gold leaf to wooden frames or adding layers of varnish to serene Madonnas. Into the mix was thrown modern ateliers and design studios. Neon signs and cubist structures graced windows and trendy bars pumped out Jovanotti rap and pop songs by Ligabue, Pausini, and Nek.

Here in my neighborhood—my *quartiere*—I was treated to an endless variety of melodies, composed and performed by a thousand musicians. From the street, I heard the roar of Vespas mixed with the insistent *Bee-BOH-Bee-Bee-Bee-BOH* cry of an ambulance and the bonging Vesper bells from Santa Maria del Carmine. As I passed by the open doors of bars and cafés, I heard the constant chattering of china cups and the hissing whistle of the quadruple-cup espresso machines. Each morning these sounds, mixed with the smell of freshly brewed coffee, brought me fully to my senses.

But the morning sounds that teased my ears the most were the staccato beats and sing-song voices of my Italian neighbors. Sometimes the sounds could be insistent and rudely demanding; other times sweetly rendered in dulcet tones. Regardless, my neighbors were an unending source of entertainment.

Usually, the first singer to open my morning intermezzo was that of an impatient mother, Signora Balestrini. Like a prima donna, her voice floated out to me, hitting all the shrill high notes. *Valentina! Basta con il trucco.*

Sembri troppo grande. E quella gonna è troppo corta. Vai subito a cambiarti."

I laughed when I heard Valentina's mother telling her teenage daughter to wipe away her makeup because it made her look too old and change her skirt because it was way too short.

Then in a crescendoing wail, Valentina's melodramatic teenage voice echoed back. "*Maaaammmmma! È come quelle delle mie amiche.*" I heard my own tearful teenage voice when I had yelled back at my mom that it was what all the girls were wearing.

From another open window came the voice of a desperate housewife as she summoned her husband, in short, staccato notes, "*Francesco. Vieni qua!*"

Uh oh, I thought. Francesco is in trouble again.

Francesco, in a booming bass, responded impatiently, "*Che cosa c'è? Faccio tardi.*"

In a prelude to a domestic squabble, his wife insisted, "*Uffa! Solo un attimo. Dai. Ti prego*"

Francesco softened his voice and sweetly crooned, "*Maria, tesoro...*

I smiled and thought: *Way to go, Francesco, buttering her up with sweet phrases of love.*

Once again I heard Signora Balestrini's high-pitched voice telling her daughter to stop dawdling, "*Vaaaleeentiiiinaaaa! Facciamo tardi. Muoviti!*"

Moments passed and then, Valentina sang out, "*Arrivo. Eccomi!*"

I rolled over on my side and thought: *Yes, the morning had begun.*

As my neighbors exited stage right and the curtain descended, their morning performances concluded tenderly.

"*Mamma! Bacino?*" Kiss kiss.

Francesco's wife, now calmed by her husband's soothing words, trilled out, "*Ciaooooo tesoro. A stasera.* See you tonight, sweetheart."

Taking a few more minutes to yawn and stretch, I rose and padded over to the window. Unlatching the sturdy brass knob that secured the shutters, I pushed them open. Leaning out the window and looking across the central courtyard, I saw Signora Moschini in her housedress and white embroidered apron ironing her son's pants. The small black-and-white television in her kitchen played the theme song from the morning talk show *Unomattina*.

When she heard my window open, she looked over and waved her hand frantically. Calling out across the courtyard, she said, "*Ehi, Sophia!* Wanna few zucchini? Zio Angelo brought me too many." She pointed to a basket of emerald green vegetables sitting on her table and picked one up for me to admire.

I called back. "*Grazie, signora.* I'll stop by this evening."

Turning on the radio, I began singing along with the Italian pop singer Giorgia. *Tu mi porti su poi mi lasci cadere...* You lift me up and then let me fall...When I met you, the game of seduction was on...You've charmed me, and I'm in love..." Whirling about my apartment I dressed quickly, gathered my belongings, and descended the stone steps to the cool, dark atrium. In America, people lived in apartment buildings, but here in Florence they were called *palazzi.* It made me smile to think that I dwelled in Renaissance stone palace, just like a Medici princess.

Pushing open the heavy medieval door, I stepped out into the street. It was already alive and bustling with brisk morning traffic. People on bicycles passed me, calling out *"Buondì!"* and rang their bells—*ching ching*—to warn me not to step into their path. I walked down the sidewalk, passing fruit stalls, flower vendors, and a small laundromat, where I now washed my clothes. On either side of the street, jewelry and leather shops were opening their doors.

Continuing down the street, I saw the glowing green neon cross that hung outside the corner pharmacy. In direct competition in the window of the *tabaccheria* shop next to it, flashed a *"Super Enalotto"* sign. If you stepped inside to buy a lotto card, you would find all manner of things, from cigarettes to stamps. I noticed that tourists were already blocking the door, buying handfuls of postcards, featuring garishly colored photos of the Duomo.

Craving a coffee and breakfast pastry I made a beeline for my favorite neighborhood hangout, the Caffè delle belle arti—the Cafe of fine arts. Bars abounded in Florence. You couldn't throw a stone in the city without hitting one. But more than selling beer, wine, and mixed drinks, it was also a place to enjoy a delicious cup of coffee. The bar was a social scene, but not where a person stayed too long. It was a place where locals stood at a stainless steel counter and sipped frothy cups of cappuccino in the morning or slugged back tiny shots of espresso in the afternoon. Certainly, there were tables, but these came with a cover charge, usually filled with tourists used to leisurely sipping coffee, or a patron who had time to spare.

Proper etiquette required a customer first to pay for their coffee and pastry. Upon receiving his *scontrino,* he slapped the receipt on top of the bar and waited for the barista to brew his drink. Within a few moments, the whirring espresso maker spit out a shot of fragrant black liquid. It arrived on a small saucer, still hot from the dishwasher. Often the bar was quite crowded, and I bumped elbows with my neighbors. The neighborhood faces were as familiar as my own. A newcomer stood out in our crowd.

One morning, I paid for a cappuccino and shouldered my way to the pastry counter. Looking up from the enticing selection of brioche and *bomboloni*—a chocolate cream filled doughnut—I noticed such a stranger in our midst. Hmmm. Not bad I thought. He was almost as tempting the sweets in the case. He was sitting at one of the tables closest to the bar. Oblivious to the noise around him, he sipped his espresso as he read the sports page. I could tell he was reading *La Gazzetta dello Sport* because the pages of the paper were pink. He was dressed immaculately in the manner of many Italian men. His shoes were well shined and reflected the light from the colorful Venetian lights hanging from the ceiling. He wore a crisp white shirt with a handsome silk tie. His jacket was slung over the back of his chair, and an expensive leather briefcase rested near his feet. Very interesting. I wondered who he might be? He seemed quite at home in *my* bar.

I took a step closer to get a better look.

Intrigued, I watched as he turned the pages of his newspaper. Observing his profile for a moment, I was overcome by a familiar déjà vu feeling. I was sure I had met him somewhere before, but couldn't remember where or when. I remained rooted to the ground, mystified by my reaction to this stranger. With a start, I realized I was staring like a foolish idiot, much longer than was socially acceptable. I glanced back at the bar, but Tiziano was still preparing my cappuccino. Standing this close to the man, I could smell his aftershave and see how his thick, dark hair sculpted his head in waves. He had quite a fine form, and his distinctive profile reminded me of nobility.

Tiziano called out my name. My drink was ready. The man looked up and caught my eye. *Cavolo. Sono stata beccata!* Darn. I had been caught. I took an awkward step backward and returned to the safety of the counter. To cover my embarrassment I initiated a conversation with Tiziano, inquiring after his daughter and asking about his plans for the Easter holidays.

Looking down into my cup, I grinned. Every morning Tiziano took particular delight in topping off my foaming cappuccino with a unique design dribbled in chocolate syrup. Today my talented barista had decorated the froth with an image of a heart with wings. As I reached for a packet of sugar, I caught Tiziano's eye. He raised an eyebrow and smiled at me in wicked delight, before turning back to his espresso machine to fill another order. It seemed nothing got by him.

I took a bite of my pastry and chewed, savoring the sweet dough and the chocolate cream filling. I began to stir sugar into my coffee and just as I was about to take my first sip I felt a gentle tap upon my shoulder. I turned around to find the man with the distinguished profile standing next to me, jacket on and briefcase in hand. In surprise I choked and coughed into my cup, spluttering bits of foam onto his dark jacket.

Horrified at what I had just done, I reached over to grab a napkin from a plastic dispenser on the counter. On its side was an advert for Lavazza coffee featuring two lovers who sipped coffee at a table in the Piazza San Marco in Venice. In my haste to grab a napkin, I clumsily knocked the dispenser over, sending it skittering across the stainless steel surface. Finally, it flipped over the edge and crashed landed next to Tiziano's feet.

The man followed the course of the out-of-control napkin holder with a smile. I rapidly wiped my lips with the back of my hand. When he looked at me again, he studied my face for a moment, raised an eyebrow and pointed to his chin, tapping it lightly. Self-consciously I watched him, not understanding what he was trying to communicate. Then it dawned on me. *Dai... no!* He wanted to tell me something remained on my chin. Tiziano saved me, handing me a napkin. I sighed inwardly. So much for *fare bella figura* and making a great first impression, I thought.

The man regarded me thoughtfully. A slight smile played over his lips. It was starting to make me feel uncomfortable. I began to wonder if more remnants of my breakfast, foam or bread crumbs were stuck to my face or hidden in my hair. The sensation of having met him before returned. Perhaps it was the look in his eyes or the call of a faraway memory. But, as he continued to gaze at me, it seemed that he, too, was lost in a memory trying to recall if we had met before. Most likely, I thought it was only my overactive imagination at work. In all probability, he was only contemplating the graceless woman before him.

Shaking his head ever so slightly, as if to clear his head, he finally spoke. "*Signorina*, I believe you dropped this." He held out my red silk scarf. It must have slipped off my neck while I was standing next to him. I thanked him profusely, words spluttering out of my mouth as rapidly as the foam had spewed from my lips just seconds before. Patiently he waited for me to finish and then said, "*Di niente.* It is nothing." With a slight nod of his nod of his head, he turned and left the bar.

I stood for a moment looking after the man as he walked in the direction of the Ponte Vecchio. I wondered who he was and why he had chosen this particular bar to take his morning coffee. What had brought him into my neighborhood today?

A whistle from Tiziano brought me to my senses. I downed the rest of my cappuccino and set down my cup just a touch too loudly. It sounded like cymbals clashing together signaling the end of a symphony. My morning music may have concluded with the man's exit, but I found myself hoping for an encore performance.

Looking up, I flashed my favorite barista a brilliant smile. Holding my hands together I formed the shape of a heart with my fingers and thanked him for the coffee and his creative design. He shrugged his shoulders indicating it was his pleasure and said, *"Figurati! Non c'è di che. Buona giornata bella."*

I checked my watch. *"Oh mio Dio!"* I cried out, "I'm running on Bella Time again. Gotta run. I'm late!" I patted my heart a few times and blew him a kiss.

Chapter 17

Rubies from a Prince

I had lived for almost two years in the city of the Medici. During that time I had dipped my hands into the chest of Medici jewels and let the gems sparkle and glitter as they slid through my fingers, admiring their beauty. I had listened well to the advice and stories of the myriad of voices that had stepped out of their elaborate gold frames, or that had called out to me from their perches on high. At this point, I felt I had surpassed my apprentice status and was now ready to receive the title of master artist. Having judged my work, Lorenzo de' Medici had found me worthy and was now granting me access to his inner circle.

It made me increasingly happy to think I would soon graduate and wear a laurel crown just like Dante. Each morning, when I looked in the mirror, it felt like I was preparing to meet Il Magnifico himself. Soon I would sit at his Renaissance table where we would dine on duck and discuss my latest painting. Soon I would sit at his Renaissance table where we would dine on duck and discuss my latest painting.

It was true. In Lorenzo's city, I had matured as an artist. I was generating so many paintings and was running out of space in my apartment to store them. Alessandro suggested I start selling my art to the public. He pointed me in the direction of a few local restaurants and bars where the proprietors would display my paintings for a small commission. He also told me to go to Piazzale Michelangelo. He said the tourists who flocked to the piazza would happily pay for oil sketches of the Duomo and the Ponte Vecchio. After oohing and aahing and taking their obligatory photos, the tourists did indeed gravitate to my artwork. They all wanted to return home to Kansas City or Tokyo with a unique souvenir of Florence under their arm.

I couldn't believe how fast my time in Florence had flown. The cycle of holidays and festivals was repeating, and once again I was celebrating another Florentine Easter. The Sunday before the holiday, as Raffaella and I walked past the Duomo, we noticed preparations were underway for the uniquely Florentine Easter tradition—the *Scoppio del Carro*—Florence's famous exploding Easter cart. When I first asked Raffa about the peculiar practice—that of blowing up a brightly painted wagon in front of a cathedral the week of Easter—she said it had something to do with the Crusades back in 1099 and the crazy Pazzi family.

"You know *pazzi* in Italian means crazy, don't you?" She laughed and said, "Well they were certainly one crazy family. They were the ones who conspired against the Medici. They killed poor Giuliano right here in the Duomo and almost murdered Lorenzo on Easter morning in 1478."

Nodding, I told her I knew all about that, but the whole exploding cart thing didn't make much sense. She looked at me and shook her head, as if to say, did things really need to make sense to exist. Then she said, "Boh! One of the Pazzi boys brought back a sacred flint from the Holy Sepulchre during one of the crusades. The archbishop now uses it to light a dove-shaped rocket, the symbol of the Holy Spirit, and "flys" it out the window of the Cathedral along a wire to set off a decorated cart in the piazza below. If the cart exploded, it was an auspicious sign for Florence. It meant everyone would have good luck in the coming year."

Personally, this year I was hoping the cart would indeed be blown to bits. I needed all the help and good fortune I could muster to pass my exit exams. I was dreading my verbal grilling, equating it in my head to the torture of San Lorenzo who had been martyred over a bed of hot coals.

After I had officially graduated, Raffaella and I were planning to spend the month of August on the beaches in Puglia. "Just wait," she said, "Soon we will be floating in crystal blue seas, like Botticelli goddesses, as we make our way from Bari to Lecce. The boys down South haven't seen anything yet!"

With things finishing up at La Scuola, I knew I'd soon have to say goodbye to some of the friends I'd made over the past two years. Some were making plans to leave Florence, travel abroad or return home. But, I wasn't ready to go yet. This *was* my home now. The thought of giving up my life, my friends, and my colorful Italian neighbors was unthinkable.

So taking a cue from Machiavelli, the Florentine politician and consultant to the Medici, I began to plot my next move. The best idea I could think of was to approach Alessandro and make a case to continue working at La Scuola following graduation as a painting instructor. I hoped it worked because, let's face it, I really wasn't all that Machiavellian. I didn't have any other schemes or stratagems conveniently stashed up my sleeve or down the cleavage of my bodice.

Just before graduation I poked my head around Alessandro's door and asked if he had a minute to spare. Looking up, he said, "*Certo* Sophia, for you I always have time. What's up? *Che c'è?*"

Before slipping into the chair in front of his desk, I placed a shot of espresso from the school's automatic coffee machine and a plump *bombolone* I'd purchased at the bar. Looking at my offerings, he raised an eyebrow. He knew something was afoot but clearly was willing to be bribed. As he held the soft pastry up to his mouth ready to take a big bite, he looked at me quizzically. I smiled at him innocently, waiting for the sugar to take effect.

Waving the pastry around in the air, eyeing it thoughtfully, he asked in a teasing manner, "And to what do I owe this lovely act of generosity?"

I gave him a beatific smile and began my well-rehearsed speech. I reminded him how useful I had become at the school and how he would miss me when I was gone. I also pointed out that a couple of the teachers were leaving and he and Roberto would be shorthanded. "Well," I added, "this is your lucky day. It would be my pleasure, not the slightest hardship at all for me to step in and fill a vacancy." I continued listing reasons why he should hire me. I stopped just short of begging.

He took a sip of coffee and set it aside. Never breaking eye contact with me, he wiped the sugar off his hands and picked up a Captain America figurine. As he tossed it back and forth, he frowned slightly and shook his head slightly. My heart sank a little. The seconds passed, and my heart sank even deeper. My plan wasn't working. I was quickly trying to formulate my next move, desperately scraping together a Plan B. But when I looked back over at Alessandro I saw a smile spread slowly across his face and my heart grew lighter.

Alessandro tossed the action figure onto his desk and picked up the doughnut as if he were going to take another bite, but he stopped with it suspended in front of his mouth. "Really Sophi, you should know me better than this. You just wasted a perfectly good pastry on me. I was planning on asking if you wanted to stick around and work in this den of artistic iniquity."

I let out a small shriek of delight. *Che schemo!* "You are such a dope." I cried. "How could you do that." Picking up Captain America, I threw it at him. He ducked in the nick of time to avoid getting hit in the head with his own action figure.

Alessandro laughed. "*Senti*—listen, Roberto and I discussed this just the other day." Seeing my growing elation at the mention of Roberto's name, he quickly warned, "Calm down, calm down. Now, before you get too excited, the salary isn't all that great."

He popped the last bit of the pastry into his mouth, wiped his hands, and picked up a pen. While still chewing, he wrote down a figure on a piece of paper and slid it across the desk. When I saw what he was offering, I winced slightly. Looking him squarely in the eye, I suggested he raise it just a touch.

He tapped his head with his finger—the Italian gesture for craziness—and said, *"Sei matta?"* As I stared him down, he finally shrugged his shoulders. Reaching for the paper again, he crossed off the previous figure and scribbled a slightly higher one below it. He said he'd have to clear it with Roberto but thought they could swing it. Leaning back in his chair, he admitted, "And really when it comes down to it you are worth it. I'd hate to see you go...after all I'd miss all those free meals at your place."

Elated, I jumped out of my chair and ran over to hug my new boss. I told him to bring Raffaella over that evening, and we would celebrate my new position with a home-cooked meal and a good bottle of wine. Before leaving his office, I swiped a coffee mug off his desk. It was a kitsch piece, featuring Duchamp's image of the *Mona Lisa* with a mustache which I had been coveting for some time. Smiling sweetly, I said, "This is going to look fabulous in my new office." Alessandro grinned back and said, "I'll loan it to you for now, but I expect it back at some point. Now go. Get out of my office, *ladra*—thief!"

I left Alessandro's office feeling a burden had been lifted. I couldn't have been happier with my prospects if Lorenzo de' Medici, the prince himself, had offered to be my benefactor.

As the Easter crowds turned into summer mobs, when life in the city became too chaotic and noisy, I took the bus to Fiesole. There in the quiet little hill town, first founded by the Etruscans and where Roman soldiers later patrolled, I basked in its peace and quiet. I learned what it means to *staccare la spina*—pull the plug and relax.

Wandering through the olive groves in the hills high above Florence, I looked down on the Duomo, and the city spread out below like an intricately woven carpet. I fancied myself one of the characters in Boccaccio's *Decameron*, who fled the Black Death in Florence. To keep themselves occupied while waiting for the plague to pass, Bocaccio's lords and ladies had spun fanciful tales in the tranquility of one of Fiesole's villas.

Soon my fertile imagination was spinning its magic. I saw the shades of ancient civilizations weaving in and out of the rustling olive green trees. I saw girls in white flowing dresses carrying baskets of figs and men tilling the loamy, dusky brown hills. Weary travelers journeyed through the town, traversing the main roads of Etruria. Ox carts filled with grain rumbled past, and the whinnies of horses pulling the carriages of noblemen filled the air. Stopping near me, they stamped their hooves on the ground and snorted loudly before passing on down the road.

When I entered the ancient amphitheater, where the remains of Roman columns still stood, the voices of ancient thespians called out. Sitting on the benches looking down at the stage below I imagined Caesar's actors performing the same comedies and tragedies that were repeated in contemporary dramas on movie screens today. Heartache, pain, irony, and love were as much alive and relevant then as they are now.

As I sat among the ruins, sometimes Michelangelo joined me. Plodding heavily up the steps, he settled himself comfortably beside me. Removing his hat, he beat it against his leg a couple of times, shaking off the accumulated marble dust. Looking over at me, he moaned loudly, "Sophi, everyone is an art critic these days. I need a break from these annoying imbeciles. "

Cocking my head to the side, I asked, *"Che c'è?"*

Sighing heavily, he said, "Yesterday, I received a visit from Piero Soderini who wanted to take a look at the statue of David I have been working on for months. You know what that idiot said? He had the nerve, the arrogance to tell me, *me,* Michelangelo, that the nose on my David was too big."

He beat his hat upon his knee again. "But I was too tired to argue with him, so I just climbed back up the scaffolding constructed around my giant boy and pretended to hammer away at his nose some more." Giving me a sly smile, he added, "I let a bit of rock and dust that I had collected in my hand sift to the ground. Then I turned to Soderini and asked if he liked the nose better. Fooled by my trickery, he declared that the statue was now perfect and ready for public display."

I smiled at his cleverness and continued to sketch as I listened to the wind whispering through the ancient stones. To the left of me was a couple with a baby. I caught their likenesses with a few deft strokes of my pencil. Glancing to my right, I saw an older gentleman, wearing a stylish straw hat reading a newspaper. Soon he too was captured in my notebook. Raising my eyes to look at the ruins below me I noticed a tall man had just walked onto the stage. He seemed deep in concentration, almost as if he were an actor rehearsing lines for a play. Moving across the stone platform, he stopped in the center and crossed his arms over his chest. Standing all by himself, gazing out at the horizon I wondered what he was thinking. When he turned around I realized with a start I knew who he was. It was the man from the Caffè delle belle arti.

I put my pencil down and sat up, instantly alert. I noticed now instead of a formal business suit he was dressed casually in jeans and a polo shirt. I observed him for a few more minutes. For some inexplicable reason, I felt like a trespasser, watching covertly from afar. So as not to call attention to myself, as I had done before in the bar in Florence, I gathered my belongings and quietly left. During the bus ride back to town, I thought about the man. Opening my tablet I started to sketch a pair of intriguing eyes, wondering where and when I might encounter them again.

I didn't have too long of a wait as just a few days later I noticed the man again in the Uffizi Gallery. I had been visiting Eleonora and was about to exit the museum when he strode through the room. When I looked up, our eyes locked. It took a moment, but I could tell he remembered me. As he exited the room, he turned to look back at me and gave me a teasing grin. Great, I thought: *Guess I had made quite a first impression after all.*

After that, I began to see him all over town, but always at a distance. We never bumped directly into one another; either he was stepping off a bus, as I was to get on, or he was crossing a piazza, as I was walking on the side in the opposite direction. Because it was becoming a regular occurrence, I began to think of these daily sightings as an amusing game of hide-and-seek. Soon his face began to haunt my days as well as my dreams. Each morning I wondered where I would see him next.

I became more and more intrigued with my *galantuomo* and began making up stories about him. At first, I imagined him to be an Italian movie star who was hiding out from the paparazzi, on his way to George Clooney's villa on Lake Como. Other times I decided he was a secret agent. It seemed perfect. Apparently, he was concealing secret codes. Perhaps he was in league with James Bond. That could be rather exciting.

But the most fascinating persona I created was that of a reincarnated medieval prince. Yes! That fit nicely. Of course, he was a prince after all he had the good looks and the proud bearings of a nobleman and even the distinctive nose of a Medici. Imagining my mystery man to be the heir to the Medici throne, protector of its art, I grew more intrigued with each passing day.

If he had been a part of the Medici family—during the 1400s he would have played upon the knee of Cosimo de' Medici, a wealthy and powerful banker. His grandfather would have used his vast fortune, an estimated 150,000 gold florins, to control the Florentine political system. His family would have lived in the massively built Palazzo Riccardi designed by Michelozzo di Bartolomeo. He and his brother Giuliano, privileged children and heirs to the Medici Empire, would have run through the streets of Florence, considering it their personal playground. When he grew up, the people of Florence would call him Il Magnifico and he would magnanimously rule his city with a silk-lined leather glove.

Thinking of my curious stranger in this light, made me realize how much I owed the Medici prince, it seemed only fitting I should finally pay a visit to the man who had encouraged so many great artists and who in turn had inspired me. So on the eve of San Lorenzo, the magical midsummer night of shooting stars, *le stelle cadenti*—when all dreams come true—I decided to pay a visit to the prince. I packed up my sketchbooks and pencils and headed to the Medici family church named for Lorenzo, the martyred saint.

As I wandered about the basilica, designed by Brunelleschi, I admired the oldest building in Florence, consecrated in 393. Afterward I sought out the Medici chapels where many of the family were interred. Respectfully I approached the tombs Michelangelo had carved for his princes, Lorenzo and his brother Giuliano. Draping over the grave markers on one side of the room were the figures of *Dawn* and *Dusk*, on the other, those of *Day* and *Night*. All four languid guardians kept a vigilant watch over the sleeping Medici.

Feeling the urge to draw, I leaned against the wall, opened my bag and withdrew two tablets. Setting one on the floor next to my purse, I focused my attention on the elegant figures. So intent on sketching, I was oblivious to the tourists that flowed in and out of the chapel. Distracted by a flash of light, I glanced up and saw my the man from the bar had just entered the room. I smiled in surprise. The man smiled back, comically raising an eyebrow as if saying to himself, "Why do I keep running into this crazy woman?"

But almost as soon as we had made eye contact, it was broken by the arrival of a flock of Japanese tourists. The leader of the group, waving a purple flag with a fleur-de-lis, stepped in between us. As she spoke in a loud voice, pointing out the merits of the statues to her group, more people filed into the small space. Soon the room was buzzing with voices and clicking cameras.

Feeling self-conscious, not wanting the man to think I was stalking him, I picked up my bag and slipped through the crowd and into the adjacent octagonal-shaped chapel, the Cappella dei Principi. There in the larger chapel, I was blissfully alone again. I looked up at the high ceiling into the dome and back down at the slick, polished floor. The entire room was one enormous marble jigsaw puzzle created out of colorful semi-precious stones. It was somewhat gaudy for my tastes, yet undoubtedly a remarkable work of art and craftsmanship.

Inhaling, I breathed in the musky scent of oranges and cloves. Recognizing the fragrance of a man's cologne, I realized I was no longer alone in the room. I smiled at the thought of meeting Lorenzo, the Medici prince. I turned around and saw him standing just a few steps away.

He was dressed in a red tunic and across his broad shoulders was draped a richly embroidered cloak. His hair was cut short, revealing a smooth, broad forehead that emphasized a strong, aquiline nose. His beard and mustache were carefully groomed, giving him a debonair appearance. Around his neck hung a gold chain from which dangled an oval medallion inset with six round balls, the emblem of the Medici princes. Looking into his gray eyes, I could see reflected a rare intelligence.

Raising his arms widely he stepped up to give me a hug. Smiling, he said, "*Benvenuta Sophia*. Welcome to my home. I'm pleased you are here." Stepping back, he eyed me thoughtfully, and I looked delightedly back at him. We stood for several moments, not saying a word, content to have finally met.

Il Magnifico had died in 1492, the year Isabella of Spain had funded Christopher Columbus's voyage to the new world. He would never have learned of its outcome. He couldn't have known on the other side of the ocean existed the Americas, a state called California, or a valley named after the moon. Nor have imagined that his impact would span hundreds of decades and thousands of miles, to influence a girl from Sonoma.

The Prince raised one eyebrow and said, "Oh, but I do know, Bella. I know everything. I've been watching you all this time. It is I who has been calling you to Florence."

I smiled at the thought. Of course, it had been Lorenzo all along, guiding my path home to Italy, for his was the voice of Florence. His call had been the strongest. I watched as he studied me, taking in the long velvet skirt and vintage lace blouse I had bought in the street market just outside his front door. He scrutinized my face as if checking for signs of happiness. Finally, he looked down at the sketchpad I held in my hands and observed with pleasure the drawing I had been making.

"Ah," he said, turning his gaze back to me. "What talent. May I take a closer look?" Together we sat down on a stone bench, and I watched as he slowly turned the pages.

He studied each one carefully, and when he reached a drawing of Eleonora de' Medici, he looked up and nodded his head in approval. "Your work is quite exceptional. These are rapid sketches, *schizzi,*" he said, pretending to draw quickly in the air, "but I can see the strength of your designs. You have a real gift. *Molto particolare. Molto bello. Complimenti!*"

I was extremely pleased he thought my work accomplished, as well as a little avant-garde. Closing my sketchbook, he said, "Never be afraid to try new things or break the mold of previous thinking. Take what you learn from artists before you and boldly create something uniquely your own."

He looked around the room and gestured broadly. "Sometimes, Sophia, being a visionary can be difficult. Some will challenge you. They might criticize you and try to hold you back. But Bella, my dear, dare to forge on. Continue to inspire us with your work."

The Prince rose and held out his hands. He clasped mine lightly and drew me up from the bench. "I can see you are happy, Bella. You have traveled far. We may not meet again for I am a busy man, but know in your heart, I am always near."

He held my eyes a few moments longer as if to be assured I had understood him. Then from his pocket, he pulled out a small satin bag cinched with a velvet cord. "I have something for you." he said, holding the bag up and shaking it slightly, "My wife, Clarice, selected these out of her jewel box especially for you. Accept them as a token of our esteem." He laughed and then added, "Think of them as a commencement present."

Untying the satchel he spilled its contents into his open hand. There, resting in his outstretched palm, were two ruby earrings set in gold. As the sunlight caught the gems, they sparkled and shimmered, sending prisms of light dancing about the room. Gently I lifted the earrings and fastened them to my ears. I enjoyed the weight of the small jewels as they dangled against my cheeks.

The Prince lifted his hand and touched one of the earrings. "Clarice has chosen well. The earrings suit you nicely, indeed." He let his hand trail along the side of my cheek in a gentle, fond caress and then leaned over and kissed me on the forehead. With a start, I realized the moment was ending, and I hadn't yet thanked him properly for all he had done for me. I reached out and lightly touched his sleeve. He paused and tilted his head.

Finally, I was able to thank him for all he had done for me. *"Grazie per tutto quello che hai fatto per me. Questo è un regalo per te."* Proudly I extended my sketchbook to him. It was time for me to stop receiving gifts and offer one in return. Seeing the determined look on my face he took the tablet, thanking me as he tucked it under his arm. As I looked up at the lofty ceiling, feeling the weight of the ruby earrings against my cheeks, Lorenzo melted away back into the shadows.

I felt at peace. I had survived. I had made it. And the very reason I now stood in this chapel in Florence, at this precise and pivotal moment—strong and whole again—was because of my parents. My father had encouraged me to fly away, and my mother had insisted I dream. It had been a difficult path but along the way I had discovered myself. Now I could now walk forward on my own with confidence.

I was awakened from my reverie when I heard the light step of someone behind me. Slowly I swiveled around. This time, instead of a vision of the Medici ruler, in front of me stood the man from the bar. In the late afternoon light filtering through the chapel's windows, despite being dressed casually in jeans and a white button-down shirt, he was as striking as the Prince in his embroidered robe.

I smiled.

He smiled back.

In his hand, he held a sketchbook. He said, *"Scusi signorina,* I fear you have dropped something—again." In Italian, using the proper formal tense one uses with strangers, he asked, *"Questo è il suo quaderno di disegni, no?"* Repeating in English, not sure I had understood him, he said, "This is yours, right?"

I recognized my second drawing tablet in his hand. In my haste to escape the other chapel I had left it on the floor. I looked back into his eyes and regarded him thoughtfully. With a start, I realized I hadn't answered him. Remembering my manners I reached out to take back the sketchbook. *"Sì, sì! Certo. Grazie."* Quickly I added, *"Salve. Mi chiamo Sophia."*

Pleased I had spoken in Italian, he said matter-of-factly, *"Lo so."*

He knew? How could that be?

When he saw my puzzled face, he pointed to my name on the cover of my sketchbook. Reaching out his hand again, he firmly clasped mine and shook it. Looking me directly in the eye, he said his name, *"Salve. Mi chiamo Lorenzo."*

My eyes opened wide with astonishment. "Lorenzo," I whispered under my breath. I looked at him and nodded my head in agreement. Of course his name was Lorenzo!

Seeing my expression, he smiled and said, "Looks like you've just seen a ghost." Holding my gaze a moment longer, he asked, *"Senta Sophia*, we have to stop meeting like this. Listen, would you like to go for a drink with me?"

"Yes. *Sì, Lorenzo. Ha ragione."* I nodded setting the rubies dancing and thought, yes, Lorenzo, you are absolutely right. It's high time we had an *aperitivo* together.

Chapter 18

Amici

Sitting in an outdoor café waiting for our Aperol Spritzes to arrive, observing the man across from me I was struck again by a comfortable sense of familiarity. I knew nothing about him but couldn't shake the feeling I had met him somewhere before. The connection that had sprung up between us was so spontaneous and natural, on the short walk from the church to the bar, we found ourselves discarding the polite—*darci del tu*—signaling the beginning of a new friendship.

As we began to talk, I learned Lorenzo had been named after a Medici prince, just as I had been named after the queen of the Italian silver screen. He had grown up in Florence where he began his formal education, continuing it in Rome and later at Cambridge. Coming from the cradle of the Medici world, naturally, his field of concentration was Renaissance art. He spent several years doing an internship at the Tate in London and then had been hired as a temporary curator at the National Gallery.

I was impressed with Lorenzo's credentials and discovered the day we had first met he had been on his way to meet the museum directors at the Uffizi Gallery to assume a new position as lead curator for their special events exhibitions. He had chosen the bar precisely for its name, Caffè delle belle arti, believing it to be a good omen.

Soon I found myself telling him my story and how I had come to live in Italy. His genuine interest caused me to ramble on and on. It seemed my tongue had become unhinged. At one point looking over the rim of my glass I felt I could trust him and found myself telling him about my parents. He listened intently; the empathy in his eyes comforted me. Shaking my head, surprised at having gone down this path so quickly, I redirected the conversation back to my present life in Florence.

When he learned I had attended La Scuola and I now worked there as an assistant painting instructor, he said I must be well acquainted with Alessandro Mazza. *"Siamo amici d'infanzia!"* he said. Smiling broadly, he repeated in English, "We've been friends since we were kids."

"*Davvero?* Really?" I smiled widely, delighted to learn he also knew Ale. "He was the first person I met in Florence, I will never forget that moment, after all, I went through to get here."

When Lorenzo smiled at me, my face flush slightly, and I knew it wasn't entirely due to the Spritz I was currently sipping. Until this moment, the man had been a complete stranger. He had been someone for whom I had invented extravagant personas—a spy, a movie star, and a prince. But now the fantasies had all but been dispelled. Here we were, sitting in a caffè in Florence, making a connection. For the first time, I had to admit I was finding the real story much more compelling than the one I had invented in my head.

Watching the throngs of tourists headed toward the Galleria dell'Accademia, I wondered how Lorenzo would react to a bit of teasing and whether he had a sense of humor. Would he pass my next test? But seeing he was a friend of Alessandro, I imagined he would take the bait. Leaning over I said in a confidential tone, "I was so happy to see Alessandro that first day at the train station," continuing in a stage whisper, "I thought him very dashing and handsome." Switching back and forth between English and Italian I said, "In fact, he taught me how to kiss like an Italian. *Infatti mi ha anche insegnato come baciare come un'italiana!*"

I relaxed back in my chair, interested to see how he would react to the information that minutes after arriving in Italy I was kissing an Italian man, *his* friend. Lorenzo merely raised an eyebrow and said, "Knowing Alessandro, I imagine he was a very adept teacher, and he has quite an eye for lovely young women."

Smiling at his response, I quickly clarified it had been all very innocent and rather awkward, ending with us bumping our noses. "Ale was very polite about the whole thing. Ever since that day, he has been the best teacher. I have learned *so* much him."

Lorenzo laughed, but by the scrutinizing look he gave me I wondered if he thought I was referring to more than just knowledge of Florence. Suddenly I felt the need explain. In a rush of words, I added quickly, "He's a great guy! I think he is an incredible painter. He's dating my very best friend, you know. They are quite an item. The three of us are always off on some wild adventure—up to no good."

Swirling my straw around the ice in my drink, I continued, "Oh, and not only that he also introduced me to something much more important. He bought me my first Italian gelato. My education was practically complete after only one hour in Florence."

Taking the last sip of my Spritz and feeling a little foolish to have babbled on about Alessandro, I decided it was time to change gears. Looking over at him, I laughed and said, "Enough about me! Tell me about your family!"

Using his plastic straw, he pointed in the direction of Campo di Marte and said, "See those hills? My older sister Rossella lives up there in Fiesole with her husband and little girl."

Noticing I was done with my drink he motioned to the waiter to bring us espressos. All of a sudden I made the connection and realized that perhaps that was why I had seen him among the Roman ruins a few weeks back.

While it was obvious, he loved his sister he admitted she was a real pain in the neck and very bossy. He said, "I call her, 'Ross la Boss.' To this day she continues to be a know-it-all, *una vera saputella.*"

I laughed at this description of his sister, so did he when I told him that was what my mother used to call me.

When I asked him about his parents and what they did, he pointed in the opposite direction and said, "They are retired and live in Bagno a Ripoli, the suburbs of Florence. My father, Alberto, used to be a doctor and my mom, Marta, she was a teacher." As he continued talking, I discovered his mother now in her free time wrote mystery novels, and his father dabbled in winemaking. Lorenzo confided rather proudly, "His wine is quite good. But his homemade limoncello is even better. He makes it from the lemons that grow in the trees on the hill behind our home. You should try it!"

He leaned back in his chair. "Those hills hold many treasures. Sometimes we go truffle hunting with my beagle, Leonardo—Leo to the family. He's a great little guy. Very affectionate and has the softest brown ears and a killer nose. He can sniff out truffles like no other dog." Leaning over he admitted, "I'd like to get my life in order soon rather than later so I can bring him into the city with me. But for now, he is better off living in the country with my parents."

From the impassioned way he talked about Florence and his family, I could tell he was happy to be back home. He seemed content and relaxed to be once again walking the medieval streets of Florence, working at the Uffizi. But when I jokingly asked him if he had returned because of a *fidanzata*—an Italian girlfriend—hidden about somewhere in Florence, he began to fiddle with his small silver coffee spoon.

Hesitating a moment, he said, "*Sì*...I have a girlfriend, but she is British, not Italian."

I tried to hide my disappointment. It didn't matter though because

Lorenzo hadn't looked up. "We've been seeing one another for a while..." Clearing his throat, he added, "Her name is Judith. She's an art restorer at the Tate. I was new to the city and didn't have many friends. We just sort of hit it off..." His voice trailed off, leaving me to fill in the blanks.

I simply nodded. I had monopolized the conversation up to this point, and suddenly I was at a loss for words.

With a smile and a shrug he said, *"Adesso le cose sono un po' complicate."* Switching back to English he repeated his last comment, "Things are a bit... well...let's say complicated. She wasn't all that happy when I decided to move back to Italy. She tells me she can't seem to find a suitable position or, rather, ones that interest her in Italy, and well..."

Again he left his sentence unfinished. I got the distinct impression Judith was in no hurry to make a home for herself here in Florence, and it was not boding well for the relationship. *What is wrong with this woman?* I wondered. *Clearly, she was an idiot.*

"Hmmm," I said trying my best to keep my response light, "sounds like trouble in paradise." Then added, "I tried that once—keeping a long-distance relationship going. Well, I'm probably not one to ask for advice in that area. It didn't work out so great for me."

Lorenzo flashed a half-smile, "It certainly isn't easy. We've been splitting time between London and Florence and traveling between cities is getting kind of rough. But London is fantastic! Here take a look."

Picking up his phone, he began swiping through his photo library. Moving a bit closer to me he held the screen up so I could see the images better. As he continued scrolling, I recognized shots of the Tower Bridge, Buckingham Palace, and Westminster Abbey. He hesitated when he came to a picture of himself standing next to a tall, slim woman. Giving me a sideways look he told me that was Judith.

I examined the photo with interest. Judith was an attractive woman with a symmetrical face and sleek blonde hair. Before I could say anything, Lorenzo clicked the phone off and slid the device back into his pocket. As he did, I reached up and smoothed back strands of my own out-of-control hair. Glancing down at my nails, seeing the remnants of paint, I clasped my hands together and hid them under the table.

We sat in an awkward silence for a few moments. Wow, that was a conversation stopper, I thought. Leave it to me to ask if the man had a girlfriend.

I cast about for a new topic and soon was telling him about my home in California, describing for him the Valley of the Moon. Lorenzo relaxed back into his chair again, and we resumed our lighthearted conversation. When I thought about it later, I wasn't entirely sure which language we had used to communicate.

Glancing at my watch, I couldn't believe we had been talking for over an hour. *"Non ci posso credere!"* I said. "Where has the time gone? This has been really nice...but now I've gotta run. I'm supposed to be meeting up with a friend at the *Officina Profumo*—you know, the old perfumery shop near the church of Santa Maria Novella—and I'm late...again!"

"Anch'io devo scappare," Lorenzo said as he looked at his watch. "I really should go too. They are expecting me back at the Uffizi."

Despite this admission, he didn't seem to be in a hurry to leave. Seeing the waiter, he casually raised a hand to summon his attention. As he paid the bill, I observed him from behind my dark sunglasses. It hit me again how easy it was to be with this man. It was all so serendipitous...the random encounter at the bar...losing my sketchbook...our meeting in the chapel...drinks. And now this instant attraction. Well, at least on my part. What was going on here? Wasn't I usually the one who was always so picky, reluctant to open up to a perfect stranger? And wasn't I the one who was quick to find fault and dismiss a relationship if I found a man wanting or short on intelligence and humor?

But Lorenzo had captivated me from the first moment I had seen him reading the soccer scores in the Caffè delle belle arti. It was as if some inexplicable energy had been drawing us together for weeks. Then I remembered he had a girlfriend. Reality crashed over me, and I felt terribly self-conscious. Standing up quickly, I stumbled slightly, knocking into the table.

Lorenzo reached out a hand to steady me. Embarrassed by my clumsiness, I said, "I'm fine. Really. Thanks again for the drinks." Glancing again at my watch, I said, "But now I'm running on Bella Time!"

Raising an eyebrow he asked, "Bella Time?"

"Oh," I said with a shrug, "it's nothing really. Very silly in fact, but I'm always late. It's one of my biggest faults." I zipped up my bag and hoisted it on my shoulder. "My father is the one who started calling it that. He used to call me Bella. Because I have this tendency to dally a bit—I'm always late, forgetting about everything and everybody—he coined the term 'Bella Time.'"

Lorenzo laughed and said, *"Allora,* so then, let me get this straight. Your nickname is 'Bella' and you are always running late, so..."

Interrupting him, I exclaimed, "So...it makes my friends so angry when

I leave them waiting—like right now, for instance. Raffaella is not going to be too pleased. And I'm always missing trains and buses!"

He looked amused and said, "Well, you've certainly come to the right place," he said, resting his briefcase on the table. "Here in Italy you can be thirty minutes late to anything, and no one will ever mind."

It was a common stereotype, but I had to admit there was a bit of truth to what he had just said.

Smiling he added, "What an enjoyable way to go through life—aside from missing trains and all. You seem to throw yourself into your work but also live in the moment, noticing things other people miss because they are in too big of a hurry going who knows where."

I looked at him and marveled a bit. His ability to turn what I considered my biggest fault into a compliment was impressive. Trust an Italian man to have mastered the art of flattery.

Reaching out a hand, I smiled and said, "Well, now that we've broken the ice, don't be a stranger. Let's do this again. It was nice." Then I mentally kicked myself thinking: *Sophia, stop! The man has a girlfriend.*

But Lorenzo seemed unfazed. He shook my hand and said, "I'll look for you at the bar. Perhaps we can share another espresso together."

Before turning away, he leaned in and kissed me on the cheek in the proper Italian manner. Whispering first into my right ear, he said, *"Sì, Bella, sai baciare bene."* Turning to kiss my other cheek he repeated in English into the left ear, "You really know how to kiss well."

He was teasing me of course, turning the tables and beating me at the game I had started earlier. I stepped back and eyed him thoughtfully. Then realizing I was staring, I turned and began to walk away. But I paused a moment and looked over my shoulder. As I did, Lorenzo glanced back at me, too. Saluting each other once again, we finally parted ways.

A few moments later, rushing across the piazza in front of Santa Maria Novella, I was glad to see Raffaella wasn't mad I was late. In fact, she hadn't even noticed, as she was deep in conversation with Alessandro. I was pleased to see he was with her because I couldn't wait to tell him I had just met his friend Lorenzo. He listened for a moment as I gushed on about his friend. I paused mid-sentence when he began to wag a finger at me. Raising an eyebrow, he said, *"Stai attenta! Ama gli scherzi! Da bambino era sempre un monello!* Be warned! He's very clever! Always up to something. I know. As kids, we were partners in crime."

Trying not to be too obvious I pressed him for more details. He was more than happy to fill me in on all the ridiculous stories of how he and Lorenzo had outwitted their teachers, skipping school, masterminding elaborate pranks and teasing the girls.

I shook my head at his stories. It seemed hard to believe we were talking about the same person. The Lorenzo I had met appeared to be a forthright man, after all, wasn't he an influential museum director? Moreover hadn't he told me up front about his *fidanzata?* But, soon I understood what Alessandro was talking about when I became the target of his teasing and realized just how clever he could be. Lorenzo liked the element of surprise and was forever finding ways of sneaking up on me undetected.

The first time it happened, I was in the Uffizi. As I leaned in closer to study a Botticelli painting, my reverie was interrupted when an authoritative voice admonished not to touch, *"Non si tocca, signorina! Stia attenta!"* Startled, I jumped, embarrassed to be reprimanded once again by my nemesis, the ever-vigilant museum guard. Turning around, however, I discovered it was Lorenzo.

Another day I was painting in front of the Ospedale degli Innocenti. Brunelleschi had designed the Renaissance orphanage, and the columns he used were, again, a nod to the past and classical Rome. As I worked, I could almost hear the crying babies and the cooing matrons who received them on the other side of the wall. I was so absorbed in my painting and thoughts about orphans and columns, light and shade, colors and hues, that I didn't hear Lorenzo step up behind me. When I felt someone touch me on the shoulder, I screamed, and my paintbrush flew high into the air. Lorenzo narrowly escaped being christened in paint from my heavily loaded brush. Enjoying the expression on my face, he quickly apologized, offering to buy me a gelato to make amends.

That fall, sitting next to Lorenzo on the steps of Florence's porticos and loggias eating an ice cream, or sipping Aperol Spritzes, our friendship deepened. We talked about art, soccer and politics, but mostly we laughed and told silly jokes. During our casual encounters, I learned Lorenzo was a competitive man, as I was a competitive woman. Soon we were playing silly games, daring each other to say a *scioglilingua*—those tricky, slippery tongue twisters—the fastest. We worked ourselves into a frenzy, repeating childhood rhymes like *"Trentatré trentini entrarono a Trento, tutti e trentatré trotterellando."* Eventually we gave up, collapsing against one another in laughter.

Sometimes when I told him a story about the Sonoma Valley, Lorenzo corrected the use of my past tense, other times my pronunciation. I frowned, suddenly conscious of my American accent and the many mistakes I still made in the language.

Gently rocking into me with his right shoulder, he said encouragingly, "*Forza!* Your Italian is very good, Sophia. You express yourself well *and* you have an excellent vocabulary. Plus you have an adorable accent."

I made a face at him. "Great," I thought to myself. I had hoped after living in Florence for two years I would have lost my flat American tone. When I said this to Lorenzo, he replied, "But that is what makes you so interesting, and really, it isn't all that distinguishable as long as you remember to properly pronounce *le consonanti doppie.*"

Ah, the dreaded double consonants!

Laughing at me when I gritted my teeth, he continued, "*Comunque,*" and then switching to English, "at any rate it is your foreign accent that makes you so charming. It sets you apart from everyone else."

When I told him, it was precisely the sound of my voice that I didn't like he said, "*Ma dai!* Come on! That's your signature style—just like your brushstroke." He paused and watched a young couple walking hand in hand across the piazza. Then turning his attention back to me and said, "You know, Sophia, an artist never really needs to sign his own canvas because his style should be so...unique and inimitable...the way he applies paint to canvas is his calling card."

Adding with a grin, "But what matters, Sophi, are your ideas and that you are able to express yourself in interesting ways. There, *mia cara amica,* believe me, you have no problems. You have a mercurial and vivid imagination. Plus," he said with an elbow to my side, "you are never at a loss for words."

At that I laughed. I was absurdly pleased that Lorenzo found this an appealing quality. I looked over at him and caught him studying me thoughtfully. "What? What is it?"

He smiled and said, "You know, Sophia, the true sign that someone is fluent is if they dream in the language. Tell me, Sophi, do you ever dream in Italian?"

I threw my head back with a laugh. "*In realtà, Lorenzo*...if you really want to know...I have been dreaming in Italian my whole life."

Chapter 19

Trick-or-Treat

*W*hen La Scuola opened its doors in the fall, I took Alessandro's place at the airport and Santa Maria Novella train station greeting new arrivals. Now I was the veteran, indoctrinating students and introducing them to Florence.

Before I could begin collecting a paycheck, however, I had to apply for a work visa and a *permesso di soggiorno*. It was a permit guaranteeing that I, a foreigner, wouldn't be thrown out of the country on my keister. Kind of a handy thing to have in one's back pocket to prevent and cushion the fall. But to obtain this Holy Grail was a nightmarish process. Once again I was led down a dark bureaucratic rabbit hole. This time, however, the warren was much deeper, filled with even more government offices, bored civil clerks, long lines, and never-ending stamps and paperwork. When I finally acquired the *permesso*, I triumphantly waved the document in Raffaella's face, and we proceeded to the nearest bar to celebrate my success with a stiff drink.

With my residency status official, it seemed more than ever my benefactor—Prince Lorenzo—was conspiring to help me. People were starting to take notice of my work, and soon I was invited to hold informal art shows in postage-stamp-sized galleries in the Oltrarno. At the beginning of the fall, I was contacted by a gallery owner, who was a friend of Roberto's, asking if I'd like show to my work in his gallery in Trastevere. It would occur in February during the off-season—nevertheless, I would gain more visibility in the bigger arena of Rome.

I slipped easily into my role as a painting instructor at the school and began organizing plein air painting outings in the countryside on weekends. I was also proving to be a popular sounding board among the students, helping them with their creative highs and lows. After my own experiences during my first year in Florence, and my own personal meltdown with Bèbè, I could relate to the challenges they were encountering.

Toward the end of October, a group of American students approached me asking if they could throw a costume party in the main studio. In Italy,

Halloween was a relatively new and imported holiday. For the most part, Italians thumbed their noses at the *fare-dolcetto-o-scherzetto-trick-or-treat-scene*. Not even children, let alone adults, celebrated it. But I tended to agree with them—throwing a costume party was a great idea. It was one of the American traditions I missed most.

I was sure Alessandro wouldn't mind, but to ensure success, I enlisted Raffaella's help. Confronted by two strong-willed females, Alessandro threw up his hands in mock defeat, saying he could say no to one of us, but faced with two femmes fatales he was *all'angolo*, painted into a corner—how could he refuse?

A few days before the party, I bumped into Lorenzo at the bar and told him about the Halloween festivities. I asked if he wanted to join us, emphasizing it was a costume party. As further incentive, I said there would be a prize for the best disguise. Surely a bottle of Prosecco was worth getting dressed up for. He eyed me a bit skeptically as he stirred sugar into his coffee, but I could tell he was intrigued. I continued to encourage him, "Oh, don't be a *guastafeste*, no one likes a party pooper. Loosen up. Come on! It will be fun." Elbowing him, I teased, "Hey, you can come as Lorenzo de' Medici!"

At the mention of the Medici prince once again he regarded me with a raised eyebrow, "Well perhaps it's not such a terrible idea. But dressing up in costume...masquerading and fancy dress balls? That's all for Carnival. Here in Italy, we throw *our* masquerade in February, not October. We over-indulge, eat too much, drink some more—and then sober up and repent just in time for Easter."

At the mention of Carnival, I drifted off, imagining what it would be like to be in Venice and dance at a fancy dress ball. I envisioned myself in silks and lace and of course a beautiful mask. The idea that a place existed where once a year people covered their faces to hide their identities and assumed another persona...well, that was just too fabulous and exciting.

Lorenzo snapped his fingers in front of my face and said, "Hey! Wake up, Sophia." Coming back down to earth, I smiled sheepishly. But Lorenzo only shook his head in amusement.

"You know," he said, "I do enjoy a good party. Maybe I will stop by. I'd like to see the costume you've got dreamed up. I'm sure you already have plenty of ideas floating around that head of yours...but here's a suggestion for you. Why don't you dress up as Eleonora de' Medici?"

I paused mid-sip and looked at him in surprise. Narrowing my eyes, I asked, "Eleonora de' Medici? Why would you say that? How do you know anything about Eleonora de' Medici and me?"

He raised an eyebrow. "How do I know about Eleonora? Hmm...let's see...could it be the many times I see you studying Bronzino's painting at the Uffizi? You get so lost in your thoughts; you never see me watching you. It's as though you are deep in conversation with the de' Medici duchess—as if the two of you share a secret."

Smiling mysteriously at him, I said, "Perhaps we do." It seemed the museum guard wasn't the only one keeping tabs on me. But thankfully Lorenzo hadn't thought me touched in the head, or not that much at least. I hadn't scared him off. Yet.

I rolled the small espresso cup around in my hands for a moment. Then I told him about my connection with the painting and the lady. I confessed my obsession with her dress and described for him about the costume my mother had made for me one year for Halloween.

"You know," he said, "I've been a swashbuckler myself back in the day. My parents used to take Rossella and me to Venice for Carnival. One year I was a knight in shining armor, and the next a terrifying pirate with an eye patch." With a mischievous grin, he added, "That costume was the best. I used to terrorize my sister by threatening to cut her throat or make her walk the plank."

I could see Lorenzo as a small boy, brandishing a sword and exclaiming, "Ahoy, matey!" I felt a little sorry for his sister with his relentless teasing. He must have been a bit of a brat.

Thinking about Venice again, I said, "You know, I've seen a good bit of Italy, but Venice...that's one place I still need to visit. I would *love* to attend Carnival." Arching an eyebrow, I added playfully, "Romance! Intrigue! Handsome men in beautiful silk coats and satin pants...shapely legs! Now that's something I'd like to see." Adding wistfully, "How does one *even* get a ticket to one of those swanky balls?"

Lorenzo smiled at my forlorn expression. Reaching for his briefcase, he said, "Yes, there are plenty of Casanovas floating in gondolas all over the place in Venice. A lady can take her pick of the lot. As for a ticket to the ball... those are like gold. Very hard to come by. You'd have to be a very prominent museum director like me...someone with connections."

I rolled my eyes at that and brushed the biscotti crumbs from my hands. I reached for my bag too, and I wagged a finger at him, "See you later, hopefully. And don't show up without a costume!"

The afternoon of the Halloween party I helped the students push aside easels in the big studio. While I set out food and wine, the others decorated the room with orange pumpkins and grizzly ghouls crafted out of paper. Someone had even provided a boom box, and now the studio pulsated with rock music.

Once everything was all set up, I grabbed my bag and ran down the hall to put on my costume. Even with the door to the ladies room closed, I could hear "Monster Mash" pumping through the marble corridor. Unzipping my bag, I pulled out my costume and the makeup I'd stashed inside. On such short notice, there was no way I could dress up like the Medici duchess as Lorenzo had suggested. So instead I improvised a simple cat costume, *una bella gattina*.

Hearing laughter and a few shouts, I realized people were arriving, and things were getting underway. Annoyed for having taken so long over the party preparations, I quickly put on a pair of black tights and a leotard, jumping up and down to adjust the tight spandex. In my haste, I stumbled and crashed clumsily into the sink. Some *femme fatale*, I thought.

Surveying my tangled hair in the mirror, I smoothed it down and swept it back with a headband to which I'd attached feline ears. Finishing off "the look" I outlined my eyes in thick, dark eyeliner, adding a few whiskers across my cheeks. Last, but not least, I secured a long swooshy cat tail.

When I entered the studio, I first noticed Alessandro, laughing and telling jokes, as he poured out glasses of wine. He was dressed in jeans and a white shirt but had risen to the Halloween costume challenge by adding to his usual attire a sombrero and a large fake mustache. I gathered he was dressed as a Mexican bandit, à la Clint Eastwood in a 'Spaghetti Western'.

Raffaella, standing next to him, wore a stunningly form-fitting purple dress and a pointy witch's hat. Pinned to her chest was a large red paper heart. She had told me earlier in the day she would be dressing up as a good witch and doling out love potions. She advised me to watch out because her spells were sure to be very potent.

As I moved toward Raffa, I recognized Lorenzo's familiar form. His back was to me, so he didn't see me approach. I smiled to myself, pleased he had decided to come, despite his protestations. The evening was off to a great start.

When I drew closer, Raffaella looked over at me, but before she could say anything I put up a finger in front, silently urging her to keep quiet. She took her cue and continued chatting with the others, providing just the right amount of distraction so I could sneak up undetected. How could I pass up this opportunity to turn the tables on Lorenzo?

Slipping up behind the esteemed museum director and standing on tip-toe, I placed my hands on his shoulders and crooned, "Meeeeeeooooow." Lorenzo turned around in surprise. Wiggling my hands before my face like cat claws, I purred like Catwoman shimming my body and swinging my long black tail.

Lorenzo laughed out loud and gave me an appreciative whistle. It vaguely reminded me of Marcello Mastroianni's reaction to Sophia's strip tease scene in one of their films. Encouraged by his response, I turned around to show off my costume, delighted with the game we were playing.

When I stopped, I cocked my head to one side, looked him up and down and then shook my head in disbelief. Zero attempt to wear a costume. He shrugged his shoulders and apologized, "*Mi dispiace*, but my royal robes are still at the cleaners! I didn't want to disappoint you completely...so I came as a very important Italian businessman."

Pursing my lips, I said, "Well, I'll let it slide just this once, Mr. Important Businessman." I had been so involved in clowning around that I hadn't noticed the woman standing next to him. As I focused my attention on the newcomer's face, I realized with a start I had seen it before on Lorenzo's cell phone.

As when a DJ drags a needle over a spinning turntable, our lighthearted moment came to an abrupt and screeching conclusion. I was instantly embarrassed to realize this cool, professional woman was Judith. Immediately I muttered, *"Porca miseria!"* Once out of my mouth, the words only served to deepen my humiliation. I was grateful, once again, Adriana wasn't around to hear me. How was I going to claw myself out of this one?

Clearing his throat Lorenzo turned to his girlfriend, placing a hand on the small of her back he propelled her forward to make introductions. As Judith and I shook hands, he informed me she had arrived unexpectedly that morning.

Looking from Lorenzo to me, Judith interjected, "Yes, I thought it was time to pay Lorenzo a visit. I haven't seen him for weeks. The new Titian exhibit at the Uffizi gave me the perfect opportunity to pop down and surprise him."

Feeling heat flush my face, I tried to think of something brilliant to say. Words failed me. I only nodded. I watched as Judith grabbed Lorenzo's arm, holding it a bit possessively. She offered no comment on our silly antics or the exchange of witty innuendos, apparently dismissing it as childish absurdity. Turning to whisper something into Lorenzo's ear, she seemed to dismiss me as well.

Pleasantries dispensed, Lorenzo disengaged his arm from her grasp, and he stepped off to the sidelines to talk with Alessandro. By their body language and the way they moved their hands, even once pretending to kick a phantom soccer ball, I could tell they were talking about the latest match.

As Raffaella and I observed the partygoers pointing out the most creative costumes, I saw Judith glancing over at Lorenzo. She waved her hand trying to catch his attention. When their eyes finally connected, she pointed to her watch. Lorenzo acknowledged with a nod and then splayed all ten of his fingers, indicating they'd leave in ten minutes. Shaking her head slightly, Judith swiveled her attention back to Raffaella and me. She smiled politely and sipped wine from her plastic cup as she tapped her shoe ever so slightly, indicating her impatience.

With the unexpected arrival of Judith, I felt like the odd man out. Even though Lorenzo had told me about her the first day, we had met, until this moment she hadn't seemed real. Suddenly I didn't feel so playful or alluring. It was utterly ridiculous, but I realized I didn't relish the idea of sharing Lorenzo with someone else. But who was I? Lorenzo and I were just friends. We weren't dating. Our relationship didn't extend beyond a few shared cups of coffee and idle conversation.

Now standing in the same room as Judith, I realized I had allowed myself to step over the friend line. I had invented something that wasn't quite real—again. And this Hallow's Eve, Judith had yanked off my mask and snapped it back in my face, making sure I knew just how things stood.

Raffaella, seeing my confidence waver, took her cue from the *Girlfriend's S.O.S. Guidebook*. She quickly stepped in and began engaging Judith in trivial conversation, giving me a moment to recover and assess the woman's appearance.

The first thing I noticed, was Judith's conservative, navy blue suit and the fact that her hair was slicked back in a severe bun. I couldn't help but think she lacked an overall sense of spontaneity and pizzazz. Seeing her designer shoes, I begrudgingly admitted the girl had good taste when it came to fashion, *and* she was going out with a pretty great guy.

Perhaps she was lovely, but I didn't see what Lorenzo saw in her. By the way she stood with arms crossed tightly over her breasts, she seemed uptight and uncomfortable. Listening to her conversation I could tell she had a sharp mind, but she came off rather humorless. I observed this when Raffaella, trying to lighten the mood, had jokingly said, "*Santo cielo!* Thank goodness for Halloween! All of a sudden the cobwebs in my house are decorations." Pent up and nervous myself, I let out a small snort of laughter. When I looked at Judith, however, she offered no smile or witty retort. Raffaella and I exchanged a look, silently telegraphing: She's not our kind of gal.

Oblivious, or choosing to ignore our female solidarity, Judith glanced down again at her silver antique watch and said, "You know, we really can't stay too much longer. I have an early morning flight back to England. I don't want to stay out too late..." As her voice trailed off, she turned again toward Lorenzo, hoping to catch his eye. When she succeeded, he frowned slightly. This time, he held up just one finger, pleading for another minute.

Raffaella stepped over to the table to nibble on the appetizers. From behind Judith's back, she began bobbing her head mimicking Judith's prissy mannerisms perfectly. I rolled my eyes at my friend but quickly turned my head away so as not to laugh.

Leaning closer to Judith, I said in a pleasant tone of voice, "So...you must find your work in London very interesting."

That was all the incentive she needed. With an exasperated frown, she outlined all the annoying problems she was currently facing. She considered her colleagues, from the highest executive to the most humble janitor, incompetent fools. I tried to focus on her words and make polite responses, but as the music began thumping and people started dancing, it became increasingly difficult to sustain a conversation. With relief we stopped trying altogether. Instead, we watched, as on cue to Michaels Jackson's 'Thriller', the students started bouncing in unison, taking four steps to the front and four steps to the back, nodding their heads, raking the air with their hands raised like claws.

Alessandro and Lorenzo, having solved the week's soccer problems, bravely returned to our group. Seeing I hadn't started drinking yet, Alessandro quickly offered to get me a glass of wine. Gratefully I thanked him, needing a bit of fortification. When a new song began, Alessandro and Raffaella moved a few steps away. Their heads bent close together they started a lively conversation. After a while, Alessandro draped his arm around Raffaella's shoulders and nuzzled his nose into her cheek. She, in turn, patted his rear playfully and put her arm around his waist. Together they swayed in unison to the music. When the song concluded, they came back to the table to refill their glasses.

Sidling up to me, Raffaella casually asked, "So, Sophi, what are your plans for tomorrow?"

When I replied I had none, she asked if I would like to accompany her and Alessandro on a wine-tasting day trip to Lucca. Without hesitation, I agreed. Hoping to sleep in the next morning, I looked over at Alessandro and asked if we could take the 1:20 p.m. train out of Santa Maria Novella.

Alessandro shrugged his shoulders. Looking over at Lorenzo, he slapped him on his back and invited him to come, too. He smiled innocently at his friend, saying he would love to have his company, but it would be even more fun if Lorenzo were to drive us in his new Alfa Romeo. We turned to Lorenzo. He tilted his head and looked shrewdly at us. Seeing he was being coerced, he leaned over to Judith and asked if she would like to extend her visit and go too.

She shook her head no, reminding him she had to get back to London, but to her credit, she urged him to go without her. Lorenzo turned back to Alessandro and studying him for a moment as if trying to figure out what game he was playing. Ale only sweetened the deal by saying he would pay for the gas himself. At that, Lorenzo rolled his eyes, not believing it for a minute. Nonetheless, he agreed. We all cheered and raised our glasses in a toast to Lorenzo.

When Judith finally managed to tear Lorenzo away from the party, I watched from across the room as he helped her with her coat. He appeared the perfect gentleman, polite and deferential, but lacked the jovial attitude I was used to seeing. They were a lovely looking couple, but they didn't converse in the lively, affectionate way of Alessandro and Raffaella. I watched as Lorenzo murmured something into Judith's ear. Instead of smiling or turning to look back, she frowned and fumbled with her purse, searching for something inside.

Lorenzo raised his hand and saluted us from across the room. Ale called out to remind him we would all meet up in front of the Ponte Vecchio the next day around one o'clock. Lorenzo nodded and shrugged his shoulders apologetically, as if reluctant to leave the party. Feeling a tug on his arm, he turned back to Judith.

I stared after them, not pleased at all that Lorenzo had left so early with his girlfriend. The evening had taken a dismal turn. I didn't feel quite so festive anymore.

Alessandro knocked into my side on purpose, causing me to slosh a bit of my wine onto the floor. When I turned to look at him, he winked and then called out to Raffa to join him on the dance floor. She set down her glass and reached out her hand for mine. As she backed herself into the crowd of dancers, seductively wiggling her backside at Ale and shaking her shoulders at me in time to the music, she pulled me onto the dance floor with her. Together the three of us danced late into the night: the outlaw, the witch, and *la bella gattina*.

Rococo

The Rococo is an Eighteenth-century artistic move-ment characterized by elaborate but light and grace-ful ornamentation, often containing asymmetrical motifs. Rococo art was a more jocular, florid, and graceful approach to art forms than the Baroque. The style, besides being fancy and ornate, had play-ful, witty, and romantic overtones.

Chapter 20

The Devil in Me

*T*he next morning I tried to sleep in but was woken early by my Italian neighbors. I blinked back the bright light filtering through the shutters and gently rubbed my throbbing temples. I rose and wandered about the apartment, picking up laundry and depositing it in the hamper on my way to my tiny kitchen, where a week's worth of dirty dishes greeted me. *"Che noia!"* Faced with boring, mundane chores the morning seemed to drag on forever.

Shortly before noon I grabbed my leather jacket and wrapping La Loren's red scarf around my neck, I checked my watch before heading out the door. As I hurried along the sidewalk, I checked my watch again. I couldn't believe it. I was ahead of "Bella Time". When I reached the designated meeting spot, the bridge was swarming with tourists. Standing on my tiptoes, I searched for my friends, worried their tardiness would delay our departure.

When Lorenzo pulled up in his car, Alessandro and Raffaella had yet to materialize. I looked over my shoulder in the direction of the school, but there was no sign of them running down the sidewalk apologizing profusely for being so terribly late.

Then it dawned on me. Suddenly I understood Ale's wink and all the conspiratorial whispers exchanged between him and Raffaella the night before. They had never intended to come today. Now it seemed transparently obvious that Raffaella had once again drawn her cupid's bow. This was another one of her setups.

Leaning down to talk to Lorenzo through the open car window I told him my suspicions, "I think this was a set up. I don't believe they are coming. Do you?"

Lowering his sunglasses, he looked up at me and nodded, "Ah, *sì*, it makes sense. Well, let's go just the same. Who needs those conniving schemers? They'd just slow us down."

Inwardly delighted that he wanted to continue, I stepped around the car and slipped into the seat beside him. Lorenzo adjusted his Ray-Bans and smoothly set the car in motion. Maneuvering through the narrow streets, he drove to the outskirts of town. At the entrance to the autostrada, he turned up the volume on the radio and shifted into high gear, heading west to Lucca.

It was a relatively short drive, cut even shorter by the way Lorenzo drove his new car taking just under an hour. He snuck up on slower vehicles, swerving to pass them at breakneck speeds. I said a little prayer, *"Oh mio Dio!"*

Hearing me, he laughed out loud assuring me he was an excellent driver. *"Non preoccuparti! Sono un ottimo autista."*

When a familiar song by Zucchero started playing on the radio, Lorenzo began tapping his fingers on the steering wheel. Soon I, too, was swaying to the music, that sounded like American blues infused with Italian words. I hummed along, as the singer crooned in a voice like oak-aged whiskey, about his restless soul and an angel who had awakened the devil inside him.

When the chorus repeated, Lorenzo, looking rather devilish himself in his dark sunglasses, grinned at me and we began to sing off-key: *Your eyes hypnotize me...your lips tantalize me...You shook my very soul...baby, I find myself in love with you...I've got the Devil in me now!*

Due to the speed of Lorenzo's driving and the distraction of the music, the time passed quickly and soon I noticed the signs for Lucca popping up along the side of the road. Exiting the autostrada, we skirted the circular medieval wall and found parking near the soccer stadium.

I had been to Lucca on several occasions. The first time had been in the company of Alessandro. We had visited the year before to attend the annual Lucca Comics and Games convention, the largest geek-cultural event in Italy. How could I resist hanging out with Ale in a Renaissance-era gem of a town surrounded by a plethora of fantasy superheroes parading through the streets in costumes and role-playing?

But Lucca is best known for its impressive fortified walls. To me, it seemed the bricks of Lucca exuded history and I could see traces of Roman antiquity in its original foundations. But best of all, the town was less crowded than Florence, and there was a peaceful serenity that was perpetuated by the green trees that lined the boulevard at the top of the wall.

We entered the city through the Porta Elisa and made our way to the city center, passing the Roman amphitheater. Once the site where Roman gladiators had engaged in mortal combat, tourists now drank frozen espresso concoctions. Continuing, we turned down Via Fillungo, pausing every so often to look into the store windows, admiring the elaborate displays and elegant, designer fashions. I stopped for a moment to swoon over a pair of red stamped-leather shoes. As I was ogling the merchandise in one window, Lorenzo paused in front of another. Looking sideways over at him, I saw he was admiring a well-tailored dark charcoal suit. As my eyes drifted from the mannequin to the man, I thought how well the suit would fit his shoulders.

When we came to a music store, I nodded my head in the direction of the door, inviting Lorenzo to join me inside. Together we sorted through the banks of records and CDs. As he worked his way down the alphabet, he finally hit upon the "Z" section. Holding up the CD that included Zucchero's devil-in-me song, he asked if I'd like to add it to my collection. Before I could respond, however, he was moving to the cash register to buy it. I followed along, uttering useless protests.

He casually leaned over and said, *"Stai calma. È solo un piccolo pensiero."* Switching to English he added, "Don't get excited. It's just a little thing. I'm not making a devil's bargain here. You don't owe me anything." Then smiling mischievously, thinking better of his words, he said, "Well, maybe I should reconsider that. I'll have to think of something I can claim from you at a later date."

Still joking he teased, "Take the CD. Listen to it again. I think you need some practice. You sing a bit out of tune."

In mock offense, I cried, "Hey! I'm a starving artist, buddy. There's not much you are gonna get outta me. And for the record, I'm not a musician—and you could do with a few voice lessons yourself."

Laughing, we stepped into the street again and walked to Piazza San Michele. At the same moment we paused and looked up, struck by the lacy stonework of the church in the center of the piazza, framed by an intense blue sky. As we rounded the church, I glanced down the narrow street and saw the Guinigi Tower peeking up over the buildings. From my vantage, I could just make out the trees that grew out of the top of the medieval high-rise. Once upon a time the tower had been the tallest in town, but when a rival family had built one even higher, not to be outdone, the Guinigi planted trees at the top to forever guarantee theirs would be taller.

Ale had told me a different tale about those trees. According to his version, a rich and powerful Guinigi had married a beautiful *fanciulla*. She had been a charming young woman, but the man, being insanely jealous, had kept her locked in the tower. He wasn't taking any chances he'd lose her to another man. The girl cried for days, pleading to be released. She begged her husband to let her walk among the trees again. The man, tired of his wife's complaints, capitulated. His solution, of course, was to create a garden at the top, thus ensuring her imprisonment.

When he heard the story, Lorenzo only said, "Sounds like something Alessandro would invent. At any rate, *se la ragazza fosse mia moglie...*" He paused and said in English, "if she were my wife, no matter how *bellissima* she was, I would have no need to lock her away in a tower."

"Ohhh, Lorenzo! So you think no woman would ever develop a wandering eye and leave you for another man?"

Lorenzo looked at me in mock offense, at the suggestion, any woman would *mettere le corna*—cheat on him. Indignantly he said, "Well, *mia cara...* if I were a duke or a prince, I would never have reason to lock *my* wife in an ivory tower, let alone a tower with a tree on top. Naturally, I would need to let her leave the house so she could buy the food for my evening dinner."

I could tell he was joking, but just for good measure, I punched him hard on the arm for being such a male chauvinist.

Then tilting my head to the side, I said, "Do you want to climb to the top? Do you think you can make it up all those stairs."

He scoffed, "*Certo! Volentieri!* Let's go!"

We picked up our pace and started competitively climbing the stairs. At the top, we both stopped to draw in great gulps of fresh air. Catching each other's eye we laughed at our silliness. Pointing north, toward the purple and turquoise hues of the Garfagnana Mountains, Lorenzo traced the rugged ridge with his finger revealing to me the profile of the "sleeping" giant. I gasped in delight. I had never noticed it before. Listening now, I could almost hear the mountain man's snores.

Turning back to me, he gestured off to his left and asked, "Have you ever been to Borgo a Mozzano? It's over there in that direction."

When I shook my head no, he said, "In Borgo a Mozzano you will find the Devil's Bridge that crosses over the River Serchio."

Slipping his black sunglasses onto the top of his forehead, he continued, "Originally it served as an important medieval pilgrimage route, but the thing that makes it so unusual is its shape. It was built using three asymmetrical arches, to withstand the high floodwaters. But the resulting effect is that it appears to be lurching to one side." *"Va bene,"* I said. "Okay, okay, all simply fascinating...but what has that got to do with the Devil?"

Lorenzo leaned back against the rail again and said, "It's so nice to have such a captive audience. Back at the Uffizi, I have to pay my staff to listen to me."

Giving him a look, I reminded him, "Well, unlike the poor Guinigi bride, I am free to leave the tower anytime I want." To prove my point, I turned, ready to retreat down the ladder.

He laughed and quickly reached out and caught my arm. Pulling me back to his side, he began to tell me the local legend about a king, an architect, the Devil, and this oddly shaped bridge.

"*C'era una volta*," Lorenzo began, "once upon a time, a king asked his master architect to build a bridge over the River Serchio. The poor guy, he ran into many problems, and the bridge kept crumbling and falling apart. It was quite a disaster. The king fed up with the architect's failures, finally gave him an ultimatum: Either you finish the bridge in three weeks and be given a big sack of money...or off with your head."

At that point, he stopped and made a gesture with his finger, slicing it across his throat.

"Poor architect, indeed!" I laughed.

"Well, yes, *era proprio spaventato.* He was scared silly. Shaking in his boots, I believe you say. The architect was at his wit's end. At that moment the Devil appeared promising to finish the bridge for him—on just one condition: The first soul to cross the bridge would be mine forever." Lorenzo continued, "The architect was quite happy to agree to the Devil's deal and, true to his word, the bridge was finished on time and to perfection. It was a beautiful bridge, elegant and perfectly symmetrical as if Pythagoras himself had calculated its dimensions."

Raising an eyebrow, I waited for the punch line.

"Everyone was happy," Lorenzo said with a broad smile. "The architect's reputation was saved, and he became a very rich man."

"*Un lieto fine,* a very happy ending indeed, except for one small tiny detail," I said. "What happened to the Devil?"

"Exactly. The Devil still needed to be paid for his work." He grinned back at me. "Imagine the architect's distress when the king announced to all his people that he would be the first to cross the new bridge. *Che incubo!* What a nightmare."

I couldn't hold in my laughter at his dramatic exclamation.

"The architect, how do you say it? He completely freaked out. If the king crossed the bridge first, the Devil would snatch his soul. This would definitely not be good for future business, no?"

"So," I said, "how did it end?"

Lorenzo ran his thumb along the side of his jaw, indicating just how clever the architect had been. "As the king approached the bridge with his entourage, the architect saw out of the corner of his eye a small dog wagging his tail. He kicked the dog, sending it skittering over the bridge. The Devil, who had been crouching at the opposite side, was so furious he had been tricked, he hauled back and kicked the bridge too."

I smiled when he concluded with a dramatic flourish, "And that, *mia cara,* is why to this day the central arch of the bridge rises high into the sky, giving it such an unusual shape—like the high arch of a donkey's back."

He leaned back and crossed his arms, satisfied with his storytelling abilities. We lingered a few moments, in a comfortable silence, looking out over the mosaic of red tiled roofs below us. But as more people began crowding the top, we descended back to the street.

Making our way to the outer wall, we passed by an open bike shop. Stepping into the tangle of rentable bikes parked in front, I began to ring a couple of the bells. Lorenzo, following my lead, started jangling a few bells himself and soon we were making a delightful, if not raucous, tune The owner, hearing the commotion, poked his head out of his shop and said he'd be more than happy to set us up with two rentals. Readily, we agreed.

Nimbly I mounted my bike. Pushing off, I first took the lead. Glancing back, I saw Lorenzo was still adjusting his bike seat. I called over my shoulder, "Come on, *vecchiotto!* Stop poking around like an old man. I won't hold it against you if you can't keep up with me."

Pedaling faster, I raced up the path onto the wall. Soon I was sailing down the tree-lined boulevard with Lorenzo in hot pursuit. The breeze was fresh, and the exercise was exhilarating. The view from the top of the wall, while not quite as high as the one from the Guinigi Tower, gave me a lovely new perspective of the city. I slowed my pace and Lorenzo zoomed ahead. He called over his shoulder, "Catch me if you can!"

Not to be left behind in his dust, I dug in, pedaling fiercely, narrowly avoiding knocking into a small group of nuns. When I finally caught up to him, he slowed his pace, and we began to ride together in unison. We cycled past joggers in orange T-shirts, boys with blue kites, and young mothers with well-used strollers.

Around and around the city we went, passing by strategically placed turrets. Calling over his shoulder, Lorenzo informed me, "As impressive as the wall and its ramparts are—quite a feat, you know, being constructed by massive mounds of compacted earth—fortunately, the Lucchese never had reason to put them to use." Teasingly he added, "They were afraid their Medici neighbors to the east would eventually overrun them. Well, *we* let them off the hook, so it appears."

Waiting for me to catch up to him, he said, "It was Princess Luisa of Bourbon, the daughter of the Duke of Parma, who decided to transform the walls of Lucca into this playground."

We continued biking a while longer, passing by the botanical gardens and La Casa del Boia, the sinister-looking house where the medieval executioners of Lucca had once lived. By now, long shadows were falling, and Lorenzo looked over and asked if I was hungry. I thought to myself not only was he a connoisseur of art and teller of fascinating stories but also an appreciator of good food as well. He seemed to know all the right restaurants in town, even here in Lucca.

I laughed and said, "Sure. I would also like a very big glass of wine. I deserve it after all the exercise I've had today."

Soon we were comfortably seated at a table in a garden terrace of a restaurant near the *anfiteatro*. Perusing the menu, Lorenzo said we couldn't go wrong by starting off with two bowls of *farro* soup. Next, he suggested that we sample the *tortelli*, pasta stuffed with meat and vegetables and topped with thick, creamy sauce. We finished the meal with *vin santo* and *cantucci*, the delicious sweet wine made by monks accompanied by small crunchy cookies, a Tuscan delicacy.

Finishing the meal we fell into a contented silence. I swirled the amber liquid around in my glass as I looked up at the full moon now illuminating the night sky. Lorenzo, seeing me lost in thought said, "Sophia, did you know that a beautiful ghost haunts the walls of Lucca?"

I sat up, put my elbows on the table, and leaned in.

Now that he had my full attention again, he smiled and began telling me about Lucida Mansi, a noblewoman who had lived in Lucca in the early 1600s. At a young age, she had married Vincenzo Diversi, who died within the first year of marriage. "There are some who claim," Lorenzo said with a raised eyebrow, "that it was she who had poisoned him."

I leaned back again and arched an eyebrow. Waving my wine glass before taking another sip, I encouraged him to continue.

"*Povera Lucida!* She remained a widow until the ripe old age of twenty-one. Luckily for her, she caught the attention of the very wealthy, but very, very old, Gaspare di Nicolao Mansi."

Together we chuckled a little evilly at such a mutually self-serving pairing. "You see," he said, "Lucida was quite beautiful. She turned many a man's heads. It seems she also had a couple of vices. She loved expensive things and lavish parties almost as much as she enjoyed being surrounded by lovers and suitors. Some claim Lucida sat for hours admiring herself in the mirror. Can you imagine that, Sophia?"

"*Boh*," I said with a shrug, "some women can be so vain." Picking up a shiny silver spoon off the table, I held it up to my face as if it were a mirror. Flipping back my hair, checking my appearance I said, "Really, I have no idea what you're talking about. But don't let me interrupt you."

Lorenzo laughed and continued, "Well one day, Lucida, after studying her reflection in the mirror for hours was horrified to find a small wrinkle on her brow. Suddenly the thought of growing old and losing her beauty made her quite desperate. At that moment—poof! The Devil appeared, promising Lucida she could remain beautiful for forty years in exchange for her soul."

"And we're back to the Devil," I said with a smile.

"Yes we are," Lorenzo said. "At first Lucida was quite enthralled by the Devil's bargain." Imitating her high-pitched voice, he exclaimed, "Signor Diavolo, I think it's a fantastic. *Geniale! Fantastico!* You are so clever. Of course, I accept."

Lorenzo laughed at my eye roll before continuing, "Lucida lived for forty blissful years. But true to his word, one dark, stormy night, the Devil appeared once again—poof! Ready to claim her soul. The Devil's deal didn't seem like such a great idea to Lucida anymore."

I nodded, "*Schema! Che sciocca!* Such a silly girl. She should have known when you play with the Devil, whether you are a starving artist or a vain pampered woman, there is always a price to pay."

Theatrically Lorenzo went on. "As the winds began to howl and lightning flashed, Lucida sat in terror as the Devil stepped closer to claim his prize. But just as he reached out to touch her pearly white neck, Lucida dashed away and jumped into her waiting carriage. Cracking a whip, further scaring the frenzied horses she began racing around the walls of Lucca trying to outrun the Black Lord himself."

Mesmerized I looked at Lorenzo. In my mind's eye, I imagined the macabre scene.

"As the horses raced, the rain poured down from the heavens. As the carriage careened around a curve, thunder cracked, and lightning flashed, frightening the horses, once again. Leaping high into the air, they fell over the wall and into the lake below. And that is where Lucida drowned."

With a flourish, he snatched a candle off the table. Holding it under his chin, it illuminated his face eerily, and he whispered, "Some people claim that if you go up on the wall on the night of the full moon, you can still hear Lucida's screams. They even say you can see her face reflected on the surface of the lake where she died."

I shivered in delight at the spooky tale and only jumped slightly when Lorenzo abruptly whispered a staccato, "Boo!"

The force of his breath blew out the candle, and we sat in darkness. Slowly I let out my breath. Warmed by the *vin santo* and fascinated by the story, it seemed a new incantation had been cast. We sat gazing at one another a few beats longer, unaware of the other diners on the patio.

Inside the restaurant, a wineglass crashed onto the ceramic pavement breaking the moment. I blinked and felt my cheeks grow hot. Picking up my cell phone to check the time, I exclaimed a little too brightly, "*Caspita. Guarda che ore sono!* Wow, look at the time. We should probably get going."

I excused myself and went off in search of the ladies' room.

While washing my hands at the sink, I studied my image in the mirror. I barely recognized my own face. My eyes were large and luminous. My tousled hair, windblown from our bike ride, gave me the appearance of one of those models in the Italian Vogue magazines.

I pulled my scarf out of my bag and knotted it loosely around my neck. Tilting my head, I checked my appearance and added a touch of gloss to my lips. Then realizing I was staring at my image a trifle longer than necessary, I chided myself. If I didn't watch it, I would soon become as conceited as Lucida Mansi. Besides, Lorenzo already had a girlfriend. Case closed.

When I returned to the table, I discovered that Lorenzo had already paid the bill. I thanked him profusely and said, "Next time *tocca a me.*" It will be my turn." I felt a little guilty. He had already done so much for me— buying me the CD and doing all the driving.

He just shrugged his shoulders and repeated, "*Non preoccuparti. Tranquilla.* You are a starving artist, no?"

As we strolled in the direction of the parked car, I asked Lorenzo where Lucida's accident was supposed to have occurred.

He replied, "She fell into the *laghetto*, the little lake in the botanical gardens, very close to where we are now."

We walked a few more steps, and I stopped. I looked back up at the moon and then back at Lorenzo. He eyed me suspiciously. Then I took a step backward and placed my hands on my hips I said, "I double dare...no, wait, I triple dare you to walk up onto the wall with me to where Lucida Mansi fell to her death."

Without saying a word, he offered me his arm and we walked to the top of the wall. The trees that had seemed serene and friendly earlier in the afternoon sun now looked menacingly evil by the light of the moon. As we strolled down the wide path, the only souls we encountered were an old man and his dog. As we passed by him, he pulled up his scarf to hide his face and impatiently tugged on the leash.

Drawing nearer to the botanical garden, Lorenzo stopped and pointed to the spot where Lucida was said to have careened off the path. I dropped his arm and gazed down at the lake, feeling the cool night air wrap its fingers around me. Unexpectedly a night bird swooped low over the path, letting out a piercing screech.

I let out a nervous giggle and cautiously took a few steps closer to the edge of the wall. As I continued looking down into the lake, the breeze picked up again, causing waves to ripple across its surface. Out of the murky darkness, I saw an alluring face rise from the depths. Her haunting visage glowed and undulated. Slowly her mouth opened and she formed silent words. It seemed she was attempting to say something.

Taking one step closer to the edge of the wall, I leaned over, straining to hear what Lucida might have to say. I screamed when I felt a tap on my shoulder. In terror, I spun around, my heart beating out of control, I half expected to see the Devil himself looming large behind me.

Catching my breath in relief, I realized it was only Lorenzo smiling wickedly at me as if he were ready to collect on his devil's bargain.

Chapter 21

Sogno nel Cassetto

*W*itches and devils soon gave way to *Babbo Natale*—Santa Claus and Christmas trees. By the time December arrived, the streets of Florence were less cluttered with tourists. They were now filled with large, starry luminaries that dangled from lampposts. The lights stretched from building to building in zigzaggy, glittery strands all down the street. In the Piazza del Duomo, a giant *albero di Natale*—the city's Christmas tree—had been erected. People bustled about, continuing their normal routines but with a lighter step amongst the festive trappings.

I had seen Lorenzo a couple of times throughout November. He had joined Ale, Raffa, and myself for pizzas at our favorite hangout near the Santa Trinità bridge. During one of our impromptu get-togethers he had told me in December, he would be traveling around Europe on business. With a teasing smile, he had said, "Try not to miss me too much while I'm away."

Laughing at that, I said I'd do my best to struggle on without him. But now as the Christmas holidays were fast approaching, I thought glumly, I would see him even less. I imagined he would be spending more time with Judith in London.

The evening before Christmas Eve, as Florence took on a magical fairyland quality, when I least expected to see him, I plowed straight into his arms. It happened in Via Sant'Antonino as I was coming out of a bakery near the Medici prince's basilica. I had been perusing the delightful trays of almond cookies and tempting sheets of *croccanti* before purchasing the *panettone*, the Christmas cake I would take to the Poglianis for our holiday dinner.

As we collided, we laughed at the sight of ourselves and wished each other "Buon Natale! Merry Christmas!"

Seeing the colorful, ornate box the baker had just wrapped up for me, complete with a big silver bow, he asked what was inside. When I told him to stop being so nosy, he only smiled and repeated his question. Giving in I said, "It's a *panettone* of course. It wouldn't be Christmas without one."

When he heard that, he rolled his eyes and quickly proclaimed he much preferred a moist, star-shaped *pandoro* Christmas cake. He said eating a *single* slice of buttery *pandora* was a thousand times better than eating *five* dry *panettone* cakes filled with hard raisins any day of the week—Christmas or otherwise. We looked at one another and narrowed our eyes in a square off. We had just stepped into the middle of an age-old debate that often split Italian families: *Panettone vs. Pandoro.*

I shook my head and laughed, inviting him to join me at the bar. Seated cozily at a little table I told him the big news about Alessandro and Raffaella. Ale had just bought a ring and was intending on proposing to my best friend on New Year's Eve. Earlier that morning he had shown me the gold band, set with an amethyst and had told me the plan he had cooked up to surprise her. Admittedly I was impressed by the romantic ambush he had in the works.

When I said as much to Alessandro, he had grinned mischievously and said, "Sophi, you should know me by now. I never do things in an ordinary way."

Hearing that, Lorenzo laughed too and said, "Yes, Alessandro and I know how to invent marvelous ways to fool people, as well as get ourselves out of trouble...and, well, sometimes it doesn't turn out so great."

Then he told me a story from their high school days. It had something to do with switching places, mistaken identities, and a car that ran out of gas on a deserted highway near Siena *and* two rather indignant young ladies. At one point I lost track of all the complicated details. I rolled my eyes at their stupid plot and how it had all backfired.

"Well," he said with a laugh, "*that* didn't work out quite as we had intended."

It was easy to imagine Alessandro and Lorenzo being the heartthrobs of their class at the *liceo.* Curious to know about his holiday plans, I opened my mouth and out popped the question, "So are you going to see Judith over the holidays? How is she?"

I groaned inwardly. *Wow,* I thought, *really, Sophia? For such a bright girl, you sometimes say the stupidest things.*

Lorenzo paused for a moment and then in a matter-of-fact tone told me she was doing well. He admitted because of his recent travels he hadn't seen her recently. Their schedules had been too busy, and they hadn't found the time to meet up. Looking me in the eye, he said, "I'll be going to England for New Year's. I have some business to take care of, but I'm coming straight home to Florence as soon as it is done."

I nodded absently. Suddenly I was depressed. I took another sip of coffee but didn't savor its taste. Putting it down, I stared into my cup. But when Lorenzo started clinking his spoon against the side of my cup I looked up in surprise.

"So what are your plans for Christmas?" he asked.

Rallying my holiday spirit I told him my family was expecting me in Campo di Marte for Christmas dinner. When I asked him where he'd be, he said he'd spend the day at his parents' home and that his sister and her family would be joining them. Soon he was painting a picture of what Christmas in Bagno a Ripoli would be like, launching directly into a mouth-watering description of the food his mother would prepare.

"First," he said, "there will be antipasti with cuts of cured meat garnished with olives and cheeses, served with homemade red wine. Followed by several kinds of baked pastas, including *lasagne verdi alla Bolognese*—one of my father's favorites—made with spinach and cannelloni filled with meat and baked with béchamel sauce."

Tantalizing me further, he said, "After that, a veal roast served with potatoes and an excellent Brunello. My sister, Ross *la boss*, has put me in charge of bringing the wine."

He continued to describe all the side dishes, reminding me that Leo the Beagle, throughout it all, would be lurking under the table hoping to steal some table scraps. At the end there would be an assortment of delectable sweets, cakes, and cookies made with sugar and nuts, to finish off the meal." When everyone is stuffed and ready to pass out," he said, "we make toasts with glasses of my dad's limoncello."

Seeing I was about to open my mouth, he quickly interjected, "But wait there's more! When everything is cleared from the table, my dad will uncork a bottle of *Amaro*, a bittersweet liqueur made from herbs—his favorite brand is Lucano. He always tells me it helps the digestive system recover from overindulgence at the table."

I thought that at this point, everyone sitting around Lorenzo's holiday table would need more than a couple of shots of *Amaro*.

Seeing me shake my head in wonder at the thought of so much food, Lorenzo paused. Perhaps he heard my stomach rumbling, or maybe he remembered the promise he'd made that someday I should taste his father's limoncello. Whatever the reason, he asked, "Hey Sophi, why don't you join us for Christmas dinner?

His offer was tempting. Well let's face it, what he had just described sounded divine. But unfortunately, I had already made plans with my Italian family. Hadn't I been the one to offer to bring the *panettone*?

Looking at him, I said, "Well, you know the old saying: *"Natale con i tuoi, Pasqua con chi vuoi."* In Italy, there was an unwritten law that Christmases should be spent with one's family, but Easters could be spent, with whomever you wanted.

But as I looked into Lorenzo's imploring eyes, I hesitated. I could clearly imagine the holiday festivities at his family's house as well as the loaded dining room table. Not only did the dinner plans sound delicious, I so wanted to meet his family. Seeing my hesitation, Lorenzo quickly added there would be games and charades sweetening his offer.

I wanted to accept, but thought: *could I break my plans with the Poligianis?* My next thought was: *how could I not the meet his family?* I knew my family would be disappointed and there would be a fair amount of teasing, but in the end, I was confident they would understand. Looking at Lorenzo, I decided it was worth it.

As we stood up and prepared to leave, I put my hand on the collar of his camel hair coat and tugged at his wool scarf. "Hold on there, *signore!* I have a couple of conditions. I don't want to be a complete freeloader."

He crossed his arms and waited for my terms.

Holding up my beautiful bakery box, I said, "First, I'll come if I can bring my cake. Second, I want to help your mom prepare the dinner." He agreed to the latter condition but rolled his eyes at the thought of the former. As he turned to go, he called over his shoulder that he'd would bring his *pandoro* as the better choice to my *panettone*.

I yelled back, as pulled on my coat, "I bet you a million euro, my dessert will be more delicious than yours."

He didn't turn around. He only raised his arm and made a puppet with his fingers and thumb opening and closing them as if it were babbling out useless threats. The last thing I heard him say was *"Vedremo!* We'll see about that!

On Christmas day Lorenzo picked me up in front of my flat and drove me out to Bagno a Ripoli. When I entered his home, I was warmly greeted by his mother and father. As Lorenzo helped me off with my coat, I noticed a curly haired little girl standing in the corner of the hallway holding a doll.

When Lorenzo turned around, she ran to him, and he picked her up and tossed her into the air. Looking over at me, Lorenzo said, "Sophia, this is my niece, Francesca." I waved to the little girl, but she only looked at me with her big eyes, too shy to respond. When I held up the box with the big bow containing the Christmas *panettone,* however, her face broke into a broad smile. I could tell I had just made a new friend.

I chatted politely with Lorenzo's parents, but was interrupted when Lorenzo's sister clamored down the stairs, crying out, "Eh! Lorenzo is that you..." She stopped on the bottom step and looked me over. She nodded her head at her brother and said, *"Ah bene. Hai portato la tua morosa americana..."*

Lorenzo cut her off quickly saying, "Watch it! She speaks Italian." Looking at me, he said with an apologetic smile, "Sophia meet Rossella, my *older* sister."

Smiling innocently, she greeted me with a kiss on both cheeks and then said, *"Sì,* I'm Rossella, Lorenzo's *much wiser,* but not *that* much older sister. *Buon Natale,* Sophia."

Looking at Lorenzo, she demanded, *"Ehi, deficiente, hai portato il vino?"*

I laughed in spite of myself to hear Lorenzo called an idiot before he had even hung up his coat.

Indicating a crate of wine bottles as evidence that even annoying younger brothers could be trusted with such simple tasks, he retorted, *"Che Strega! Tranquilla, Ross, tutto a posto. È tutto qui. Buon Natale anche a te."*

Never having had a sibling to banter with, I was amused to hear Lorenzo call his sister a witch and then tell her to relax and chill out. But I also noticed he did so with affection. Then he leaned over and kissed his sister on the cheek, reminding her not to forget to wish *him* a Merry Christmas, too.

With an ear-to-ear smile, she gave him a big thumbs-up and then lunged into another series of barbs and juvenile insults. I watched in fascination as the two bickered like teenagers. Losing interest in the teasing game they were playing, Rossella turned to me and said, "Let's you and I get to know one another better." Linking arms she escorted me into the kitchen where her mother was busily stirring boiling pots on the stove.

The air smelled heavenly as fragrances of the holiday meal wafted through the large, open room. Lorenzo's mother fussed about me, welcoming me into her kitchen. In no time at all, she pulled out an apron from a drawer and tied it around my waist. Then she presented me with a large wooden spoon and directed me to a sauce simmering on the stove.

I chatted comfortably with the two women, happy to answer their questions. As the inquiries kept coming, I quickly realized I was receiving a not-so-subtle third degree from the most important women in Lorenzo's life. I couldn't blame them. I'd be curious, too, to know why he had brought a girl, a practical stranger, home to the house for Christmas dinner.

Saved from further interrogation Lorenzo entered the room and pulled me into the dining room to help him push the tables together in preparation for the big feast. When everything was ready Lorenzo's father opened the holiday meal with a toast. As soon as he had finished his last word, Lorenzo eagerly grabbed a platter and began passing plates.

At first, dinner conversation was light and casual. We spoke about the weather, Lorenzo's mother's latest novel, and the renovations Rossella and her husband were making to their home. Rossella told me they were expecting another baby. I looked down at Francesca and asked if she was happy about becoming a big sister. She bobbed her head enthusiastically.

Smiling down fondly at her daughter, Rossella said, "*Sì,* Francesca! You will be a wonderful big sister, just like I am to Zio Lorenzo."

Lorenzo let out a loud guffaw.

Narrowing her eyes first at her little brother, Rossella turned to me and said, "Sophia, do you have any siblings?"

I shook my head.

"Well," Rossella said, "I can only hope Francesca has a baby sister." She looked back at Lorenzo and shook her head. Then she said, "Sophia, did you know my little brother was really, really, really, annoying when he was little?" She paused a moment then added, "Well perhaps he still is today."

I raised an eyebrow and agreed, "*In effetti lo fa ancora.*" Rossella laughed when I confirmed her suspicions.

Lorenzo only snorted and looked momentarily insulted, but Rossella continued to smile. She turned to Lorenzo and said, "Should I tell her how horrible you were to me and what an obnoxious little brat you were?"

Not appearing at all fazed, he shrugged his shoulders. Lorenzo's mother said, "*Santo cielo,* these two. Oh, how they squabbled—*battibeccano*—like cats and dogs...always trying to outdo one another." Rolling her eyes in the direction of her children she admitted, "They used to drive us insane. And they still do."

"*Senti, mamma,* it was always Renzo who started it," Rossella said and took a sip of her wine. Leaning over to me, she whispered indignantly, "Sophia, what would you do if you found your most precious doll's face covered in marker?"

Oh, the most hideous of offenses, I agreed. I could tell that although the incident had taken place years before, Rossella still hadn't let that go. Across the table, Francesca clasped her doll to her chest and gave it a tight squeeze as she looked at her uncle in horror.

Lorenzo assured his niece, "You have nothing to worry about, Francesca. I have long given that up. As a respectable art director, I have the highest regard for valuable works of art…as well as for the faces of dolls."

Rossella then exclaimed, "Oh, and then there was that time when he ran over my music books with his bike. On purpose. *Cretino!* Jerk." She smirked then turned to me and said in a tone dripping with sarcasm, "What a sweetheart he was. A real prince. So I wanted to teach him a lesson, and came up with a plan to strike back."

Leaning forward, she said with a sinister grin, "One night when my parents went out for the evening I decided to give Lorenzo a really good fright. On TV that night they were playing Alfred Hitchcock movies, so I invited Lorenzo to watch one with me, you know the one where the birds go crazy and terrorize the town."

Lorenzo leaned back in his chair and crossed his arms. "*Sì, sorellona mia*, and how did that work out for you?"

She sipped her wine again and rolled her eyes. Clearing her throat, she admitted with a rueful smile, "Well, not so great, let me tell you why. Later that night, I woke up to the sounds of birds pecking and scratching at my door." From across the table, Lorenzo started to claw at the tablecloth and in a high-pitched voice let out little caw. Rossella laughed and said, "Yes! I was terrified. I screamed out *Aiutami* Lorenzo! Help!'"

I looked over at Lorenzo, who was now laughing uncontrollably. Then I said to Rossella, "But it was him, wasn't it? It was Lorenzo at your door, scaring the living daylights out of you? He certainly has quite a talent for sneaking up and scaring poor innocent girls."

Raising our wine in a salute to female solidarity, Rossella and I clinked glasses. We downed the last drops and then looked back over at Lorenzo, who raised his hands in mock defeat.

As we stared at him in feigned annoyance, he exclaimed, "Okay, okay! *Che cosa volete. Mi arrendo.* What do you want? I give up." To make amends, he poured us both a bit more wine.

When the meal concluded, Lorenzo declared it was time for us to prepare our desserts. Together we retreated into the kitchen to put the finishing touches on our Christmas cakes. I rolled up my sleeves, determined to win our bet. Deliberately I began to drizzle the sweet sugar sauce I had made earlier over my *panettone*. When I was satisfied with my confectionery masterpiece, I looked up. Lorenzo was slicing his *pandoro* horizontally, creating a tower of offset, star-shaped layers. Picking up a sieve filled with sugar, he began dousing it with a coating of white powder.

Curious to have a better look, I took a step closer. As I leaned in, without looking up, Lorenzo turned the sieve on me and dusted my face and hair too in a sweet white cloud. Gasping in surprise, I immediately retaliated shaking the spoon I still held in my hand, letting fly a spray of gooey icing. It landed smack dab in the middle of his forehead.

Surrounded by a sweet haze of sugar, we looked at each other and broke into laughter. When Lorenzo's mother poked her head through the door and saw the mess we had created, she tsked into the air. We came to attention like penitent children. To make amends with his mother, we cleaned up the mess and then proudly returned to the family, carrying before us a wobbly, sliced *pandoro* and a majestic *panettone*. Trying several slices of each, then conferring amongst one another, the family voted my *panettone* the winner and loudly toasted my success, Rossella the loudest one all.

After the dishes had been cleared, we made ourselves comfortable on the couch while Lorenzo's father read a book. With our feet propped up on the table before us, I let my head fall back upon the soft cushions, and my body sank deeper into the couch. Leo jumped up next to me and nuzzled his head into the crook of my arm. It took just a moment before he began to snore. As my eyes drooped closed, my head lazily lolled against Lorenzo's shoulder and unconsciously we settled closer together.

Soon I, too, succumbed to the irresistible temptation of a new dream. My mind began to drift and to turn around and around in a circle I found myself standing in a field of sunflowers. In front of me was an easel upon which rested a painting. From a nearby meadow, I could hear the sounds of children's voices calling out to one another. High above my head flew a colorful kite. I followed its graceful path through the sapphire sky. Turning my gaze back to the painting, I saw I had been working on a portrait of a man.

As I reached up to touch his hair, I heard a voice call out, "Sophia...wake up! Let's play a game of *Tombola*—Italian bingo."

Opening my eyes, I saw the face of Francesca only inches away from my own. Pleased I was awake she climbed into my lap. I hugged her tight. Lorenzo opened one eye. Seeing his niece nestled in my embrace, he inched his fingers along her arm before diving in and tickling her belly. The bouncing couch and Francesca's squeals awakened Leo the beagle, who started to bark excitedly.

Putting her small hands on my face, she looked me in the eye and urged again, "Sophia come on! Let's play a game. Let's make believe."

Around midnight, tired from the many rounds of charades, card games and *Tombola*, Lorenzo and I finally said our good-byes to his family. I hugged his parents, promising I would return in the spring and paint the view of Florence from their terrace, as well as collect some of their lemons. I wished Lorenzo's sister good luck with her pregnancy agreeing to drop in for a chat the next time I found myself in Fiesole. Turning around I was delighted to see Lorenzo holding up two sacks bulging with leftovers, as well as several bottles of Alberto's wine. Fully loaded with great food and good cheer we headed back to the city in his Alfa Romeo.

When we entered the city, it seemed deserted except for a few Christmas cats hanging out on ledges in alleyways waiting patiently for their owners to return home from their holiday dinners. Coming to a smooth stop, Lorenzo parked directly in front of my doorstep. Wrapping his hands over the steering wheel, he peered out the windshield and up at a new winter's moon that was just peeking over the tall medieval buildings.

With a nod, he said, "*Guarda!* Look. Isn't that beautiful?"

Bundled in overcoats, with scarves tightly wrapped around our necks, we sat in the chilly car looking at the moon, watching as our breaths merged into a single cloud, fogging the car's windshield. I was reluctant to break the moment and open the door. We sat for a few more minutes without saying a word, listening to the rumble of traffic in the distance and the whine of a lonely Vespa. Suddenly the evening seemed to take a melancholy turn.

I thought this is ridiculous. Rallying to end the evening on a high note, I brightly thanked him saying it had been a lovely day. He smiled and agreed. Then as if he realized that he, too, needed to add something, he wished me a Happy New Year, asking, "So what are your big plans for *Capodanno?*"

I shrugged and said, "Nothing much, I'll be spending the evening with some friends."

He nodded absently. Silence descended again. Then because I couldn't think of anything else to say, again I stupidly suggested the next time Judith was in Florence we all get together. He didn't look at me or make a reply.

I thought *it is time to leave before I ruin a beautiful evening even more.* Touching his coat sleeve, I said a shade too brightly, "Thanks again. *Buon anno!*" adding lightly, "See you next year!" Not waiting for an answer I quickly opened the car door, ready to beat a hasty retreat to the safety of my apartment.

Before I could swing my foot out the door, however, Lorenzo reached out and grabbed my arm. Hesitantly he began, "Sophi, wait a minute..."

I stopped and faced him again. He held my eyes for a few moments and then gently lifted a strand of hair and tucked it behind my ear. It seemed he was about to speak when a motorbike thundered past the parked car, causing me to jump. The moment was broken. Lorenzo shrugged his shoulders and waved his hand in the air and said, "*Niente.* Never mind. I'll tell you later. It can wait until after the New Year." Then leaning over he kissed my cheek and said, "*Buona notte, Bella. Sogni d'oro.* Good night and sweet dreams."

Turning quickly back to the steering wheel, he started the car. Feeling confused, I slipped out of the seat and onto the sidewalk. After the New Year? What did that mean?

With a hand to my cheek, I watched the taillights of the Alfa Romeo move slowly down the narrow cobblestone street. I stood there in the dark as the car turned the corner and disappeared into the cold Christmas night and whispered back, "What are your golden dreams, Lorenzo? Do you have a *sogno nel cassetto?*"

Chapter 22

Blackbird Days

*I*n a small apartment near the Santa Trinità bridge, I rang in *Capodanno* in the company of friends. We wore silly paper party hats, ate lentils for good luck, and at midnight threw streamers, making a ridiculous ruckus with little tin horns. Drinking one glass of prosecco too many, I tottered home to my apartment near the Pitti Palace. Laughing hysterically with my girlfriends, I staggered down the sleepy streets of Florence, awakening neighbors who angrily shouted down at us from their windows to shut up, "*Basta, che baccano!* Enough with this racket!"

Once or twice, during the first frosty weeks of January, I was greeted by a flurry of snow when I stepped out on my way to the studio. It sugarcoated the city and dusted the red bricks of the cathedral. It reminded me of Brunelleschi's snow globe, which sat on the window ledge in my apartment. According to my Italian friends, the last days of the month were called the days of the blackbird—*i giorni della merla*. They were considered the coldest time of the year. As I bundled myself up to protect myself from the frosty morning air, I thought of *la merla*—the blackbird who once had feathers white as snow. But one bitter, cold January, feeling the bite of the icy wind, it had sought shelter inside a warm chimney. It emerged several days later covered with black soot from the hearth fires below. According to legend, its feathers were permanently changed; to this day they remain the color of night.

I took comfort in the notion that the story also predicted, if January days were fiercely cold, then the following spring would arrive early. But I had no time to lose myself in daydreams, or gaze absently at snow globes. I was so caught up in preparations for my Rome show.

One morning focused on my to-do list I barely heard Alessandro call out to me as I rushed past his office. Backtracking down the hall, I stuck my head through his door. I saw him leaning back in his chair with his feet propped on his desk, waving a thick envelope in front of his face.

Glancing at my watch, I said, "I've just got just a sec so make it quick."

Seeing my impatience, he swung his feet to the floor and leaned over and said, "*Guarda!* Look what I just got in the mail."

Unwrapping the scarf from around my neck and unbuttoning my coat, I shrugged it off my shoulders and looked at my watch again.

"Just imagine this," he said dramatically. "Behold. Here in my hand is a ticket to the Ballo del Doge, held every year at Palazzo Pisani Moretta in Venezia." Sitting up, resting his arms on his desk he said, "It is only *the* swankiest, most exclusive masquerade ball in all of Venice, perhaps in the entire world."

Smiling at me, he said, "Over the top doesn't begin to describe it. You can't even begin to imagine the waiting list and what people will do to acquire one of these prized invitations. Only the crème de la crème attend the ball. Together in one room, you will find the most favored darlings of the moment all dressed in period costumes." Looking a bit smug he cleared his throat and added, "And, of course...now me."

This *was* intriguing. Suddenly I didn't mind being late for class. I sat down in the chair in front of his desk and asked, "*Caspita!* Where did that come from?"

A coy smile spread across his face. "Wouldn't you like to know?"

I rolled my eyes, preparing myself for a loaded story.

"Let's just say," he began, "it is a complimentary gift, sent to the school based on its stellar reputation." In a voice dripping with mock modesty, he said, "You see? This is just further evidence of my importance in the Florentine art community."

"You mean Roberto's importance, don't you?" At his crestfallen expression, I grinned.

Casting his eyes heavenward, as if he were suffering from a great pain, he said in a mournful voice, "Well, as wonderful as this news is...unfortunately, I can't, I mean, we can't go. Raffaella slipped and fell, it seems she has sprained her ankle."

"What?" I exclaimed. This was news to me. I had talked to Raffaella last night, and she hadn't mentioned anything about taking a bad spill.

When I said as much to Alessandro he quickly replied, "Umm, right, it just happened this morning. She can barely curtsy, let alone dance at a Carnival ball."

Looking sorrowfully at me he lamented, it wouldn't be fair to attend the party without his lovely bride-to-be. He added, there would be hell to pay if he did. Slowly he began waving the thick, expensive-looking, cream-colored envelope. With a sly smile, he asked, "Wanna go to the ball and represent La Scuola in my place?"

Before he could say anything more, I reached out to snatch the invitation from him. He was too quick for me though and whipped it away. Continuing to taunt me, he slowly pulled out the gold-embossed card and began reading in a self-important, exaggerated accent, "*Cari Signori,* you are cordially invited to attend Il Ballo del Doge at Palazzo Pisani Moretta on February..."

He stopped and glanced back up at me with a taunting smile. Pulling out two tickets, he looked at one of them and said, "Since we can't go, this one has been promised to another associate of Roberto's, but this one is yours if you want it. If you do go, you will need to find a splendid costume. I mean it has to be *exquisite*. Do you think you can do that? You understand La Scuola must be well represented."

"Ha!" I scoffed. "This is me you are talking to. Of course I can find a magnificent costume. I've been training for this ball my whole life. But if you really want me to go in style," I said with a twirl of my hair, "perhaps the school needs to help me foot the bill. You know those things don't come cheap."

I fully expected my idea would be shot down, but he surprised me by nodding his head in agreement. Further debate wouldn't be necessary I realized when he reached into his wallet and counted out a couple of hundred euro. He tucked it, and the invitation into the envelope and theatrically handed it to me.

Had I died and gone to heaven? A masked ball in Venice! On top of that, the school was going to help pay for my costume. January was turning out not to be such an awful, chilly month. Things were starting to heat up. Only in Italy could you find yourself one day in the City of Gladiators and the next, riding a gondola in the City of Doges.

I began exploring the tiny boutiques and vintage shops in my neighborhood in hopes of finding *the* dress. I put in several days of searching, but, still was getting nowhere. Feeling disheartened I was beginning to think I'd have to settle for something less than perfect. But one afternoon, taking an alternative path home from La Scuola, I found myself wandering down a narrow street I had never noticed before. Peeking into the display window, which featured hand-painted masks and mannequins dressed in elaborately crafted costumes, I had a hunch I'd stumbled into the right place. Seeing the name of the shop etched on the window, *"Sogni d'Oro"*—Golden Dreams—I knew inside I'd find my dress.

When I entered the store, a little bell above the door jangled musically. A woman sitting at her sewing machine looked up and greeted me with a pleasant smile, *"Buona sera. Posso aiutarLa?* Can I be of help?"

I told her about the fancy dress ball in Venice and began describing the type of costume I wanted. When I finally took a breath, she cocked her head to one side, as if she were quickly running down the inventory of gowns in her shop. Standing up, she said, *"Sì, signorina.* I have many beautiful dresses. Let's take a look."

Moving to an overstuffed rack of velvet and satin costumes, she pulled out a shimmery, reddish-purplish brocade trimmed with a silver braid. I shook my head vehemently. Clearly, she hadn't been listening, so I started all over again carefully describing in more detail the fabric, pattern, and style of the gown I was seeking.

"Ah, sì! Sì. Sì. Ho capito. Ho capito. Okay, okay yes I get it." She put back the magenta dress and began rummaging through the rack, flipping through the hangers, pausing now and again to pull out a dress to show me. When I shook my head, again and again no, she finally stopped and planted her hands on her hips. Then as if struck by inspiration, she exclaimed, *"Aspetti!* What a minute."

She ducked behind the heavy velvet curtain, separating the shop from the back room and when she returned she held in her hands a gold-and-black dress embroidered in silver and gold thread. She told me she had started this dress for another client who had just changed their mind. Looking at it, I immediately knew it would be perfect. It somewhat resembled Eleonora de' Medici's gold brocade dress. I clapped my hands together in excitement and nodded my head vigorously in approval.

The woman smiled and invited me to try it on. Slipping behind the curtain, I stripped off my jeans and eased the dress over my head. The garment hung a bit limply around my shoulders and was much too baggy around the middle. The seamstress only waved her hands in the air and said not to worry. Then settling her glasses upon her nose, she set about pinning the waist and shoulders. She told me to come back at the end of the week when the alterations would be done.

As I dug around in my handbag for my wallet to pay for the dress, I admired the Carnival masks displayed on the wall behind the register. I was struck by the vast array of shapes and quirky images. There were traditional harlequin masks as well as ones shaped like maple leaves and butterflies. There were also others, more grotesque, with long, oddly shaped beaks. Seeing my interest, the woman explained that during the middle ages, doctors had stuffed herbs into the nasal cavities of the long-nosed masks to protect themselves from the plague.

Then she pointed to another type of mask. In contrast to the others, these masks were much simpler and downright ominous and bleak in their austerity. Instead of colorful hues and intricate patterns they were painted in solid colors: gold, black, and white. She told me these were the "Bauta" masks and had been designed to cover a man's entire face—as well as his social status. Winking at me she said, "It is just the kind of mask Casanova might have worn. I imagine it would have come in handy on more than one occasion to hide his true identity in an attempt to seduce a young lady."

I smiled at the thought. Spying a gold half-mask embellished with jewels and feathers, I couldn't resist and added it to my purchase. I thanked the woman for her help and left the shop feeling lighthearted. With my costume taken care of, I could refocus my attention on my show and finish the mountain of work I still had left to do.

One afternoon as I was hurrying back to my apartment, I chanced to run into Lorenzo. Seeing my load, he offered to help. I told him I'd happily repay him with a cup of home-brewed coffee. It didn't take long for him to make himself at home in my apartment. As we sipped our espressos, he shared the news of his family as well as recent developments at work. I, in turn, filled him in on the million details that were keeping me occupied as I prepared for the gallery show in Rome.

"I'm sure everything will go smoothly. It sounds like you have things well in hand."

When I asked if he would be coming, he paused and said he would try his best adding, "I have a couple of business trips coming up, but I will try to fit it into my schedule."

Feeling extremely disappointed I feigned indignity and said, "Well, Mr. Very Important Museum Director, I wouldn't want you to put yourself out. After all, it's only my very first, very big, and very important show. Quite possibly *the* show of the year, of the century even. But don't you worry. I'll manage just fine on my own."

He smiled contritely and shrugged his shoulders. I waited, curious to see if he would tell me what had been on his mind in the car a few weeks back. His words had been weighing on my mind. But, Lorenzo seemed to have forgotten. So, I probed him by asking, "Didn't you have something you wanted to tell me? Remember Christmas..."

Lorenzo looked at me and then quickly set down at his coffee. He began stirring it, suddenly more interested in the drink than me. Still looking down at his cup he hesitated a moment and said, "*Sì, sì,* I was just thinking...yes, there is something...*allora*..." Clinking the spoon against the edge of the cup, he glanced briefly about the apartment and then over at the armoire where my carnival gown hung. Seeing it, he said, "Well, now! What is *that*? Looks a bit fancy to wear to work."

Looking over at the dress a huge smile spread across my face. I had picked it up a few days before and was quite pleased with the results. It fit me perfectly. Jumping up, I exclaimed, "Lorenzo, you have to see this dress! Guess what? I'm going Venice! I'm going to the Doge's ball. And get this. I'm going as Eleonora de' Medici."

With obvious excitement, I told him about Alessandro's ticket to the swanky ball in Venice and how it was now mine. "Can you believe it? Just like that, Alessandro hands me this ticket—well come to think of it, I kind of swiped it out of his hands—and asks me to represent the school in his absence." Holding the dress up in front of me, I did a little pirouette, letting the wide skirt sway around me. Smiling at Lorenzo, I said, "Remember when I told you I wanted to see Carnival? Well, it seems *this* dream is going to come true.

Lorenzo didn't reply he only smiled. I watched, as he toyed again with his coffee cup. What was up with him today? First, he was non-committal about the Rome show and now he seemed highly amused by something— about what—I hadn't a clue. Before I could press him further about what he found so funny, Lorenzo pointed over at the gold mask I had purchased and asked, "Is that your Carnival mask? Can I see it?"

Delightedly I picked it up and put it on, tying the satin strings securely at the back of my head. As I did, I described for him the shop where I had found both the gown and the mask. "The woman who runs the store is a sorceress with a needle and thread. You should see her creations."

I gushed on for several more minutes until finally Lorenzo held up his hands and said, "*Ok. Basta!* Enough already. One would think you were just a little excited about this Venice trip." Looking back at the dress, he said, "No doubt about it, you will be *la donna più bella della festa*—the fairest of them all."

Then, eyeing me carefully he warned, "Be careful, Sophia. You will turn many a head at that ball." He wagged a finger at me almost like a jealous suitor, "Don't go falling into the clutches of any wayward Casanovas."

As I untied the mask I laughed and said, "Don't worry, what happens in Venice," I paused, "stays in Venice."

Chuckling, he agreed but then countered, "Perhaps. And then again, perhaps not." I laughed at the comical way in which he raised his eyebrow.

Realizing it was getting late, I stood up and shooed him out of my apartment. "Begone, kind sir. I've got work to do. This Cinderella has to pay the rent before she can go to the ball." Then I added, "I hope you can make it to Rome. It would mean the world to me if you did."

Lorenzo said, "Don't worry, Sophi, even if I don't make it to Rome, we will get together. Soon. I promise you that."

Before stepping away, he said, *"In bocca al lupo!"*

It was the Italian idiom for wishing someone good luck. It meant "in the mouth of the wolf". It was a funny remark, similar to "break a leg" in English, but in Italian to ward off bad luck, the proper response was *"Crepi,"* wishing death on the wolf before he could eat you.

As I watched Lorenzo descend the stairs, I called out to him, *"Crepi!"* to ensure my luck would stick.

Calling over his shoulder as he descended the steps, "The days of the blackbird are behind you now, Sophia. *Il peggio è passato.* The worst has passed, and better things are headed your way."

Then he stopped and turned around. With a smile lighting his eyes he said, "I hear spring is due to arrive early this year," he said. "It seems you will have good weather in Rome, but I think it will be even better in Venice."

Chapter 23

Roman Holiday

*B*efore I knew it, I was in Rome. *La città eterna!* A city founded by emperors, from whence all civilizations *and* art, flowed. It was a sprawling metropolitan jungle, and despite being big, loud, and dirty, I found it utterly fascinating. It was a place where everything was exaggerated, from the enormous marble statues to the trompe l'oeil fantasy ceilings that blew the tops off buildings through clever artistic tricks and illusions. Nothing disappointed or failed to dazzle. It was a melodramatic orgy of bold, swirly spirals and heavy chiaroscuros that drew the eye ever upwards. Rome simply popped and exploded with ornament and color.

Even though I painted in a modern, minimalist way, something inside me responded to the drama and exuberance in the paintings, architecture, and fountains so typical of Rome. When I stood before Bernini's statue of the goddess Daphne as she fled from Apollo, I felt her fear, as well as her astonishment, to be turning into a tree. I chuckled at the expression on the face of Caravaggio's St. Matthew. He seemed like a drunken, middle-aged man caught unaware during a poker game, who when asked by Christ to follow him, responded incredulously, "Who, me?"

Whether it was a mythological creature, a stocky Madonna with dirt under her toenails, or frothy cotton candy interpretations of heaven, the drama conveyed was as good as any Broadway play. But the sense of grandeur was never more awesomely felt than when I stood in the middle of St. Peter's. Standing in front of Bernini's Baldacchino, illuminated by sunlight that filtered in through the high altar windows, I felt dwarfed and overwhelmed by the church's interior.

I arrived in Rome on a crisp winter afternoon in early February. Despite the brisk temperatures, the sun was bright, and my heart was light as I set about unpacking crates and hanging paintings. I worked diligently to complete the show's installation. When everything was all set up, there was nothing left to do but relax and enjoy my Roman holiday. Unlike the summer months when the city was bursting with tourists, I practically had the place all to myself.

Putting my free time to good use, I decided to explore the Borghese gardens near the Piazza del Popolo and the shops in Trastevere. But before striking out into the city, I first made a pilgrimage to the Vatican museums. There I wandered about the rooms, unhampered by crowds, free to study Raphael's *School of Athens* without feeling like a sardine jammed into a can.

But suddenly I felt something was missing. There really was no one here to disturb me. Come to think of it lately, my mind had been occupied elsewhere, entrenched in the details of the show, hurrying from one appointment to the other, I had stopped taking the time to gaze around me and enjoy life. It had been quite some time since I'd turned around to find a surprise visitor ready to have a quick chat.

What was wrong with me? What had happened to all the fantastic visions? Where had they gone? Here in the papal galleries, I thought I might have the chance to catch up on a bit of gossip with Caravaggio. But it appeared he had other things to do than speak with me today.

As I left the museum and stood in the piazza in front of St. Peter's, admiring Bernini's massive colonnade. I waited. Still, I encountered no one. Apparently, Bernini had stood me up too. Pausing a moment I perked up my ears, but all I heard was the subdued chatter of street vendors hawking their wares and the shrill wail of a *carabinieri* siren. It seemed the only company I was to keep in St. Peter's Square today was the army of stone saints who looked down on me from the top of the church.

I walked on. Picking up my pace, I passed Castel Sant'Angelo and crossed over the bridge that spanned the Tevere River. I stopped briefly in Piazza Navona, hoping to see Marcello Mastroianni coaxing Anita Ekberg out of any one of Rome's famous fountains, it didn't matter which one. As I gazed around the square, nothing appeared out of the ordinary.

Feeling deflated by my lack of *fantasia*, I proceeded on to the Pantheon, the dome that had inspired Brunelleschi. I shut my eyes tightly, hoping to see a familiar face or smell the smoke of the architect's cigar. But when I opened them, all I saw was the cool winter sun glinting off the portico, and I smelled the aroma of freshly baked brioche from a nearby bar. I glanced over my shoulder to the fountain behind me. No artist peeked out from behind the monument, just a couple of birds strutting about, looking curiously at me. Who was the crazy loon now?

The Prince had said he wouldn't abandon me. Where had they all gone? Once again, I closed my eyes and waited. This time, my efforts were rewarded. Soon I began to hear the strains of music and voices singing. As I listened, other voices joined in. I could hear calls of Roman architects, Florentine artists, Tuscan poets, Italian generals, Medici duchesses, and last but not least, the strong, salient voice of Prince Lorenzo himself. I smiled. The muses they all were still there. I just had to listen with my heart to hear them.

On the night of the gallery opening, I carried the voices with me. I was pleased by the large turnout of friends and colleagues, as well as by a curious public who came as a result of a nice write-up in the arts section of *La Repubblica* that had described my work as "inspired by a sense of modernity, but with classical tendencies."

For the show, I wore a blue satin dress that reminded me of something my mother, or perhaps Sophia Loren herself, might have worn. It made me feel like a bona fide diva. Earlier in the day, in the Via del Corso, I had splurged on a pair of spiky high heels to match the dress. Dressed to the nines, I welcomed my guests with glasses of bubbling prosecco and followed them about the gallery, conversing with them about my paintings.

Several hours later, as people began to leave, I kicked off my heels, ready to relax. Rubbing my foot against the back of my leg as I studied one of my paintings, I took a sip of prosecco. My throat was dry from too much talking. I took another long drink to quench my thirst. It tasted so good; I chugged down the entire glass in one swallow. The bubbles tickled my nose, making me sneeze. Then before I could help it, I hiccuped even louder.

It was then I felt a gentle tap on my shoulder.

Finally, I thought.

I turned slowly around, curious to see who my next guest might be. A smile broke out across my face when I saw Lorenzo standing behind me. At that moment I couldn't think of a more welcome visitor to step out of my dreams to surprise me. By his amused expression, I gathered he had also heard my prosecco-induced hiccups. I bit my lip, thinking I'd never measure up to his polite and proper English girl. If I didn't have a smear of chocolate on my face, I was making noises like a drunken fool. I looked at him and shrugged my shoulders, but he only laughed and offered to refill my glass.

"You deserve a toast. *Questo merita un brindisi,*" he said, raising his prosecco glass to meet mine.

"A toast indeed!" I agreed and looked him directly in the eye as we clinked our glasses to ensure good luck. I was thrilled he had made it to my show.

Surveying the room, he raised his flute again, and said, "I think we should also make a toast to Alessandro." Looking back at me, he raised an eyebrow and said, "It appears he has done his job and taught you well."

I laughed in agreement and lifted my glass to Ale.

Then growing serious, Lorenzo said, "*Caspita!* Wow, Soph, this show is truly impressive. Well done." I was absurdly pleased by his comments, seeing as he knew a thing or two about curating a show. Lorenzo had seen some of my sketches, and he had caught glimpses of many paintings mid-progress, bumping into me in the street. But this was the first time he had seen everything professionally framed and presented for public viewing.

As we strolled about the galleries, he whistled softly. At one point he leaned over and asked, "What if I told you I wanted to buy one of your paintings to hang in my new apartment?" Without waiting for a response, he indicated with his glass a view of the Ponte Vecchio silhouetted against a lavender sky. "That one. That is the one I'd like to own."

I was particularly happy with his choice. It was one of my favorites. It had been done at a tricky time of day, moments before the afternoon melted into evening dusk. I smiled approvingly and said, "I do believe the gentleman has excellent taste." Touching his arm, I added, "Exquisite taste, in fact." Standing on tiptoes, I whispered into his ear, "Listen, I happen to know the artist, and I think she'll give you a fair price."

Taking a sip of his prosecco he laughed and said, "*Davvero?* Really? *Fantastico!* Tell her I'm very interested."

"Still, I'm afraid it won't come cheap," I said with a tilt of my head and a raised eyebrow. Placing both hands on my hips, I looked back at the painting and said, "I was thinking about keeping that one for myself and hanging it in my apartment. But for you, *amico mio,* I might just make an exception."

"Your friend, yes? Well, I'm sure it would look very nice on your wall, but I think it will go even better on mine. Perhaps we can come to some kind of agreement to satisfy us both. Shall we make a deal?"

I nodded my head delightedly. When he asked the price, without blinking, I stated a number. He whistled quietly in response. But seeing I meant business, he rose to the challenge and began in earnest to negotiate a better one, as art curators are ought to do—especially good Italian ones. He played his game for a while, but in the end agreed to my terms.

"Affare fatto," I said with a grin. Extending my hand to shake on the deal, I repeated in English, "Done deal. *Grazie, signore*. Always a pleasure doing business with you.

We smiled at one another, and I squeezed his hand, and he responded with a decisive, shake. But as I withdrew mine from his grasp he held for a few seconds longer, making me look up at him in surprise. He shrugged his shoulders in a teasing way and finally let go. Moving to refill his wine-glass, he made himself comfortable in the gallery's reception area. I perched myself on the table next to him, careful not to knock off the silver tray full of discarded prosecco glasses and empty bottles. Idly I began twisting a long lock of hair between my fingers, letting my legs swing back and forth.

Lorenzo followed my movements, continuing to sip his wine, he seemed far away. I snapped my fingers to attract attention. Looking up he apologized, "Sorry. Just thinking about a project I'm working on. So tell me. What's new with you? Besides this latest triumph, I mean. How are your plans for Carnival shaping up?"

Delighted to be talking about Venice again, I immediately plunged into telling him the time of day I'd be arriving, which train I'd be taking, even where I'd be staying. "Things have fallen into place. Alessandro pulled a couple of strings and just like that he found me a room in the heart of Venice somewhere off Piazza San Marco."

I paused when I saw a broad smile spread across Lorenzo's face. "I believe," he said, "Alessandro deserves another toast. It seems he has been quite attentive and helpful with this Venice trip of yours."

Leaning forward, he gestured again with his glass, waving it in a circle as if to encompass the entire gallery. "Sophi, I just want to tell you again how impressive your show is. Your hard work has paid off." Then looking back at me he said, "You know I was teasing you back in Florence. You must know I wouldn't have missed this for the world."

I looked at him thoughtfully, "But surely you are here in Rome on other museum business too, right? Not just for me?"

He looked at me a bit obliquely and said, "Oh, you know me, always in search of a rare piece of art," he said. "I've discovered a real treasure right here in Rome."

He wouldn't give me any more details than that, diverting my attention by talking about his work colleagues and changes to museum policies. I, in turn, confided that I had received another invitation to hold a new exhibit in the fall, this time in Milan. We covered a lot of territory, but the one topic we both avoided was Judith. I had no desire to ruin my perfect evening by bringing up her name. Lately, the thought of her flawless face irritated me more and more.

As we talked, I noticed a couple who had entered the gallery earlier, beckoning to me. Out of the corner of my eye I had been watching them as they strolled through the room. I had observed with pleasure their apparent interest in my work. Repeatedly the woman had stopped in front of a painting, bent in close and then with a gloved finger had indicated a detail to her companion.

I had been struck by the woman's tall, lithe figure. About her neck was a red scarf and her face was obscured by a broad-brimmed felt hat so I couldn't see her features. Normally I would have approached the couple immediately, introducing myself, welcoming them to my show. Somehow, I had let myself be distracted by Lorenzo, forgetting my responsibilities.

Seeing the man tilt his head and wave at me again, I slipped off the table and stepped back into my shoes, resuming a more professional guise. I turned to Lorenzo and gave him a quick hug good-bye. As he buttoned up his coat, he smiled at my sudden change in persona from that of a slightly tipsy artist to a more sober businesswoman.

Looking directly into my eyes, he said, *"Ci vedremo presto!"* He said it again in English, this time a little more forcefully, "We *will* see each other soon."

I squeezed his arm. "Yes, of course. See you back in Florence. Don't be a stranger."

Before I could turn away, he reached for my hand and raised it to his lips kissing it lightly. I looked at him again in confusion, feeling the blood rush to my face. It was definitely time to stop drinking prosecco tonight. I watched a little sadly as he disappeared again into the cold winter night.

"Signorina," the man called out. *"Un attimo per favore!"* Switching to English, he said again, "Miss, a minute please!"

I came back to my senses and turned my attention to my clients. Walking over to the couple, I introduced myself as Sophia, the artist. Gesturing to the painting that held the couple's interest I quickly launched into an explanation of where and when I had painted the picture. When I glanced to my left, directly into the woman's face, my mind drained of all logical thought. I stopped talking and stared dumbfounded as I recognized those dark brown eyes.

Before me stood Sophia Loren. The living, breathing woman—as elegant in person as she was on the silver screen. For the second time this evening, my fantasies had come to life.

When she saw the expression of disbelief on my face, she laughed. Then reaching out to shake my hand she said, "*Ciao!* My name is Sophia, too. Pleased to meet you Sophia, the artist...I am Sophia, the actress."

I shook my head, trying to regain my composure, racking my brain for the right words to say. But instead, I blurted out, "I can't believe it! It's you. I'm *named* after you."

Smiling again, La Loren leaned over and whispered into my ear, *"Senta, in questo caso dovremmo assolutamente darci del tu, no?"* Repeating in her lovely accented English, "Look, my dear girl, in that case, we absolutely must use the familiar term of address, don't you think? We Sophias must stick together."

I nodded, still unable to form a single coherent sentence in either English or Italian.

Turning back to my painting, she said, "Sophia, I just adore this piece. My son, Carlo, and I were having dinner around the corner. As we were passing by the gallery, we decided to pop in and have a look around. Your work is beautiful. *Complimenti!* I adore this painting. It reminds me of a simpler time and the things that make Italy so beautiful. I would like to buy it."

Could this be happening? Here I was in Italy, in a Roman gallery and Sophia Loren had just walked in and wanted to buy one of my paintings.

When she saw me shaking my head in disbelief, La Loren arched an eyebrow and asked, "Is there a problem? Is the painting not for sale?"

Thinking back to my conversation with the Medici prince in San Lorenzo, I knew what I wanted to do for this legendary actress. For the very same reasons I had given Prince Lorenzo my sketchbook, it was time for me for me to give something back to her.

I looked at her and said, "No, Ms. Loren. This painting isn't for sale."

Seeing her face drop in surprise, I hastened to say, "It isn't for sale, but please accept this painting as my gift to you. You have been an inspiration, to me all my life. And not just to me, but to my mother also, she loved you so. How I wish she could have been here tonight to meet you, she was an artist too."

Caressing my cheek, she said, "Such a sweet gesture, Sophia. If you must...I will accept gratefully—*volentieri*. Now, won't you please tell me about your mother, *cara*. She must have been a very special woman to have produced such a talented *and* generous daughter."

I smiled and stepped over to the wall to remove the painting. As I wrapped the picture in protective tissue paper, I said, "She was an amazing woman. I can't remember a time when she wasn't showing me a new way to look at things and to find joy in life.

Hearing that, Sophia laughed and said in a voice that sounded curiously like my mother's, *"Ma certo. La fantasia ed i sogni sono cose importanti per dare sapore alla vita."* Nodding at me, she said again in English, "Yes, dreams and fantasy are very important to flavor one's life. But you, Sophia, I can tell, you have a good head on your shoulders and have found a way to walk the line between the two."

I slid the painting into a sturdy bag stamped with the gallery's logo and handed it to her. *"Grazie*, Ms. Loren. Thank you...thank you for everything. You have made a dream come true."

Winking at me, the actress leaned over and kissed me first on one cheek and then gently on the other. *"Stammi bene, cara!* Be well, my dear. Your mother has done a good job."

Picking up one of my business cards, with a firm nod of her head, she added, "I'll keep my eye on you, *cara,* you are quite gifted. I look forward to your next show."

She moved gracefully to the door and called back, "Sogna! Sogna, Sophia. Keep dreaming! I believe in dreams. Dreams become reality."

Venetian Renaissance

For centuries, Venice has been the point where East and West meet. Painting, sculpture, and architecture produced during the Venetian Renaissance reveal the intermingling of the two great cultural forces. Venice, more than any other location due to the dampness of the city, helped make oil paint on woven canvases popular. Frescoes are nonexistent. Rich, sensuous colors, golds and deep reds, complex chiaroscuro, and elaborately detailed exuberant themes are typical of the Venetian Renaissance.

Chapter 24

La Serenissima

A week after the gallery show closed in Rome, I boarded a train back to Florence. I dumped the contents of my suitcase onto my bed and refilled it with clean clothes, lacy bras, and satin slips. The last thing I added was the damask embroidered Carnival gown, carefully wrapped and protected in its linen bag. As I gathered my toiletries and finished packing, I turned up my radio and sang with Francesco Renga: It is you who gave me my most beautiful day in the world, you who offers me a smile for no reason, you who opens all the doors...*a toccare con un dito questo cielo che spalanca l'infinito*... to touch the sky opening wide into infinity...

Continuing to hum the song, I, too, felt as optimistic and serene as *La Serenissima* herself the name Venetians use to describe their fair city. In just a few days I would be attending a Carnival ball in a city made famous for its gondolas, canals, and Byzantine palaces. Oh, and lest we forget Casanova— one of the world's most charming lovers. On his reputation alone, Venice had been branded the capital of intrigue and romance.

How deliciously exciting to be traveling to the place where the famous philanderer was rumored to have had more than one hundred and twenty assignations, including a dalliance with a nun. *Oh, mio Dio!* Yes, the city had quite a reputation as being a hotbed for womanizers. Even Vivaldi, one of the greatest baroque composers *and* an ordained Catholic priest, had been rumored to have had a love affair here with his beautiful servant girl.

With these thoughts in mind, I stepped off a train at the Santa Lucia terminal in Venice. Lucia was the patron saint of sight. I thought it perfectly poetic that the station had been named in her honor. It was through her portal that people had their first magical glimpse of the Grand Canal and the city.

Standing at the top of the stone steps that led down to the water, I watched all manner of boats chugging along Venice's main waterway. Late afternoon sunlight shimmered across its surface, intensifying the color of the water, casting long inky shadows. I had seen pictures before and heard other people's stories, but still, I hadn't expected to be so completely bowled over by the enormity of her beauty.

Venice was a unique and remarkable city that had risen out of the Adriatic Sea. It had been built up from reinforced islands floating in a boggy, saltwater lagoon. What an incredible idea, I thought, to solidify the foundations of the city by driving wood pilings into the mud, causing them to petrify. Who could ever have imagined, that from such humble, muddy beginnings, a magical fairy tale city would emerge?

As flocks of partygoers poured out of the station, jostling me from behind, I came back to my senses and walked down the steps to catch the next transport to Piazza San Marco. When it arrived, people called out to one another, joking and laughing as they pushed and shoved, carrying the party they had started on the dock onto the idling waterbus. Finding a spot on the crowded bench, I wedged myself between a woman wearing a strawberry costume and a man in a powdered wig and blue satin evening coat.

The boat took off a bit roughly, lurching forward, causing me to lean heavily into the man to the left. I apologized and was treated to an invitational wink and a knowing smile. Not wanting any further advances, I turned away. Craning my neck, I gazed out at the arched windows, lacy grillwork, and richly colored façades that lined the canal. Each building was more elaborate than its neighbor. They appeared not to be made of marble and stone at all, but rather impossibly thick slabs of wedding cake.

I watched with interest as a smaller boat passed by and a man in a black tricorn hat doffed his cap and called out to me. "*Signorina,* you are the most beautiful woman I've ever seen!"

I waved back and blew him a kiss. "*Grazie, signore. Sì, è vero. Io sono davvero Bella!*" I laughed at my own joke, as I agreed with him. Here in Venice I was indeed my father's beautiful daughter, Bella.

At the next stop, as people disembarked, I moved over to make room for a man dressed as a plump red lobster complete with over-sized claws. As he squeezed in beside me, I felt my old persona take a backseat as a new, fascinating woman stepped forward. Perhaps she was an artist or maybe an enchantress who might seduce Casanova himself. No one really knew who I was and there was no one to call my bluff and say, "*Ti conosco, mascherina!* I know who is hiding behind that mask."

By the time the boat docked in Piazza San Marco, the lights of the piazza were flickering on, illuminating the crowds of fancifully, dressed tourists. As I approached the Doge's palace, I slowed my steps. From the porticos, I could hear strains of violins playing from outdoor cafés. Children bumped into me, hopping and skipping and startling flocks of pigeons, sending them fluttering into the air, in frenzied gray clouds.

Under the loggia of the piazza, I stood taking in the scene. All around me were small tables full of costumed people sipping their cocktails. As they conversed they dipped their fingers into small bowls of Venetian appetizers called *cicchetti*—bowls of nuts, olives, and dainty sandwiches.

Tired from my train ride, I found an open seat and collapsed into it. Looking at the menu, I considered my options but in the end decided on a Bellini in honor of my parents. How could I resist enjoying a drink that had been created right here in the square at Harry's Bar to honor the Venetian artist Giovanni Bellini? I relaxed and let the bubbles go to my head. Warmed by the liquor—it tasted so good—I threw caution to the wind and ordered another. When I had downed the last delectable drop, I picked up my suitcase and stood up. The colors in the piazza swirled together like a spinning kaleidoscope.

Taking a few unsteady steps, I gathered my wits and pushed through the crowd to the other side of the piazza. Not at all sure I was headed in the right direction, I launched into a side street in search of my *pensione*. I paused briefly to consult my map. Tilting it this way and that, I finally got my bearings and proceeded confidently forward. But, as I began to notice the yellow markers with arrows pointing to San Marco over and over again, I got the sneaking suspicion I had been walking in circles.

At first, I didn't mind. It was lovely getting lost in Venice. I relished the sensation of drifting back in time with each bridge I crossed over. I continued meandering down the small *calli*—the narrow side streets—that ended in a small courtyard or led me into another secluded alleyway. Whenever my path dead-ended, I walked around a fountain and retraced my steps back to the main street and re-orientated myself. But instead of re-establishing my bearings, each turn seemed to draw me deeper into Venice's labyrinth. I soon realized I had entered a part of town more accustomed to seeing working class people, college students, and grandparents. Here people weren't armed with cameras, and only Italian was spoken. But even I had trouble recognizing their words, as they were all in Venetian dialect.

I slowed my pace observing the soft, faded colors of the buildings and the watermarks left from *l'acqua alta*, the high tides, and flooding. From the windows high over my head, I heard the clinking of plates, the tinkling of glass and mothers calling their children and husbands to dinner. The smell of rich fish broths and fragrant risottos wafted out into the night air, making my stomach rumble, signaling that I, too, was ready for a good dinner.

Night had fallen and I still hadn't located my *pensione*. In the dusky eve, I stopped for a moment on top of a small bridge. The waters gently lapped beneath me, reflecting a heavy full moon. I dreamily watched as a long, black gondola glided under me. I listened as the oarsman dipped his paddles into the water, propelling the flat-bottomed boat forward as he hummed an ancient Venetian song.

Looking up, I admired the evening sky illuminated by stars. There was a nostalgic ache inside me. Right now I would have given anything to have Lorenzo appear beside me. Then I smiled at the thought of meeting Casanova. What would I really do or say if the man should approach me? In this dreamy state of mind, and yes, slightly tipsy, I certainly was ready and ripe for the picking. I might just succumb to the man's fatal charms.

I pulled out my map and turned it around again a few more times. Looking up for someone to help me, I realized I was all alone. In the dim light I squinted at the names of the streets, trying to get my bearings. Hearing the sound of a man clearing his throat, I looked over my shoulder in surprise. I thought I had been the only one on the bridge, but below me in the shadows stood a tall, dark figure. His face was covered entirely by a gilded Bauta mask, giving him a sinister almost unearthly air. A tingling sensation ran up my arms and down my spine.

The mask, devoid of expression, gave little clue as to the man's identity. His form was further concealed by a tricorn hat and a flowing dark cape. In the manner of an eighteenth-century nobleman, he wore fashionable short pants, cuffed at the knee, and thick white leggings. At his neck I could see a touch of a lace cravat and in the man's breast pocket was a small red rose. But what made his costume truly stunning was the gold-embroidered vest beneath his coat.

He didn't say a word. He simply stood observing me from afar. I watched him curiously, but said nothing myself, hesitant to break the spell. I couldn't see his eyes through the inky black eye holes, so I couldn't determine what thoughts he might be entertaining. Several heightened moments passed before he placed his foot onto the bridge and moved toward me. With a little trepidation I realized he had made the decision to engage me in conversation.

As he approached, he said in a rich, deep voice, made even huskier by the mask, "Well, well, well, *bella*, it looks like you are lost."

I was momentarily taken aback when he called me by my nickname. Had the man recognized me? Then I remembered here in Venice everyone thought I was *bella*, beautiful.

I shook my head to clear the fuzziness. The spirits and shades of Venice had just conjured up a very fine, elegant specimen of a man, indeed. I relaxed into the scene, letting my overactive imagination run wild. It appeared Casanova had just made an entrance, and I was to be his next conquest. Well, look out, *signore*. I can play your game and perhaps even turn the tables.

I settled against the railing of the bridge, tossed my head, and replied, "So what if I am lost, kind sir? Will you take pity upon a poor maiden and help her find her way back home?"

Perhaps it was the magic of the lagoon, or maybe it was those two Bellinis I had downed so quickly back in the piazza—whatever reason, feeling emboldened, I pushed away from the railing and sashayed toward him, swaying my hips seductively. I leaned forward, as if to plant a kiss on his mask but paused before I did. I quipped, "Or perhaps you, Signor Casanova, would like to take me back to your apartments and offer me a drink instead?" I rose back up and batted my eyelashes to make my flirtatious act appear even more vampy.

The man hesitated. He seemed a bit taken aback by my suggestion.

"You recognize me, *signorina*?" he asked in surprise. "Has my identity been found out?"

"But of course," I said with a laugh. "You, dear sir, can be none other than the great lover Casanova."

The gentleman mulled over my words, relaxed, and then chuckled. "Ah, dear lady, so you think you know the man behind the mask?"

I hesitated a moment and replied, "*Mi scusi, Signor Casanova*. Really, I mean not to offend. It is Carnival, and everything goes—*ogni scherzo vale*—every trick, every joke, is acceptable."

"Yes," he said, "this is the season for pranksters and merrymakers in Venice. But you, my sweet thing, appear to have lost your way *veramente*. Seriously, my lady, this is no laughing matter. Perhaps I can assist you in locating your lodgings."

Wanting to prolong the charade, I agreed and held up my map. As the man moved another step closer and bent down to take a look, I caught his scent. It seemed oddly familiar. A shimmer of suspicion clouded my mind. I wrinkled my brow and concentrated but the bubbles in my head made me dizzy, and I swayed woozily. Shaking my head back and forth, I tried to re-align my thoughts to the game we were playing. Picking up my suitcase, the man offered, "*Signorina*, this way. Let me direct you to your quarters."

We walked on in silence for a few minutes. As always, my mind began to wander and once again I was captivated by the narrow canals, the boats and the paint peeling off the sides of ancient buildings. I was so caught up in the charms of the city I ran right into the man's back when he stopped suddenly. Looking over his broad shoulders, I saw we had arrived at a cheerful, bottle-green door with a shiny brass knocker shaped like a lion's head. He rapped a couple of times, and we waited for someone to greet us.

I could hear movement inside, and someone called out "*Un attimo*, just a minute. I'll be right there." As we stood waiting for the owner, Casanova pulled the rose out of his pocket. Picking up my hand, he kissed the back of it. Then turning it over gently, he laid the flower in my open palm.

Looking at me through the dark holes of his mask, he said, "*Cara mia*, I leave you now, but be assured we will meet again."

The sound of the door being wrenched open made me turn around. I glanced over at the owner of the pensione, who stood on the threshold.

"*Permesso?*" I said, asking for permission to enter. I introduced myself. He nodded and moved out of the way so I could enter. "*Si accomodi*. Yes, yes! Come in. We've been expecting you."

I turned around, but just as I had assumed, Casanova had melted back into the night. Lorenzo had been right, here in Venice I was attracting suitors left and right, and I'd been in the city only a couple of hours.

The next day, I wandered about Venice enjoying the spectacle unfolding around me. I watched as a girl swung from a wire like an angel, descending from the bell tower in San Marco. In a smaller piazza off the main square, I attended a puppet show. Along with a crowd of children, I cheered as Arlec-chino, the sneaky servant, tried to steal a kiss from Colombina, the beautiful innocent servant girl. We booed when Pantalone, the rich and stingy mer-chant, tried to separate the two lovers. And then at the end, we applauded when Pulcinella, the lazy chatterbox, saved the day.

Leaving the show, I pushed through throngs of people, admiring the creative costumes and masks. From the stalls lining the square I purchased a T-shirt emblazoned with "I heart Venice", a couple of cheap trinkets, and a few picture postcards. In upscale shops, I admired the blown-glass vases and baubles, the hand-painted masks, and the colorful *millefiori* beads. Venice indeed was a floating bazaar, filled with all kinds of decadent things for sale.

As the sun sank into the lagoon, I returned to the pensione to dress and prepare for the evening's festivities at Palazzo Pisani Moretta. Carefully I removed the gold brocade dress from its linen bag and shook it out, separating the heavy brocade from the crinolines underneath. Slipping the dress over my head, I zipped it up. Then I fluffed up the skirt and adjusted the folds. Next, I entwined Lucrezia's strand of beads around my neck, I clipped the Prince's ruby earrings to my ears and slipped Eleonora's ring onto my finger. Standing before a glass mirror, I brushed my hair to a rich, luxurious shine, capturing it at the nape of my neck with my mother's coral clip.

Then I began painting my face, adding blush to my cheeks and thick, dark liner to my eyes, exaggerating their almond shape. I finished with dark mascara and a light dusting of powder. Picking up the gilded mask laying on top of the dresser, I shook it gently, letting the gold satin ribbons gently untwist and dangle free. It almost seemed a pity to cover up my artfully made up eyes. But then again, what was a masquerade ball without a Carnival mask?

I fluffed up the plumes and shook the mask again, causing glitter and a small feather to drift onto the dresser. Humming under my breath the Venetian tune I had heard a gondolier sing, I placed the mask delicately on my face and tied it around the back of my head. Then I faced the oval mirror in the corner.

I smiled in pleasure. The creature gazing back at me was not me at all. I had been transformed completely into the Duchess Eleonora de' Medici. The embroidered brocade dress fit smoothly and evenly over my form, and the wide, full skirts swooshed about me in a soft, rustling whisper. The pattern was vibrant and lively and the bead work exquisite.

Turning slightly to the left and then dipping back to the right, I studied my reflection for a few more moments. I let myself be transported back in time to a bedroom in Sonoma, where a small Sophia curtsied in front of her mirror as her mother watched from the doorway. Now as I gazed at my reflection, I saw my mother's face in the shadows. Stepping up behind me, she wrapped her arms around me and hugged me tightly. Listening carefully

I thought I heard her say, "*Figlia d'oro, sei bellissima!* Look at you my golden girl you are beautiful!"

I closed my eyes and touched the gold band with the fleur-de-lis, turning it around on my finger a few times. Lifting my hand to my lips, I kissed the symbol of unbroken love and said, "*Un bacio mamma.* Love you, Mom."

I searched for my shoes and slipped them onto my feet. And just like that, the Medici duchess was ready for her first ball. Still humming softly to myself, I reached for my beaded purse and the invitation. Holding up the embossed card, I thought, this is my passport to another new and fantastic world.

Just before flicking off the light, I noticed the rose Casanova had given me the night before. It was sitting on the dresser next to the feather that had come loose from my mask and was now covered with a dusting of glitter. I picked it up and waved it under my nose. I closed my eyes. The fragrance was still sweet, even though the petals were starting to tarnish, turning brown around the edges. If I took care of it, this token of love would surely last through the night and well into tomorrow. Carefully I placed it in a glass of water and set it on the table next to my bed.

Touching the velvety petals, I marveled at the thoughtful gesture. Such a lovely gift. Casanova might just turn out to be a gentleman, after all.

Before walking out the door, I adjusted my mask, making sure it was securely tied. The woman behind the mask had a secret identity. Here in Venice, I was Bella. It was a magical night, and anything could happen. A waltz was about to begin, and I would have my pick of partners. A smile spread across my lips. Who would the lucky man be? It was time to find out.

I was ready to face the music and whatever new surprises La Serenissima held in store for me on this wild and beautiful Carnival night.

Chapter 25

Casanova's Mask

By day the streets of Venice were a jumble of color and garish festivities; by night they turned silver with mystery and intrigue. As I walked along the canals that glinted with shards of moonlight, bubbles of excitement welled up inside me. When I arrived at the fifteenth-century Venetian palace where the Ballo del Doge was taking place, I was greeted by an attendant dressed in sparkling livery. He checked the guest list, and with a sweep of his arm, he invited me to enter the party that started on the main floor, the *piano nobile.*

The room was lit entirely by candles. I paused on the threshold and was offered a flute of champagne. As I took in the scene, my eyes widened in pleasure as I observed other guests in fancy costumes and masks serenaded by singers and a small string quartet. Moving into the next room, I saw nimble acrobats performing tricks, swinging from multicolored ropes dangling from the ceiling. They danced, sang songs, and flattered the beautifully dressed ladies.

The costumes at this party were colorful and extravagant, but unlike those I'd seen roaming the streets earlier, these were more finely made using exquisitely expensive materials. All around me ebbed and flowed a sea of silks, velvets, and sparkling jewels. In my beautiful brocade gown, I fit right in. With my shoulders straight and my head held high, I glided through the mirrored room at home among the other elegant revelers.

Passing into the *sala da pranzo,* I took in the banks of mouth-watering delicacies. Crowding the crisp white linen-covered tables were silver platters filled with roast pig, quail, and game hen. An orgy of cheeses, grapes, olives, and pastries was laid out in an overwhelmingly obscene display. And the sweets, oh my! Cookies, marzipan, and gooey yellow lemon cakes made my eyes glaze over. I also noticed a tray of *chiacchiere,* a typical Carnival *dolce.* *"Chiacchierare"* means to chit chat and indeed when I bit into one of these deep fried crackers, it seemed I really was having a crackly conversation with my sweet.

In the center of the room stood a magnificent fountain guarded by a figure of Cupid sculpted out of ice. A bubbly river of golden champagne flowed from the upturned urn at his side. Waiters passed through the crowd, offering up glasses of his sweet wine. I helped myself to a little gold plate and filled it liberally with pâté and flaky meat pies, duck, lamb, and goose.

Wandering around the room, I rubbed shoulders with Venice's elite, easily striking up conversations with other partygoers. Making jokes and conversing, never a hardship for me was made even easier tonight. A gilded mask now hid my identity, and a golden gown was my armor, making it easy to slip into the role of a fascinating enchantress. I could laugh and flirt and say many ridiculous things to perfect strangers, and no one would be the wiser.

Leaving the sumptuous banquet with my newly acquired suitors, I entered the ballroom where an orchestra played a lilting waltz. I twirled around the room, passing from one set of arms to another. Just as I nodded thanks to one gentleman, I turned my head and accepted the light, gloved touch of another. We bowed and curtsied and then circled around and around the room some more, under a massive sparkling crystal chandelier. On this magical night, in this incredible ballroom, I could be held in the embrace of as many fascinating, unnamed strangers as I could fit on my dance card.

Who could guess who resided behind the black-and-gold Bauta masks and fabulous bird beaks? Only at midnight would I know for sure, when we would all be unmasked at the bewitching hour.

Pleasantly occupied by my swarm of suitors, the evening quickly melted away in a blur of color and music. Shortly before the clock struck twelve, as the anticipation for unmasking was mounting, I found a secluded corner of the ballroom where I could catch my breath and relax for a moment. Slipping out of my high heels, I wiggled my toes and did quick pliés. I rolled my neck and shoulders, adjusting the weight of my gown. Eleonora had been right. These long brocade dresses were rather unwieldy.

From my hidden vantage point in the corner of the room, I observed the dancers. The entire room swayed to the music, an effect enhanced by the light that sparkled off mirrors and brass sconces. It all seemed like a magical dream, almost too impossible to be real. If I closed my eyes and opened them again, would I see La Signora standing in front of me holding out a forgotten book?

I laughed softly and decided to test out the theory. I allowed my eyes to flutter shut behind my mask. Placing my hands on my hips, I tapped my foot in time to the music. As I counted out ten beats, I listened to the murmur of conversation, the trill of laughter, and the music of violins flowing all around me. I opened my eyes slowly. A figure came gradually into focus.

But it wasn't my Italian teacher.

Before me stood Casanova.

Why was I not surprised? Once again it seemed the man had materialized out of thin air. He was as impressive as he had been standing at the bottom of the bridge in the moonlight, dressed in the same dark jacket and gold brocade vest. Just as it had the evening before, the Bauta mask concealed his features entirely. Well, this was certainly a welcome development. A warm smile spread across my face at the thought of dancing in *this* gentleman's arms.

Seeing my lips curve up in delight, Casanova placed his white, gloved hands lightly upon my shoulders. Leaning over he whispered into my ear, "*Ciao, bella.* It is wonderful to see you here tonight. I told you we would meet again."

The hour was growing late, and the clock was ticking its way toward midnight. People were moving about, plucking glasses of champagne off silver trays and clinking them with those of their neighbors. The din of the room rose even louder. I became aware of a familiar scent and took another step closer to the man, comfortably drawn into his embrace. I peered curiously into the mask, but I still couldn't see his face or make out his identity.

Speaking a little louder so as to be heard over the crescendoing noise, he said, "You are so lovely. *Che bella donna! Guardati!* Just look at you."

Slowly he turned me around to face the gilded mirror on the wall behind us. Staring into the glass, I saw the images of Eleonora de' Medici and Casanova reflected back at me. As the clock began to chime the midnight hour, the orchestra picked up a frenzied Vivaldi melody and the man slowly twirled me around to face him again. He raised his arm and tugged at the black silk ties that held his mask in place. It released and dropped effortlessly into his other hand.

The image of Casanova evaporated into the night, and before me stood Lorenzo. I inhaled my breath in surprise. The man behind the mask had been revealed to me at last.

"*Caspita! Che ci fai qui?* What on earth are you doing here?" I asked in shock. I playfully pushed his chest with the palms of my hands. But instead of replying, he reached up and untied the mask that still covered my eyes. He tilted my head up with his hand, looked into my eyes, and exhaled heavily.

"Oh, wow! *Che occhi!* Why cover those amazing eyes with a mask? You look sensational tonight, Sophia. Or should I say Eleonora de' Medici?"

"Well?" I said as I slipped back into my shoes. Putting my hands on my hips, I waited for an explanation.

Lorenzo laughed. "You should see yourself now. The expression on your face is priceless."

Reaching for my hands, he raised my arms out wide so he could get a better look at my Carnival costume. "You are beautiful," he said. "You were right. Eleonora's dress was the perfect thing to wear to your first ball. You look like you stepped right out of her gilded frame."

Slightly placated, I looked at him, hardly believing he was here in the same ballroom as me. I shook my head trying to make sense of it all.

As if reading my mind he looked deeply into my eyes, "I know how much you wanted to come to Venice, Soph *and* how much you wanted to attend Carnival. I wanted to invite you myself, but couldn't resist surprising you. You know me! It's carnival after all...*Ogni scherzo vale*—all manner of tricks and intrigues are acceptable at this time of the year."

I took a step closer to Lorenzo and pushed him gently again, this time letting my hands rest comfortably on his chest. I shook my head, "You planned all this? This was your idea? The invitation to the ball...it was yours, *not* Alessandro's. This was all your doing!"

Suddenly I remembered the evening before and exclaimed, "And that was you on the bridge last night."

Lorenzo nodded. With a self-satisfied grin, he said, "Personally I think this has been one of my more successful schemes. It's worked out perfectly. I fooled you completely."

I couldn't believe it, how had I not put everything together before tonight? Looking back, it was all so obvious. The clues had been there for weeks. But why hadn't I recognized him yesterday? I paused for a moment and replayed the scene in my mind, remembering that I had been tired and fuzzy from the train ride, as well as a little tipsy from drinking. Plus I had been caught up in a fantasy, gazing up at the moon and the stars, my head a million miles away in the clouds.

Then a thought occurred to me. I narrowed my eyes and asked, "Hey, wait a minute. How did you know where to find me yesterday?"

Lorenzo rolled his eyes and said as if it was obvious, "Remember back in Rome? You told me which train you were taking. I was waiting for you in Piazza San Marco. I watched you get off the water taxi and walk into the piazza. I wanted to make sure you had safely arrived in Venice."

I eyed him skeptically.

"I even wore the damn costume so you wouldn't recognize me. It was all I could think of to do. I didn't want to spoil the surprise I had planned for this evening. There were so many people in the piazza yesterday...you passed right in front of me. You were too busy looking around to see me. I admit I was a little offended you didn't notice such a handsome specimen of a man. I watched you from inside the loggia as you drank your Bellini... or should I say Bellinis—plural. Wow! You know how to put away the prosecco," he said with a grin.

I nodded, recalling the many revelers in the square, all dressed in bright costumes.

"I followed behind you," he said, "and soon realized you had lost your way, so I decided to help." He laughed again, telling me how awkward he had felt. "I thought at first you had recognized me. You talked to me as if you knew me. You called me Casanova, almost like you were talking to the ghost of Casanova himself. I thought I'd given myself away and I'd blown the surprise altogether."

I shrugged sheepishly at the mention of Casanova's name and the flippant game I had played. I was in awe he had taken the time to invent such an elaborate ruse to lure me here to Venice and this elegant ballroom. Clearly, Lorenzo had an imagination that rivaled my own. He had taken a page out of my own creative book and had written an entirely new chapter. It was all so thoughtful and romantic.

At that moment I was flooded with my feelings for him and admitted to myself how much I loved him. By masterminding this whole thing, it seemed he reciprocated my feelings. Ever since we had first met, it seemed we had been slowly and gradually building up to this moment.

But there was one tiny complication.

"*Aspetta un attimo, signore.* Hold on there, mister," I said again, "What happened to Judith?" I took hold of the collar of his coat and shook him firmly, as well as a little possessively.

He looked at me with a sheepish smile and said, "Ah, *carissima*, I think you know the answer to that. I admit it. I was a complete idiot. I really don't know what I was thinking. Rest assured we've said our good-byes."

Pulling me a little closer, he added, "She was replaced by an artist with paint under her fingernails, a lovely woman I had coffee with one afternoon outside the church of San Lorenzo. I hope," he said, "that from tonight on, I will be holding her in my arms for a long time to come...paint and all."

He traced the line of my jaw with his finger. Tilting my face up, he kissed me on the forehead. Then he kissed me softly first on one cheek and then the other.

I breathed in slowly, enveloped by his familiar scent. We blended into a comfortable embrace, fitting naturally together. I pulled back just a little bit, just enough so I could look into his eyes, and whispered, "*Sai che Eleonora è pazzamente innamorata di te?* You know Eleonora is crazy in love with you, right?"

Caressing my cheek with his finger, he laughed and softly said, "Well, now...that's a very good thing. Casanova *ti ama alla follia!*" Tucking a strand of hair behind my ear, he said again, "Casanova is pretty crazy about you too."

His voice trailed off, and he leaned down and kissed me. As our lips touched, I thought, *this feels right.* It was the same sensation I had felt when I first stepped off the train in Florence like I was coming home.

Noticing the music had started again, Lorenzo leaned back and looked over his shoulder at the couples gliding onto the dance floor.

"*Senti,*" he said, "I've been extremely patient this evening, letting you enjoy the Doge's Ball all on your own. I wanted you to have a taste of the glamor and enjoy the entire party *a modo tuo*—in your own way." Looking a little putout, he raised an eyebrow and said, "I have to say, it's been torture watching you from the shadows, dancing and basking in the warm embraces of all your admiring suitors. Now, *mia cara,* it's my turn. There will be plenty of time to talk later. Right now I want to feel you in my arms, close to my heart."

"What took you so long?" I asked with a laugh while grabbing his hand.

"It's about time you cut in and claimed your dance."

With a formal bow, he drew me into his embrace again. "May I have the next dance, my fanciful Medici duchess? My beautiful, bella Sophia?

"*Aspetta! Aspetta.* Wait a minute." The words bubbled out in a rush.

"*Che cosa?*" Raising his eyebrow, he asked, "What is it now?"

I smiled at Lorenzo, thinking back to Marcello's advice in the mailroom. I heard the screen legend say: Kiss often *and* kiss like you mean it.

"Come here," I said. "Let's try that again."

"What?" he asked again a little too innocently.

Reaching up, I intertwined my fingers around his neck, and said, "*Baciami ancora!*"

Without further encouragement, he leaned down and kissed me again.

Chapter 26

A Private Language

*L*orenzo and I were in no hurry to rush home, preferring to linger a few more golden days in the city set in a silvery lagoon. We welcomed the opportunity to steal a few moments from our busy lives, to explore our newly found intimacy. I moved out of the *pensione* and into the elegant hotel suite he had booked weeks before, in anticipation of luring me to Venice and hopefully into his arms. There we spent the following days lounging between silky sheets and listening to the love songs of the gondoliers paddling their boats in the canal beneath our window.

Eventually, we rose from our bed and left the privacy of our room, venturing into the public streets of Venice. By now the Carnival crowds had dissipated, and the streets were nearly empty. The only indication that Venice had thrown a party was the *coriandoli*, the bright colored paper confetti, which still powdered the stone walkways and floated on the canals.

Hand in hand we explored the city together, finding tables in cozy *trattorie* where we nibbled on *cicchetti* and sipped Bellini cocktails. We visited the Accademia and the Guggenheim and wandered through the Doge's church and palace, tiptoeing over the marble mosaics that embellished the floor. We also explored the Venetian prison and walked through the Bridge of Sighs, where prisoners drank in their beautiful last view of Venice before being taken to their cells.

Sometimes we slipped into empty churches and listened to priests practicing their hymns in preparation for the evening mass. As we exited the sacred spaces and meandered along the canals, we heard music just as heavenly coming from the violins of street performers, in the piazza of San Zaccaria.

As we walked, I was content to have Lorenzo by my side. Inevitably, however, when some bit of architecture or a detail of a painting caught my eye, I wiggled out from his embrace and pushed him gently away. Momentarily distracted by the ascent of a Titian Madonna or the elaborate scrollwork on the façade of Santa Maria della Salute, I moved closer to observe the intricate details more carefully.

In the Sala Superiore at the School of San Rocco, to avoid craning our necks to view the ceiling paintings, we accepted the large mirrors the docents handed to us. Seated cross-legged on the floor, I tilted mine this way and that, studying the details. After a bit, I was distracted by the sight of Lorenzo's face looming above me. I watched in amusement as he gave me a broad smile. Once again, he had snuck up on me, catching me unaware. But this time, unlike the others, he crouched down beside me, brushed back my hair, and kissed the nape of my neck. Wrapping his arms around me, together we gazed at the reflection of two happy people, set against a backdrop of luminous colors and Venetian splendor.

During our walks, Lorenzo explained that from the first day he had seen me in the bar, he felt as if his life had been turned upside down. He had come home to Florence from London seeking stability but instead had been sent into a tailspin of self-discovery. He realized he'd been listlessly floating along in a relationship that no longer sparked or inspired him. It had been a casual affair he admitted, one he'd allowed to drift on far longer than he had intended. But even from the beginning, he had never felt the true contentment that comes from simply holding someone's hand.

That all changed, he said, the day he had picked up my red scarf in the bar in Florence. He chuckled and said, "You caught my attention immediately. And that chocolate smeared on your cheek—I was completely taken in. After that, I knew I was a lost man."

I laughed and confessed how awkward and silly I had felt that day. He smiled and reached for my hand, and while tracing my gold ring with his thumb said, "From the very first moment I knew you were different. *Qualche volta un po' lunatica...ma sempre una sognatrice—always a dreamer.*"

"I think somewhere in there is a compliment," I said with a sideways glance. Smiling over at me he agreed, indeed there was.

He told me that he had returned to London after Christmas, specifically to break things off with Judith. This is what he had almost shared that night in the car. Before making a new beginning with me, first, he had wanted to break things off definitively with her. "It was the right thing to do. I wanted to start the New Year off with a clean slate—Anno nuovo, vita nuova—as the saying goes."

He recalled at midnight—when the clock chimed in the New Year, although he had been walking along the Thames looking up at the London Eye, he had been thinking instead of the Arno, the Palazzo Vecchio, and a girl named Sophia.

Knocking into him playfully, I said, "Well, I'm glad you finally came to your senses, you big art director idiot. Of course, you should have been dreaming of your Sophia!"

He squeezed my hand. "I was planning on telling you the moment I got back." He paused a moment, and a familiar devilish grin spread across his face. "But on the plane ride back, I opened my briefcase and saw the invitation to your show and beneath it the invitation to the Masquerade Ball, and I got this really great idea."

Still holding my hand, he said, "I remembered how much you wanted to visit Venice at Carnival. So I cooked up this idea to get you here, to surprise you." Raising his eyebrows a couple of times he added, "I thought, let's do this up right and in style. Let's create something she will never forget."

"I have to hand it to you," I said. "You have some serious bonus points with me. They should last you, well...at least a couple of weeks. But I warn you! A girl could start getting used to this kind of treatment. I'm interested to know what else you've got up your lacy sleeve, my dear Casanova. Perhaps I'll demand a repeat performance."

Lorenzo laughed at that. Leaning down, he whispered into my ear, "Well...meet me back in the room in about an hour."

Smiling back, I said, "Okay, that just bought you another week's worth." Raising an eyebrow, I teased, "Lucky for you that I can be so easily duped. What would you have done if I'd fallen under the spell of some other Casanova before you decided to take off your mask?"

"Good thing you didn't," he joked, "otherwise I would have been forced to call the cad out for a duel."

With his arm around my shoulders and mine about his waist, we continued our walk through Venice, engrossed in a new, private language we were both beginning to learn.

We drifted idly in the 'Floating City' for a few more days, but remembering work commitments and family obligations, we eventually headed back to Florence. As we navigated the autostrada, we sang to the radio and made jokes. I told him for the umpteenth time about meeting Sophia Loren at the gallery in Rome, and he listened to me patiently, as if he were hearing the story for the first time. When I caught his eye, however, and saw his raised eyebrow, I realized I was running on and immediately closed my mouth.

But a few minutes later he had me laughing again when he leaned over and innocently asked, "By the way did you meet anyone interesting in Rome... besides me, of course? Please do tell me about it. Again."

Then he imitated the face I had made the night before at dinner when I had tried *sarde in saor,* the Venetian dish made with onions, vinegar, and sardines. He puckered his lips and bulged out his eyes, sending me into another fit of laughter.

I told him it was almost as bad as the tripe they served in Florence. He looked momentarily offended and promised to take me to his favorite *lampredotto* truck as soon as we returned to the city. At the thought of that, I rolled my eyes and began making gagging sounds. He shrugged his shoulders and said my disdain for tripe, one of *his* favorite dishes, was my only fault.

Reminding him it certainly was not my only fault, I added, "Wait until you discover all the other fascinating sides of my personality." Then in mock chagrin, I exhaled my breath, making the bangs on my forehead flutter.

"Listen, *mia cara,*" he said with a smile, "I think I have a pretty good idea of what I've gotten myself into here."

When a new song began to play on the radio, he reached over and turned up the volume. Looking over at me, he seductively crooned, *Parole! Parole! Parole!* Words. Words. Words.

I quickly joined in his duet singing: Here's my destiny, speaking to you, speaking to you like the first time.

When we passed a sign for Verona, I cried out, *"Guarda!* Look. We have to stop. *Per piacere, amore mio."* I paused for a moment noticing how easily the words *"amore mio"* rolled off my tongue.

Then grabbing Lorenzo's arm in excitement I continued pleading. But no matter how many endearments I might come up with, I could see he wasn't about to take an unexpected detour. He looked at me as if I was crazy and said, *"Ma tesoro. Sei pazza.* At this rate, we will surely hit rush hour. We will never arrive home at a decent hour. *Che incubo!* What a nightmare."

He tipped his dark glasses down his nose and observing my pouting lips, he only chuckled and said to try again. Rising to the challenge I appealed to his stomach, saying it was time to take a break for lunch. Glancing at the clock on the dashboard and then back at the road, he sighed heavily and finally agreed to my plan.

We entered Juliet's fair city and headed straight to Piazza delle Erbe— the town's central square. There we ate a pizza and drank a full carafe of wine. When we finished, we walked down the street in the direction of the Capuleti courtyard.

Passing by Piazza dei Signori, we paused to gaze up at the statue of Dante Alighieri. I silently thanked the Tuscan muse who had originally inspired me. Following in his footsteps, I had started a journey that had taken me from a kitchen in Sonoma to this Italian piazza, to be holding the hand of a man who had captured my heart and my imagination.

Together Lorenzo and I walked around the poet admiring him from every angle. When a group of American tourists joined us, we slipped into Italian. We laughed and called out to one another, commenting on their blinding white socks and tennis shoes, *Guarda quelle calze bianche e le scarpe da ginnastica così pulite."* Throughout our good-natured teasing, the tourists never realized they had been the target of our jokes.

Before exiting the piazza, I looked back up at the statue of Dante and saluted him, blowing him an affectionate kiss. In return, the poet winked and wiggled the fingers he held under his chin. It seemed he had overheard our teasing comments and Dante, the father of the Italian language, had a sense of humor.

When we came to Juliet's house, we stepped inside the small courtyard. In front of us was the fabled balcony, underneath which stood a bronze statue of Shakespeare's tragic heroine. This had been the playground of my Italian teacher. Closing my eyes and listening carefully, I soon heard the voices of children calling out, "But wait! What light through yonder window breaks? It is the east, and Juliet is the sun."

In my mind's eye, I saw a younger Signora Zeffirelli standing under Juliet's balcony playacting with her friends. Turning her head in my direction, she waved at me and beckoned me to join her. I heard her call out, "Sophia! I'm so glad you came." When my lids fluttered open again, the image was gone.

I smiled remembering that when I had stumbled and fallen, it had been Signora Zeffirelli who had picked me up and encouraged me to keep moving forward. It was in her classroom I had awakened to new possibilities.

Looking up at Lorenzo I squeezed his hand, conveying how pleased I was to have him now walking beside me. He smiled in response. Our silence communicated volumes, much more than words could express.

Modern Art

Modern art includes work produced roughly from the 1860s to the 1970s. The term is usually associated with art in which the traditions of the past have been thrown aside in the spirit of experimentation. Modern artists explored new ways of seeing and developed fresh ideas about the nature of materials and functions of art.

Chapter 27

Finding Joy

Summer had arrived again in Italy. Standing on the front veranda, holding a cup of freshly brewed coffee, I gazed out over the fields of ripening grapes. Before me spread Val d'Orcia. I drank in its beauty, recalling the first time I had seen the rolling fields of Italy from a train window. The mist. The fresh air. The golden hills. I closed my eyes and saw another valley set between two rugged mountains where cool ocean breezes blew in from the Pacific—the Valley of the Moon. It was where my parents had sat in rockers on the veranda watching hawks glide on updrafts of air. I opened my eyes and smiled. Like a bird on outstretched wing, traveling on a high current, I had come full circle to rest in a new home, set in another golden valley.

I took a sip of my coffee, enjoying the rich aromatic flavor. What a treat it was to be free of responsibilities and to have the time to focus on my own work. La Scuola had closed its doors for the summer, and I was on holiday. To rest up and have some much-needed solitude to paint, I had decided to rent a place in the country. I would head back to town at the end of September to start my third year at the school. I was now a full-fledged professor.

As if that weren't enough to keep me busy, I was also selling my paintings online. It was a portal through which I also accepted private commissions. With Raffaella's design skills, I had put together an attractive website. Now I was also thinking about organizing *plein air* outings for tourists. But that plan would have to be put on hold for least another nine months until I could figure out all the logistics.

I had driven down from Florence the night before in a car loaded with bags and boxes, filled with all the necessities I would need for the summer. Arriving late in the evening I was tired and a little light-headed from the heat and the motion of the car. Deciding to leave the unpacking for the morning I promptly crawled into an empty unmade bed.

It was refreshing to wake up at dawn and feel the cool morning breeze, instead, of the oppressive heat of the city. My alarm clock was now, the cooing of doves and the whirring of cicadas, instead of the angry whine of Vespas.

Pulling on a T-shirt and a pair of faded blue jeans, I noticed they had become just a little bit tight. Leaving the top button undone I padded barefooted into the small kitchen, going straight for a box stamped with the logo of my favorite Florentine bakery. Opening the lid, I lifted out a pastry and took a big bite. I closed my eyes and savored the sweetness.

Licking the sugar off of my fingers, I dug through boxes until I found my favorite silver espresso pot the one Adriana had given me. Following a well-versed routine, I measured out coffee and filled the small pot with water. Setting it on the stove, I turned up the heat and waited. Soon the pleasant sounds of spluttering coffee began bubbling up—always welcome notes in my morning symphony.

Searching inside another cardboard box, I pulled out a large mug decorated with the whimsical image of Mona Lisa with a mustache that I had stolen from Ale's desk. Leo da Vinci meet Marcel Duchamp. Marcel meet Leo! Once again the past meets the future, and the future looks to the past for inspiration. Didn't Vasari and Brunelleschi teach me that? I think you two cool cats would have liked each other very much. I smiled thinking of Glenninghall.

Pouring coffee into the mug, I added a splash of steamed milk. Then wrapping my fingers around the cup, feeling its warmth, I walked to the porch and sat on the steps to enjoy the view. I could have remained there all day, but suddenly I was filled with a burst of energy. I turned back inside to set things in order.

Leaving the door open, to allow the Tuscan breeze to blow through the house, I moved to the guest bedroom that I planned to use as a studio. I began first by sweeping the debris from the floor and dusting cobwebs from the corners. I set up my easel and emptied boxes filled with my painting supplies, dumping them in a massive pile on the table.

My nose wrinkled, as I inhaled deeply, at the familiar oily smells, more pungent than usual. I peered into the bottom of one of the boxes and saw a soggy mess. I picked up cans of linseed and turpentine that had leaked during the bumpy ride down from Florence. With a rag, I began wiping them down. Waving the cloth under my nose, like smelling salts to awaken my senses, I breathed in the fragrance of creative possibilities.

I filled an empty jar with my favorite well-used sable brushes, and against the far wall, I neatly stacked primed boards and canvases that I had stretched back in the studio at the school. Finishing, I stood back and surveyed my new headquarters. The blank canvases beckoned me to fill their faces with images of the sunflowers and smoky violet horizon I could see from the veranda. My fingers tingled in anticipation.

Happy with what I had accomplished, I turned my attention to the kitchen. I had brought with me the essential pots and pans I would need to prepare simple lunches and dinners. Later in the day, I would drive into the nearby village to purchase wine, vegetables, and pasta. I would chat with the townsfolk and learn the names of my neighbors, stopping in at the local bar to make friends with the barista. Soon he, too, would prepare my cappuccino with frothy designs created especially for me.

As I puttered about putting things away in the cupboards, I listened to the radio and hummed along to classic favorites sung by Zucchero and Giorgia. When the DJ switched to a classic Patty Pravo song—La Bambola"—I began to dance around my kitchen, singing into the back of my spoon, just as I remembered my mother had done.

Giddy and laughing I spun around and around until finally, out of breath and severely dizzy I collapsed onto a wooden chair. My stomach was doing a series of little flip-flops, and although I had stopped moving, it continued dancing all on its own. Resting a hand upon my midriff, I glanced over at the table and noticed there was still one more cardboard box to empty.

I stood up and folded back the lid. This time what I saw inside did not frighten me. Instead, I welcomed its presence. I reached into the carton and drew out the wooden box with the fleur-de-lis. As I gently brushed my hand over the surface, feeling the smooth wood, thoughts of my mother enveloped me. With my finger, I traced the design and the name engraved on top, *Gioia*.

My whimsical and free-spirited mother, who had studied in Florence at a time when the Mud Angels saved Florence, had been named Joy.

I carried the box to the living room and set it on the table in front of a small love seat. Gently I inserted a small brass key into the lock and listened for the gentle click that would unlock the past.

When I opened the lid, I saw a packet of Luciana's letters tied with a satin ribbon. Over the years there had been many, but these were my favorites—they contained the most precious stories about my mom.

I reached back into the box and pulled out a gold ring with a fleur-de-lis. I held it up to the light to read the engraving on the inner band: *To Joy and our daughter Sophia. With love, Michael.* It was the ring my dad had given my mother the day I was born. The morning she left for Italy she had placed it in my hands, reminding me that a circle of love would always connect us.

As I slipped the ring onto my finger, a bittersweet smile spread across my face, and my eyes glistened with tears

Peeking into the box, I pulled out the items one by one: the marble stone, the red silk scarf, the Venetian beads, the gold button, the leather-bound volume of Romeo and Juliet, and the ruby earrings. Along with these was a collection of seashells my mother had collected, perhaps in Viareggio, or maybe it had been in Amalfi.

I toyed with one of the shells, and then seeing the red coral clip I picked it up and fastened it in my hair. I smiled a bit wistfully at the memory of former loves.

Placing my hand once again into the box, I pulled out Brunelleschi's globe and shook it vigorously. I watched as the snow fell back down over the miniature cathedral inside.

Last but not least, I removed a black-and-white photo of my parents. They were sitting at a table with their heads close together, holding in their hands two Bellinis. It appeared they were toasting the photographer.

I gently placed the snapshot on the table along with the other treasures. Each item symbolized a step on a journey that had led me to this place. They were pieces of Italy my mother had collected and that had been passed on to me for safe keeping. I picked up the piece of Carrara marble. As I rolled it around between my two hands, I heard my mother's voice quoting La Loren, "Never block out the memories of the past, even though some are painful. Everything you live through helps make you the person you are now."

As I sat bathed in the warm afternoon light, surrounded by the fields of Tuscany, I felt at peace. The Italian dreams my mother had first encouraged me to dream, still inspired and pulsed within me. I had tried to reject them, but their pull had been too strong. My Italian muses had guided me out of a dark place into the light of Italy.

Now every time I picked up a brush to paint I knew they and my mother were guiding my hand. Whenever I stopped to look at my work, astonished by what I had created, not consciously knowing from whence it came, I knew they were whispering into my ear. My feet might be more firmly planted in reality, but I wouldn't let that stop me from hearing their siren song. I would continue to be Dreaming Sophia, never forgetting that true creativity only came when I dreamt with my eyes open.

Just then, from down the lane, I heard the pleasant crunch of tires on loose gravel. I glanced up in surprise to see a car slowly approaching the house. Billows of dust filled the air as it came to a full stop, next to several over-sized terra-cotta pots filled with rosemary and lavender.

The car door opened, and a beagle with the softest ears came bounding out. Tearing across the lawn, he ran up to the house and leaped into my arms. Close behind, a familiar and well-loved man stepped out of his Alfa Romeo and walked up to the door. As he watched the scene play out, he leaned against the door frame. Removing his dark sunglasses, he smiled and said, *"Ciao, Bella!"*

I smiled back. He was not an apparition or a figment of my imagination. Standing before me was my Lorenzo.

Still patting the dog, with a heart bursting with delight I looked up at him and said, *"Ciao...bello anche tu!* You're kinda handsome yourself."

"Sorpresa!" Then with an even bigger grin he added, "Bet you weren't expecting us so soon. I got back from my trip a day early. I...we..." he corrected himself, glancing down at Leo, "couldn't wait to see you."

Laughing in pleasure, I realized once again this man would be a constant source of surprises. But I too could compete with the best. Gently I touched my midriff and thought: *Just you wait, amore mio, until I tell you my news. Oh, what a bella surprise I have for you!*

I stood up to embrace him, welcoming him back with open arms. Of all the gifts I had received thus far, the love I had found with Lorenzo and the life inside me were my greatest creations of all—*i miei capolavori*. Never would I forget my parents or the inspiration they had given me. They were the ones who had created Dreaming Sophia. I would carry them in my heart forever, but now I was ready to take off in a new direction. I was ready to grab hold of Lorenzo's hand and touch the sky opening wide into infinity... we were ready to fly. *Volare, volare, volare.*

Together in this golden valley, keeping the laughter and love alive, we would create new dreams—never once forgetting we had been brought together by Joy.

To Sophia Loren I extend my heartfelt respect and admiration. I had the pleasure of meeting Miss Loren on March 26, 2016. She is as gracious and lovely in person as she is on the silver screen. I kissed her on both cheeks, spoke with her in Italian and told her about Dreaming Sophia. What a thrill it was to hear her say:

"I believe in dreams. Dreams become reality."

Thank you Sophia for being a role model and source of inspiration. You have helped turn my dreams into reality.

MATTA

PRESS

Acknowledgements and thanks to:

Edith Pray, my mother who encouraged my interest in art and writing and who inspired me to write this book!

Francis Pray, my father who gave me sage advice and wings to fly.

Patrick Muldoon, my husband who embraces and supports my big, crazy Italian dreams.

Ryan, Michael and Kyle Muldoon, my three sons, my three masterpieces—*i miei capolavori*

Harland Goudie, my art history and painting professor at Knox College—the one who first opened my eyes to the world of art. For the love of Mike, he was one cool cat!

Gloria Acerboni, my friend, my *"Luciana"*, who listens to all my stories, corrects my Italian and lends a helping hand with all my Italian projects! *Grazie per tutte le chiacchierate e la tua amicizia!*

Elizabeth Bosch, special heartfelt thanks to Lizzy. She was the first to read the initial draft and the first to read the finalized manuscript. Together we read the last chapter out loud together. What fun we had getting Sophia ready for her publication date.

Laura Fabiani, Dianne Hales, Laura Morelli, Mary Osborne, accomplished friends, writers and published authors who also inspire me to write. They offered support and valuable advice.

Debby Billings, Paula Doherty, Caroline Eitzen, Karen Henderson, Barbara Rindge, Carol Marcantonio Sansone first readers who provided invaluable feedback. *Grazie ragazze!*

Leslie Goudie Warner, friend, artist, bridesmaid and college senior art show partner. Special thanks for sharing memories and letters about her father Harland Goudie.

Patty Kelbe, my Texan friend who is "all in", who has accompanied me to Italy—as well as on my journey to meet Sophia Loren in real life. I can always count on her to lift me up!

Dorie Nelson, Lunette Rawlin, friends who always provide encouragement and make me laugh.

Angela Vita Campanella, my friend and Italian teacher from Puglia.

Francesca Mazza, my friend and Italian teacher in Lucca.

Daniela Bonaccorsi, Angelo Giannini, Antonella Martini, Eva dal Porto, friends and teachers at Lucca Italian School, and collaborators for my *Italian Lucca Language Programs.*

Vittorio, Tonia, Francesca, Graziana and Roberto Mirabile, my Italian family in Puglia.

Rossella Rebonato, my friend in Bardolino, my Italian sister—*la mia carissima sorella italiana.*

Marta Guerrieri, my darling friend in Lecce—*la mia ragazza del sole.*

Kelly Medford, friend, plein air painter in Rome and Italian language program partner. Her paintings truly speak to me. Keep mixing, squinting, mixing!

Massimo Balestrini, friend, teacher multi-media artist in Verona and Torbole who inspires me with his creative work and wit.

Sharon Sanders, the friend who inspired me to begin the *Studentessa Matta* blog—starting everything—blogging, Youtubing, podcasting, Italian immersion trips and book writing!

Mons. Marco Domenico Viola, Priore della Basilica di San Lorenzo, thank you for your insights.

Ilaria and Federico of *Finestre sull'Arte,* thank you for answering my arcane art history questions.

Freya Middleton, friend and art historian & tour guide in Florence, thank you for your insights.

Gloria Acerboni: Italian editor, *Elizabeth Bosch:* content editor, *Michelle Fabio:* story/title consultant, *Jess Resnick:* proofreader,

Heather Debling, Jane Friedman, publishing consultants

Debbi Stocco, My Book Designer: e-pub formatter. Thanks for your expertise & attention to detail

Special thanks to all my Italian friends—from the tip to the toe of the boot. The decision to learn Italian and travel in Italy has connected me with so many warm generous people. I treasure our friendships. Vi voglio bene tutti quanti!

Grazie also to the readers of the Matta blog, followers of the Matta YouTube channel and Matta Facebook page. I am so pleased to have you with me on my journey, as I continue to explore Italy and deepen my knowledge of the language.

Melissa Muldoon is the Studentessa Matta—the crazy linguist! In Italian, *"matta"* means "crazy" or "impassioned". Melissa has a B.A. in fine arts, art history and European history from Knox College, a liberal arts college in Galesburg, Illinois, as well as a master's degree in art history from the University of Illinois at Champaign-Urbana. She has also studied painting and art history in Florence.

Melissa promotes the study of Italian language and culture through her dual-language blog, *Studentessa Matta* (studentessamatta.com). Melissa began the Matta blog to improve her command of the language and to connect with other language learners. It has since grown to include a podcast, *"Tutti Matti per l'Italiano"* and the *Studentessa Matta YouTube* channel. Melissa also created *Matta Italian Language Immersion Tours*, which she co-leads with Italian partners in Italy.

Dreaming Sophia is Melissa's first novel. It is a fanciful look at art history and Italian language and culture, but it is also the culmination of personal stories and insights resulting from her experiences living in Italy, as well as her involvement and familiarity with the Italian language, painting, and art history.

As a student, Melissa lived in Florence with an Italian family. She studied art history and painting and took beginner Italian classes. When she returned home, she threw away her Italian dictionary, assuming she'd never need it again but after launching a successful design career and starting a family, she realized something was missing in her life. That "thing" was the connection she had made with Italy and the friends who live there. Living in Florence was indeed a life-changing event! Wanting to reconnect with Italy, she decided to start learning the language again from scratch. As if indeed possessed by an Italian muse, she bought a new Italian dictionary and began her journey to fluency—a path that has led her back to Italy many times and enriched her life in countless ways.

Now, many dictionaries and grammar books later, she dedicates her time to promoting Italian language studies, further travels in Italy, and sharing her stories and insights about Italy with others. When Melissa is not traveling in Italy, she lives in the San Francisco Bay Area. She is married and has three boys and two beagles.

Melissa designed and illustrated the cover art for *Dreaming Sophia*. She also designed the *Dreaming Sophia* website and created the character illustrations that can be found in the book and on the *Dreaming Sophia* websites.

www.DreamingSophiaBook.com
www.pinterest.com/dreamingsophia
www.facebook.com/DreamingSophia

www.studentessamatta.com
www.facebook.com/studentessamatta
www.youtube.com/c/StudentessaMatta_MelissaMuldoon

44107637R00131

Made in the USA
San Bernardino, CA
06 January 2017